IN PRAISE OF N

"Alternately heartbreaking and uplifting but consistently inspiring. Wardell recreates a lamentably bygone era when traditional orphanages served as places of refuge . . . for children abandoned by parents who could not or would not care for them . . . a poignant reminder that 'homekids' ultimately found stability and the feeling of being wanted—not from the attentions of social workers but from each other."

> — William F. Shughart II,
> Frederick A. P. Barnard Distinguished
> Professor of Economics, University of
> Mississippi

"With prose that inspires and tingles the spine, Wardell tells how two women created an orphanage with little more than dedication to transform the lives of children . . . an authentic story . . . stands as a testimonial to what women accomplished decades ago."

> — Richard McKenzie, Walter B. Gerken Professor,
> University of California, Irvine
> Author of *The Home: A Memoir of Growing Up in
> an Orphanage*

"*Naomi's Place* is a real-life, Southern, female-view version of *Cider House Rules*. Young Jennifer's love and admiration for Naomi, the founder and mother of the children's home and school, fills the pages. Even as she recognizes Naomi's weaknesses that would lead to her undoing, Jennifer's affections remained fervent. A touching and very interesting book."

> — Heidi Goldsmith, Founder and Executive Director,
> Coalition for Residential Education, Washington, D.C.

"A compelling story of the culture of the hollows, bittersweet relations and naive loyalties."

> — Bob Chitester, President,
> The Idea Channel

"Wardell grounds her story in reality—not only of her own childhood but also that of thousands of other abandoned children that grew up in orphanages . . . explores the true dynamic of a children's home."
— Nurith Zmora, History Professor, Hamline University
Author of *Orphanages Reconsidered*

"Wardell deftly weaves together Jennifer's coming-of-age story . . . a beautiful and absorbing work."
— Nikki McCaslin
University of Colorado, Denver

NAOMI'S
PLACE

To Marguerite,

Hope you enjoy this
personal story.

Fondly,

Dee 1/01

NAOMI'S
PLACE

Delores Wardell

SEVEN LOCKS PRESS

Santa Ana, California
Minneapolis, Minnesota
Washington, D.C.

Seven Locks Press
P.O. Box 25689
Santa Ana, CA 92799
(800) 354-5348

Individual Sales. This book is available through most bookstores or can be ordered directly from Seven Locks Press at the address above.

Quantity Sales. Special discounts are available on quantity purchases by corporations, associations, and others. For details, contact the "Special Sales Department" at the publisher's address above.

Printed in the United States of America

Library of Congress Cataloging-in-Publication Data
is available from the publisher
ISBN 0-929765-89-3

Cover and Interior Design by Sparrow Advertising & Design

AUTHOR'S NOTE

There was a period of time in North American history when hundreds of unconventional, independent women blazed trails into remote regions to bring education and ideology to the underserved. Many came alone, shunning marriage and convention, to fulfill a vision spurred by idealism. Some came with religious zeal, sowing either good or ill in their well-intentioned paths.

From the late 1800s to the early 1960s, there was room for creative, enterprising efforts to save those who might not even know they needed saving. This book is about one such effort, a children's home, nestled deep in the Appalachians, and the bright and unconventional woman who started it; this is the story of her struggle to realize her vision, her ability to survive unthinkable tragedy, her triumphs, and her failures. But it is also, in part, the story of someone who grew up in that home.

Jennifer's story, told herein, could have been told by any one of the numerous people who grew up in the children's homes that were scattered across North America from the late 1800s into the 1960s. Over the years, I have talked with many individuals who, like myself, grew up in "orphanages." As we began to tell our stories, I was always surprised by the similarity of our experiences.

This book is dedicated to all the grown children who share a common legacy. Although every story is unique—some better, some worse—a common bond is instantly formed when one "home kid" meets another.

Naomi's Place is a fictionalized story based on some real events and in some cases on my own experiences. But the names, places, and events have been altered to protect the privacy of those who wish to put the past behind them.

Many people helped make this book possible. I must thank my brother, who gave his unrelenting encouragement and support through numerous drafts and pushed me to speak from the heart. I must also express gratitude to my husband, David, who, for over twenty-five years, has sat through many dinner parties hearing anecdotes about my child-hood home again and again, meeting the people on whom some of the characters in this book are based, and forever responding to my stories with "You know, you really should write these down." His love and reassurance erased any doubt of my own worth.

Numerous others also need to be mentioned. First are the people I met along my journey to adulthood who, through their deeds, taught me the value of offering friendship and a helping hand during difficult times. I also want to acknowledge Patricia Yglesias, whom I trusted enough to read a first draft and who was courageous enough to suggest changes. Special thanks go to Jim Riordan, my publisher and a wonderful human being, whose optimism and dedication to his authors is impressive. I also wish to thank my editor, Sharon Goldinger, who sliced through my ramblings to make a readable story.

Last, but never least, my greatest thanks go to my "Naomi," who believed in me and loved me.

PROLOGUE

I was raised in an orphanage in the heart of the Appalachian Mountains. I suppose my childhood home isn't what first comes to mind when people think about an American childhood, but it was the only real home I knew. I never thought I'd be writing a book about it, but one day I received a package that changed my life. Inside a manila envelope with my name on it was a poorly typed manuscript written by Naomi—my mother and the mother to hundreds of other children. As I read about her early life and the unexpected adventure of starting an orphanage, my hands shook and my eyes filled with tears as the sounds, scents, and sights of my childhood flooded back.

Naomi's memoir was written in her eighth decade, when memory dims. In reading about events that I remembered myself, I recognized some inaccuracies and the condensation that inevitably occurs when one memory fades into another. Many stories, however, were just as I had heard them numerous times during my life with Naomi. I was enjoying the reading, never expecting to do writing of my own, until I realized that Naomi had given only one paragraph—three empty, unrevealing lines— to an event that changed the orphanage and all of our lives forever. Right then and there, I knew that I had to finish the story.

Naomi came to the Appalachians with missionary zeal, determined to do right. At first, she might not have intended to start a children's home, but that's what she did. I think of her like a shooting star blazing across the heavens. The light she brought with her was bright and sudden but all-too-soon extinguished in an atmosphere of bureaucracy and regulation.

The story told is not meant to be factual history. I have generously used my imagination to portray the beginning and end of an era, with realistic accounts of personalities and events, but not hesitating to alter them for fictional needs. It is a story told from differing perspectives: Naomi's, Miss Ruth's, her nemesis (there always seems to be one in every home), Jennifer and multiple other children who arrived with varying backgrounds and stories of their own.

Naomi's manuscript was sent to me by someone I'd never met, her last living relative, who knew intuitively that I would treasure it and perhaps, in loving memory of Naomi, do something with it. The gift was greater than the giver knew. For in reading Naomi's words and retelling the story of her life, I have found the voice to tell my own as well.

PART I:

IN THE BEGINNING: NAOMI, 1935–1940

CHAPTER 1

No human sound could be heard that afternoon other than the firm, steady rhythm of the traveler's feet, crunching on the gravel of the railroad bed. Although the year was 1935, the hills were quiet—no hum of electric wires. No soft, distant purr of a car motor. No airplane overhead. No sound of a neighbor's telephone or unwelcome music from a stranger's radio. The young woman had been walking for nearly three hours and had not seen a house for almost two.

Only days ago, Naomi Fraser had left upstate New York, bidding farewell to friends and family and everything familiar, as she boarded a train bound for the Appalachian foothills, a few hours' travel from the Cumberland Gap. When after three days of hard travel, lugging a washtub the entire way, she had finally arrived in the small mining town of Madison Creek, not even fatigue could hold her back from getting started doing God's will. Unwilling to wait for the train from the town to the mission, she had set off along the tracks, determined to cover the eight miles to Mission Creek by foot. Why wait around the railroad station when she was so close to her destination—her destiny?

As she walked deeper into the hills, Naomi felt as if she were entering a holy sanctuary. The railroad tracks stretched ahead, blazing a path through the labyrinth of the mountains. The narrow bands of steel were flanked by thick patches of pine, birch, walnut, and beech trees, and the pinks and whites of dogwood blossoms graced the variegated greens of the new growth. Clouds were gathering overhead and birds called to one another. Naomi paused, breathing in the clean, sharp air of the place that was to be her home. Then, shifting the bag on her shoulder, she pulled her sweater close around her, smoothed her cotton Sunday dress, and trudged on.

Before leaving the station, she had changed out of her traveling clothes. Anticipating the walk ahead, she had put on white work shoes—the footwear of nurses and waitresses—but she had placed her dress shoes atop her Bible in the shoulder bag, close at hand so that she could slip them on before she reached her destination. The blue of her only sweater matched the forget-me-nots printed on her dress and set off her eyes. The effect was pleasing, but her reasons for changing were purely practical. Often mistaken for someone younger, she had donned her Sunday best so that when she introduced herself she would appear up to the task that had brought her to this isolated country. The rest of her things, she'd left at the station.

The stationmaster had assured her that he would send her belongings—a small trunk, a suitcase, and the washtub—on the four o'clock train to Mission Creek. The trunk had all she would need for teaching: textbooks, maps, notepads, pencils, construction paper, colored pencils, and chalk. The suitcase held the rest of her wardrobe: two dresses for work, underwear, an extra pair of shoes, a small satchel of toilet articles, and a coat. The washtub was for the mission. She had ignored the looks from fellow passengers during train transfers as she struggled with it. But the stationmaster at Madison Creek seemed to find the tub a perfectly understandable piece of luggage. The McCalls, who ran the mission, had written, urgently requesting her to bring as large a tub as she could manage because the one they used for laundry and baths had finally given out.

Naomi planned to reach the mission well before the four o'clock train brought her things. Although she did not have a watch, she had been walking about three hours now and knew that she should be nearing the turnoff. The stationmaster had given her careful directions. "It's a piece past eight miles. There'll be a post office with a sign that reads 'Mission Creek.' Turn right, and up the road 'bout near a quarter of a mile, you'll see it. Can't miss it."

A sudden sound made her stop once again along the track to listen. Was it rifle fire? Then she heard it again, rolling over the mountains like a wave crashing overhead—thunder.

She quickened her pace and shifted her bag to the other shoulder. As the first few drops of rain began to fall, she gathered the bag close to her body and sprinted down the track. If the rain became heavier, she'd duck into the woods and wait it out. Meanwhile, she'd try to make it to the next bend in the tracks. Maybe the post office would be there.

As she rounded the bend, her hopes fell. She saw no building. The tracks stretched ahead for another half mile. The clouds were arriving dark and fast. She looked to the side of the tracks, searching for shelter, and was surprised that she had missed seeing a small shanty nearly hidden among the trees. Smoke curled from a tin pipe in the roof. She ran toward the shelter, hopeful, for the rain was coming down hard, bouncing off the ground, soaking her dress.

As she neared the structure she noticed a small wooden sign, swaying and creaking in the wind. The words carved in it were barely legible: Mission Creek. The post office! She pushed open the door and nearly fell inside.

Three mountain men, warming their feet around a potbellied stove, acknowledged the stranger who had stumbled through the door, giving her a slight nod but saying nothing.

Flushed and breathing heavily from having run the last eighth mile, Naomi stood awkwardly before her expressionless audience, too relieved to be at her destination to remember her plan of making a good first impression. Her dress shoes remained in the bag along with her Bible. Some wet strands of hair had escaped from her long braid, and she pushed them out of her face, revealing her lively blue eyes. Noticing the men watching her, she buttoned the sweater over her wet dress and looked around.

A small boy leaned on a counter, which held a few jars filled with hard candy, some pouches of tobacco, and a couple of cartons of cigarettes. Behind him hung a shelf with a meager array of toilet articles. A few bags of flour and sugar were stacked against the wall underneath. Behind the counter was a tall metal box with a lock hanging from its rusted hasp and the word "mail" stenciled across the front.

Naomi took in the whole room with one sweeping glance, and just as a garment might tell plenty about a person, the room said all she needed to know about the hollow: poverty and scarcity prevailed. It made no difference to her. Her father used to tell her, "Use it up, wear it out, make it do, or do without." Material possessions meant little to her for she was more concerned with spiritual gifts.

The boy spoke before she could introduce herself, interrupting her reveries. "Kin I git you anything, ma'am?"

She was pleased that it was a child who was the first to speak to her. It was the children that she had come for. She smiled at him. This was an auspicious beginning. "Yes," she said warmly as she made her way closer to him, her back now to the men. "I've come to help the McCalls. I'm to be the new teacher. Can you tell me how to get to the mission?"

There was a derisive snort behind her.

The boy looked steadily into her eyes. "I kin take you there after the rain quits."

One of the men spoke to the boy. "Buddy, you tell her about the McCalls leaving?"

Of course he had not told her. The men had heard the only two sentences he had uttered. But he understood.

"The McCalls, they ain't staying. They be leaving on tomorrow's train. Good thing you got here today so they can show you the schoolroom."

Before Naomi could respond, a large woman in overalls and a man's plaid shirt stomped into the room, shaking off the rain. She stepped out of her high rubber boots, leaving them by the door, and moved behind the counter. Naomi couldn't tell her age. Women here had children young and the hardship of the hills took its toll early. But her face seemed kind.

"God almighty weather," the woman complained. "Still, I should be thankful or else I'd have to be hoein'." She caught sight of Naomi and her voice filled the room with a warmth that made whatever fierce goings-on outside seem insignificant.

"Howdy. Ain't seen you around before. What brings you back up this way?" It wasn't that she didn't expect strangers, because they came occasionally to the mission, but their appearance came with the two daily train stops, one at 8 A.M., coming from the west, heading toward Madison Creek, and one at 4 P.M. coming from Madison Creek. It wasn't one o'clock yet.

"I'm Naomi Fraser. The new teacher for the mission."

"I'm Cora. I run the post office. And this here is Buddy. He runs the store. Nobody can cheat him out of half a cent." She nodded toward Buddy and flashed him a smile of pride. "No train's been by here for hours now. How'd you git here?"

"I walked—from Madison Creek. It wasn't raining when I started out."

Cora laughed. "It sure does come sudden. Can catch you clear by surprise if you're not watching. You just make yourself at home and dry out by the stove. This'll pass soon." Her voice suddenly changed, taking on a confidential tone, as she leaned forward over the edge of the counter in Naomi's direction. "I reckon you won't be staying now that the McCalls are leaving. Too bad. We need a teacher in a worst way."

Naomi expressed her surprise. "I didn't hear anything about the McCalls leaving. Why?"

Cora pulled her body up, dwarfing Naomi. "They'll tell you. But it probably won't be the truth."

Naomi had worked in other hollows briefly and knew their customs. Outsiders were suspect and confidence had to be earned. She didn't have this woman's confidence and there was no use probing for more information.

The thought of being alone at the mission sent a wave of uncertainty through her, which she quickly suppressed. When you're called, you're called. And besides, she had no other place to go. It was here she planned to stay.

With an air of forced determination, she replied, "Well, if you need a teacher, you've got one. That's what I came for and I don't see any reason to leave."

The men sat silent, leaning back on their chairs. One of them got up and looked out the door into the rain. "It's movin' fast. Should be gone soon."

Cora spoke to him. "Hiram, take a rest. You should be used to sittin' a spell by now. You ain't going nowhere anyhow."

The men laughed.

Cora brought forth a hidden key hanging from a string around her neck and opened the tin mailbox. "Might as well take them their mail as you're headed that way." She handed two envelopes to Naomi. One was an official-looking letter from the county superintendent of schools; the other appeared to be a personal letter. Naomi felt even more impatient to get to the mission. She wanted to know why the McCalls were leaving.

The men made no effort to invite her into their circle. They sat staring at the stove, their boots smelling of overheated leather. Naomi talked to Buddy and Cora.

Bold and cheerful, Cora freely gave advice and asked personal questions. "Why ain't you married?" "Don't you miss having children?" "Why did you come to Mission Creek anyhow?"

Aware that every word she said would be spread throughout the community, Naomi answered Cora's last question carefully. "All my decisions," she explained, "have been directed by God."

Naomi hoped that Cora would be satisfied with her answer. From the woman's line of questioning, Naomi could tell that Cora found it difficult to understand how a woman could choose a life that didn't include a husband and children of her own, but nonetheless the young woman felt that Cora accepted her in spite of her seemingly unnatural choices. She was pleased when, before parting, Cora told her, "Now you need anything, you let me know, you hear?" Perhaps she was beginning to win Cora's trust.

When the rain let up, Buddy and Naomi set off along a narrow road, which seemed about to disappear into the underbrush. The boy hopped from side to side, avoiding the worst of the mud and the ruts filled with water, navigating the road with ease. Naomi tried to follow, picking her way carefully, hoping to save her shoes from becoming further encrusted with the heavy, claylike mud. When she wasn't hopping about, Naomi hummed absently to herself. Humming was a habit she'd had ever since childhood, whenever she was lost in thought.

As the two came into a clearing, Naomi suddenly caught her breath. "Oh, Buddy, look. A sign from God." She grabbed his hand as she pointed excitedly to a rainbow that arched across the valley, touching down on one side near a small house sitting on a rise above a harvested cornfield. Unable to restrain herself, she told him the story of Noah's ark. "The rainbow is a sign of God's promise to never flood the world again," she pronounced with certainty.

The boy kept silent with his eyes fixed on the house. Then he spoke. "That's my house. There's no pot of gold there though," he said, "just me and my grandparents."

"No, no pot of gold." She laughed. "That's just a folk story. Not true, like the one about Noah. What a wonderful promise God gave us. He loves us, you know."

"I guess."

She heard his doubt. "You do believe he loves you, don't you?"

"I guess."

"Well, you come to my Sunday school class this Sunday and I'll tell you many more true stories about his love." She paused. "You believe in God, don't you?"

He considered her question seriously, thoughtfully, and replied, "No, ma'am."

She was taken aback. A child who did not believe in God? In a Christian country? She had not expected that the first heathen she met would be a child.

Naomi launched into a well-rehearsed, enthusiastic speech, telling all about the love of God. Her passion imbued her with a soft radiance that drew the boy to her. When she finished, she stopped and bent low to study his face. She rose abruptly, slightly disoriented, for the eyes staring back at her reflected a place that she knew—a place where she had been before, a place she never wanted to see again. What was it she saw? Doubt? Disbelief? No, it was more than that; it was what happens to the soul when reason prevails, when faith and hope surrender to rational thought. She was an intelligent woman, and once she herself had waged a battle between reason and spirituality. She saw in the boy's eyes that for him, reason had won the battle. Her heart quickened with the realization that he might have doomed his soul for eternity. Gently, she placed her hand on his shoulder, resolving within herself to resurrect his soul if she could.

———

Buddy walked along beside Naomi, weighing her words. He didn't want to hurt her feelings, but her words made no sense to him. He had heard it all before, in many versions, and it didn't sound the least bit logical or realistic. In the long twelve years he had been on the planet, he had seen enough of death and hardship. People died and those left behind suffered. Those who believed in God didn't seem to get a better deal. His own mother—who had been a believer—died before she could suckle him. In time, Buddy had concluded that the world was just what it seemed—a cycle of life and death—and there didn't have to be a fancy reason for it all. That's what his granddaddy said, too. Buddy didn't tell the new teacher his beliefs. He liked her. She smelled sweet, not like his grandma, who smelled sour. He wished he had a mother like Naomi, one filled with such happiness, who was so certain about herself. He wanted to be close to this new schoolteacher. He had heard talk about God from a lot of the traveling preachers who came to the hollow. All of them had a little different picture of God, and it sounded to Buddy like he was pretty hard to please. But Buddy promised Naomi that he would come to her Sunday school class. In his heart he knew the real reason was to listen to the music of her voice.

———

They came farther out of the woods into the open plain, and Buddy pointed to a cluster of shabby wooden buildings surrounded by wild undergrowth that spread up a rising mountain. The scene gave the impression that this was the last vestige of civilization on the edge of an abyssal wilderness. "We're here," he said.

Naomi sucked in a quick, sharp breath, surprised at how crudely constructed, forlorn, and rundown the mission looked. A sanctuary neglected! For an instant she wondered if its shabbiness reflected the spiritual work that took place there as well. Ashamed of such a thought, she began to picture how the mission would look after she planted flowers, moved the woodpile to the back of the house, cut the weeds. This was a mission, a place that represented God, and she resolved that soon its appearance would do him honor.

Eager to look around, to see inside the church and the schoolroom, she turned toward the house instead. She knew her first obligation was to meet the McCalls and learn why they were leaving.

CHAPTER 2

Naomi walked alone to the main building. Before she climbed the stairs to the porch, she turned and looked back. She could see Buddy jumping the stream as he made his way toward the house on the hill. From this perspective, his house was screened by rows of uncut, dead corn stalks not yet removed for spring planting. Anxiously, she scanned for other houses, but none were visible. For the first time since her journey began, she felt completely alone. Just a few days before, her father had held her face in his hands and said, "Naomi, it hurts to part with you. You've been a big help to us. But go, do the Lord's work. We'll be fine." Now, for the first time since childhood, she needed her parents more than they had needed her.

The depression had spread like a wildfire, consuming the country's soul, swallowing up jobs, and sucking the oxygen out of men. Her daddy was a hard worker, and he took whatever work he could find, switching railcars, carpentry, stone masonry, laying bricks, driving a milk buggy, sales, and most recently working as an overseer of a farm and a greenhouse. She was sure he had had more jobs, but those were the ones she remembered. Whether it was the times or her father's wanderlust, the family often found themselves living from hand to mouth, packing up and moving on when he heard of another job. Several times he gambled his savings on a business he was sure would succeed. Each time something went wrong and they found themselves broke again, starting over. The family wandered from Iowa down to Louisiana and up to New York. That is where she had left them, settled down with her mother's family.

She felt an ache spread through her as she thought of them so far away. Numerous times her schooling had been interrupted to help support her parents. She had finally graduated with help from her church and the three, sometimes four, jobs she had held. Her raw determination seemed to work miracles—not that she would ever believe herself to be a miracle worker. She was just an instrument to be used by God. But at this moment, she was no more than a lonely, vulnerable twenty-seven-year-old. She swallowed hard, then mounted the stairs, ready to introduce herself to the McCalls.

Naomi knocked politely on the uneven door and waited. From inside came sounds of someone scurrying about, moving things, but no one came to the door. She knocked again and called out, "Hello. Anyone home? It's Naomi Fraser, the new teacher."

A short time later the door opened. "We weren't expecting you," said the woman who stood half-hidden by the door, as though Naomi might be a threat.

Beyond her, articles of clothing and household items lay scattered about the room, waiting to be put into boxes. Naomi stood motionless at the sight—not so much at the signs of their leaving, for she had been warned, but at the wretched figure that stood before her. Mrs. McCall appeared to be in the same condition as the dilapidated mission: run-down, haggard, neglected. Fortunately, Mrs. McCall took the look on Naomi's face to be shock at the news of their departure.

"We sent the church a letter telling them not to send you. Guess you didn't get it," Mrs. McCall frowned.

Naomi shook her head.

"Nash, my husband, took another job, over in Cumberland. It's going to be a lot better for us."

An awkward silence followed and Naomi thought the woman was about to turn her away.

Finally, Mrs. McCall spoke again. "Might as well come on in. You want some tea?"

Naomi nodded. She was led into the kitchen, which was nearly empty of kitchenware. The cups, plates, and even the kettle were missing. Mrs. McCall wandered into the front room to retrieve the kettle, along with a few cups.

The magnitude of the decision before Naomi began to slowly sink in. What was she to make of this? What was she to do?

"Were you the teacher?" she asked Mrs. McCall.

"Was until the parents boycotted the school."

"What do you mean?"

"Well, they don't send their kids often, anyway. Keep them out for hoeing corn and harvest times. They don't care if the kids get an education. They'll do anything they can to undermine you." Mrs. McCall stared bitterly into her cup, and in a measured, cautious way she added, "Maybe there is something you should know about these people. They are mean. I'm just warning you."

Before Naomi could respond, Mr. McCall entered. He was a dark, stocky man. Overhearing his wife's comment, he added, speaking in the same bitter tone as his wife, "You don't want to stay here among these people. Not alone. You're free to stay here tonight and go back on the train with us in the morning."

Naomi was too confused to answer right away. Even if she had the fare to go home, she was reluctant to surrender a dream so readily. "Well I'll need to think it over. I'm thinking I'll stay on. My things are coming on the four o'clock. I'll need a few days to decide what to do."

"Not wise. You don't know these people. Let me just tell you a few things. Ol' Hiram, lives down the road, just got out of the penitentiary. The next-door neighbor to the right would kill anyone for five dollars. Ol' grandpa, across the road, sleeps with a rifle. It's not a fit place for a woman alone."

Two thoughts passed simultaneously through Naomi's mind. The first was that she hadn't seen any evidence of neighbors, except for Buddy's house, around the mission property. The second was an image of the man Cora called Hiram. Could that be the convict? Cora didn't seem to be afraid of him. But these thoughts could wait. The immediate problem was whether to stay or go.

They had their tea, and Mrs. McCall returned to packing. Mr. McCall disappeared. Naomi sat alone, wrestling with her decision. Faith prevailed as the verse came to her. Softly she repeated it: "In the time of trouble he shall hide me in his pavilion, in the secret of his tabernacle shall he hide me; he shall set me up upon a rock, and there shall my head be lifted up above mine enemies round about me." Then and there it was settled. God had called her to this place, and whatever trials he had in mind for her, she would prove herself worthy. With that decision, another thought swiftly followed: If she was to stay, she would need some of the household items that she believed belonged to the mission and were being concealed among the McCalls' belongings.

She approached Mrs. McCall with a sweet, firm voice. "I have prayed about my decision and God tells me that I am to stay. He has also said that he will provide. I have looked around the kitchen and surely there are some things that belong to the mission. Would you know where I might find them?"

Mrs. McCall looked a bit uncomfortable. "There's not much. Most of it we supplied. But I'll look and see if by mistake some were packed."

"I'll be happy to help you. Once we get your boxes to the station, maybe you can show me around."

They worked together for several hours and the whole time Mrs. McCall complained about the hill people, how uncooperative, dishonest, and mean they were. Fear gripped Naomi at times, but she silently repeated the Bible verse about being set upon a rock and calmed herself. "Since I'll be here alone, isn't there anyone I can turn to, to count on for a friend in case I should be sick any time?"

Mrs. McCall shrugged, then said, "Well, maybe Mrs. Miller. She's just around the bend, but she's not well."

They worked until dark, packing, carrying boxes to the station, retrieving Naomi's belongings from the four o'clock when it arrived. Mrs. McCall finally gave Naomi a quick tour of the grounds. Naomi learned she had to draw water from the well and carry it by bucket to the kitchen; the outhouse was between the main house and the church; she had to make sure the woodpile was kept stocked because the cooking stove was wood-burning, but she could also walk down along the tracks and pick up coal that fell from the train. She learned where the chickens were kept and the eight cows that belonged to the mission. The dog was quite good about herding the cows and bringing them to the fenced area at night, she was told. They needed to be milked in the mornings and at sundown.

That night in bed Naomi's spirits began to falter, and dread replaced confidence. She had not been trained at the other missions for this kind of work. She was a teacher, not a farmer. How does one milk a cow? Max, her minister, the leader of the congregation that had so dutifully supported her through college, had once spoken to her about her two strongest traits: her passionate belief that love could overcome all obstacles and her raw, sheer determination.

"Don't let your strengths become misdirected, Naomi," Max had said.

Maybe this project was too much—a young, single woman alone in the outback, far away from the rule of law and social niceties. Naomi had at times felt these conventions to be burdens, but now she longed for them. She knew a little about the hills. Twice, during brief internships, she had gone to missions in the hills to train for foreign missionary service, but these places had been well established and well staffed, and the men did the farmwork. The people she had met at those missions had been wonderful, not like these people, at least the way the McCalls described them.

A fleeting pang of resentment passed through Naomi. Why wasn't she in Africa, the place dearest to her heart, the place most dreamed of since age seventeen when she found God? The passion to work in Africa had driven her from other loves that fill the hearts of adolescents. But the dream had unraveled a few months earlier, all because of an invisible, barely audible heart defect. Sometimes she lay on her side and covered an ear so that she could hear her heart beat, the steady, slow rhythm reminding her of the drums of Africa. Her heart sounded strong, sure, reliable, like herself, but the doctor had said it had a murmur, which disqualified her from foreign missionary service. How could a heart so passionate be so fragile? She had made him listen again and again. He finally said, "Young lady, God has another plan for you."

It had taken her weeks to climb out of the despair into which she had fallen and to consider her situation. She had been willing to give up everything for this calling. Was it only a few months ago—it seemed like a lifetime ago—that she had to find another dream, another reason for her existence? Then a friend working in the Appalachian Mountains wrote about an opening for a teacher at Mission Creek, and Naomi had seized the offer.

Her parents had seen the opportunity as salvation from the despair that gripped Naomi and encouraged her to go, even though they needed her with them. Naomi heard herself utter aloud, "Trust in the Lord with all thy heart, lean not unto thine own understanding. . . ." And peace began to fill her again.

Now, as she lay in the dark and quiet of her mission room, she decided that if it was God's will that she should be here, perhaps even die here, what greater honor, what loftier privilege could there be than to suffer in his name? And with that comfort, she fell into a deep slumber.

The next morning, the McCalls left on the eight o'clock train. Naomi walked back to the mission from the station surprisingly refreshed, her spirits lifting as time and distance separated her from these strange, bitter people. How could danger linger among this much beauty? The air was sharp and clean from yesterday's rain; the trees were alive with the activity of birds preparing their nests. She picked an armful of flowers for her house but then wondered whether she had a container for them.

Once home, an eagerness overtook her. She had much to do—unpack, clean, move that dreadful pile of wood to the back of the house. What day was it? Friday. Two days to get organized before Sunday services. She looked forward to meeting the minister; the McCalls had said he came from Walnut Creek, a few hollows over. She also wanted to meet the neighbors and invite their children to her Sunday school and to encourage the children to attend school on Monday morning. Yes, there was so much to do. She would also have to pick up the mail.

The mail! She suddenly remembered that she had forgotten the two letters that had come for the McCalls. She would have to return them to the post office. Maybe Cora would know where to send them.

The first task was to fix a cup of tea before starting the day. It was a familiar, comforting routine—a cup of tea, a quiet time for prayer and Bible reading, and then the day could properly begin. She had retrieved a few miscellaneous pieces of crockery, a few mismatched plates and cups, and some jars for drinking glasses from the McCalls' possessions. This collection wasn't much, but it was enough should company drop in.

As if her thoughts had brought company, she heard a knock on the door. At first she mistook the knock for a sound peculiar to the house, but the second time it was a bit louder. She went to the front door and found a small shoeless child, about four years old, wearing a hand-me-down dress too large for her. With her thin legs barely visible, she appeared to be standing on tiny stilts.

"My mommy sent you this," she said as she thrust out a jug of buttermilk and a tin of corn bread.

Naomi invited her in. "Thank you, dear. Will you join me in having some?"

The child could not resist the warmth in Naomi's voice and the sparkling blue eyes that seemed to say "You are about the nicest thing that has ever happened to me." The child looked shyly over her shoulder toward the underbrush near the road, then slipped eagerly inside.

Naomi brought two jam jars to serve as glasses and set them down before the child. "Now tell me, what is your name?"

"Innia."

"Innia?"

The child shook her head. Naomi tried again, "Ina?"

Again the child shook her head and said slower and louder, "*Innia.*"

"That's a very pretty name," Naomi replied, fearful of offending the child by mispronouncing it again.

Hearing muffled giggles, Naomi looked to the front door and saw three girls with their hands over their mouths. As she started toward the door, they turned to run, but she called them. "Please come in. Have something to eat."

They came in eagerly, their eyes fixed on the new teacher. Naomi soon learned that these were the Miller children, a small flower garden family. At thirteen, Lily was the oldest, slim, fair, and fragile; then Daisy, age eleven, her bright, round face full of mischief; then came solemn Violet, age seven; and finally "Innia," almost five, who Naomi then realized was named Zinnia.

The flower sisters first question to her was, "You gonna stay?" Naomi was touched by the hope in their voices. She smiled at them and said, "I just reckon I will."

The children helped her find an empty tin can large enough to hold her flowers, then settled at the table to eat. Naomi had never eaten corn bread so delicate, so cakelike. "No one makes corn bread like Mama," Daisy said. The children told her that it was their mother's specialty, apparently the envy of the other women in the hollow because they tried to copy it. But their mother told them that no one could make it the way she did because of a special ingredient, called love, that she stirred into the batter. To Naomi the story sounded a far cry from the ones told by the McCalls.

"Come home and meet Mama," Lily said, and Naomi's plans for the day's work ended.

Naomi was not going to hide in her house for fear of her neighbors. So she went with the children to the small lean-to that sat hidden off the road behind a cluster of trees and shrubs.

Maddie Miller was a frightfully slender woman. Naomi had seen the signs before—the cough, the thin bead of perspiration, the hollow fatigue. Consumption was a death sentence. Naomi's heart fell. Maddie's husband had died two years before in a shooting accident. Within a short time, these children would be orphans. Who would look after them?

Naomi put aside her concern for the moment. "Will the children be attending school?"

"Miss Naomi, my children were given to me by God," Maddie said simply, "and they need all the learnin' about his world that they can git. But I need the two older ones at home."

"We open with a prayer and verse, then say the pledge to the flag. The first class of the morning will be reading. Surely they could come for the first hour so they can learn to read for themselves what God wrote."

Maddie reflected on Naomi's words, then consented by replying, "That's a mighty powerful way of puttin' it. I reckon I can spare them for the morning."

The rest of the day Naomi spent walking up and down the hollow, stopping by each house to introduce herself. Her arrival seemed to be anticipated, as the women called out to her before she got to the front porch, "Come on in, an' set a spell." To Naomi's surprise, most of them were eager for their children to get an education, but she was told that during planting and harvesting, every available hand—young and old— was needed in the fields, and that was the way it was. It began to occur to her that the school schedule would have to be flexible to fit their lives.

Naomi met Maddie's sister, Mae, who followed the pattern of naming her children by category. The oldest was a girl named Opal, then came Ruby, a boy named Perl, and the youngest, still a baby, who was called Emery but named Emerald because of his green eyes. Naomi recognized Mae's husband, George Watson, as one of the men at the post office the day before. He began questioning her so closely, she felt she was on trial but she had no idea why.

"How did you come to know the McCalls?" he asked.

"I never met them before yesterday. My friend, Esther, is a missionary over near Harley. She wrote me about the mission needing a teacher. So I came."

"You know the mission gets closed down if there is no school?"

"No, I didn't know that. But that's why I came. The children seem so eager, so bright, I know they can benefit from it."

George stared hard at her. "The property belongs to ol' man Nobel, across the way from the mission. He don't care about no church; but if there is no school, he'll take it back right now. He don't stand for no cheatin', either."

She didn't understand his remarks. "No, I won't have any cheating. That's wrong. I'll do my best to have a proper, well-run school."

So it was Buddy's grandfather who owned the mission property. And it was his inspiration that made it happen. She learned that it was he and the men in the community who had built the structures for the mission.

George's tone gradually changed. "You need any help? I don't guess they left you much when they left. I'll bring Perl and a couple of other boys over tomorrow and we can help you clean up. The boys can cut the grass. Shame how they let the place go."

Naomi agreed wholeheartedly, but she would never allow herself to say so aloud.

She thought about her conversation with the McCalls. Was this the man who would kill anyone for five dollars? People here seemed wary of strangers but not unwilling to meet kindness with kindness, listen to her, or lend a hand. Why were the McCalls' experiences so different from her own?

Not everyone, however, was so accepting of her mission. Mr. Sturgis informed her that his children would not attend the Sunday school. "I don't hold with such goin's on. They can come to the school, but after that Bible talk is over."

Naomi learned that other adults also disapproved of Sunday school and adult prayer meetings, not because they didn't believe in God but because the old-time preachers did not believe in such activities. Many of the preachers could neither read nor write; they had learned about the Bible from those who could, and they preached what they had heard others preach. Although they never admitted it, these new college-trained women invading their world threatened them. Tradition dies hard, and no harder than among isolated people—strangers to change.

Back in the mission at the end of the day, Naomi repeated the words of Solomon. "Give thy servant an understanding heart to judge thy people, that I may discern between good and bad."

CHAPTER 3

The next day, Saturday, a man on his horse emerged from the thicket at the edge of the mission. Naomi knew it was four o'clock because she heard the train's whistle announce its arrival at the station. The sun had begun to slip behind the mountain, and the shadow over the valley gave the illusion that the mission was a lonely island, a place set apart from the world around it.

All day Naomi had pulled weeds; she had intended to end her day's work outside when the shadows fell, but the magnitude of the task kept drawing her to the next patch. With stiff, tired muscles she rose unsteadily to greet the approaching rider.

"Howdy. You be Miss Naomi?" the rider said as his horse strode slowly in her direction. A beard and a hat with a brim hid most of his face. A rifle balanced across the saddle seemed to be a familiar companion.

"Yes. And who might you be?"

"Hiram Stone."

"Didn't we meet at the post office?"

"'Twas there."

"What can I do for you?" Naomi's heart was quickening. Could the man before her be the one who just got out of the penitentiary? He didn't seem threatening in the post office, but now, outfitted with a rifle and peering at Naomi with his narrow, hard eyes, he had the look of a convict.

Attempting to ease her fear, she started an elaborate account of her plans for a garden, but as she looked around she realized her day's efforts had scarcely made a dent. She faltered and Hiram broke in.

"My brother Clay died last night. We're havin' a sittin' up for him tonight. We thought it fittin' to have a missionary there. It ain't gonna hurt to come up and see what you kin do."

He was inviting her to the wake. She was touched. Eagerly she responded, "I'll be pleased to come. What time? Where?"

"It's startin' now. I'll take ya when you're ready."

She had no time to bathe and groom carefully for her first community event. With a quick washing, she did her best to clean the dirt from beneath her fingernails. She quickly changed into her dark blue Sunday dress and wore her walking shoes, since she was to follow behind Hiram's horse. After a short walk, they left the road and moved along the bank by the stream until they came to a clearing. They climbed a hill, passing a pigpen and a barn, and finally came to a clearing where a large house constructed of logs leaned slightly forward, as if bowing to greet the visitor. A sizable group stood outside, waiting for a space inside the crowded house to open. When Hiram dismounted, people scattered and a path formed as he walked with Naomi toward the front door.

Inside, more people stepped aside and Hiram led Naomi straight into the front room, where she saw the body dressed and laid out on the table. Clay Stone's wife and children sat in chairs nearby. Naomi went to them to offer her condolences. The wife stared straight ahead, nodding slightly at Naomi's words. The children modeled her, sitting silently and stoically beside their mother. No signs of grief were evident. Naomi opened her Bible to say a few words of comfort, but her words were drowned out by a sudden outbreak of moaning and wailing. The sounds rose and fell as each newcomer approached the body.

When she realized her attempt to read from the scripture was futile and closed her Bible, someone steered her to a table that was piled high with a variety of bean dishes, platters of pork, potato dishes, vegetable mixes, and desserts. Through a small window opening on the backyard, she could see the men passing around a jug. A dread filled her, as she remembered her last mission stint, when alcohol and passions led to a man getting killed over at Pog's Hollow. Hoping the men wouldn't get drunk was as futile as wishing that flies wouldn't swarm around garbage, she knew. An event such as a funeral provided a short reprieve, an escape from the burden of the hard mountain life. Still, Naomi would never understand nor ever approve.

Wandering among the grieving, she was delivered from feeling useless when someone called upon her to lead them in song. She stood reverently in front of the body and began "Nearer My God to Thee." Halfway into the song, a man stumbled forward and broke into "My Dear Departed Husband Is Gone, and I Shall See His Face No More," robbing it of what little rendition it had. The audience inside the house joined in with equal tonelessness. Not knowing the song, Naomi remained silent. As soon as this song ended, the men outside with the jug began a sonorous melody of "Goin' Up Cripple Creek" and that was the end of Naomi's attempts to sing what she considered proper funeral hymns. The noise and heat inside the small house drove her outside. In the lantern light, she recognized Mae Watson with her son Perl and moved eagerly toward them, welcoming a familiar face. She asked Mae politely, "How did he die?"

"He fell off his horse, but we guessed it was because he was so drunk he couldn't find his legs to git up. He was always a-thinkin' stupid. He died half-mile down the road, facedown in the crick."

"Oh." For a moment Naomi was speechless. Then, "How long will this go on?" she asked, nodding toward the raucous group inside.

"I reckon, like always, all night; probably until the buryin' tomorrow. But ain't nobody crying their eyes out of hurtin'."

"I don't think I can stay that long." Recognizing she had no role here, Naomi was eager to leave. With the thought of the journey home, she realized how foolish she had been to leave without a light. She turned to Mae, "I didn't think to bring a light, and I'm not sure I can find my way home in the dark."

"Don't worry, Perl will take you when you be ready." She nodded in Perl's direction and he flashed back a smile.

Naomi wanted to leave right then, but she waited a bit so as not to seem overly eager to escape. When she was ready, Perl led her in the darkness, knowing every turn and obstacle along the way. He saw in the dark more than she could see with light.

Naomi was in low spirits. She keenly felt her separateness from the people. Reverence for the dead had not been on the night's agenda, the way she believed it should have been. She had failed in her first attempts to be a missionary, failed to offer solace to the grieving.

Thankfully, Perl kept up a steady chatter all the way back, unaware of her loneliness, proud to be escorting the new teacher home. He had his own reasons for wanting to be alone with her, for he had long wanted an answer to a puzzling dilemma unanswered by teacher McCall. He turned to her seriously with his academic problem, "Miss Naomi, kin I ask you something? It's really been bothering me—what one teacher said. She said the earth is round. Now in the Bible, it says there are four corners in the earth, and I never saw a ball with corners."

Perl's faith in the scripture delighted Naomi. Here, at least, she could help. She carefully answered the question he had been struggling with by explaining that God meant the four directions when he talked about the four corners. "If you come to school," she offered, "I'll show you where the Bible mentions the circle of the earth." Perl promised he would.

She could tell by his relieved expression that her answer had set the boy's mind at ease, and by the time they entered the path to the mission, her heart had lifted. At last she had been useful. This was why she had come. Before entering the house, she turned to say good night, but Perl had disappeared into the wild darkness, leaving only a nightingale's song on the night air.

Naomi's body ached from the pulling and lifting and cleaning that she had done for the past few days. She had not worked entirely alone. As promised, George Watson had brought a few boys that morning, and they had helped move the woodpile and cut the grass. Troy, a tall blond boy of about sixteen, had promised to come each morning and evening to milk the cows. In exchange, he would take some eggs and milk home. She had more than she alone could use. She knew enough about the mountain people to know there was dignity in their poverty and they did not accept charity. Bartering, however, was acceptable.

She built a fire in the stove and heated a large pail of water. It was a good night to try out the washtub that she had lugged all the way from upstate New York. She slipped off her clothes, her strong youthful body softly lit by the one candle flickering on the kitchen table. She blew it out, less out of modesty than frugality. Candlelight was unnecessary, and she was already learning about scarcity. Although she had two kerosene lanterns, they were to be saved for necessary lighting. Making a pillow of a towel to rest her head, Naomi eased her body into the hot water and gradually surrendered to its warmth.

Her mind relaxed along with her body and drifted home. How far away the world seemed. She wondered what her parents were doing this night. Probably tending the sick, she thought. When young, her mother had worked for a time with a doctor who taught her to be his assistant. Wherever they moved, knowledge of her work soon became known, and the role of nurse was thrust upon her. Naomi's father waited patiently long hours in cold or heat, outside or in dimly lit halls, to take his wife home. When Naomi wanted to place them somewhere in the universe, it was this scene she visualized. They had moved so many times that no place had come to feel like home. Home was in the glow of her parents' relationship, the way they depended on each other. She was grateful that her mother had taught her not to be afraid of the sick and wounded and that she had shown Naomi a few tried-and-true remedies for cuts, broken bones, and other common maladies. She was proud of her parents for their bravery and the way they didn't shirk adversity.

A loneliness swelled within her. She needed companionship. She must write her dear friend Hope Beatty and tell her to come. Oh, she needed a friend, someone to ease the formidable separateness that she felt. Would she always be an outsider, a respected missionary and teacher, but never a *friend*? Yes. She would send for Hope—for a friend—and she wondered why the idea hadn't occurred to her sooner. The thought excited her and her tired body felt a surge of energy. She sat up, unbraided her long dark hair, and poured water over her head. She lathered and scrubbed, feeling such happiness with the discovery that something as simple and natural as a bath could restore one's soul.

She toweled off and wrapped herself in a heavy bathrobe that she had found in the attic of the school earlier that day. She had discovered a room filled with articles of clothing and household items, such as blankets, still in unopened boxes sent from churches who donated to the mission. Why had they not been distributed within the community? Was it another indication of the strain between the McCalls and the local people? She was hesitant to lay blame for she remembered from her short stays in the hills the harsh pride of the people and their reluctance to accept charity. Her heart warmed as she thought of many with whom she had worked in the past, how little they had materially, but how much strength and faith they possessed. At that moment, she resolved to embrace their values. She too would not ask anyone for anything—except the Lord, of course. He had promised that in time of need he would provide; she would be calling on him to keep that promise.

She saw light falling into the living room, and it drew her outdoors, onto the porch. A blue moon was making its way over the mountain, nibbling at the edges of the trees until it hung like a Chinese lantern, flooding the valley with light. She trembled at its beauty and absently tightened her robe around her as though it could stop the thoughts that were starting. Why did the moon touch her so? Why did it take the lid off a hidden part of her soul and let all the longing and despair run rampant?

She breathed his words, the ones that he had written before she left. "'Your leaving is as if God has turned off the light and left me in an eternal darkness—without warmth, without meaning, without hope.' Oh, Max," she murmured. She heard a noise and blinked away the hot tears that were forming in an effort to see who was there.

Buddy sat a few steps beneath the porch railing where she was leaning. This allowed her to slam the lid shut on her ache and come back to the present.

"It's pretty, huh?" It seemed that was the only reason he needed for having arrived in the dark—to share with her the beauty. Together they sat in silence, watching the fireflies and listening to the crickets. The moonlight flowed across the valley and draped across the mountains like a gold-and-silver garment.

Buddy saw it differently. "It's like a pot of gold being poured out."

"Oh, yes, yes. Even more precious than gold," Naomi murmured.

Many nights thereafter Buddy would arrive in time for a spectacular sunset or the full moon, and together they would seek metaphors for the beauty around them.

———•———

The day after the wake, Naomi opened her first Sunday school class to a roomful of girls, except for Perl, who had kept his word that he would be there. Although the girls had attended the wake, they did not stay throughout the night as had the men and boys. Nevertheless, the girls arrived tired and listless. Naomi hung a little felt cloth over the back of a chair and using paper cutouts told the story of little Joseph being sold by his brothers into Egypt and how he overcame adversity with forgiveness.

When Joseph was sold into a foreign land, did he feel as separate from the people around him as I do now? Naomi wondered.

The hour-long class ended at eleven o'clock, giving the children time to go home for lunch and return at one o'clock, when Preacher Sawyer would arrive from another hollow where he performed an earlier service.

The congregation gathered in the small church for the afternoon service and filed into pews made of planks nailed to a sawhorse at each end. A small potbellied stove sat in the corner like a sentinel, and a crudely made podium stood alone in the front of the church—a lonely martyr.

Nothing was colorful in this setting, except the preacher. Preacher Sawyer was an uneducated man who got his calling for the pulpit after recovering from a particularly bad bout with moonshine. Many a time he told his congregation how the Lord Almighty had revealed himself to him when he lay facedown in his own vomit. A voice came forth from a bright light that nearly blinded him and commanded Sawyer (like Saul) to arise and spread the gospel, and if he didn't he could die right there in his vomit for all the Lord cared. Sawyer thought this offer was a good trade and found the will to get on his feet and the courage never to take another drop. Some of the church members resented the way he held himself out to be special because of his meeting with the white light and figured his vision was no more than the light of the moonshine. Others embraced him as the father embraced the prodigal son.

Preacher Sawyer declared himself to be a "Hardshell Baptist," which meant he did a lot of preaching about the temptations of Satan, the consequences of sin, the horrors of hell, and the importance of deeds. His words fell discordantly on Naomi's Methodist ears. Other listeners echoed "Hallelujah" and "Amen," and most forgave him when he mixed up his parables, confused the disciples, and blended stories from various books of the Bible. They overlooked his lapses of knowledge, for his calling had been recent and God loved best the reformed sinner.

Again, a sense of estrangement came over Naomi as she tried with all her heart to feel the presence of God in the midst of this clamor. She found herself thinking of Max, how he would stand tall and elegant before the congregation, speaking eloquently with a message of compassion and tolerance. He didn't badger and shame his congregation into believing the way Preacher Sawyer did. Instead, Max's eyes rested on each member of the congregation as though he were speaking to each one alone—encouraging, forgiving, inspiring. Max reached out to touch each soul—just as his soul had touched hers. Warmth spread across Naomi's face at the thought, and she bowed her head to her Bible diligently, fervently seeking a passage that would bring her mind back to the matter of worship.

When the service was over, she accompanied the procession to the cemetery not far from the mission. The coffin preceded a long line of mourners, who gathered at the small fenced cemetery for another round of preaching. Two ministers presided over the funeral: Preacher Sawyer and Preacher Maddox. Maddox, who belonged to the sect called "No-heller" because they didn't believe in hell, began first. To Naomi's shock, he began his opening remarks by saying what a godless, wicked villain Clay Stone had been. He continued to drone on about Mr. Stone's misdeeds for nearly thirty minutes before ending with "But I'm here to tell you, his spirit has gone back to the God who give it."

Preacher Sawyer stood up, and being a "Hardshell" who believed in hell, went beyond the "No-heller" in describing the misdeeds of the deceased. "Everyone here knows Clay Stone was the meanest, vilest, rottenest, lowest of God's creatures. Nary a one would deny he beat his wife, never did a lick of good for his kids; he drank and cursed and cheated his whole life. You all knowed it, too. God gave him many a chance to git right, but he lived in a way that forced God to finally turn his face away. God gives up, too, you know, if you don't do no listenin'." The offering of remembrance to the deceased continued along these lines for some time, with Preacher Sawyer sweating from the passion of his words. Naomi looked about in alarm, only to find people nodding in agreement or paying respectful attention.

Preacher Sawyer then turned to the "No-heller" and pointed. "I have deep respect for my friend here, a man of God, but when he says Clay didn't go to hell, he's a-lyin' and he knows it."

This remark caused an outburst among the family members, not because of the misdeeds of the deceased or even the public acknowledgment of his sins but because of the fine theological point that separated the "Hardshellers" from the "No-hellers": not whether Mr. Stone was in hell but whether there *was* such a place. They took their theology seriously, Naomi discovered, and their uncompromising positions separated them as righteously as any family feud—and could have even led to one.

Naomi motioned to Maddie's girls—Zinnia, Violet, Daisy, and Lily— to follow her as soon as a brawl broke out. Lily turned reluctantly. Wearing a clean pink dress, which gave her porcelain complexion the color of a pale rose, she was set apart from all the other girls in beauty. Naomi had seen her casting shy looks at Floyd, then retreating behind lowered eyes. Naomi could tell that Lily wanted to remain at the cemetery, to stand there in front of the handsome boy, but she also noticed that Floyd saw Lily's beauty and that worried her. Naomi had seen Floyd drinking with the men the night before, and he was by far the most eager offender. Lily was so young, so innocent, and Naomi felt the need to shelter her from the reckless boy who probably was harboring not-so-innocent thoughts toward Lily. Maddie would surely disapprove, if she knew, and Naomi thought it her duty to keep a protective eye on Lily.

The girls were talking about the fight, taking sides in the theological debate: Daisy decided there was a hell; Violet, who would take the opposite side no matter the issue, disagreed. They asked Naomi to be the tiebreaker.

She said, "Hell is in the Bible. I have to accept it." But under layers of theology was an inner troubled place, for Naomi was a woman who believed completely in a God of love. The belief that Catholics and Africans and Jews and children and pagans who had never heard the Word or never been exposed to someone like Preacher Sawyer would be condemned to an eternal life in hell disturbed her. If she allowed herself to dwell upon such ecclesiastical matters, which she did not, she might be taken back to the old battleground she had abandoned when she wholly embraced faith. She tabled such conflicts by signing them off to God's mysterious ways, acknowledging that sometimes his ways were hard to understand.

They walked in silence until Zinnia spoke. "When Mommy dies, can I be your little girl?"

How could Naomi answer such a question? Teaching was as close as she thought she would ever come to motherhood. What should she say to the child? False reassurance is no comfort. But she wanted to grasp at it just the same and tell the child, "Many people get sick for a little while and then get better. Mommy will get better." But a lie would undo trust, and trust was the magnet that drew the little hand into hers. Nor could she offer, "Of course you can be my little girl." What if there were other relatives who would insist on taking her?

Muddling her thoughts were doubts about her ability—no, she reconsidered, her willingness—to commit to such an awesome request. She was single, a teacher, a missionary. But a mother? Somehow motherhood loomed greater, holier even, than teaching or ministering.

The three girls stood silently waiting for her answer. She replied, "'Behold the fowls of the air: for they sow not, neither do they reap, nor gather into barns; yet your heavenly Father feedeth them. Are ye not much better than they?' God has a plan, Zinnia. His ways are hard sometimes to understand. If he calls your mother home, he will make sure you are cared for, provided for. Don't worry."

It was this for which she had come: to give comfort to the weak, to sustain souls battered on the rocks of life, to shore up faith in times of uncertainty and grief. She didn't know whether the four young figures trudging along with her toward the mission felt restored, but there is no doubt that her own spirits lifted.

CHAPTER 4

Twenty-three students enrolled at the tiny schoolhouse. Eighteen were in the lower grades and five were in the high school—all boys. The students arrived barefoot, the girls wearing clean starched dresses and the boys in clean bib overalls. Most carried only a small paper bag holding a meager lunch, most likely a piece of corn bread and a slice of cured beef or a hard-boiled egg. Naomi supplied textbooks, writing paper, and pencils, which she collected at the end of the day. She had been warned by George Watson not to give the boys homework. They would be working in the field after school; she knew there was no electricity for late-night study. What they learned had to be mastered during instruction time.

Maybe this necessity accounted for the students' eagerness to learn and for the encouragement and assistance the older ones gave to the younger ones. As the weeks went by, Naomi was amazed at the talent before her. The students were bright, some more so than others. Buddy astonished her with his knowledge of mathematical figures. He never missed a math question and never seemed to lack understanding when she pushed him to the next level. Perl had a photographic memory for history and geography. The boys were industrious, but she worried about the girls. They became shy and anxious when asked a direct question. She knew that at times they deliberately gave a wrong answer.

Once she asked Lily to summarize from the reading how the ancient Greeks had lived. Lily turned crimson and stumbled through her answer. "Oh, you know, it was like this—they didn't do things like us. Well, they were, well, I just can't say what I mean."

One of the boys finally spoke up. "Oh, hush. You know you don't know a thang about it."

Lily glanced shyly in Floyd's direction, clearly proud of how she had replied.

Naomi tried to hide her disappointment. In this world girls were not supposed to know much about academic subjects and must never, never

know more than one of the boys. Naomi was determined to instill
another way of thinking, so she instituted a rule that exam papers were
not to be shared. Since each student learned according to his or her own
ability, she told them, no one's work should be compared to someone
else's. She wrote encouraging comments on the girls' papers, hoping
praise would inspire them to put forth genuine effort.

Naomi's patient, thorough instruction, her careful review of the previous day's lessons to identify who was lagging and who was ready to
advance, made her a good teacher. However, she was exhausted at the
end of each day; it was too much to teach both elementary and high
school grades. She had to rely on the older students to help the younger
ones. She worried that the older students were not benefiting fully
because of the time they gave to the younger ones. It troubled her also
that she had a liberal arts degree. Was she adequately prepared to teach
the upper grades, particularly in math and science?

She wrote again to her friend Hope Beatty, who had a bachelor of science, urging her to come or, if she couldn't, to please recommend
someone who could teach the high school classes. Her original letter to
Hope had gone unanswered so far.

Naomi made it a daily ritual to walk to the train station at four
o'clock to pick up the mail, but her true purpose was to mix with the
locals. The shack that served as the train station was the community
gathering place. The children came to play, the older girls came to steal
furtive glances at hopeful suitors, and those already courting came to
make secret plans for meeting. Naomi came to be with the people, for
she was lonely and longed to put aside differences and be accepted as
part of this close-knit community, which she had begun to love.

On a warm afternoon, a month after her arrival at the mission,
Naomi was picking up the mail and visiting her neighbors when she
heard the train stop. She looked up and saw something that made her
heart pause for a moment. It was Hope! Hope Beatty leaped from the
train. Naomi and her friend ran toward each other with abandon,

forgetting they were adults, forgetting they were missionaries, forgetting they were being observed. They hugged and danced and kissed and cried and laughed as people do when filled with surprise and overflowing with happiness. The reserved onlookers caught the mood; some came rushing forth to help with Hope's bags. Others began to talk excitedly. The children drew close and happily stood next to Naomi, asking, "Is she the new teacher?"

"Oh, yes, yes," she answered before even asking Hope. Introductions came forth like tossed confetti, overwhelming Hope with the attention and confusing her with the strange-sounding names. Naomi felt that she could not have planned a better welcome. Hope had arrived before her reply to Naomi's letter. She had been wavering about whether to join a mission in Indonesia, but Naomi's letter had resolved the uncertainty, she told her friends.

All the stored-up longing to share and the deprivation of communion with a like mind fueled Naomi's need to talk. She could not stop speaking until she felt emptied. Hope heard the stories of the neighbors and their struggles, the children and their abilities, Naomi's dreams of what might be done and the limitations she felt within herself. "Oh, Hope, there is so much need. Life is hard here, but the work feels more honest than anything I've known before. I am happy. You will stay, won't you?"

"If you will let me get a word in—yes."

They continued to talk as they undressed for bed, daring sleep to separate them. They lay side by side in the dark, talking in a whisper as though someone might overhear their secrets. The conversation finally turned to home. Naomi felt a pang as she realized that she had failed to ask about her parents. She searched her memory for a trace of the self she left behind—only a month ago? Slowly the ache deepened as home came into focus, flooding her with memories of touches, sounds, smells.

Hope said she often dropped by to see Naomi's parents. Naomi was glad they treated her like a daughter because Hope's own parents had rejected her after she got her "calling" and especially after she joined the missionary church.

The news from home disturbed Naomi. Dad hadn't found work yet, but her parents were making do mainly through the help offered by Naomi's maternal grandparents and the church. Naomi felt herself tighten at the mention of the church. She wanted to ask about Max, but she didn't. She fell silent—the first time since Hope's arrival—her quietness seeming like an unwilling confession.

Finally Hope broke the silence. "I also saw Max before I left."

With feigned indifference Naomi replied, "Oh, and how is he . . . and Madeline?" Her voice tightened against saying his name. Oh, she wanted to. She wanted it to roll across her lips, bringing him close again, but she dared not awaken futile longings.

"He looked terrible. Unhappy. He said to tell you he sends his love."

"Is Madeline any better?"

"The same. Poor Max. To be stuck with a wife so sickly."

"It's hard to know why we are given the burdens we must carry."

Hope rolled over onto her side, rested her head on her bent elbow, and looked into the dark at her friend. "He misses you terribly," she said. "I have no right to pry, and really, I didn't know about how he felt until I saw his face flinch with pain when your name was spoken." She paused, then quietly added, "I'm sorry—for you both."

Naomi wanted to take the high road and deny any feelings. But her friend lay too close and perhaps had observed the slight tremor that had passed through her body at the mention of his name. Hearing it had shaken loose her defenses, and she had a powerful, overwhelming need to confide in someone.

"Please don't think poorly of him," Naomi said. "We never meant for it to happen—to care for one another. When we both realized how the other felt, it was agreed we would not speak of it again." That was not exactly the whole truth, but she was not lying either; she was just putting a proper face on an untidy business. In fact, he had pleaded with her to talk to him, to help him find some comfort in knowing that she felt as he did—but *she* would not speak of it.

"Oh, Naomi, I wish I had your strength. I'm afraid I'd never make a good martyr if called upon. But you—your ability to deny your own passions, to suffer for what you believe. It's admirable. I'm afraid I'd go screaming into the fire." Hope paused.

Naomi reached for Hope's hand and gently squeezed it, "Don't. Don't put me on a pedestal. I'm not perfect. I sometimes wonder whether my 'suffering,' as you call it, is not also my weakness." There were times when she felt it held her captive, a burden that prevented her from ever reaching a state of abandoned joy. Hope was the opposite of her and Naomi loved her for it: Hope's lightness, her laughter, the way she saw humor in the ordinary. Naomi had a vague sense about herself that, unlike Hope, even when she was happy, she always felt a heaviness.

"No, it is for the best that you both just acknowledged your feelings and it went no further. If only you had met him first. It's sad when I think of how he would have cherished a good helpmate and how you would have flourished in that role."

"Don't be sad for us. I am meant to be here." Naomi said it with such conviction that for a moment her pain eased.

Hope agreed. "You are meant to be here. I'm glad I'm with you—to help."

Naomi was again aware of why she loved Hope. They said good night and Naomi rolled over on her side, hiding her grief and tears for Max from her closest friend.

———

Hope's friendship lifted Naomi's burden of solitude and overwork, bringing an unexpected comfort, like the soft chime of a clock breaking a monotonous ticking. Now Naomi taught the lower grades in the schoolroom and Hope taught the high school students in the kitchen of the main house.

Mr. Nobel had taken upon himself the role of defender of the constitution to assure that church and state were kept separate. Naomi had battled hard with Mr. Nobel about allowing the prayer and Bible verse. He had finally compromised by allowing her to call the Bible recitations "chapel" and declaring that school officially began with the pledge to the flag. Naomi could tell he was a practical man and feared losing another teacher. And she sensed he liked her. But every day, the eighty-plus, arthritic Mr. Nobel hobbled to the mission to place himself at the rear of the class to remind her to keep church and state in their proper places. It was clear to her that he approved of her teaching and was more eager to learn than to criticize, as evidenced by his ignoring the occasional slips when boundaries between religion and science blurred. Now with classes in two buildings, it made his entertainment more difficult for he had to shuffle between the two. Naomi came to feel at ease in his presence and missed his intense, interested expressions when he was absent to attend classes in the kitchen.

About two weeks after Hope arrived, a stranger appeared at the front door of the main house and asked for the McCalls. His unusual attire—for the hollow—of a suit and hat and his officious-sounding voice alarmed Hope. He introduced himself as Mr. Stanton, superintendent of schools for the county. Hope dismissed her students for recess then took Mr. Stanton to Naomi's classroom. Perl headed across the field in the direction of home, but the others lingered nearby, curious and sensing a mischief-maker in their midst. Hope and Mr. Stanton stood in the back of the room next to Mr. Nobel and waited for Naomi to acknowledge them.

Naomi was struggling with seven-year-old Violet, who just couldn't grasp the concept of subtraction. "Let's try it another way," sighed Naomi. "If you had twelve chickens and two of them died, how many would you have left?"

"I don't right know. But we'd sure have some good dinner."

The boys snickered and Naomi silenced them with a stern look. She tried again. "Now what do you do when you have twelve chickens," she said as she drew ten alive chickens and two dead ones, "and two die?" She underlined the dead chickens for emphasis. Naomi was looking for the answer "You take away," but instead, Violet suddenly brightened for now she certainly knew the answer. She blurted out, "You bury them." The children's laughter filled the room and Violet looked pleased.

Naomi agreed with Violet that you could either eat them or bury them, but then she asked Violet to count how many would be left. Violet eagerly counted the ten chickens, without making the connection that the dead ones were once part of the group of twelve. Naomi thought it was best to take a break, for she was eager to meet the stranger standing with Hope in the back of the room. She collected the math books and excused the class for a recess.

The children scattered, some eager to return to the sunshine and some lingering nearby to overhear what the stranger wanted. Mr. Stanton repeated that he was there to see the McCalls. Naomi told him they had left quite suddenly, taking a position, she believed, somewhere around Cumberland.

"Who are you?"

"I'm Naomi Fraser, the teacher they sent for—before they left."

Drawing himself up, he said in his most authoritative tone, "Well, they were notified by me in writing that the school was to be closed. This school is not accredited by the state. The students are not passing the requirements to enter high school. And the McCalls were under investigation for fraud—submitting reports for funds for more students than they had enrolled. This school is to be closed immediately and not re-opened until we authorize."

Naomi suddenly remembered the mail. The official letter she had forgotten to give to the McCalls! Did they suspect it would be coming? Had they deliberately hid the information from her? Confused and worried, she blurted out, "Oh, my. I didn't know. They didn't say. I—well, is there anything that can be done?"

At that moment Naomi heard a cane tapping on the floor as it made its way toward Mr. Stanton. Mr. Nobel tipped forward, his thin, frail body filled by a firm, strong voice. "This school will not be shut down. Now we can discuss this peaceably or without peace. The school stays open. These here teachers, they ain't nothing like the McCalls. I don't think they even knowed about funds for teaching. They came to give it free, and they teach honest, too."

Mr. Stanton waved Mr. Nobel away, as one might an annoying mosquito.

Mr. Nobel moved closer and said a little more firmly, "We ain't closing the school."

Mr. Stanton asked imperiously, "And who are you?"

Just at that moment the door flew open and there stood Perl, his father, George Watson, and four men close behind, each cradling a rifle.

"I'm the one who donated the land for the school. My name is Nobel. Now we don't want no trouble. This here has got to be worked out somehow."

Well aware of how disputes were handled in the hollows, Mr. Stanton saw a need for compromise. Someone from the community had contacted him complaining about the McCalls, but bureaucracy moves slowly and he had arrived too late. The McCalls were gone, and the situation had obviously changed. Being an intelligent man, he could see that the community felt differently about the new teachers and that tact was required.

In a conciliatory tone he addressed Naomi and Hope. "Of course, you didn't know. It is not your fault. You can teach until the end of the year and your students can take the tests offered over at Madison Creek to see how they place. I'll inform the principal there, Mr. Ness. I'm sure he'll be glad to work with you. You understand, these children have the right to an education equal to other children's. That means they should be able to pass tests. It's the new state regulation."

Mr. Nobel tapped his cane and shook his head. "Won't work."

Naomi felt panic rise in her throat. She was angry at Mr. Nobel for meddling. A compromise was on the table, a way of letting her keep her school open. She could get the students ready, she thought, even though there wasn't much time left and the children were woefully behind. She turned to Mr. Nobel. "I can try. Let us try. I think we can get them ready."

"They'll be ready. That's not the problem. Problem is only a few can pay the train fare—to git over yonner to take the test. I reckon it's fair that the tests be brought here. No need to trouble the families with the cost. We pay taxes, this is a proper and fittin' school, so, like I see it, it is the government's job to bring the test here, not have the younguns go to the test."

Mr. Stanton hesitated. The men outside with the rifles took a few steps toward the school door. George Watson, who was leaning against the doorframe, lowered the rifle in his arms so that the butt rested on the floor and let the weapon gently rock back and forth between his fingers.

Mr. Stanton loosened his tie and turned his hat nervously in his hands. "Well, we will talk to Mr. Ness. See what can be worked out."

Naomi could see what was happening, and she didn't feel right about forced negotiation. On the other hand, these threats reaffirmed the local people's confidence in her and their determination to have their children educated. She passionately agreed that these children should have the same education as other children, and she knew, too, that bureaucracy could be indifferent to the rules that governed unique communities. She would have to find a balance between the two.

She thought quickly. "Suppose I go tomorrow and meet with Mr. Ness. I will work out lesson plans that complement his—to make sure the students are being taught the same material. Then I could give the tests and take the results to him."

Mr. Stanton's eyes were on the exit and he didn't argue. Mr. Nobel agreed that tomorrow was just right because it would be the first day of corn planting and most of the students would be in the fields anyway. The dispute ended peacefully and Mr. Stanton made his escape.

Naomi should not have worried so because Mr. Ness turned out to be a most understanding and kind man who quickly understood the situation. He himself had grown up in the hills and knew the sacrifices that families made to allow their children to receive an education. He readily agreed to become her ally in keeping the school open. Whenever she went to town, which she rarely did, he made sure that she was treated to the rare luxury of a restaurant meal and introduced to other important community figures—such as Dr. Jackson, the physician who visited the hollow once a month; Mr. Phillips, the bank president; Reverend Charles; and others. Mr. Ness wanted Naomi to stay and he wanted her to keep her school.

Naomi did keep her school until providence handed her another role.

CHAPTER 5

Time seduced Naomi, leading her to believe life at the mission would go on forever just as it was. She forgot the words of the preacher who saw that "the race is not to the swift, nor the battle to the strong, neither yet bread to the wise, nor yet riches to men of understanding, nor yet favor to men of skill; but time and chance happeneth to them all." She rejoiced in the days, in the weeks, in the seasons, that unfolded like a well-told story in which calm and excitement, tension and relief, were perfectly balanced.

First came the routine of school. Most of the children passed their examinations and were admitted to the next grade, and those in the high school received credit toward a coveted diploma. The community was pleased that honesty and trustworthiness had been reinstated in their teachers, for these values were the very ground on which they firmly planted their feet.

Summer brought a new routine. One morning a week Naomi laid out all the clothing and household items sent by churches and offered them to the neighbors for prices from as low as a few pennies to as high as a quarter. Nothing cost more than a quarter because fifty cents could be an entire family's weekly wage. But for many, her low fees were still too much so she accepted the local bartering system—jams, a chicken, or a side of pork could be exchanged for selected items. The result was just enough money and food supplies for Naomi to live comfortably. Everyone benefited.

The mission gradually became the gathering place for young and old. First Maddie brought a basket of green beans to string and hang with Naomi. One by one, other women came at the end of the day to snap and string the beans. During the day, bushels of Kentucky wonder beans were picked and dumped on Naomi's front porch. After supper the older girls would snap off the ends of the beans and the women, using a long needle, would string the beans onto a long piece of twine and hang them to dry. It took experience to know when the beans were just right. If they became too dry, they popped. In the winter these shucky beans, as they called them, would be soaked all night and then cooked to a dry, chewy consistency.

The children played kickball and hide-and-seek in front while their mothers visited. The word spread about the evening gatherings at the mission, and gradually the boys started coming around, too. Naomi welcomed them. She set up a volleyball net and the boys played, showing off for the girls, and after their game the girls joined in. Naomi used the schoolroom for taffy pulls and popcorn night. The parents welcomed having a safe place for the young to meet and court—safe for everyone but Lily. Lovely Lily, Naomi called her. Lily grew more beautiful by the month—and handsome Floyd grew more interested.

When fall came, Hope told Naomi that the only pang she felt about not going to Indonesia was that she wondered if it was wrong to choose a life she so thoroughly enjoyed.

Fall was the time for the community celebration of making molasses—the "stir off." First, the sorghum cane was cut, brought to the yard near the small mill out by Hiram's place, and dumped into large piles. Next, a mule was hitched to a long pole that turned two large rollers. As the mule walked obediently around and around, a young boy fed the cane stalks into the rollers until all the juices ran out and were collected in a pan. Then a large trench was dug in which a fire was set. Over the fire was placed a galvanized pan, about twenty feet long and four feet wide with multiple partitions. This special pan was passed around from year to year to the various farms, which took turns having the "stir off." After the juice from the cane was collected, it was placed in the pan over the fire, where it flowed through the partitions, guided by a man using a large wooden paddle. The juice thickened and foamed as it moved across the heat, finally coming to the end of the pan. When the molasses became the right consistency, it was stored in five-gallon tins or large lard containers.

The children snapped off pieces of fresh cane, taking the joint and dipping it into the yellow foam to suck. This sweet, sticky substance worked as a glue on the community, bringing them together until feuds were almost forgotten. Games and music and dance in the moonlight celebrated the end of this annual autumn event.

Life in the hollow alternated between routine and emergency. Once when passing Mr. Sturgis's house, Naomi observed him eating a large raw onion. It didn't surprise her when his boy came running to the house soon afterward shouting, "Come quick! Pa is a-goin' to die."

Naomi grabbed some medicine to ease stomach pain and rushed over. As she neared the house, she could hear Mr. Sturgis wailing like a chant, "Lord, have mercy on my poor soul."

When she entered, he cried out, "Oh, Miss Naomi, can you do something for me? I'm sure to die."

She placed a large spoonful of medicine in his mouth and prayed for him. The rapid relief the medicine brought made Mr. Sturgis her first convert. Her status in the community went up a notch right then and there, for everyone knew Mr. Sturgis was an ardent nonbeliever who had kept his promise not to allow his children to come to her school until after the prayer and Bible verse. The day after the healing, his children were present at "chapel."

Not all the emergencies were so easy to cope with. Naomi found herself carrying a child eight miles to Madison Creek for medical care that couldn't wait, as well as treating children with broken arms, stomachs full of poisonous mushrooms, and burns. Her protests that she knew little about nursing did not dissuade her neighbors from bringing all their maladies to her. They came to her for healing—and for prayer if her healing failed.

Dr. Jackson, who visited the hollow once a month, came to rely upon her for assistance, knowing she had the confidence of the people. He trusted her, too, and would leave her samples of medicine to have on hand for emergencies. Liberally he shared medical information with her and discussed his patients' conditions. Naomi did not question his decision to send her home with a syringe of morphine to give twenty-year-old Sarah, who was dying of cancer.

He told Naomi, "When the time is close, don't let her suffer anymore. This will end her pain. It'll return her to her God."

"How will I know the right time to give it?" she asked trustingly.

"The family will guide you. And you'll know. Some go peacefully, some do not. I expect she will suffer."

The family called for Naomi when the suffering became unbearable for Sarah and for them. They gathered around the bed and prayed as Naomi inserted the large needle in the young woman's arm. It wasn't complicated. They all knew that Sarah was going to heaven, and helping her get there with less pain seemed compassionate and sensible.

As the months passed, Naomi gradually wove herself into the life of the community, a thread that stood out shining and strong, as though it might be the one thread that kept the fabric of this isolated society from unraveling. She didn't see it that way or believe it about herself; the reality was that she created synergy within the community, making the sum of its parts a little greater than it had been before.

Winter came with a vengeance. Heavy snows held prisoners inside homes for days, swollen waters destroyed well-worn paths, and even daylight seemed unwilling to linger. For weeks the skies were gray and heavy, blotting out light, erasing the difference between twilight and dawn.

Feeling housebound and craving fresh air, even if it came bitter and harsh to her lungs, Naomi made her way through the dim light and dirty snow to the small house around the bend. Somehow she knew before she knocked on the door that death was inside. Daisy's swollen face greeted her at the door and confirmed her fears. Seeing Naomi, Zinnia ran to the corner to gather up a small knotted bundle.

Quietly and reverently, as though sound might disturb the dead, Naomi approached Maddie's bed, hidden behind a suspended blanket.

The children followed, their bodies pressed close to hers, as though the life within her could shield them against death's presence. She gathered them in her arms and they stood silently gazing down on a thin, tired face that looked as though it needed a long rest. Naomi reached over and touched the cold body.

"When did she pass on?" Naomi asked.

"We just woke up and she didn't git up."

Naomi took Lily's hand. "Come, let's make something warm. There's a lot that must be done." Naomi knelt next to the wood-burning stove and added wood to a stubborn fire.

Lily, being the oldest, took the responsible role. "Me and Daisy was going over to Uncle George's. Him and Aunt Mae don't know yet."

"Of course," Naomi said. She heard the urgency and the mimicry of adulthood in Lily's voice.

A chill deeper than the January morning had settled over the house, squelching both the life of the fire and the energy of the children. A quartet of frozen, frightened flowers stared helplessly at Naomi, unable to organize themselves to do what was needed.

Naomi took charge, transferring her energy and will to them. "Pack a few things, children. I'll take Zinnia and Violet back with me. They can stay with Hope. I'll come back for you, Lily and Daisy, then we'll go to Aunt Mae's."

Lily stared vacantly out the window. "I reckon I can wait, or maybe we could walk with you and then go to Aunt Mae's."

Naomi silently admonished herself for her lack of sensitivity. Lily was still enough of a child to be frightened. "We'll all stay together," Naomi said. "You can stay over with me or at your aunt's."

Zinnia had not let go of her bundle or Naomi's hand. "I'm stayin' with you. I'm your little girl now for a while."

Who could argue with that determination? Certainly not her sisters. They had lived for five years with Zinnia and knew that once she got something in her mind, that was how it was and reason or persuasion couldn't change it.

Naomi kept Zinnia's hand in hers as the five of them trudged back through the snow to the mission, where Hope was waiting with oatmeal. Food can sometimes help fill the overwhelming emptiness brought on by death. At least it would give sustenance for a long day ahead of waiting and preparing the deceased.

Lily would not leave her sisters, so it was agreed that all the children would stay with Naomi until other arrangements could be made. Naomi gradually learned that no other arrangements would be possible, at least not until their Uncle George added another room to his house. The house Maddie lived in would pass on to her husband's brother, who needed it badly. He had not asked Maddie to leave after her husband's death because she had been so ill and he knew that time would take care of the matter. When Naomi understood the situation, she moved the children into the mission.

Within days, Naomi realized she could never let go of Zinnia. The child's bright disposition and easy manner filled the dark winter days with sunshine. Her small psychic antenna picked up the mood of those around her, and she seemed to say just the right words to bring on a smile. She was so different from her sisters—dark and moody Violet, practical and matter-of-fact Daisy, and elusive and dreamy Lily. Zinnia was pure joy. At night, when Naomi seemed lost in worry, Zinnia would appear by her bed, still and quiet. She would wait until Naomi sensed her presence.

"Zinnia, is that you?"

The small ghost of a child waited in the dark as she asked, "Can I sleep in you's bed?" Once she had permission, she climbed in, not so much to be comforted as to comfort.

Behind her joy at the child's presence, Naomi worried that Zinnia did not seem to grieve for her mother. Should she urge it? What was the right thing to do? Not being sure, Naomi waited. One day Zinnia suddenly asked, "Can we have a conversation?"

Naomi chuckled softly. Zinnia was holding her glass like a grown-up and now talking like one.

"I've been thinking that you might need a new house," Zinnia said. "You might get more kids to come live with you. I think Buddy wants to live with you. You need a place for girls and a place for boys because boys don't get along good."

Naomi listened with amusement. "I have enough kids now, don't you think?"

Zinnia shrugged. "Well, I've just been thinking—"

Naomi interrupted her. Maybe now was a good time to bring up Zinnia's mother. "Zinnia, I'm very happy you are here and you can be my little . . ." She paused. Saying "my little girl" made her feel disloyal to Maddie. "Do you miss your mommy?"

Zinnia shook her head and said brightly, "I'll see her again. That's what the man said." Naomi thought she must be talking about the preacher, something he said about all being reunited one day. Oh, what faith!

Zinnia went on, "The man who came the morning mommy died. He looked right at me and said, 'Don't be sad, Zinnia. You'll see Mommy soon.'"

A shudder passed though Naomi. "What man? Who came?"

"I don't know his name. I never saw him before." Zinnia got up from the table to put her glass away. She was finished with the conversation.

Naomi asked Lily, who said, "There weren't no man. That's Zinnia. She's been saying that, but there weren't no man. You know how she is. It's her imagination."

Yes, she did have quite an imagination—that was part of her magic. But it seemed unnatural to use denial as a weapon against grief. Naomi talked over the situation with Dr. Jackson, and he said it was natural, that grief came in all sorts of forms and Zinnia didn't have any signs of emotional problems.

"Oh, my, no," Naomi responded. "Zinnia is one of the most cheerful, well-adjusted children I've ever known."

But Zinnia was right about Naomi needing a new house. Two months later a man in the hollow shot his wife and left eight children. They had no family to take them, so they came to the mission. Naomi put them up in the school at night, and Hope slept there to supervise them.

Something had to be done. The answer was right under their noses, but Naomi didn't see it until she received a letter from her father. She read between the lines and knew he was still not working, and she knew without seeing his face how the shame filled up the creases and made him avert his eyes. She must be careful, very careful how she phrased her letter to him. She wrote first about how much good God had provided, then about all the children she now had—twelve—and how desperately she needed a new building. The men were starting back to their planting, she wrote, and hands were scarce, but she knew that God would provide, and she had made an agreement with herself that she would ask for nothing. She would wait for God's answer.

Putting the problem like that gave her Scottish father a way to respond. "God has his reasons for my not having work," he wrote. "He has made it so that I should come and help with your mission. I will build and plant, and your mother can cook for the children to free you for your teaching." It was just as she had wanted—indeed, planned—for she had lived long enough with her father to know how to reach him without wounding his pride.

Her parents arrived within weeks and the building began. The mountain men helped when they could. They supported the mission because it had become the vital center of the community. But the work also served to assuage the guilt the community felt over the breakup of its marriages and the abandonment of its children.

First built was a large school building with a second story to serve as a dorm for the boys. Then the new main building was constructed with bedrooms upstairs for a worker and the girls and a large room on the main floor, next to Naomi's, to serve as a nursery. Before it was completed, the home was already full. Men were leaving the hollow to look for work, promising to send support as they entrusted children to reluctant relatives, who eventually made their way to Naomi's place.

Naomi worked for two more years trying to manage teaching and running a home that by this time had grown to twenty-five children. No sooner would a family member return for one child than a new arrival would appear. Naomi wrote to the church, pleading for workers. They responded with a nurse, two single women, and finally, a teacher who could replace Naomi.

Over the years, Naomi felt obliged to correspond with Max. She kept her letters formal and informative as she knew they would be read to the congregation. Its members were generous and Naomi told them how their gifts were used. The women's missionary prayer group was especially thoughtful and creative in the personal items they selected to send around the holidays. A year earlier the group had sent a camera, so Naomi enclosed in her letters pictures of the new structures and the children. On an ordinary day in 1940, she received a letter from Max that disarranged her contented, safe, inner world.

It began, "I have been asked by the congregation to urge you to visit. Everyone is enchanted with the pictures of the children and the stories you report of the work you are doing."

Naomi scanned the page. Only fragments filtered through the chaos that erupted in her mind: I can't go; can't leave my work. Oh, to see him. No, I mustn't see him. Oh, yes. No, no, no.

She handed the letter to Hope.

"This is wonderful," Hope responded eagerly. "They want you to come and make a presentation, to stop at some of the affiliate churches on the way up. Look, a generous check, too, to cover your expenses. Of course, you must do it."

Naomi was shaking. Her safe ground was here, not in New York. She was silent throughout most of the discussion that took place after dinner when the children were in bed. Her parents and Hope recognized the opportunity to raise additional support, and there was no question that it would be foolish not to go. Now she had the staff to free her for travel. Only Hope understood Naomi's hesitation.

"*You* go," Naomi pleaded with Hope when they were alone. "Just say I couldn't get away. You will make a splendid presentation. You've been here from the beginning. You gave up your dream of going to Indonesia to help me. This mission is as much yours as mine. You haven't been home, either. Please. You would be the better representative."

Hope smiled. "You won't get off so easy by manipulating me. This is *your* place, Naomi's place—that's what everyone calls it. It's not even called the mission anymore." She paused. "Sometimes things aren't the way we imagine them. People change. You've changed. It might be the most healing thing you could do—to go back and see him."

Naomi lay awake long after sleep subdued the others. She could not imagine the world outside the hills. It had been five years since she had been outside the mountains. She tried to remember the sounds of life beyond the hills. She thought of motorcars, of shoes, hundreds of shoes, moving along sidewalks, and of the numerous sounds that came with electricity—refrigerators, radios, mixers. She thought of the sound of flushing toilets, the rush of water coming from indoor pipes and of nights filled with light and people acting as though it were day. These images were now foreign to her. Once she had taken them for granted—now they seemed bigger than life. She was frightened by the thought that she would no longer fit into her old world. She had come to count on natural light and darkness and sounds no louder than laughing children—and the silence, especially the silence. She had come to love the silence because as it grew in her, it seemed to crowd out confusion, unwanted desires, and vanity. Her life had enough complexity as it was without the sounds created by human ingenuity.

But it was another image, the one that she fought against, that won the debate. She must see Max. She would go to New York, but not entirely out of selfishness. She needed to raise funds for the home, for she had only recently recognized that she was running a children's home.

CHAPTER 6

Naomi announced her trip at the evening meal, telling the children the purpose and informing them that Hope would be left in charge. They offered prayers for her safe journey, and a few even prayed that she might not die while being so far away. Zinnia came to Naomi's room the night before Naomi left. Zinnia was nine now and slept in a room with the other girls her age, but now and again she would find her way to Naomi's bed, which was often occupied with another grieving child. Naomi could always squeeze over to make enough room for Zinnia. She tried not to show favoritism, but magic dust had been sprinkled on Zinnia and how could one not openly adore such a lovely, bright, self-contained child? Zinnia possessed a wisdom that astonished newcomers, but those who knew her accepted her prescience as being as natural to her as the freckles scattered across her nose.

"I came to be with you, to tell you not to worry," Zinnia whispered as she crawled beneath the covers.

Naomi hugged her. "And don't you worry, either."

"I won't. I'll be okay. I love you." Several times during the night she moaned in her sleep and rolled close to Naomi. Oh, Naomi thought, how I will miss her. I wish I could take her with me. Like a lightening bolt it occurred to her: why not? A child would bring the home closer to the hearts of its supporters. Next time, she thought. Zinnia could sing, and with her excellent memory she could memorize any passage of scripture and recite it. The thought thrilled Naomi. Yes! Next time.

The realization that she could take some of the mountain life with her on future trips sustained Naomi as she boarded the train. The first trip was a practice run. If it went well and she was invited back, then she would bring a child.

Naomi stopped at three affiliate churches on her way to New York. She was taken aback by how eager and generous the members were. She grew more confident with each presentation, making the children real to the audience by showing slides and telling stories of how they came to her. When Zinnia's face appeared on the screen, Naomi paused—words failed to describe how special Zinnia was. To speak of her threatened to diminish her. But the audience knew, for when Zinnia's face filled the screen in the darkened church, there was a gasp.

Naomi said, "This is my precious Zinnia." The longing that swelled in her chest choked off her words. No more needed to be said.

By the time Naomi reached New York, she had collected over $500, an incredible sum in a nation still in the throes of the Great Depression. The churches were eager to support her cause, and several members privately told her they were glad to have money going to "our children" rather than overseas missions.

The closer Naomi got to New York, the farther away Max seemed. The effect of the trip, the recognition, the praise, the accolades, filled her with a sense that she needed nothing more than her work. Seeing the results of her work through the eyes of strangers filled her with an even greater passion to serve God. She had no room for Max. She stepped off the train in New York confident that she could face him and need nothing from him.

She was greeted by a small reception committee. Naomi was grateful because the awkward first moment of looking into Max's eyes was postponed. She had wondered if Max would meet her alone, and the thought had filled her with apprehension. Instead, she was distracted by meeting people for whom she had worked—baby-sitting their children, scrubbing their floors, cooking their meals—while she attended college. Their names—and those of their children and parents—easily returned to her. The distance, the estrangement that she worried about, dissolved as quickly as morning fog in the sun. It was as though she had gone away for only a few days instead of years.

Hope was wrong about her being changed, Naomi realized. She was dangerously the same. The same. She tried to steady herself by thinking of Hope.

She faltered as Max approached. He was less boyish in appearance: the gray that gathered around his temples, the soft lines forming around his mouth and between his brows, and the few extra pounds gave him a compassionate fatherly image befitting a pastor. A quick stride and he stood at her side before she could find a diversion. The warmth of his voice—and his smile, the open, wide smile—pulled her unwillingly to him.

"Welcome home, Naomi," he said as he extended his hand to her. When she took it, he grasped her hand tightly.

"Hello, Max." She quickly turned away from him and spoke to the audience. "It's good to be back. How kind of everyone to be here. Thank you all." As she turned, she struggled to free her hand from his. Max made a short speech in honor of her return, and then they became separated as friends made their way forward to share news and to ask questions. Naomi looked for Max's wife, Madeline, but she was not among them. She pushed aside a small panic fighting to surface. *I love this man too greatly,* she thought. *What will I do alone with Max if just the touch of his hand can undo my balance?*

A few hours later she found herself sitting alone with him at the dining room table. An awkward silence filled the air, reminding Naomi of the last scene between them, when they had fought courageously against their longing for one another. Unconsciously, she began a nervous little hum. The click-click of the typewriter coming from the small office on the opposite side of the living room became irritatingly loud. Max rose to shut the door. The act shot a bolt of fear through Naomi, making her abruptly aware of how dangerously alone they were. His eyes met hers, and now there was no mask. His face was full of love, and he said again, "Welcome home, Naomi."

Frantically, she cast about for a distraction. "What do the doctors say about Madeline? Do they know what the problem is?"

"There is nothing physical that they can find. Depression. A sickness of the soul."

Naomi did not know much about depression and was sure that being in the good grace of God—or Max—should relieve it. It was incomprehensible to her that this could happen. But she was not one to judge.

She had to get away from him. "May I see her?"

"Certainly. But stay with me a bit. Let me just look at you."

She rose quickly and turned to the window, clenching her fists tightly and shutting her eyes against a flood of tears. "No." Her voice sounded strange, harsh. "I can't—we can't. Don't."

He rose to stand near her and she moved wildly, like an animal about to be caught.

"Stay away. I shouldn't have come." She tried to get past him and find the door.

His large frame blocked her. He reached for her arm and said, "It's okay. It's okay. I'm sorry." They stood beside one another for a moment. When her trembling stopped, he said, "Tell me what you would like me to say to the congregation tonight when I introduce your work."

They kept the conversation on safe ground for the next hour, and gradually Naomi regained her self-control.

Max then took Naomi to his wife's bedroom. The room was darkened by heavy drapes, keeping the glorious, bright sunshine outside. They found Madeline lying still with open eyes. Max leaned against the doorframe, watching the two women—one radiant, the other dull; one full, the other shriveled; one effervescent, the other listless. Then he turned and left them.

Madeline's face brightened when Naomi approached. "I wanted to come to the reception. Forgive me. I was so tired. I'm glad you've come."

Naomi stayed two hours with Madeline's hands in hers, telling her stories about the children and her home. At one point Naomi thought she felt energy flowing from herself into Madeline, but she dismissed the idea. She observed that Madeline rose to a seated position in bed but made nothing of Madeline's increased questions or sudden bursts of laughter. Madeline had always loved Naomi.

Naomi prayed with Madeline before she left. The prayer was simple and brief. "God, please bring Madeline your warm light."

Max knocked softly on the door to tell Naomi that they had thirty minutes before the evening service. The church had scheduled a special Saturday night program. Naomi ate a light supper and collected her slides and equipment for the presentation. As was customary, all returning missionaries stayed at the parish, where simple quarters consisting of a bedroom and small sitting room were available to them. Until she entered the room to change, she had not given any thought to where she might stay. With her feelings toward Max, it seemed indecent for her to sleep under his roof. It wasn't that either of them would violate the social code, but she would be more comfortable elsewhere. Maybe she could make arrangements to stay with a former college friend—if one showed up at church.

––––––

Max led one of the largest nondenominational churches on the East Coast, with over five hundred members. He inspired in them a zealous need to spread the gospel to all corners of the earth. An active social committee raised money for the projects they sponsored.

The large audience surprised Naomi. Slowly she learned how they had looked forward to her letters, waiting with anticipation for each month's news about the mission. She realized the congregation had begun to feel personally invested in the growth of the mission, as though their spiritual worth moved up a notch with the success of her work. The woman running the women's missionary prayer group announced that the group was committed to fulfilling one Christmas request for each child at the mission.

When Naomi rose to give her presentation, she held back tears. With words full with emotion she expressed her gratitude for their care and concern. As she was concluding one of the most moving and amusing accounts of her work, a member suddenly asked if any of the children in her pictures could be adopted—especially Zinnia. Naomi stumbled.

Struggling for a proper answer, Naomi feebly replied, "Well, most of these children have families or relatives who are trying to get back on their feet so they can eventually provide for them. In time, someone comes for the children. We have none free for adoption at this time."

After she finished, she sat on the stage listening to Max's concluding remarks and scanned the audience for a familiar face. She spotted Myrtle Wilkinson, a sister of her former college roommate Katie, and hoped her conflict about staying at Max's was resolved. After the service Naomi maneuvered her way through the crowd that gathered around her until she finally found Myrtle.

Myrtle threw her arms around Naomi, her eyes sparkling with admiration. "Wait until I write Katie. She will be so thrilled to hear about your work. You know she is in Africa, with the Wycliffe group, helping to translate the Bible."

Naomi knew about Katie's gift with languages, and it seemed natural for her to use it for translating the Bible into an African dialect. "I would love to see the family again," Naomi said. "Are they here?"

"No, Mom is helping a neighbor. Dad is working."

"Oh. I thought we might get together so that I can catch up on Katie's life. I'm here for only a few days. I was hoping tonight . . ." She dropped her sentence as she saw a troubled look cross Myrtle's face.

Suddenly Myrtle brightened. She pulled the young woman standing beside her forward and thrust her close to Naomi. "Naomi, meet my friend Ruth. Ruth Lewis. This is her *first* visit to church." She said it in a tone that meant "she is an outsider."

Ruth was an attractive, fashionably dressed woman; her hair and makeup were stylish. Naomi felt the stranger's air of superiority like a chill. As Ruth reached for Naomi's hand, something inside Naomi recoiled, but she quickly recovered her poise.

Their brief conversation was ended by others pressing forward to talk with Naomi. Later, Myrtle found Naomi, and as she hugged her goodbye she whispered, "I would love to have you come home with me tonight. But I have a bit of a crisis on my hands—Ruth, you know . . ." She looked away. "Sorry. Hope we can see each other before you leave. I'll drop by."

With no alternative, Naomi was left to stay with Max. On the way to the house, she chatted nervously with him, filling the silence with thanks for the generosity of the members of the congregation. She praised the work Max had done and the support he had given to her.

Max sat silent, drawing out the ten-minute drive from the church to the parish. "It's you they love. Everyone loves you."

What could she say? She knew what he meant and she was afraid her heart murmur would become a loud cry. Distance, yes, she needed distance to regain her equilibrium. As soon as they were inside the house, she excused herself, pleading fatigue from an exhausting day.

His look of disappointment did not escape her. But he let her go. "I hope we have more time to talk before you leave," he offered reluctantly.

The next morning she spoke briefly in church. All that was collected from the offering plates that morning and the night before went to her. She would return to her mountain home rich.

After the morning service a lunch was served at Max's house. Several church board members were present. Max's secretary, who served as hostess instead of Madeline, prepared the meal. Max was keenly aware of Naomi's beauty. As he glanced around the lunch table, his eyes continually returned to Naomi. There is no beauty like that of a woman contented with life, fully living up to her potential, and completely unaware of herself.

It was early fall, just a few days into October. The sky was shockingly blue, the gold and crimson leaves hung in unnatural beauty, as though they had been traced against a blue page to accent their splendor. Off the dining room, the doors that led to a garden were open, and the curtains stirred, softly lifting and falling with the same gentle rhythm as the conversation.

Suddenly, a powerful longing for Mission Creek gripped Naomi. Her mind drifted back to her home. How different this world was from the one she had left, she thought. At the mission, there would be no silver and china gracing the table. The conversation would not be about committee meetings but rather about some small crisis in the life of one of the children. For a moment she thought she heard the mission's bell.

Max rose to respond to the doorbell, rousing her from her reverie. She smiled and nodded as he excused himself. He returned shortly and handed her a telegram. "It's for you."

———

His words kept bouncing through her brain like a clanging gong and Naomi closed her eyes against the moment. She did not want it to be for her. No. It should never have come. She remembered Max handing the telegram to her. She remembered opening it. She could not remember how she got to the couch in his study. When she opened her eyes, she was alone with him. He was sitting close to her, holding her hand and rubbing her forehead.

"Dear, dear Naomi," he kept repeating.

She remembered only one word of the telegram—*Fire*—then closed her eyes and mind again. She fought to stay conscious, to take the pain in bits, but it came too strong and too hard, beating at her until she was sure it would kill her if she stayed conscious. The next time she opened her eyes Max was holding her head and gently offering her water. "Drink," he said, and she did. Sweet, pure water to wash the taste of ash from her mouth.

She was obedient for she had no will of her own. A pill went down with the water and she saw the doctor standing over her. Before the pill took effect, she remembered more:

> Mission destroyed by fire. *Stop.* Five children and two
> staff lost. *Stop.* Zinnia, father, and Hope among. *Stop.*

She heard a cry come out of her, an anguished sound she had never heard before, like the wail of a wretched, tormented animal.

———

It was night when she awoke. Max still sat beside her. She felt groggy, medicated, but she struggled to sit. She reached for the water on the table, but her hands shook, so he held the glass for her. She looked into his eyes as she drank. Her eyes were wide, searching. When he set the glass down, he took her in his arms and held her against his heart. Finally, with her face close to his, she asked, "Why?"

"I don't know," he breathed into her hair.

She was grateful that he didn't lie or try to make her accept the unacceptable. They were silent in their embrace and he stroked her hair gently. She heard his words, his throat full of pain, "Oh, my dear, if I could only take your pain, I gladly would bear it to spare you."

"But it is mine, isn't it? Oh, Max, how will I bear it?" She pushed away from him and started toward the desk, where the telegram lay open, waiting to destroy her again with the impersonal words inked on the page. She drew back and walked to the doors that opened to the garden outside. She opened them and welcomed the cold night air on her face. She felt cold, hot, cold, hot. Then she retched. Max was at her side with more water. She felt weak. Max lifted her in his arms before her legs gave way and carried her back to the couch, where he sat with her, rocking her, soothing her. "Your strength is in the Lord," he said.

She felt the first wave of anger, but her voice came out like a pleading child's. "Where was God? Where was God at five o'clock this morning?" Her body shook uncontrollably. Slowly out of her medicinal haze one thought stood clear: I must get home.

"Max, send a telegram that I am on my way. Take me to the station." The recognition of what she needed to do gave her a sudden strength.

"Naomi, it is late. You must rest. Stay here until you are stronger." He wanted to tell her that he could not bear to let her go, never again, now that he had held her. He wanted to be her protector, her comforter, to see her though this. That was his job and there was never a time that he wanted more to fulfill that role—for his beloved.

She steadied herself as she rose, propelled by the urgency to move, to act. Her voice was low and determined. "If you do not take me, I will walk. I would rather wait at the train station than be with someone who will not help me." She faced him squarely, waiting for his answer.

"I cannot." The two regarded one another for a moment, then Naomi grabbed the telegram from the desk and ran for the stairs. She felt wild and at the edge of entirely falling apart. In her room she sat on the bed, folding and unfolding the telegram, not daring to look at it, trying desperately to collect herself. Sucking in deep breaths, she kept repeating, "They need me." Repeating these words like a mantra, she began to gather her belongings and throw them into the single satchel that had been her traveling companion.

As she left her bedroom she could hear Max and Madeline in conversation. She heard Madeline say, "If you don't drive her, I will. You can't keep her here. She needs to go."

Madeline walked out of her room and down the hall toward Naomi. "My dear, I will take you to the station, and then I will go to the telegraph office and send a message saying when they can expect you."

Max spoke reluctantly, "I will take her."

He did not put her on the train until he found another traveler going to the next station. He told the young woman Naomi's story and asked if she would stay with Naomi and see that she boarded her next train. He also requested that she look for someone who would go on the next leg of the journey with Naomi, and so on until Naomi was safely home.

That is how Naomi went home, guarded, guided through each portion of her journey, under the watchful eye of fellow travelers whose only reward was the belief that they were playing a small part in a tragedy that would be in the headlines of the next day's news. Naomi did not thank them for their part in protecting her, for she was unaware, lost in the depths of her grief.

CHAPTER 7

Naomi sat stoically upright, staring straight ahead. The lady beside her was speaking. "Are you all right? Can I get you something, dear? Some tea?"

Gazing vacantly, Naomi shook her head and the woman fell silent.

The train raced purposefully ahead, its wheels clacking, first vague and muffled, then becoming louder until the noise roared in Naomi's ears: clickity-clack, clickity-clack. *It should have been me, it should have been me.* At first her numbed will gave in to the rhythm, letting it wash across her mind like a great soothing wave until it nearly drowned her. Finally her mind broke free and pushed forward in a desperate debate with God. *Why not me? You know I would have given my life for any one of theirs; seven times—one life for each one. This pain is greater than death, for it will not end, it will go on for an eternity. Is this my destiny? Is this your plan for me?* A small groan escaped her, and the woman beside her reached over and gently squeezed her arm.

I told you to go. Oh, Hope, why didn't you go? If only you had gone instead of me. Always thinking of someone else. How can I go on without you? Why? Why? Why? Where were you when the fire came? Did you see Zinnia? Did she cry? Did she suffer? Papa would have been there first. It happened in the early morning. He would have been milking. He would have seen the flames. Did he see her? Did she scream? He would not have let her suffer. She died in his arms, resting against his strong shoulders. Oh, Papa, I remember when you lifted me on your strong shoulders above the crowds at the circus. "Look, Naomi, you can see more than everyone." I could see the merry-go-round, the clowns walking among the crowds, people eating large puffs of colored cotton candy and throwing balls for prizes, and I could see behind the tent where the girls in sparkling dresses were standing with the animals. I screamed when I saw the man swallow fire and you said, "It's a trick; don't be afraid." Oh, Papa, could this be a trick? Don't leave us. You are our safety. Clickity-clack, clickity-clack. *It should have been me.*

I wish I could sleep. Two days before I get there. Madeline said she would send notice—when to expect me. Two days. Oh, God, was it pride? Pride goeth before the fall. Or vanity? I didn't want to leave. I didn't want more than what we had. Was it so wrong to see Max again that they should die? I didn't come on this trip for me. It was for the children. The children. My responsibility. I should not have gone, should not have given in to my desires—to see him. I knew it could come to no good. Oh, why didn't you stop me, God? I cannot feel your presence. Only the pain. Don't abandon me for I cannot go on, cannot go alone, without your strength. Where is my comfort? Where is my light in this darkest hour?

Naomi looked absently into the night. The wheels of the train kept humming. *It should have been me.* She saw a tiny spider work its way along the window ledge. She watched vacantly, aware of her power of life and death over this small intruder. She could determine its destiny. Was it that simple, being in the wrong place at the wrong time? Abruptly she squashed the spider with a finger. She jerked back her hand in disbelief—the aggression had slipped out of her as uncontrollably as the earlier groan. She hadn't meant to kill it. Doubts began to seep up from the chasm that she had sealed long before. Could it be that tragedy occurs without reason? That it happens randomly to both good and bad? She felt her heart beating in her chest like a quivering, captured bird wanting freedom. She plunged on. Then what about God? How did he fit into man's life? Maybe there is no—*Don't say it, Naomi. You are close to losing your soul.*

At that moment, as clear and real as the conductor who paused at her seat each time he passed, Hope sat across from her. *Naomi, don't try to understand the unknowable. You have not lost me. I will be with you forever. There's something I never told you—not outright, but maybe you guessed. I never really wanted to go to Indonesia. I knew after one day at the mission that I belonged there for as long as I was needed. Don't grieve so for me or Papa or Zinnia and the others. Their suffering is over. If you give up, if you stop your work, you will have used up your life in self-absorption. You will be a hollow martyr.* Hope threw back her head and laughed as she always did when she saw irony. *Imagine me, a martyr. I always thought it would be you, Naomi. You were a natural for it.* Naomi shuddered. She blinked to clear away the vision. It would not leave. Maybe she was asleep and this was a dream. She heard her own voice sounding dead and distant, "Have you seen Zinnia?" She realized she was not dreaming and she felt foolish for letting the words escape. The woman sitting next to her patted Naomi's arm. Hope disappeared.

Oh, Hope is right, I cannot question God. His ways are mysterious. But the pain. I don't think I can bear the pain. The children. My responsibility. What did she mean, I was a natural for a martyr? I don't like to suffer. I only try to be kind, understanding, selfless. I must ask Mother. She will tell me. Mother—was she with Papa when he died? Mother was probably looking after the burned who were alive.

As though an angry lightning bolt had jolted her, Naomi was suddenly thinking of how selfish she was to feel such pain, for she had not heard the screams, seen the dead, held the disfigured, lived the tragedy. She turned to her God. She would ask not for herself. *God, give them strength. Sustain them with thy love. Be close. Give me strength, not for me, but for them.*

———

She did not question how it was that upon changing trains another person always appeared who was attentive and helpful. She believed that God's watchful eye was upon her, intervening, interceding, interjecting his will. She must trust.

Waiting for her next train, Naomi felt distracted by the lonely, loud announcements of departures and arrivals in the sleepy early morning hours. She went into the clean Harvey station restaurant for coffee. It seemed that lost and unattached souls traveled in the late night hours. Those who belonged to someone were placed on trains early in the morning, traveled by day, and were met by family or friends before bedtime. A young woman traveling with a child said she was waiting for the next connection and would wait with her, if Naomi didn't mind. Naomi was not one to say no. She was too accustomed to accommodating others.

This train is quieter. How kind the woman was who helped with my connection. Do I carry my grief as a poster? Is that why the people in the restaurant were looking at me? She gave me a copy of the newspaper; how did she know? Not yet; I will read it before I get there—when I feel stronger. The names are not right; they called Zinnia "Ina." They wouldn't think that she was named for a flower. Zinnia—happy, sunny Zinnia. Oh, my little flower. My small bright ray of sunshine, my joy. My little girl. To never see your face again. My children. My responsibility!

"Oh, thank you." She nodded as the woman handed her a handkerchief. Naomi had not been aware her tears were falling.

A kind woman—I cannot explain these tears to her. It would break me in two. How is it that I stand, sit, move, breathe? How is it that a heart that has a murmur does not fail? Oh, God, you still ask everything of me when you have taken all. Am I unworthy? Is that the lesson? I am unworthy to be a mother? Did I abandon my calling out of pride? Was it wrong to want more, to want to do more? I went beyond myself and I am brought low. Is that it? They call it Naomi's place, but it was not mine. It was yours and in my pride I called it mine. Do you want me to leave? Oh, such pain, such stupefying pain—to leave the mountains, the people, the children. The children. My responsibility! What would I do? Where would I go? I must leave. I cannot stay amongst the ashes. That is all that is left. Ashes of all whom I loved. Don't they know that my heart is but cinders? Blackened, smoldering coal. I wonder if it was the coal that started the fire. The conductor told me they intentionally let more coal fall from the train when they passed because they saw us with our buckets in the cold late afternoons. They wanted to help. So much good.

"Joy to the World." That's what they sang on Christmas morning as they came down the stairs, each carrying a lit candle, singing and eager to receive their Christmas gift—a piece of fruit—at the bottom of the steps. The children in their white robes. Zinnia, be careful of the fire.

PART I

Hold your candle away from your dress, sweetheart. How bright her eyes look, shining—like stars. What? I can't hear you above the noise. Her lips were moving.

Naomi leaned forward toward the vision, the face in the window. *I am with my mommy. Thank you for being my other mommy. I needed one for a little while. You'll be a mommy to more children.*

No. I can't do it again. The child nodded her head, her wise eyes smiling. *Yes, you will, because they need you.*

Zinnia, your dress, it's on fire. Come back! Gone! Gone! Oh, my little girl.

"Would you like to hold her?"

Naomi was startled by the voice. She must have spoken again. She realized she had been staring at the face of the child who was resting against her mother, watching Naomi with large sad eyes. Did she know? Naomi wondered. Naomi shook her head. There was only one child that she wanted to hold.

The train's wheels made a rushing sound. Now its rhythm echoed the words *I will fear no evil, I will fear no evil.*

My thoughts won't stay inside my head, they leap out of my mouth. I need some relief from the pain. Maybe I will see Zinnia again in my sleep. Maybe Hope. Maybe Papa. "Shall we gather at the river, the beautiful, the beautiful river." *No one can sing it like Mother. I need to see Mother. She will tell me how to get through.*

It was the image of her mother that began to turn the tide and brought rest at last. The train rocked her as gently as her mother's arms when she had sought them in the past. She heard her mother whisper. *My child, be strong, be strong in the Lord.* "The Lord is my strength and my shield: my heart trusted in him, and I am helped; the Lord is their strength, and he is the saving strength of his anointed." *Lean hard upon him. Lean hard. Lean hard.*

What time is it? It is approaching night. I must have slept.

Naomi's tortured thoughts continued. It was the feeling she had failed in her responsibility to the children that tormented her. Would she be suffering more if she had given birth to them, she wondered? She thought not, she thought that for a child to die while in one's trusted care magnified the pain.

She would never go further with the anger against God than she went during the two-and-a-half-day train ride. Belief and trust in a higher authority than her own had been securely fixed in her since childhood. She had learned well the lesson that a kind, caring authority knows better than the child what it needs. Before she arrived at her destination, she had again surrendered her will, her longing, her outrage, to a loving and fair God. Yes, he must be fair. This horrific happening in her life must come from a need to balance the books for a reason mysterious to her.

———•———

George Watson met the train eighty miles away from Madison Creek. He could not let Naomi make another transfer, for she would have had to wait until the next day to make the connection.

She spotted him in the big terminal, standing out of place wearing clean but stained overalls, twirling his hat awkwardly, nervously pacing like a caged animal in a zoo. He rushed to her. The kindness and concern flooding his face brought tears to her eyes.

"Howdy, ma'am. I—we—couldn't let you wait. Thought you might need some company on the trip home."

"Oh, thank you, George. You are an answer to a prayer. How is Mae? The children?"

"Let me help you git your things in the truck. I borrowed it from Mr. Ness. He would have come—wanted to—but he paid for the gas." She understood; she was touched by how quickly she must have come to their thoughts. She knew he'd had to leave his grieving wife—Zinnia was her niece, after all.

"I'll tell you everything I know." He paused briefly and added, "If you want to know. Whatever you want to know, I'll tell you."

She was grateful to him for hiding nothing. She was tired of feeling protected. She wanted the freedom to choose how much pain she could endure. If he could stand there before her breathing, talking, going on with the responsibilities of life, she could, too.

Her breathing was shallow, for she didn't want to go too deep inside or feel too much of herself. "How did it start?" she wanted to know.

"Well, they found some oily rags near the potbelly on the second floor. After the morning fire was set, the door must have not been closed all the way. It seems the rags caught. It went fast."

She didn't ask—she could never ask—who had set the morning fire.

The story came out haltingly and in bits. But she finally saw it all and lived it through George's eyes. Her papa had seen the flames as he was coming out of the barn, and he rushed to the building. He threw the milk on the ground and ran for water. The bucket of water he frantically drew from the well to use on the flames was mostly lost to the earth again as he ran toward the burning building.

He stripped off his shirt and soaked it in the half-full bucket and he ran into the flaming building screaming, "Wake up! Fire! Fire! Wake up!" Hope was the first with him; he gave her his shirt to put over her face. They ran up the stairs and both carried a child out. They screamed for the children to wake. Some were already full of smoke and did not respond. They got out as many as they could. Hope didn't follow her papa out the last time. He thought she had. Zinnia was outside with Lily. Suddenly she pointed to the second story and called, "There's the man!" She freed herself from Lily and ran toward the burning building. Lily looked up in the window but could see only Hope, standing there screaming; she was on fire.

George spoke in a steady, firm voice. "Your pa knew he couldn't save her, there was no more they could save. But when he saw Zinnia run into the building, he went tearing after her; he was yelling at her, real mad, 'Little flower, you git back here right this minute.' But she kept running. She was halfway up the stairs when he got her and the stairs collapsed. He died holding her."

He had finished the story. His face was grim and taut. "I'm awful sorry, ma'am. She killed him. She was right quare. Don't think she ever was in her full mind."

Naomi reached for his arm and touched it lightly. "Oh, George, she was a special child. I loved her like my own. Papa would not have had it any other way. He would rather have died saving the children than to have wasted away in old age."

Naomi knew her papa. She knew what she said about him to be the truth. For a fleeting moment she felt envy for the dead because their pain was over. But she knew the wrenching pain of their departure would be dulled by the responsibilities of living. Already she could feel the ache begin to be pushed aside as she prepared to meet her mother and the rest of the survivors.

PART II

WHITHER THOU GOEST: RUTH, 1941–1950

CHAPTER 8

The train began to slow a mile before its destination. A young woman looked anxiously out the window, searching for some evidence of beauty, one small indication of something uplifting in the view outside that would lighten the heaviness that had settled over her. *Bleak. Brown. Bare. No beauty, civility, or development.* Those were the words that drifted through her thoughts as she tried to prepare herself for her destiny. The heaviness deepened as the train gained distance from the last town and burrowed into the hills. It was the late fall of 1941 and nature was in hibernation. Cold had obliterated the beauty and charm of the land, leaving a barren, worn-out place.

Her fellow travelers who had boarded in Westchester, headed toward Mission Creek and beyond, were so strikingly different from those with whom she had left New York two days ago that she began to withdraw deep into herself, barely able to nod in response to their howdies. Her clothes—a fashionably tailored suit with wide lapels and padded shoulders, a tidy handkerchief peeking from the breast pocket, a hat tilted enough to partly cover one eye, and shiny matching shoes—were in stark contrast to the overalls, homemade flour-sack dresses, and threadbare and dated suits around her.

Have I made a mistake? she wondered. Will I ever feel close to these people? Will I ever belong? Well, God had not sent her to be happy or to make others happy, she concluded. He had sent her to do his work. That was the bargain she had struck with him, and she was determined to keep it. At twenty-four, she had put youth, frivolity, and happiness behind her. Her face had begun to accept this fact, for small, tight lines near the mouth were settling in, and the eyes had given up the sparkle that once danced in them. She had a lovely face with clear porcelain skin and thick honey-colored hair that complemented the golden flecks in her dark eyes. Her bearing did not invite, it commanded. And because she was not yet sure of herself with this new calling, she donned a haughty look in an effort to keep the old self suppressed.

The train let out a loud, long exhalation as it came to a stop. The conductor cried out, "Mission Creek, all off for Mission Creek." She stepped off the train into the four o'clock dusk. A light drizzle had begun to fall and the bare trees along the stream bank looked like angry infantrymen with pitchforks. She had been unable to get soldiers off her mind since her brother Lee had been assigned to the Philippines. She stood on the gravel along the tracks, looking for a familiar face. Naomi came running toward her, breaking free of a small group surrounding her.

"Ruth, Ruth Lewis," Naomi called as she ran. One year had passed since Ruth had last seen Naomi; Ruth noted that Naomi was a little heavier and the vibrant glow that had radiated from her the night of her presentation at the church was no longer there. But as Naomi came nearer, Ruth could see her eyes were still warm and eager. Ruth felt the same odd stirring she had felt when she first met Naomi. She wanted to be near this woman—wanted to possess something she had, to be like her.

"My dear, what a long trip you have had," Naomi said. "I trust it was not a difficult journey."

"No. I took a sleeper most of the way."

Naomi turned to the woman accompanying her, "This is Linda— 'Miss Lindy' the children call her. She takes care of the little ones. And I might add is loved by them all."

Linda blushed and brushed off the compliment. "My job is easy because the children are so special," she said.

Self-consciousness suddenly came over Ruth and she felt a need to tell them straight out, "Well, I don't care much for children. I wrote you that I came to cook." It was not entirely self-consciousness that made her confess. She was responding to Linda's humility. Ruth had an inordinate need to set herself apart from others, to not be swallowed up in the average, and the average here, she believed, was humility.

Linda gave Naomi a grave look. Naomi responded, "Well, you may not have been around many children. I am sure you will come to love these children. Your luggage?"

The conductor had set a large trunk and several suitcases along the track. The train stopped only long enough to let off the passengers and to take on new ones. It was already moving slowly down the track, picking up speed. The three women walked back to gather the luggage. Naomi and Linda strained as they lifted the trunk. Ruth stood reluctantly next to the two suitcases, showing no sign of intending to pick them up.

Naomi looked around for help and waved toward Floyd, who was leaning against the rail on the post office porch. "Floyd, can you give us a hand?"

"Sure," he said, and the first southern word that reached Ruth's ears was a soft drawl that made "sure" sound like it had two syllables.

"This is Ruth Lewis, our new cook. Ruth, meet Floyd. He's married to one of our first girls, Lily. How is she, Floyd?"

"Well, you ought to know. You see more of her than me," Floyd said and he laughed.

"Yes, I know," Naomi acknowledged. And a bitter silence fell as the four of them set off down the muddy road.

Floyd shook his head and grinned as Ruth tried to preserve her high-heeled shoes from the mud. She carried nothing but a newspaper folded under her arm.

"Oh, you brought a paper," Naomi noted. "We never see one. What fun we'll have after dinner, Linda, catching up on the world." She turned back to Ruth, "We get the news in bits—mostly word of mouth from visitors or neighbors who have been to town. When we go into town, we get a little more from Dr. Jackson, who has a radio."

Linda chuckled, "That is, if we remember to ask."

Ruth did not understand how far away the world was in the hollows. Even concerns about local politics in Madison Creek seemed remote— much less events going on across great waters and wide continents.

Linda's attitude again made Ruth want to set herself apart. "A lot of people don't seem to care," Ruth said. "People that don't think we should get involved. But we will—already are. Hitler's monstrous hunger to take whatever he wants, must be stopped. We already have troops overseas. My brother is in the Philippines. I have no doubt we will go to war."

Linda didn't reply. She was too consumed with the daily activities of the children in her care to have time for world events.

"Well, we'll just go on over there and show that scoundrel a thing or two," declared Floyd. "Hell, give me a chance and I'd take him out with my Betsy."

"Watch your language, Floyd," Naomi cautioned. "And violence doesn't solve problems."

"Who's Betsy?" Ruth asked him.

"My rifle—its name."

"Oh," Ruth said. She was looking at this lanky, uneducated, ungroomed man of about twenty-one and comparing him to her brother, who had just graduated from West Point, who was so handsome, so magnificent in his uniform, who understood the complexity of international affairs far more deeply than this ignorant stranger.

———

Naomi was eager to help Ruth feel more comfortable. She had reread Max's letter before meeting the train, but now she understood his warning. "She is a new convert, eager to serve; she is a close friend of Myrtle, your friend Katie's younger sister, and Myrtle, it seems, has rescued Ruth from a difficult situation. Myrtle assures me that Ruth is a dedicated, determined young woman who just needs some love and friendship to bring forth her potential. I could not place her in better hands. I have told you often of how your presence here was like a miracle for Madeline. Every day we bless you in our prayers."

Although the ache was smaller, it sat like a small acorn in her chest, looking for soil in which to grow. Naomi was always surprised to find it still there; she was ever hopeful that it would shrivel and die.

"Not all who receive the call to serve are fully prepared or understand the sacrifice involved. Whatever the outcome, God has a plan. We fully support your work and have much gratitude for the numerous missionaries who have served under you and gone on to other missions."

"You probably don't remember me," Ruth said, turning to Naomi. "It was the first time that I attended the church—the night you gave the presentation. The night before . . . the fire."

A frosty stillness fell. No one in the hollow talked of the fire after the dead were buried, even though scars remained on the arms and faces of a few survivors.

No one spoke, so Ruth continued. "I came with Myrtle, a friend who was a member of the church. It turned my life around. I saw the pictures that night and I knew that I, too, wanted to do something of value—I mean, something meaningful. After the fire, I joined the women's group and helped collect blankets and things to be sent on to you—to help with the rebuilding. But I was waiting to be used—really needed. And then you wrote and asked for a cook. God spoke to me and said it was time. So here I am."

Summaries present only a skeleton of the truth. Although what Ruth said was true, there was much more to the story. Her desperation had been touched by inspiration that night and hope awakened within her. She wanted to be free of her evil, of her sins of recklessness and fleshiness. She wanted to be whole, to have the certainty and self-assurance she saw in Naomi. She believed—without knowing why—that if she was near such goodness it would rub off on her and she would be redeemed. She arrived in Mission Creek with that expectation.

The answer she gave was interpreted differently by each of the three listeners. Naomi thought, God led her there that night at my highest moment. He used me to touch this woman's life. I will do my best to fulfill his plan. Linda thought, She's come out of selfishness. Come for her own glory, not for God's. She will never be like Naomi. Floyd thought, She is running—and she is a liar.

They neared the mission and Ruth got her first look at the crudely made buildings that had been reconstructed after the fire. Light from kerosene lanterns filled two big dark holes, like eyes peering across the veranda at the approaching party. The children who had lingered on the large porch waiting for their dear Naomi ran forward calling "Nam" and "Miss Lindy." "Nam" was the affectionate blend of "Naomi" and "Mom" that had become the title by which they respectfully addressed her.

Ruth was slightly unnerved by their noise, their rambunctiousness, and by the name *Nam,* which seemed to her ears disrespectful. And, oh, she respected Naomi and felt that everyone should honor her with the same regard. Ruth heard her mother's voice, "Children should be seen and not heard," and for the first time in her life, she agreed.

Naomi and Linda set down the trunk to greet the children. When they were introduced to "Miss Ruth," they became shy and deferential. It was Martha, the youngest in the group and the dirtiest, who reached for Ruth. "I ain't never seen nothin' so nice," she said as she extended a filthy hand to touch the designer suit. Linda intervened with a quick movement to embrace the child. Ruth gave Linda a look of thanks and the tension that had been present dissolved.

Supper was almost ready. The luggage was left on the front porch as the adults and children hurried to the dining room. The menu was special because they were welcoming a new worker: soup served with beef, corn bread, and coleslaw. The dining room was crowded with twenty-five children and four adults—three women and a man. Nathan Bush, the sole male worker, timidly nodded when introduced to Ruth. He was a slight man with watery eyes and a reddened nose that gave him the appearance of having just finished crying.

Ruth studied him briefly and summed him up with one word—"ineffectual." She filed the description safely away in her mind. She did this whenever she met someone new. Her one-word record of her first impression would remain unaltered until she had reason to expand it. Naomi had been summed up as "holy" when Ruth first laid eyes on her. Tonight "tired" was added.

Ruth looked around the dining room. The children were scrambling to find seats next to their friends. Then they stood behind their chairs, waiting for the blessing of the meal. Before sitting, they sang their welcome song—simple, commonplace words sung to the tune of "Happy Birthday." "We welcome you here, we welcome you here, we children of the mission, we welcome you here." Then the room filled with the voices of happy children, sometimes calling to a friend at another table. When the noise level increased, Naomi stood and asked that they lower their voices. This occurred three times during the meal.

After supper Ruth was eager to see the kitchen since she had come to cook. What she saw was small and bare. Water pails were lined up along a crudely constructed shelf. As soon as one was emptied, Ruth learned, it was set by the door so the next person going outside could fill it at the well. As soon as a meal had finished cooking, a pail was quickly placed on the stove to heat water for washing dishes. The cook was also responsible for keeping the fire burning for all meals.

It was a meager kitchen, but she could make it more functional. It appealed to her because it was small and set apart from the dining room. In the kitchen she would have full control. She could maintain a semblance of order. Ruth decided that she would remain in the kitchen during all meals. The noise of the dining room offended her. She cringed when she thought of the lack of order. How much more gracious, more splendid would be the work of the Lord if it was done neatly and with order.

———

Later that night as Ruth lay in bed, she had difficulty relaxing. Her nerves were raw from the day's journey. Her body jerked with small spasms as she lay in the dark, questioning her choice. The mission was nothing like she had imagined. As time had passed, Naomi had become bigger than life in her mind—mother, saint, healer, who out of ashes had created a miracle that housed small, clean, well-behaved, silent angels. Instead, she found herself in a shoddy, small, crudely constructed place with unruly, unclean children speaking with mangled grammar. Could she find deliverance in such an inadequate setting? It was too much to ask of her. But where else would she get the esteem, respect, and admiration that the congregation showered on Naomi, who was eulogized above all the other missionaries?

She bitterly thought of the members of the congregation. Why did they venerate perfection? Did it make them seem less flawed? But she was guilty as well. Oh, yes, she was flawed and she needed to be valued by the woman in the other room. She had dreamed of coming to Naomi to befriend, to aid, to be her servant. Instead, Naomi had seemed reserved with her. As usual she was confused by the way most people treated her with aloofness. Why didn't they like her? Why didn't friendships last long? Myrtle had screamed at her that it was she, Ruth, who used up people and then discarded them, long before they grew weary of her. Was it true?

She listened to the rise and fall of Naomi's and Linda's voices in the other room, excitedly devouring the paper she had brought. She tried to suppress the aching "left out again" feeling. She had come hoping for closeness, desiring to be Naomi's best friend. The feelings of aloneness, of being friendless and bereft of all support, swept through her until she sensed she was standing alone in a parched desert. Tears came suddenly, out of control, until the sound of her sobs filtered into the next room.

Naomi rushed in. "My dear, what is it? Is there anything wrong?" Linda had rushed in also, but when they saw that Ruth was in no physical danger, Naomi waved her away.

Ruth was trembling, taking in loud gasps of air as she tried to regain control. After several attempts she finally formed the words. "Will you be my friend?"

Naomi loved imperfection, as Christ had loved it, and her heart opened to the vulnerable, crying woman she saw as someone that needed to be nurtured. So kindly, respectfully, she said, "Of course, I will."

"Forever?" Ruth asked.

"Forever."

CHAPTER 9

Ruth felt free in her new life—comforted in the shelter of the hills, a cocoon that served as protection from the temptations of the world. She did not mind the harsh, cold mornings when she rose at five to set the fire for breakfast. She had grown up in Maine, where residents took pride in their ability to endure hardship. In fact, she preferred the early mornings because she retired early. Seldom did she join Naomi and the others who gathered in the living room after the children were in bed to play board games or to discuss the events of the day. The staff looked forward to these few hours to draw from one another the support and the courage to keep at their work. And they had fun. Their laughter sounded inappropriate and childish to Ruth; it was almost unbearable for her to listen to Nathan's attempts at humor and Linda's full responsive laugh. On occasion, Ruth managed to delay Naomi from joining the others, believing that Naomi truly preferred more serious conversation.

As the weeks passed, Ruth amazed Naomi with the clever way she managed to make meals out of so little, how she could barter with one of the neighbors for a slab of ham and make it do for several meals. She saved money by feeding the children oatmeal every day except Sundays, when they could have an egg. She learned from Mr. Nobel that he would sell her oatmeal in bulk for a few cents cheaper than the price in town.

After she had done the shopping, Ruth would piously display the receipts to Naomi, showing how much she had saved in comparison to the months before she had arrived. Ruth secretly hoped her example would inspire the other staff to think creatively and accomplish more. Naomi was truly appreciative, for she had longed for someone with good organizational abilities, strengths that Naomi lacked. And Ruth wanted more than anything in the world to see Naomi as director of a dignified and respected institution. It never crossed her mind that she could ever replace Naomi.

Puzzled by Naomi's lack of vision, Ruth was eager to inspire her to greater possibilities. "Do you ever see your home growing, becoming a place of importance?" she once asked.

"It is important."

"Yes, yes, of course it is. But I mean, do you envision more?"

"God has brought us so far already—more than I ever imagined. Is this not enough for you?" Naomi asked gently.

"Oh, I can see so much more. I believe one should aspire to the highest limits. We owe it to God to be more perfect, to bring honor and dignity to his name. I remember a little card that was passed out at your church, and I've never forgotten it: 'Only one life will soon be past, only what's done for Christ will last.'"

"That is true, but a small task is just as important as a large one, if that is what has been entrusted to us. If God sees fit for us to do more, he will open the way."

Ruth had another idea of how the world worked. She saw that hard work and resourcefulness were basic ingredients that were lacking all around her. It bewildered her that God could call so many ineffectual laggards into his service—losers, really. Linda was sweet but not very bright. Nathan was, well, so hopeless, and Naomi's mother sat most of the day reading the Bible, hardly contributing to the many tasks that needed doing. Naomi was doing it all, running everything, making it work. Naomi needed her, Ruth was sure of that.

———————

Within a few months of her arrival, Ruth knew that she wasn't well liked by the staff or even the children, but that was all right with her because she wasn't there to be liked. She was confident she had Naomi's respect, and that was enough. Besides, her name had been included in the last newsletter to the church. Naomi had written, "Ruth's resourcefulness has been a blessing. I don't know where we would be without her. With great ingenuity she manages to keep the pantry full and to secure much-needed supplies." Ruth was satisfied. How could they turn their noses up at her now? Even her own mother, with her self-righteous attitude—Ruth longed to have her mother acknowledge just once that she, Ruth, was capable and good. She would see. She would see.

———

Two incidents occurred shortly after Ruth's arrival that should have sent a shock wave through Naomi, waking her from the trance into which she had fallen. Naomi's faith kept her in a chronic dreamy state: People were good. Society was good. Government was good. God was good. Bad came only because there was not enough love. It was her mission to dispense God's love so that bad would be defeated. When she had a dim recognition that bad could not be held back, she resolved to throw a blanket of love around those she sheltered to keep them safe from harm. The two incidents were foreshocks of what lay ahead. Naomi felt them but, like the citizens of ancient Pompeii, catastrophically misinterpreted them.

Naomi was away the day the first incident occurred. She was over at Green Lick teaching a Bible class. Linda had taken some of the children for a walk. A few of the toddlers were left in Ruth's care. Ruth looked up to see a man's frame filling the front doorway. When Ruth first saw him, she felt a warmth, like sunshine, spread over her. He stood tall, straight, and handsome in his military uniform, and he looked familiar— the same golden slicked-back hair and straight white teeth—for a moment she thought it was he, but she knew it could not be. The man spoke in a formal, firm voice with an easy southern rhythm that took the hard edge off his intensity. He asked for Naomi, but when he was told she was away, and that she, Ruth, was in charge, he seemed to relax and he spoke respectfully to her. He leaned casually against the doorframe like a confident suitor.

"You new here, miss?" His eyes traveled quickly over her body and settled back onto her flushed face.

"Well, I'm—yes." Her answer caught her by surprise as she realized how new she still felt, that she was still an outsider, not yet an integral part of the mission.

"I've been away. Just come home."

"The Pacific?"

"That's where I'll be going next. You got family there?"

"A brother. And a friend."

"Well, I wish them luck. It's going to heat up from what I hear."

He did not say why he had come and seemed to be studying her. She began to feel warmer under his scrutiny and fiddled self-consciously with the button on the front of her blouse. She wanted to talk, especially about the war. It was good to be in the presence of someone who had been out in the world.

"Tell me everything you know about what's happening. We never get news."

"Europe is in shambles. England is getting pounded to smithereens. The whole damn world—oh, pardon me, miss—seems about to destroy itself. It's going to take a mighty lot of courage to stop it."

"Yes. Courage!" She was thinking of her brother, so resolute, so brave. He was the only one she knew who could stand up to her mother.

"Well, I must say, I'm a bit surprised to find an intelligent, reasoning person here. Bet Miss Naomi don't think like you."

Ruth cringed at the grammatical error but smiled. "Well, I don't know. We don't talk about politics."

"Bet you would like to have someone to talk to. You seem like you would."

"Oh, it's okay. I get letters."

"Um." He continued to lean against the doorframe. She saw the set jaw and the hard glint in his eye—the result of the war, she was sure. War did that to men. Her brother's letters had begun to sound bitter.

"Well, what brings you here?" she asked him.

He stood straight, hesitated, but then smiled and said, "I came for my daughter."

"Oh, and who is she?"

"Nancy. Nancy Phillips."

"Why, I can see the resemblance now that you tell me. But I don't know. I don't have the authority to give her to you. Can you wait until

Naomi returns? She should be back late this afternoon. Maybe around four. Could you stay, have some coffee?"

"No, ma'am. I'm headed back north. I'm leaving her with relatives. I only have a few days leave and my sister is counting on me being there this evening. I can't wait."

The struggle in Ruth's mind began. Naomi had left her in charge. Naomi depended on her to make the right decision and she wanted to show that she could make good ones. What would Naomi do? She wished Linda would get back. "What arrangement do you have with Naomi about Nancy?" Ruth asked.

"She is just keeping Nancy until I could come back, make arrangements. Like she does a lot of the kids." He kept looking down the road in the direction of the train tracks. "You see, miss, I need to get going. And I'd be obliged if you'd just turn over Nancy to me. I am her father. I have rights." He stepped a little closer toward her and she could feel his strength. "Do I have to bring the law? I'll get the sheriff here by two o'clock if I have to. She's my flesh and blood, all I have left of my wife. She died. You understand?"

He was so polite, so respectful, so handsome. Surely there would be no reason to deny this father who wanted to be reunited with his child. What harm could there be? Naomi had always said it was best for children to be with their families. The home was just a safety net for them. Besides, it would free a bed for another child who was staying with neighbors temporarily. And with that leap in reason, Ruth went to gather Nancy from her nap. The sleepy child looked up at the man for a moment, then turned and threw her arms around Ruth's neck and whimpered. Ruth didn't like clinging, whining children and quickly detached the child from her and thrust her into the man's arms.

He paused before walking down the porch stairs. "You're mighty understanding, miss. Children belong with family. Good day to you." And he started in the direction of the post office.

Ruth leaned against the door and watched as he walked away, cradling the child in his arms. She could see Nancy's wide eyes staring back toward the mission. Ruth was thinking more about the man than the child. She shrugged and went back inside.

———·—·———

Naomi arrived at four, and Linda was to relieve Ruth so that she could go to the kitchen to prepare the meal. It was Sunday supper and would be simple to prepare, a choice of bread saturated with milk or bread and peanut butter.

Suddenly Linda rushed in, out of breath. "Have you seen Nancy? She's gone."

Ruth answered, "I was just going to tell you. Her father came for her this afternoon, while you were both gone. I had to make a decision. He couldn't wait."

She stopped when she saw Naomi's face pale and Linda's begin to redden with rage. "You didn't—" Naomi tried to find the words. Again she said, "You didn't—" and stopped. "Not to *that, that* man?"

"Why, what did I do? He seemed nice enough," said Ruth with an edge of defensiveness in her voice. She knew she had done something dreadful and it was time to begin the rationalizations.

"He killed Nancy's mother, but no one could prove it. He wasn't to know Nancy was here. She was here under the court's protection. How long ago did they leave?"

"Four hours ago," Ruth said.

Naomi turned to Linda, "I'll go on horseback to Madison Creek to inform the sheriff. I might not make it back tonight. Send for George Watson. Have him ask around, see if anyone heard anything about where Nancy's father would go."

Ruth answered. "He said he was heading north to leave her with relatives."

Naomi looked at her as if she were looking at a foolish child. "He wouldn't tell you, but I doubt he has any relatives who will have anything to do with him."

She hurried to her horse, which had not yet been unsaddled from her earlier trip. Ruth ran outside to her and held the reins.

"I'm so sorry. I didn't know."

"You never asked," Naomi said, her voice more sad than angry.

She rode away, leaving Ruth broken and praying, "Oh, God, please undo my wrong. Please make it okay."

It was not okay. They never found golden-haired, wide-eyed, scared little Nancy. She vanished like foam on water, not leaving even a breath of evidence that she had existed.

Ruth sealed herself in her room until Naomi returned, then pleaded for forgiveness, her face swollen from tears. Compassionate Naomi could not turn her back on repentance. How would Ruth have known? she reasoned. I may have made the same decision under the same circumstances. Naomi then took upon herself the blame for not having trained her staff better. "We all learn from our mistakes," she told the grieving young woman.

"No, it's more than that," Ruth said. "I thought—he was so like him—I was wrong. Oh, Naomi, can I tell you? Will you understand? I am such a horrible, despicable person.

"I couldn't see the man for the uniform—it was the uniform. I loved a man once. Nancy's father reminded me of him, just the hair and body frame, nothing more. But the feelings. I was never able to think clearly around him, Joe, and—oh, my mother was right. She said I disgraced the family. Now I have disgraced you. I pledged my word to God that if he got me through this thing—with Joe—I would dedicate my life to his work."

"What 'thing'?"

"Will you promise not to send me back? It was you who saved me, I'm sure of it. That night at church when you spoke, something changed in me. I knew how I wanted to be. I cannot go back home. My mother predicted I wouldn't last. She said I could never be anything but a har—," her breath was short and tears were coming hot and hard. The little handkerchief came out of her breast pocket and was waving like a small truce flag around her nose. She tried again. "She said a har—a har—" Taking a deep breath, Ruth forced out the word and it hung in the silence: "a harlot."

"Did you get into trouble?" "Trouble" was a polite term for any deviation from proper behavior. And it was definitely improper for there to be any physical contact other than a handshake between an unmarried man and a woman.

"I was carrying his child. The night I came to your church. Mother suspected and threw me out. Myrtle took care of me. After I heard you talk, that's when I said if God got rid of the child, I'd do his work with children."

"Why didn't you tell him? He would have married you, yes?"

"No. He was engaged to—someone else. We loved each other. He— we—couldn't figure out a way. It was impossible." The words that fell from her mouth had the same small tremble that was shaking her body. Her pain seemed less for poor little Nancy than for the awful predicament in which she had found herself.

Naomi sat quietly, reaching for words to minister to an aching heart. Her head was reeling. It was so confusing. To pledge to get rid of a child to take care of other unwanted children—was this a reason to come? The thought flitted like a shadow and passed. She was thinking of Mary Magdalene and Christ's love for her. "I'm sorry. It must have been so frightening for you to go through alone. What happened to the child?"

"Well, that's why I'm here. The next day the curse came, and I was no longer with child. It was God telling me, through you, of my direction in life. I was waiting until you needed me. And I came."

Naomi felt motherly toward Ruth and responsible for her. One child had been lost, but another was saved—Ruth. Naomi, who was always prone to see the better part of people, saw a good heart, determination— and vulnerability—beneath Ruth's hardened shell. Ruth had been such an asset since she arrived, Naomi decided to work harder to help Ruth fulfill her destiny.

Ruth resolved to be perfect and to see that perfection was achieved around her. It was this aspiration that brought about the next incident.

A few weeks later, Naomi sent Violet to the kitchen to help Ruth prepare supper. Violet had grown into a solemn and humorless teenager. She was the last of the flower family to remain at the mission. Daisy had married a local boy who was in the military. Before leaving for duty, he took her to Ohio, where she found work in a factory. Naomi felt that Violet's demeanor was the result of too many losses. It was easy to interpret her comments as negative, for she showed very little enthusiasm for anything, but she was a sweet girl who never caused one day of mischief. She appeared in the kitchen to announce in a tone that did not sound eager to Ruth's ear, "I'm here to help."

"Well, you can begin by filling the water buckets." Ruth knew that was the chore least liked by the children assigned to her. The buckets were heavy and the metal handle cut deep into the soft hands of a child.

As Violet made her way to the shelf where the buckets were kept, Ruth heard her say, "I don't keer if I do."

Ruth rushed to the girl, yanked her by the hair, and said, "You will show respect around me, young lady." As Violet tried to jerk free, her hair tangled in Ruth's hands. Violet pulled harder until Ruth was left holding a handful of hair.

Violet screamed at her, "You are crazy! I ain't workin' with you!" And she fled the kitchen.

Naomi saw Violet running across the yard toward the house, holding her head and crying. Naomi rushed to her. The story that tumbled out of her made no sense, "Miss Ruth, she attacked me, grabbed me by the hair for no reason. I'm not staying here if she stays. She is mean, Nam, she is a bad woman. She makes up all kinds of rules when you go away. You got to git rid of her."

Naomi urged Violet to go with her to the kitchen to sort out what had happened. Violet wanted to go to Lily's house. Naomi said she could go after they talked to Miss Ruth.

"Well, she was disrespectful to me," Ruth said, "and I just took her by the hair to get her attention, to tell her not to talk to me like she did, and she jerked away. It is her fault."

"I never said nothin'," Violet yelled back. Naomi kept her arm around the girl to help still her trembling. She turned to Ruth, "Just exactly what did she say?"

"She said she didn't care to do what I had just asked her to do—which was fill the water buckets."

"I did not. I said 'I don't keer if I do.' That's what I said."

"Well, isn't it the same thing?" Ruth said, satisfied.

Naomi suddenly understood. "Oh, there has been an awful misunderstanding. 'I don't care if I do' means 'I'm agreeable to it. I don't mind doing it.' I think you owe Violet an apology, Ruth."

Apologize? Ruth was stunned. However, she did not want to displease Naomi, so she muttered, "I guess I misunderstood."

Violet was not satisfied. She left to go to Lily's house, and she stayed there.

These two events, so short a time after Ruth arrived, should have been a signal to Naomi. But the only step Naomi took was to talk over the matter with her mother. Naomi was aware of how quickly Grace was aging. Since Papa's death, she had become less active, sitting most of the day in a rocker, reading the Bible. But Naomi still turned to her for guidance. Ruth had asked Naomi not to tell anyone about the pregnancy and Naomi honored her promise. Instead, she pointed out to her mother how Ruth wasn't well liked by the other staff members, and she wondered if Ruth should be working with children when she did not seem to like them.

Grace, too, had been troubled. But this was Naomi's decision and she could see how much help Ruth gave. "There is no question that things have changed since she's been here. If she stays, I fear she will be a thorn in your side. The unhappiest people are those who are in conflict with their nature. I do not believe it is her nature to be without a man or to serve others. Her need is for control, for power over others, and I'm afraid it will bring unhappiness wherever she goes."

Naomi could not ask Ruth to leave. After all, had not Ruth said that Naomi was to be her salvation? And Naomi's calling was to save lost souls.

CHAPTER 10

The three years after Ruth's arrival brought many changes to the little mountain home. The form and structure remained the same, but a subtle, elusive shift occurred, somewhat like what happens to a painting when it oxidizes. The fresh and vibrant colors disappear, leaving a dull, muted patina. The image remains unaltered, but the color is a few shades off. This process may improve some paintings, but it takes the life out of others. Ruth had the latter effect on the mission and its people; she wore them down until what was left was dour and dull.

First Nathan left. His departure came suddenly, before Naomi discovered the real reason for his decision to go. He stood before her with his few possessions in a tightly wrapped bundle and in a voice gruff with resolve announced that he had stayed longer than he'd intended and he was needed over at Green Lick to help with a new building. "You can always count on me to help you, if you need me." He placed special emphasis on the word *you*. And with that he mounted his mule and rode away.

Naomi suspected that his decision to leave had something to do with Ruth. It was probably nothing that Ruth had said directly to him, but the looks she gave him, or didn't give him, were enough. Ruth thought Nathan lazy, but, even worse, incompetent, and she went out of her way to let him know. She watched his work with a jaundiced eye, never failing to demonstrate her own ability to repair something that he had miserably failed to fix. It was true, Naomi thought, he wasn't very bright, but what a happy and willing heart he had.

Linda left shortly afterward to work at the mission over at Green Lick. She was replaced by a plain, middle-aged nurse, who kept mostly to herself. Because of the war, there was a drop in the student population at school, and Madison Creek was able to lend a teacher to the mission school.

The lethal war was now in full force, with battles breaking out across Europe and in Asia and Africa. Most of the men in the hills had gone off to join the action, even young Buddy as soon as he turned seventeen. There was a scarcity of men for labor, and the women either did the work themselves or let the bigger jobs go until they could find an able and willing man.

Lily and her three children practically lived at the mission after Floyd went away. Loneliness drove her back. But not Violet, who kept her distance, preferring to remain at the house, keeping it ready for Floyd's return. On the rare occasion when Violet did appear at the mission, she would slink around and scowl at Ruth like a security dog sniffing out hidden contraband.

Ruth paid her little mind; if Violet had any effect on her, Ruth didn't let it show. Her resentment about Lily's return took the form of complaints to Naomi about how short supplies were, especially now with the rationing, and how there was hardly enough to feed those for whom they had direct responsibility. Naomi's reply, "Yes, it is hard everywhere," offered no comfort. Sugar had long since disappeared. Shortages were everywhere; there was barely enough flour for bread, and other staples needed for a tasty meal were scarce. Even paper supplies and soap were hard to come by. To Ruth, that was the worst. She had held fast to her upbringing and refused to bathe with the lye soap made by the mountain women. Then one day she succumbed because she had no other choice, and she wept. Her skin smelled like a scrubbed kitchen floor and she longed for just a spray of lilac scent or a sprinkle of talc on her body.

Gladness filled Naomi when Lily came back, for Naomi had seen the wreck Lily's marriage had made of her. Lily, the softest, most lovely of all the mountain flowers, had become wilted, withered, and aged. Some flowers have a long bloom, and others brief. Beauty had abandoned Lily shortly after she lost her virginity. Floyd grew more handsome as Lily declined. The army food had done him good, as had the experience outside the hills. He was straight and strong and had lost some of his cocky naiveté. It was replaced with a cynical, blunt forwardness that was coated with a smooth veneer of seduction and wrapped in a soft drawl.

Floyd was stationed at an army base a few hundred miles away and was able to get home more frequently than the other men. Because of the shortage of men, Naomi reluctantly called on him to handle chores for which the women lacked the strength. He did not seem to mind hanging around the mission.

One day he was resting on the back steps after having cut a cord of wood, his sleeves rolled up high and his hard, veined muscles bulging. His shirt was wet in patches and he unbuttoned the top few buttons to let the air cool him. He rubbed his fingers through his dark hair, which was slicked down close to a nicely shaped head. His hair was shining where his damp hands had stroked it. He sat watching Ruth as she bent over the washtub scrubbing clothes, her hair hidden by a scarf tied in a neat bow at the brow. She looked up when she heard a half-laugh escape him. He was shaking his head, looking directly at her, and still laughing to himself. She glared back.

"What are you looking at?" she said disdainfully.

"At you. Lordy, how did such a refined woman as yourself ever get to be a washwoman?"

"You find it amusing, do you? Well, a little hard work never hurt anyone."

"I can see that. Matter of fact, it's an improvement, if you want my opinion."

"I don't."

"Well, I got a lot of opinions about you, Missy Ruth." His tone claimed an intimacy that did not belong to him.

"I would appreciate it if you kept them to yourself." Ruth loathed his churlish manner. She wanted respect.

"I'd like to ask you something. Why did you come here?"

"To serve the Lord."

"Well, that may have been the second reason. What was the first?"

"The first and last reason are the same."

"You are a liar. Women like you don't end up here. Not unless they are running from something."

Ruth was furious with his impertinence and his perceptiveness. She replied angrily, "My life is of no concern to you. Don't you have work you need to do? Go away. Leave me alone."

"You're a hard woman, Missy Ruth. What made you so hard? Yes, ma'am, you remind me of a dog I had once. She had been badly handled. Nothing worse for an animal—they'll snarl and bite against the next one trying to tame them. Were you badly handled, Missy Ruth?"

"Since you're so free with your opinions, I'll give you mine. You're no prize yourself. You are lazy, amoral, selfish, and"—she was searching for the spot, that tender place in a man where a word could fly like an arrow and pierce—"and from what I've seen you're no expert on women."

He flinched. She had hit the bull's-eye. He was completely puzzled over the failure of his marriage. Other women fell in love with him, and he had good times with them. There was no good time with Lily. She was so passive, so totally compliant, so completely accommodating to his will that he felt sometimes he would suffocate. But wasn't that what every man wanted? He seemed to prefer stronger women, those who could tolerate his being himself without taking on a pained and suffering bearing. He swung wildly between blaming Lily and blaming himself.

He did not let Ruth see the wound she had made. He laughed as though he were laughing at her and threw back, "And I bet you're no expert on men."

Such encounters occurred between them whenever they were alone, even for brief moments. Each lashed out at the other—he trying to discover her hidden secrets and she fighting to keep them hidden.

The heat of the summer days drove Ruth to walk along the creek in the evenings to cool herself. She came often to weep or to stare into the bubbling water, hoping to hear a divine answer to the loneliness that gripped her. Sometimes she wondered if one could die of loneliness. This afternoon, she had slipped off her shoes and was sitting on the edge of the bank with her feet in the cold current. She dipped her fingers into the water and sprinkled chilled drops down the inside of her shirt and along the nape of her neck. She was weary of the mediocrity that surrounded her. Disappointment in Naomi, with her willingness to settle for the ordinary, increased Ruth's feelings of isolation. Just today she had tried again, prodding Naomi: "Don't you want more?" The puzzled look Naomi returned drove her to the creek to wrestle against despair. She longed to be affiliated with anyone, anything, that was not ordinary, that possessed a strong, purposeful intelligence. Maybe it was the heat that made Ruth restless, that filled her with an unknowing longing.

She did not hear Floyd since he approached from her left, and she did not know how long he had been there before he spoke. In childhood she had lost hearing in her left ear, and the problem never ceased to annoy her. That something might escape her scrutiny made her edgy.

Startled, she stood quickly. Her feet slipped in the rocky sand and she almost lost her balance. He was beside her to steady her, his hands firmly on her waist. She fell back against him and nature made her recall the sublime joy of being in the strong arms of a man, of being desired. Her brief hesitation before attempting to break apart spoke to his nature and before either of them could stop what should not be happening, he buried his face in her neck and began kissing her furiously. He turned her toward him, holding her tightly so that even if she wanted to struggle, she could not.

For one brief moment she surrendered, seeing Joe's face in her mind's eye.

The moment ended quickly, nature having won the first round, and she pulled away in confusion. Her arm rose slowly to her mouth as she tried to obliterate any evidence of their act. As her mind cleared, she remembered that he was everything she loathed—an uncouth, hick mountain man. When she looked at him, she recognized something else—that he knew about her loneliness. She hated him. Slowly, she saw more: evidence that a woman could easily have power over this man's defenses. He stood before her disarmed, his eyes forgiving. She blurted out an *Ohhhh,* a sound between dread and desire, and she fled the secluded wooded terrain into the open ground leading back to the mission.

It was Floyd's last visit home before being sent overseas. Twice before he left she returned to the stream with her disgust and her desire. She could not have explained why she returned. She went as though she were being led. Each time Floyd was there waiting. She did not allow him to speak, gently placing her fingers against his mouth, then opening the front of her dress and placing her bare upper body firmly against his. She listened to the beating and breathing of his body. She guided his hands inside her blouse, to her buttocks, and between her legs. He thought he was leading her on, but she knew they were staying right where she wanted them to be. The affair went only as far as she would allow. She wanted to kiss him, to feel his arousal, and to let him touch her until the electricity surged through her. She was there to wrestle the devil, to defy his having dominion over her. And she won.

Oh, sweet revenge. She had discovered a way of repaying Joe. The power gave her a secret thrill. Her motive was nothing more complicated than that. She had no guilt when she looked at sad Lily, who looked back at Ruth knowingly. Floyd meant nothing to Ruth, and Ruth meant nothing personal against Lily. She had only borrowed Floyd to rid herself of Joe—to free herself forever of men, she thought. There was no one to warn her that what we despise in others is what we have not yet understood within ourselves. Foolishly, she felt free.

———

Lily expressed her fear about Ruth to Naomi. They were sitting on the porch in the hot afternoon—at the same time that Ruth and Floyd were at the creek. Naomi asked Lily about the deepening sadness etching its lines along her mouth, across her brow, and into the iris of her eyes.

Lily said, "I'm glad Floyd is leaving."

"I'm surprised. You've missed him so."

"He don't miss me. He's got his eye on Miss Ruth. I can tell he has. I know him."

Both women knew Floyd's nature; both put the blame in different places—Naomi blamed Floyd, and Lily blamed Ruth.

"Oh, honey, rest your fears. I don't believe Ruth would have anything to do with him." A fleeting doubt was quickly smothered, and Naomi repeated more firmly, "I know she wouldn't."

"Oh, Nam, why do you only see the good in everyone?" In a lower voice she added, "Everyone but Floyd."

———————

Winter came again, made even more bleak by the heart-shattering news that reached the small community of men missing in action or dead and buried in frozen ground at great, foreign distances. In another time these men might not have ever traveled more than a few miles from home, and now they would remain forever homeless, spiritless.

Floyd was among the dead. He had left to go overseas a confused man. Winning over Ruth had felt like losing. When Ruth heard of his death she thought, He's dead, just like Joe. She felt strangely renewed as though this sacrifice had purged her sins, washed her clean by their blood. However, the war had not killed Joe. When he married his fiancée, Ruth buried him in her heart and soul, determined to never think of him alive again.

Buddy had come home with a new bride. She was a pretty, petite, wild-spirited girl with dark hair, flashing eyes, and straight white teeth. She couldn't have been older than seventeen. She said it was her Spanish blood that gave her her fire and her gift for storytelling. She had more stories than a chameleon has colors and could change them faster; some said she was a yarn-spinner, but others just called her a liar. Buddy brought her to meet Naomi, and they had with them their son, Billy. Naomi had never seen a more beautiful child—large dark eyes like his mother's and a quiet, studied expression like his father's.

Ruth was fond of Buddy and had been from the first time she met him. He was unlike the other boys, or men, she met in the hills; he had a refined manner, and she wondered how any mountain woman could have given birth to a child who seemed to have the blood of royalty. Even the other boys seemed to respect the difference; they never bloodied his nose or challenged him, as if they knew they would be defeated.

Privately, she called him "the prince." The title came after she had observed a small encounter in town between Buddy and a store owner. Mr. Nobel, Buddy's grandfather, had relied on Buddy from age eight to purchase supplies in town. One day Ruth was in town to pick up supplies when she observed Buddy buying a sack of sugar. Its price was determined by weight. When Buddy was given the price, $2.40, Ruth overheard him say, "Your scale must be off. Could you please weigh it again?"

The owner said, "New tax on sugar."

"How much?" Buddy asked.

"Quarter cent a pound." The store owner should have known better than to fall into that trap. Buddy was renowned all over the county for his speed and accuracy in mathematics.

"Well, you best weigh it again because you are charging two cents over the tax increase."

"Now, Buddy, you don't think I'm cheatin' you, do you?"

Buddy smiled, but his quick eyes examined the scale. "I think I see the problem. It might be this small piece of wood wedged here." He reached over and freed it. "Now let's see. Weigh it again." This time he paid—five cents less than the original price.

Ruth heard the store owner mutter, "Damn smart-aleck kid." Ruth told the story to Naomi but didn't repeat the swear word. "That boy has a mind," Ruth said. "He's going places." She valued brain over brawn, but more than that, she was impressed by the refined, relaxed manner with which he handled the crusty old store owner. Buddy had a natural gift. Ruth was disappointed in his having chosen a fickle wife. She had expected more of him. The child-wife did not have a dignity and reserve that matched his. But she could see it in little Billy. He was his father's child.

———

Overall, Ruth had a freer, happier spirit in the days after Floyd went away. The few encounters with him had calmed, rather than bewildered, her. Now she resolved that she would have no rivals for first place with Naomi. Indeed, there weren't any. The nurse slept in the boys' quarters above the schoolroom. Miss Barr, the only worker who ever insisted on being called by her last name, had come to be a housemother to the girls.

She was an insecure, timid woman around whom the older girls ran circles. When Naomi was away, Ruth stepped in and took charge, demonstrating for Miss Barr how young women should be treated. She went as far as she could without offending Naomi. She gave extra work detail, restrictions, and occasionally, when Naomi was away, used physical punishment. The girls respected her, she believed. But Ruth did not understand the difference between respect and fear.

Lily was there to care for the younger children. But since Floyd's death, she had retreated deeply into herself and had grown distant from Naomi. She poured all her love onto the little ones, rocking, cuddling, and calling them flower names. She's just like her mother, Naomi thought.

Ruth began to see her home as a shelter, a closed little universe away from the insanity that seemed to have taken over the outside world. She stopped wanting more, except to be closer to Naomi.

Because the house was crowded, Ruth gave up her room to the new worker and moved into Naomi's room. Naomi's mother slept on a cot next to the window. Ruth and Naomi shared the double bed. It did not seem to occur to Naomi that this arrangement kept the children from coming to her bed when night terrors stalked them. For Ruth it provided comfort and serenity and the tenderness that she had sought, but found lacking, in her intimacy with men. In the dark, with the steady rise and fall of Grace's breathing emanating from the cot across the room, Ruth opened her life to Naomi. She told stories of her home, of her sister and brother.

Her older sister, Edith, had always been sickly with a vague disorder the doctors finally labeled as fibromyalgia. Edith's illness caused their mother to fret and overprotect Edith and, in truth, favor her over Ruth. Ruth escaped all the childhood diseases and consequently never got much of her mother's tender care. Because Ruth and her brother, Lee, had been blessed with good constitutions, their mother thought, What more could they need? Indeed, it was selfish to want more. Ruth had wanted more; she had wanted the most forbidden of all wants, her sister's betrothed. That Ruth could never tell Naomi.

Although Ruth's mother was no convert of any religion, she ruled her life by her own set of rules more rigid and less compassionate than those of any organized religion. She had her own Ten Commandments made up of pithy moral edicts, such as "Waste not, want not" and "A stitch in time saves nine." To her, a moral life was an efficient one. Now, away from her mother, Ruth began to worry about Edith as well, whether she might have a medical crisis while her husband was away on business.

The stories came out in bits and pieces in the late hours, and Naomi loved Ruth the more she understood her—for understanding brings forgiveness—and she believed the power of love healed all wounds. Freely, Naomi gave Ruth sympathy, caring, and always a tender good-night embrace and kiss on the cheek. It was the first time in Ruth's life that she felt she could let someone see virtually all of herself and not once feel judged, condemned, or misunderstood. How tender, how sustaining, how healing it was. Instead of filling her up so that she could stand alone in her own goodness, however, Naomi's benevolence became Ruth's addiction, unleashing desire and making her irritable and moody when Naomi's kindness was directed elsewhere. It was as though Ruth became psychologically attached by an invisible umbilical cord through which Naomi gave her sustenance and life. Her awareness of Naomi's life-sustaining importance came when the cord was nearly cut.

———————

One bright spring morning, Dr. Jackson arrived with a new antidiphtheria serum to inoculate the community against the deadly disease. An outbreak had occurred in one of the hollows several miles away, and he had been on his horse for days traveling through the communities, plunging the same needle into the arms of children and adults, his assistant swabbing the needle with a cotton ball saturated with alcohol between injections. Doubtless Dr. Jackson knew some people were hypersensitive to the drug, but he did not have time to perform a skin test and wait thirty minutes to look for a reaction. If he lost 5 percent of his patients from drug toxicity, he reasoned, it was better than losing a whole community to diphtheria. He may have reconsidered if he had suspected that Naomi would be the one person to react with the serum sickness.

Her symptoms came on long after the doctor had gone. Naomi took to bed with a headache and chills, then her fever rose to 105 degrees. Fear gripped Ruth and it allowed her to do what she would not have thought possible. First, she shut herself alone with Naomi in their room, having the audacity to tell Nurse Ann that it was better she not be exposed, for if others came down with the disease, the nurse would be desperately needed. Nurse Ann was too weak to protest. Ruth tried to reduce Naomi's fever with cool, wet towels. She sat at her bedside feeling the wild race of Naomi's pulse as it struggled to keep oxygen flowing. She held Naomi's hand in hers, talking softly to her. Her words were a prayer, not to God—for she had forgotten him as the fear of losing Naomi consumed her—but to Naomi. "Please don't die. You are my life. I could not do this without you. We need you. You can make it. Stay with us."

When Naomi's breathing became laborious, Ruth knew it was time to find Dr. Jackson. She had never been on a horse, but love lifted her onto the saddle, and adrenaline blocked out the pain of the heavy sheets of rain lashing at her body as she rode from one hollow to another inquiring after Dr. Jackson. She found him late in the afternoon. He had just finished inoculating the small population and was ready to mount his horse to move on. He recognized the desperate rider and mounted his horse, motioning Ruth to turn around and he would follow. He knew before she told him that it was Naomi. And they rode fast against the rain, arriving after dark.

Dr. Jackson was worried about Naomi's heart. Could it survive the assault of the disease, provide the strength her fever-weakened body would require to keep her alive? She could die of paralysis of the heart—stronger ones had. It was not the heart he would count on, but the will. Naomi's will was indeed strong.

The doctor could see by the blueness of her lips that it might be too late or that at the least he might have to do a tracheotomy, but first he would paint and scrape the throat. This step was necessary to detach the poisonous membrane obstructing the air passages. It was all he could do in this era before antibiotics.

Through the night, the doctor and Ruth sat in the dim lamplight willing death to have pity and not to take away this blessed life that brought joy and peace to people who inhabited a land of hardship and suffering. The room pulsated with a silent cry for life; it finally caused death to pause and turn away to seek companionship elsewhere. By early morning, Naomi's fever had broken and her breathing became easier. Love had defeated death. Or as Naomi would later describe it, "God was not yet finished with me."

CHAPTER 11

Naomi's recovery was slow. Dr. Jackson insisted that she remain bedridden longer than Naomi felt necessary. He did not want to give the bacteria a chance to invade her heart, for he knew that the heart is fragile and needs protection against all kinds of assaults.

Another, more insidious threat, as dangerous and destructive as *Corynebacterium diphtheriae,* permeated the air around Naomi. Dr. Jackson tried to warn his patient but had learned long ago the futility of telling his clients what was good for them; he watched as they nodded blindly and listened deafly and continued in their ways. But Dr. Jackson did try, for he was uncharacteristically fond of Naomi, and he worried about her good heart. One day, while Naomi was still recovering, he sent Ruth on an errand and had a few moments alone with his patient.

"Naomi, are you happy with the way things are here at the mission?" Questions were awkward for him, for he was not an intrusive man.

"Yes. Why do you ask?"

"It is vital to your recovery that you have as little stress as possible. That you trust your staff to run things smoothly while you recover. Do you feel you can? If there is something I can do to—"

She interrupted him, "How kind you are, Dr. Jackson, and thoughtful. I'm in good hands. Ruth almost never leaves me and is attentive to my every need. She won't let me do anything for myself." So many incompetent staff had come and gone that she was grateful for Ruth; even though Ruth had her faults, at least she was capable. So much so that there were times Naomi almost felt unneeded. Naomi quickly brushed away the thought. Ruth needed her, too. Surely.

He frowned. "It is Ruth I wish to discuss with you. Things have—changed since she has come." He watched carefully for an indication that she understood.

"Yes. Things do run more smoothly," she said, brushing her hand across the blanket, deep in thought. "There's order. Order is good."

"Order would have come on its own—in time—with or without her." He faltered, then plunged forward. "I'm troubled about some things the children have said to me—told me privately of her cruelty." He saw her eyes widen with alarm, and he backed away, for he could not distress his patient.

"Who told you? What did they say?"

"Well, Shirley, she—"

Before he could finish Naomi said, "You must know, Dr. Jackson, how Shirley is. She's so dramatic. When the other children tease her, she reacts as though they are killing her. I know that Ruth can get overly . . . zealous, but . . ."

"Perhaps it is a matter of style. Ruth's style is so different from yours that I'm worried it will cause difficulty for you." But his voice faded as he saw denial cloaked in kindness staring back at him.

"I don't know how I could do without her."

"Well, you could, if it came to that; you did before she came. Just remember it is so, if you ever need to make that choice."

Naomi was troubled after he left and her fever rose again. Ruth spent as much time with her as she could afford without jeopardizing the order and routine of the home. Ruth saw to it that the children were quiet. The change came by way of an announcement at the dinner hour. She rose as she rang the small bell that signaled silence. Her voice was grave and her posture commanding. "Children, our dear Miss Naomi is near death. It is imperative, meaning absolutely necessary, that no disturbance reach her ears. That means no running, yelling, or talking aloud while in the main building. All work activities in the yard will cease until she is fully recovered. All games and play activities will be stopped until she is recovered. We must all do what we can to make sure she recovers. I am sure none of you wish to hasten her death. If you cause any disturbance at all, you will be isolated from all the others until she has recovered."

The quiet troubled Naomi. At times she wondered if her room was a soundproofed tomb and whether eternity was a dark, silent place without the laughter and sounds of children. Their laughter and arguments were music to her ears, and her heart quickened one day when she heard Shirley speak harshly to another child. That was her Shirley! But then Naomi did not hear her again.

Timidly she asked Ruth, "How are the children? I never hear them." Not knowing why, she asked, "Are they happy?"

"Happy? Why, yes." How could they not be happy? Ruth thought. Well-behaved children are happy children.

When Naomi asked that some of the children visit her, Ruth told her it was doctor's orders that she not have visitors until she was fully recovered. When Naomi tried to resume her regular duties, Ruth guarded her protectively, telling Naomi when she looked tired, sending her back to her room for rest, intervening when a child came to her with a complaint, removing all obstacles in her path.

———

Dr. Jackson observed this jealous protection and wondered about it. He arrived on horseback one morning unexpectedly. All morning his thoughts had been on how to approach Ruth about her "style," as he had silently come to refer to it. He'd found that self-righteous people have the hardest time seeing into themselves. How can one admonish good acts? Well, good acts be damned because when they are self-serving and dished up without compassion, they are more harmful than ignorance.

The doctor had braced himself to talk with Ruth. On his way to the main building, he saw Shirley swinging in the front yard. He made his way over to her, dismounted, and sat in the sagging, lopsided swing next to her. He observed her runny nose and the encrusted sleeve of her sweater, which served as a hanky. Her legs were like small sticks, making her small shoes appear like clodhoppers.

The children liked Dr. Jackson's soft manner, but they were afraid of his needles. Shirley's eyes widened with fear as he greeted her.

"I be good. No yelling, no hitting, no fighting, no—"

"Shirley, I'm not going to give you a shot. I just came to talk, see how you are feeling. Would you like a push?"

She nodded and he stood up and gently gave the swing a small start. She pulled back and forth with all her might and the swing barely increased its motion. As he watched the small legs kick back and forth, he noticed the yellow marks on her legs. He sat down again in the swing and watched as it slowed. "Shirley, how did you get the marks on your legs?"

She shrugged.

"Did you fall? Did someone hit you?"

She came to a slow stop, got out of the swing, and approached him. She said very softly, "There is evil under my bed. It has red eyes and horns and scratches at night."

"Is that how you got the marks on your legs?"

"I'm not playing with Eddie anymore. He got me in trouble."

"What happened when you got in trouble?"

Her large brown eyes stared hard at him, then she wiped her nose again on her sleeve, leaving a long, clear thread between her nose and arm. She picked up the corn doll lying in the dirt and began to hit it against the seat of the swing. Its head fell off and she stepped back with a surprised look. He took the doll from her, placing the head back in position. "See, it's fixed. Be careful with your dolly. She needs to feel loved and . . . and safe."

Shirley took the doll and squashed it with an enthusiastic hug. "Safe, safe, safe," she giggled as she whirled in a circle.

He was going to ask her more when she was called to come into the house. Dr. Jackson pondered over the child with yellow marks on her legs. They were also along her arms, and he had seen them on other mal-nourished children. Maybe she bruised easily. He walked toward the kitchen expecting to find Ruth finishing the morning chores. She was seated with a cup of coffee.

"Hello, Doctor. Would you like a cup?"

It seemed false to sup with someone he was about to confront, so he declined but sat down heavily at the small round table.

"How are things going since my last visit?" he asked her.

"Your patient is doing great. I'm doing everything I can to keep her rested."

"I see that you are. She's ready to resume some of her activities. I'm on my way to talk with her about it. The best thing for her recovery is to feel useful." He held his voice steady and neutral. Then he changed the subject. "I just saw Shirley. She's too thin. I'd like you to mix a whole egg in her milk each day for two weeks and add some vitamins to the drink." He reached into his bag and pulled out a bottle containing a liquid mixture. "Just add one dropper full each morning."

Ruth looked aghast. "One egg? We can't afford to feed one child an egg each day. That means no eggs for the others on the weekend."

Dr. Jackson was sure that if he had recommended this prescription for Naomi, there would have been no protest. "I'm headed over to Mr. Nobel's next. I'll ask him to bring extra eggs they have from their hens. Just for the next few weeks." He rose and started toward the door. He turned and said, "I'm hoping those bruises on Shirley are the result of vitamin deficiency." Using his I-mean-business tone he added, "If they come from any other reason, such as discipline, I'll make sure the person who put them there is gone. Do you understand me?"

"You don't like me, do you?" Ruth asked. Her voice was trembling and she gave him a pained, misunderstood look. "I'm doing everything I can to help. Everything to make it easier for Naomi. I love her, too."

He turned and said half under his breath, not being a religious man, "Oh, Lord, spare the world from helpful people."

———·———

Naomi tried to resume her activities, but Ruth could not fully give up being protective and left Naomi feeling useless and in the way. She took Ruth's suggestion and agreed to go to Florida to stay with a cousin. She resolved to recover not only her strength but also her determination. Something had been gnawing at it, leaving her but a shell of herself. She had been going through the motions of daily activities mechanically, like a watch indifferently grinding out hours and days.

While Naomi was away, something wonderful and terrifying happened to Ruth. Buddy's bride arrived at the front porch to hand over her beautiful three-year-old son and a tiny, sickly, deformed infant girl. With eyes too large for her sunken cheeks and wide forehead, a rounded head that was not yet softened by hair, a swollen belly, and spindly legs, the child looked like a throwback to humans' primate ancestors. The young wife said she would return for the children when she got back on her feet. It was too much to take care of two kids and make a living, she explained—and she had to make a living because she couldn't live on the money Buddy sent her.

Ruth turned the infant over to Nurse Ann, who said, "My heavens, the child is malnourished." She began immediately to feed her small servings of warm milk. The child was passive and slow to suck and lay listless, without expression. Nurse Ann said, "If this child lives, she will need numerous feedings. You will have to help me." And she thrust the child and a bottle into Ruth's arms.

At first Ruth was repulsed by the child's ugliness and lack of spirit. The child lay passively in Ruth's stiff, fearful arms, looking steadfastly into Ruth's eyes. Since Ruth did not believe that children were really people she stared back at the "object" she held. She thought children were a bundle of instincts, responding impulsively to their environment, or lumps of clay to be shaped and formed. Ruth had no idea the process worked both ways, the child doing the shaping as much as the parent. Slowly, ever so slowly, something began to stir inside Ruth as the child began to suck, then smile, then pull herself up in her crib, reaching her arms up toward Ruth to be picked up. In time, the swollen belly began to flatten and the child's eyes began to sparkle. Within two months, she was catching up to her age of thirteen months, first walking timidly by holding onto pieces of furniture, then letting go and like a sprinter hearing the starting pistol, racing toward some imaginary finish line, clasping her hands with pure joy at the accomplishment. Ruth thought the miraculous change was due directly to herself, not the nourishment she gave five times a day, and she was overcome with wonderment. In some way

Ruth identified with this waste of a child; the idea that one could transcend a state of being, undergo a metamorphosis, had a deep spiritual meaning to her. When she spoke to the child, she spoke in "we's": "we are hungry," "we are tired," "we are happy."

When Naomi returned two months later, refreshed and strong, she was pleased with the transformation she saw in Ruth. Billy responded quickly to Naomi, sitting on her lap and pulling his thumb out just long enough to ask, "When is Mama coming?" Naomi couldn't answer. She hugged him and said, "She'll come back," and he rested against her, assured by that promise. Naomi encouraged Ruth's involvement with Billy's baby sister, believing it would spill over to the other children now that she had opened her heart so completely to one child.

It was about a year later when the mother came back for the children. The loss of the little girl caught Ruth by surprise. She felt devoid of all affection, especially toward the other children. Their presence irritated her, causing a small chronic pain like a paper cut on a finger. Naomi tried to soothe her, "You know, Ruth, they don't belong to us. We are here to offer love and guidance until their parents can come for them or until we find another home for them. All that love you felt in your heart can now be given to another child. There's Shirley. She has such a need."

Ruth could not tell Naomi that her words were no comfort and that Ruth could not tolerate the sight of the small, runny-nosed Shirley whose angry disposition was so unlike that of her little, happy, gone-away child. No, Ruth would not love Shirley or any of the others. She didn't know why, but she was sure of it.

Ruth returned with zeal to the task of molding children into prospective saints. But gradually she came to a profound realization. Her talents would be best used not in shaping individual children (they didn't like her, and she didn't really like them) but in transforming the home itself. Her talents were as an administrator, and here she would find her true calling.

With that resolution, she spent the next few years searching for every means to turn the fledgling children's home into a respectable institution.

Her vision required goods and money. Hospitals, department stores, schools, and public transportation gave free service to missionaries, orphans, and children. She would thank these supporters and woo others. Ruth began to write an inspirational newsletter that went out to the various charitable organizations that contributed to the home.

Her outreach efforts didn't stop with the newsletter. She wanted to meet these supporters in person, too. Dr. Jackson was one such samaritan. When one of the children had been accidentally stabbed in the foot with a pitchfork, the infection that followed the accident could have resulted in an amputation, but Dr. Jackson had kept the boy for several days at his home, skillfully attending to the swollen foot. After he had done all he could, he made arrangements to have the boy treated at the children's hospital in the state capital. When Naomi took the boy there the first time, she told the doctor, "We don't know how we will pay for this." The doctor replied, "Do not worry. He will be given the same care as if he were the son of the richest man in the country." And he was.

When it was time for a follow-up visit, Ruth insisted upon accompanying Naomi and the child to the state capital. She wanted to thank the doctor personally. By this time, the year being 1947, Ruth had made herself indispensable to Naomi. They were riding on the rail line of one of the home's biggest supporters. On this particular journey, riding on the same train, was the regional director of the railway. The director was a large man with a thick head of hair that immediately became unkempt after combing; although he was neatly groomed, the untamed hair gave the impression he was rumpled. He carried a small pocket comb that he used liberally, to no avail. He loved the railroad. His family had been in the business from the beginning. He had started in the trainyards, but his knowledge and dedication brought him to the attention of his bosses and he rose fast in the company, getting into management by his late twenties. He was in his forties now. His kind face was already developing crevices from worrying day and night about his job.

The director traveled in the management's personal car, and as usual he made contact with the conductor, inquiring about problems or special circumstances aboard.

"Any problems, Earl?"

"No, Mr. Roland. No special cargo." That meant no coffins or loiterers.

"That's good. All happy, paying passengers, I guess." He smiled. That's how he wished it was always.

"Well, all but three are paying passengers."

"Who's traveling gratis?"

"Two missionaries and a kid. They are out from Mission Creek, transferred at Westchester."

"Mission Creek." He started to walk away, then paused. "Didn't our employees do something for them? Around Christmas? Do you remember?" He was actually trying to jog his own memory. He recalled the small children's home along the route that went through the coal mining towns. "Yes, of course. They are on our charity list. Invite them to my car." And he pulled out his little pocket comb to attempt order once again. He was happy, for he hated the feeling he was wasting time riding the train. Even though he was going from one destination to another, he wanted to be working, doing everything he could for the company.

When he saw the little group coming, he knew Naomi was the home's director by the way she helped the boy. Naomi stepped forward and extended her hand in thanks for his invitation and told him how wonderful his company had been to them. "Why, this year there were enough presents for each child. And thoughtful presents, things children love. We cannot thank you enough for the support and for the courtesy in letting us ride free of charge. We don't abuse it. We use it only when necessary."

Mr. Roland like her immediately. "Oh, ma'am, you don't have to worry. You use our services whenever you need to. Where are you going today?"

She told him about the boy's foot and how it would have been lost had it not been for Dr. Jackson. The children's hospital had insisted on follow-up appointments, she explained. Mr. Roland chatted with the boy, then sent for the conductor to take him to see the engineer's room and to ride in the front seat. The child hobbled off on his crutches, leaving Mr. Roland alone with the two women. He ordered coffee and asked questions about the home and where the children came from and how long they stayed.

Ruth sat quietly, letting Naomi answer the questions. Her ears pricked up when she heard him say, "You know, it seems to me that I read something in the paper recently about there being proposed legislation that all children's homes be located along a main highway by 1950. Something to do with emergencies, not being able to respond to them, and loss of children's lives." He stopped suddenly, for he remembered now reading about the fire that had razed the home at Mission Creek. "Oh, I didn't mean to—"

Ruth spoke, "We haven't seen or heard anything about it. Have you heard anything?" She turned anxiously to Naomi.

Naomi's face immediately changed, as if a cloud had cast a shadow on it. She replied as reassuringly as she could, "Well, we'll be passing the capitol today. We should stop in and visit the Department of Social Services. They should know."

Mr. Roland could see his words had distressed them, and that was the last thing he had wanted to do. He suddenly thought of a solution. "You know, there is a place—it's on our route—about forty miles from Mission Creek. A place called Lookout Ridge. It was a former Methodist girls' school, closed about eight years ago. It never could recover when the depression hit. It's empty. Maybe you could inquire about it."

Ruth was suddenly transformed from a polite observer to an enthusiastic shopper. Like a prospective consumer she wanted to know the quality, the size, the amount, the value of the school. Mr. Roland could answer none of her questions, but he appreciated her calculating mind. He was wishing she worked for his company. Naomi became quiet and still, as if she had just heard sorrowful news about a friend's health, not knowing if it would mean recovery or death. She was in that in-between place—of dread.

Because Mr. Roland was so kind and also because he wanted to see the young, bright Ruth again, he said upon parting, "It's been a real pleasure meeting you both. Now if we can be of any help to you, you just let us know. I mean it sincerely."

The encounter with Mr. Roland led Ruth and Naomi to the Department of Social Services later the same day. They were told that indeed there was legislation; it was being debated but would probably not pass until next year or maybe not until the next term. Nevertheless, they were told, they should think about relocating because there was a lot of political support for the proposition.

Naomi hardly noticed Ruth's ebullience on the way home. In contrast to Ruth's excitement about the possibility of getting out of the hills, residing in a more civilized and respectable environment, Naomi was feeling despair about leaving.

Naomi was thinking, Oh, why can't things stay the same? Of course, this new legislation makes sense, but will the people of the hills come outside the hollows to bring their children? They only turn them over to someone they know and trust. Of course, there would be other children who need a place, those not from the hills. Her mind felt sluggish. She felt she was reasoning in circles. Finally she knew. I don't want to leave. I love the mountains, the people, their way of life. I love my life just as it is. She could not give a name to what made her feel afraid.

Ruth was thinking, The Lord has heard my prayers. A school already built. It has electricity and indoor plumbing. I know it can be ours. I will write letters to the Methodist council and find out about the property. I will write to Mr. Roland. Maybe the railway will help financially. I will get all the information and surprise Naomi. Oh, she will be thrilled.

Over the next year, Ruth wrote letters and gathered information. Out of the box came the carefully packed-away suit and matching shoes and the little hat that covered one eyebrow. These were for meetings with Mr. Roland, the banker at Madison Creek, and the representative from the Methodist council. When she had finished with her inquiry and the project looked like a possibility, she informed Naomi.

Ruth approached Naomi on a warm, quiet Sunday afternoon while the children were taking their regular two-hour rest period. They were lying in bed, Ruth holding Naomi's hand. "I have some wonderful news. I know you've been worried about the letter we got last month from social services. Well, I've been working on it all year. Do you remember our conversation with Mr. Roland about a Methodist girls' school being empty?" Naomi did not. "I went to see it. It is perfect." She told all the good news first. "It is furnished with a dining room to seat one hundred. It has a dorm room with beds. There is a dorm with a gymnasium across the street where the boys could sleep. There are three hundred acres of beautiful farmland and forest. Oh, Naomi, it is too good to be true. And the church is looking for a buyer."

Naomi was stunned. "We couldn't possibly come up with the amount of money they would be asking."

"But we might. Mr. Roland with the railway is talking to the board about making a sizable contribution. It helps them with tax problems. If we could get a commitment from the churches for the payment, the council might take a reasonable offer. We have a meeting next week."

Naomi struggled to put in order the raging confusion that was tumbling about in her mind. How could Ruth go over her head to take on this kind of decision? What an enormous demand to be making of the churches that had so humbly supported them. How could they fill up a place for one hundred children? There were never more than thirty at the mission. And to leave the hills, the Watsons, Lily and her children, Mr. Nobel, and all the other families that had become a part of her? To give up going to the little churches she visited monthly, little fledgling plants that needed watering and care. Who would keep them going? And then the other side. Yes, she knew it was coming, the day she would have to leave. But she had envisioned something different: to be on the edge of a hollow, along a main highway as was required in the new regulation, but not so far away, so close to a large town of over five hundred people. It would change everything. Change. Her mother used to say, when you can't adjust to change, it's time to leave this world. She was only forty, she had been in the hills now for about thirteen years. Things were changing fast since the war ended.

"You're quiet," Ruth said apprehensively.

"I'm thinking. Of course, you're right. We need to think of relocating. But I'm not sure this is the place for us. It sounds like too big an undertaking."

Ruth was dismayed. Fighting back her disappointment, she said, "You will at least look at it, won't you? The meeting has already been set for Thursday." Then she leaned on her elbow and looked into Naomi's face. "You know, I did all this for you because I love you, and I did not want you to worry."

"Yes, I know, dear. But you could have included me in the search."

Ruth's eyes stung with tears. It wasn't to exclude Naomi. It was all for her—for Naomi's glory, not for mine, she thought.

A week later, the meeting took place and Ruth was in her element. Armed with a rare combination of sexuality and competence, Ruth not only could get what she wanted from men, she could make them enjoy giving it to her. Naomi, sitting in much confusion, did not notice her friend's charms: the flushed face, bright smiles, and smooth manipulations that accompanied her words as Ruth suggested, worried, considered, and then accepted the offer the men presented. Ruth turned to Naomi and said, "If we get a commitment of a $250 monthly increase from each of our largest supporters, we can easily make the payments, and we have ten years before the balloon payment is due. You have always said God will provide, and I believe this is where he wants us."

Naomi tried to regain control by pointing out the downside of the plan, but she was met with optimism on all sides. Everyone seemed to agree this was a good idea. They had all been seduced by Ruth's charm and swept up in her enthusiasm. Naomi had looked at the property. It did not appear as magnificent as Ruth described. It was shabby, left untended for years. The roof leaked and needed repair. The boys' and girls' dorms were separated by a main highway. Wouldn't that be dangerous? The big white building was badly in need of paint.

Another big brick building stood across the street. When Naomi asked about it, she was told the county was making an offer for it and planned to use it as an elementary school. The children from the home could walk across the street to school. Although the mission would own the large field between the school and the boys' dorm, it was possible to get a small fee from the county for leasing the field for a playground, as well as rent for the gymnasium. Naomi gradually became infected with the vision Ruth and the others shared.

No other offer was on the table, nor any foreseen, and the council was eager to get rid of the property. The offer was made contingent on getting a commitment from the small mission's supporters. The process would take time.

It was a wonderful year for Ruth. She had tested herself and was pleased with the result. Eventually she secured the commitments needed from the churches and other charitable organizations. Once she even went alone on a fund-raising trip throughout the eastern seaboard that took her north to Maine, where she returned triumphant to her childhood home. She was pleased that she was finally recognized as an authentic missionary; she had survived where people thought she would fail, and she felt vindicated—even if her mother did not acknowledge her triumph.

When she returned to the mission, she discovered to her utter joy that Buddy's children—three of them by now—had been returned. Naomi had received a letter from Buddy saying he had been contacted by the Red Cross and told that the children had been abandoned. He asked if she would pick them up where they were being held by social services and bring them back to the mission where they were to remain. Buddy was filing for divorce on the grounds his wife was an unfit mother, and consequently, she was to have no contact with the children. And in that same letter he told Naomi that she could have the little girl, Jennifer. He was not claiming parentage of the youngest boy, but he would return for Billy.

Something familiar about the mannerisms of the little girl at first disturbed then thrilled Naomi. It was an ephemeral feeling, like déjà vu, that haunted her. It was not until one night while Ruth was away that she understood. The child stood at her bed trembling and whispered, "Can I sleep in you's bed?" At first Naomi thought it was an apparition, the tiny urchin dressed in a long white gown that shimmered in the moonlight. "Zinnia, is that you?" The child thought she had said "Jennifer," so she said "Yes" as she snuggled close to Naomi. Although Naomi could not accept the idea of reincarnation, she could believe that God might replace an enormous loss and give her compensation in exchange for having to leave the hills. For in this child she would be taking a bit of the hills with her. The child sounded and acted like Zinnia and even had the same sprinkle of freckles across the bridge of the nose. Naomi had been given a child that would embody all she loved about the place she would be leaving.

Ruth did not know Naomi's feelings about Jennifer. She could not see beyond the happiness that they would be moving and that Ruth had been reunited with her extended self, the child who could be better than she. But a cloud shadowed her delight. The child had forgotten her and preferred Naomi.

And so the child returned to the place that had once revived her, and her return raised the hopes of two women, each of whom was sure Jennifer would be the key to her own happiness.

PART III

THROUGH A GLASS DARKLY:
JENNIFER'S STORY, 1949–1956

CHAPTER 12

It now falls to me, Jennifer, the child upon whom such hopes of happiness rested, to tell how the beginning ended. For I am the self-appointed historian, the keeper of the record of first a mission, then a home, then an institution. This is my personal story, unlikely to be told the same by another observer. But someone needs to tell it before it is forgotten, for often it is out of the past that the present can discover itself.

Although my birth may have been an accident, my arrival at the mission was not. The great events shaking and reshaping the world in the 1940s reached far beyond the battlegrounds, forcing decisions that would snare the innocent. Thousands of young people were torn from their roots during the second great war and displaced into worlds with new rules and promises, far from home. They fell into loneliness, desperation, and they needed to insure that life would win against the massive slaughter threatening its extinction. So they married and had children and many made impulsive and unlikely choices. Like so many others, my parents awoke one day to look at each other and ask, "What have we done?" And like thousands, they fled one another, leaving their offspring scattered here and there. I do not blame them, for they were as much a product of their circumstances as I.

On my second return to the mission in 1949, I was suffering from pneumonia. I owe my life to Naomi; she told me that. Unlike Miss Ruth, who had restored my health when I was malnourished, Naomi resurrected me from the dead. She told me the story when I was good, when I was bad, when she was happy, and when she was sad. She told it like a poem, a rhythm that still echos when she comes to me when the wind rustles the leaves: "No one thought you would live. When they told me you had died, I went to you and lay my body on yours, making a vow to God that if he saved you, I would give you back to him. He saved you to serve him." After Naomi told me this, she often expressed her disappointment about not serving as a missionary in Africa.

The story rather complicated matters for me because I sensed I was to fulfill a destiny that might have belonged to someone else, like maybe being a missionary to Africa. But I can't complain because being made to feel special was a rather good feeling. At times I understood why God had especially recognized me out of all the others that made up my world and not Shirley, who was downright mean, or Millie, who was mentally retarded, or Sunny, who didn't believe in the God of Naomi and Miss Ruth. At other times I figured God had picked the wrong person because I could be as mean and dumb and unbelieving as my friends. Maybe it was the expectation that I might do something extraordinary that gave me the dream of soaring beyond my circumstances. Or it could have been good luck or genes or, most likely, love. But the idea that I was special was the legacy given me.

For me, being special was not without problems. It required careful maneuvering through a minefield of envious playmates. Sometimes I was forced to discover how ordinary I really was—like the time Shirley nearly got me drowned. The truth is she always wanted to kill me. She hated my getting more attention than she, but I was too young and too busy getting my share to worry about how it might affect Shirley.

One warm summer afternoon, the kids from the mission were at the post office in Mission Creek, waiting for the train. There was always excitement in the air while we waited, everyone, young and old alike, wondering what surprises the train might bring. The eligible girls arrived in clean dresses and stood in groups, looking down the track to where the available boys stood, also in clean shirts. Worn-out mothers, weary farmers, and friendly neighbors stood around greeting one another, sharing gossip, discussing the purpose of their rare departures or who they were there to greet. Waiting made us kids giddy and eager and restless. We ran around, challenging each other to footraces or games of skip rock at the creek, which ran parallel to the path from the mission and opened to a swimming hole behind the post office.

At the time, Shirley and I were both four and the same height, but she was heavier. We had found our way down to the creek, when Shirley bet

PART III   123

she could wade farther into the water than I could. Since we never wore shoes in the summer except for church, it was simple to hike up our dresses and meet the challenge. We waded in, shoulder to shoulder, the brown water rising above our knees, then our panties, then our waists, until suddenly the current lifted me and carried me swiftly toward the rapids that were just beyond the swinging bridge. Shirley turned around in satisfaction when she saw me drift away, glad I was on my way to the rapids and out of her life. She didn't say a word to a soul and no one knew I was missing until I appeared coughing and soaked like a beaver, in the arms of George Watson. He was on his way to the train station when he saw me bobbing by and he plucked me out of the creek. Poor disappointed Shirley.

She got into a peck of trouble, not for trying to kill me, because no one suspected that, but for not telling what happened so that I could be rescued. She said she didn't tell because she didn't want to get into trouble. And Shirley turned the story around so that she was the victim, and what a pathetic victim she could play. She tried to teach me once how to play a victim—but that's another story. After this little incident, I concluded that God hadn't been looking after his special child, but Naomi saw just the opposite—that it was proof he was watching over me.

How can I describe Naomi? How does one describe a saint? Saints are known more by their auras than their physical appearance. They all seem to look the same: a face shaped by giving to others. You know what I mean—beatific, forgiving, with no hard edges and kind, ever-so-kind, eyes.

By the time Naomi came into my focus, she was forty, carrying a square, solid body strengthened by long daily walks through the hills to call on neighbors. Her gray hair was neatly plaited at the nape of her neck and her blue eyes were enlarged by wire-framed glasses. Her face had begun to fall, giving her that soft puppy-dog look that middle-aged women tend to get. She had a very ordinary appearance for such a remarkable person. The eyes! They told a deeper story, elusive and mysterious to the child looking back into them. They twinkled like stars, and sometimes they were sad—an ocean-deep sadness. At other times came a flash of hardness—just a flash that disappeared almost immediately. Someone told me that Scots were stern; it was a trait universal to them. What did she do with her Scottish sternness? Where did she put it? Maybe she gave it to Miss Ruth.

To me, Naomi was a miracle worker—not just because she saved my life. She worked other miracles, too. Once during a bitter winter one of the home's workers came to her saying we needed blankets; there were not enough for all the children as the population had exceeded thirty. After lunch, Naomi announced that we needed a special prayer time. Now I have to be honest and tell you these prayer times were pretty boring. We children squirmed and poked at each other, sometimes using the prayers as a way to get even for some earlier injustice. When Shirley prayed and asked God to forgive Jimmy for having hit Bobby, Jimmy angrily blurted out, "And God forgive Shirley for she's a darn liar, and she knows it." Naomi was patient and coached us on how to pray, telling us it was wrong to whine and plead and try to manipulate God. I can still hear her pray:

> Our Heavenly Father, we thank you for your bountiful gifts and the blessings you have so generously bestowed upon us. You know our needs and we know you will hear our prayers. At this time, we bring our needs before you. We ask that if it is your will you will send us blankets. We thank you for every gift you send our way, for those we ask, and for those we receive before asking. In Jesus' name we pray, amen.

I walked with Naomi that cold, gray afternoon to meet the four o'clock train and to pick up the mail. I remember old Mr. Ward, a local farmer, helping unload two boxes that were marked for the mission. They were from a church up north that regularly sent donations. The boxes were full of blankets!

We rode back to the mission on Mr. Ward's horse-drawn wagon, which carried the miracle blankets. He didn't say a word as I triumphantly told him how we had just prayed for blankets, and now, here they were. Our prayers had been answered. Naomi smiled and corrected me, "They were answered even before we asked."

Naomi's certainty that all things would work out according to a predetermined plan offered a security that calmed the demons of a five-year-old who had already witnessed too much catastrophe and upheaval. The child could not see any problem in the belief that if God provided, he had heard one's prayer, and if he did not provide, a no was also an answer. As Naomi might say, "A no to a prayer might be to teach us patience." I needed to be sure the trickster of change had been tamed—and Naomi's religion reassured me.

I had been told that I came to the mission suffering from malnutrition, that my teenage mother thought babies liked Coke, not milk. I stayed long enough to become strong and healthy and to wrap a few adults around my finger. Miss Ruth told me it broke her heart when I left, and Naomi said that I would never have left had it not been for the fact that her mother died the very day my mother came to reclaim us. I found out Naomi's mother had died in her sleep. I left believing that she was sleeping and I imagine I was too excited about my journey to notice the fact that she failed to kiss me good-bye.

Willingly I left with the woman of whom I had no memory. Children with broken attachments will often fasten themselves to anyone who holds a promise to adore them. I was known to throw my arms around perfect strangers or invite myself to be their child in exchange for extra affection, attention, and candy. Off I skipped down the lane, next to my brother Bill, two years older, who seemed to have special claims on the woman. My sketchy memory of the train ride includes itching legs from sitting on the wool-covered seats and a screaming fit because the woman would not let me walk down the aisle with the conductor to greet the travelers as I always had.

Years later I was shown a picture of me taken the day I left, wearing a bonnet and carrying a favorite pink sweater, the one that became the proverbial security blanket. As I looked at the picture, a memory returned: I am standing with my face pressed against the window watching the waving adults from the mission get smaller as the train moves farther away. I am crying. Something reminds me of a dark, hollow place into which I have fallen before and makes me want to end this holiday before it begins and return to my world, over which I had a small portion of control. The woman seems angry as she tries to pull me onto her lap and I resist. Bill is mad at me and I kick him for taking her side. It was a bad start that never improved.

Bits of memories and partial sketches remain like a jigsaw puzzle with pieces missing: a sleeveless red plaid dress with a torn pocket; a blanket under a tree where a smelly, dirty baby lies crying; a small white frame house with slanted steps, one with a gaping hole where a cat hides; yellow, dimly lighted rooms that make me sneeze. Scenes of men in uniforms; sounds of fighting, clinking glasses, and loud voices that frighten me. Strangers and unfamiliar places. And then, out of the chaotic background emerges a sound so sweet that it transports me to a safe, warm place where I am blissfully content. Sweet sounds and sunset colors envelop me, but I cannot put form to this amorphous spirit. Out of frustration, I toss the fragmented pieces into a bottomless pit in my stomach, with determination that there they shall remain—at least until I drag them out and start the same futile game of trying to make them fit together.

The sharpest memory of my return to Naomi's place is the sound of a rocking chair and a little boy's heartbreaking half-song, half-sob, "I want my mommy," that filled the room like the ticking of a clock. I remember looking into the dark and seeing my brother in a long white nightgown, thumb in his mouth, rocking back and forth, his moaning song barely audible. Out of puzzlement and concern, I reached for him, wondering about his longing for the woman we called "Mommy," wondering at his broken heart and why he might choose chaos over safety. Sometimes the crying would stop long enough for him to stand by the bed and ask, "Do you miss her, Sin?"

He called me "Sin" long before we knew what the word meant. The name was his effort to condense "Sis" and "Jen" into one name.

Everyone called me "Sin" until I returned to the mission. An all-out effort
was made to break Bill's habit of using it but without success. Even when
I learned its meaning, the name never sounded like a defamation coming
from him.

––––––––––

Bill and I came to an unspoken agreement about our abandonment—
he would express the grief and I would provide the comfort. Around the
time he quit crying, I started occasional outbursts of screaming.
Sometimes there was a trigger but often not. The screams erupted unpredictably, like a geyser, releasing pressure. A scream would begin in the pit
of my stomach, like a hunger ache. Instinctively I tried to suppress it—
tighten, relax, tighten, relax—but the feeling would swell until it spilled
out of my mouth in a wail until gradually the pain subsided. Puzzled by
the scream's unexpected appearance and a little ashamed afterward over
my lack of control, I tried to hold my breath against it, but the only result
was my passing out and receiving a bump on the forehead.

One day when I felt a scream start, I picked up the toy truck I had
been running over mounds of dirt and slammed it against Donnie's head.
I suddenly found my feet flying out from under me, and I was turned
upside down and my bottom slapped so hard it expelled the scream from
me—like a shaken carbonated drink after its lid is popped. I saw Donnie
look at me with satisfaction, but I suddenly realized my scream had been
legitimized. For a time thereafter, misbehavior became my devious
method for discharging that overpowering feeling.

Gradually the tremors from the earthshaking events of the time with
my mother subsided and so did the screaming. People and images came
into focus and I attached myself to them, especially Naomi. Naomi's
arms became my shelter from the threatening shadows that played on my
walls at night. It was in those arms I learned to count. Our game began
with my saying, "I love you the most." She would say, "But I love you
bushels full." I, "I love you two bushels full." She, "I love you three
bushels full." And up we would go, as far as my young mind could
count, the numbers getting higher as I became older. The game ended

when she squeezed me tight and whispered in my ear, "We love each other just the same." Contented, I surrendered to sleep, slumbering between the two large, soft pillows of her breasts.

As much as she desired to protect me from the world, she also wanted me to know it. She awakened me one night, wrapped me in a warm blanket, and carried me outside under the starlit sky to observe a rare appearance of the aurora borealis. She taught me where to find the Nile, the Red Sea, Jerusalem, and the Indian Ocean on a map. I knew where these places were before I knew how to find Madison Creek. The way she told the story about Daniel in the lion's den made the Three Little Pigs seem like milksops.

As images began to be shaped into words, I became a storyteller to my peers, finding ways to use fantasies as balm. In the darkness of the dorm room after bedtime, when our supervisors were convinced we were asleep, I began the story of the beautiful child Jessica who had a perfect life and escaped all dangers placed in her path. In those quiet moments before sleep, someone would say, "Jen, tell us what happened after . . ." and the tranquilizer of imagination began to work its charm.

CHAPTER 13

If Naomi was the safe harbor, Miss Ruth was the storm. With Miss Ruth we had to be vigilant about the weather, watch for subtle signs of change, for squalls could come, fierce and damaging. They could stay for days or dissipate as quickly as a cloud sliding past the sun. We could usually avoid the storm's brunt if we recognized the signs and took off for a secure harbor. But sometimes the wind turned and made even the harbor unsafe. Those were the scariest times. A group of us might be in Naomi's room before school—perhaps she would be brushing and braiding our hair or helping us with multiplication tables—when Miss Ruth would appear with black flashing eyes and some excuse, sometimes pathetically insignificant, to break up our jovial gathering. One time she stood before me trembling with anger, accusing me of loving Naomi more than her. She could tell, she said, because I made Naomi's bed more carefully than hers.

Such insight this woman had. I did love Naomi more. But I took great care to hide the fact from Ruth, not because she was right, but because her knowledge made me feel afraid. What was it that made me feel she had some claim on me? It seemed important to her that I love her more than anyone else and that I think of her as a mother. It was confusing. Sometimes she would lose control and I would find myself being flung across the room because I had on the wrong pair of shoes. It wasn't as if I got the worst of it. I got the best, but the best was like being the prisoner most favored by the jailer—it is not a welcomed privilege.

When Miss Ruth was not raging about something, she was not so bad. If you stayed to the left of her, you could get away with quite a lot. The deafness in her left ear was a discovery passed on to the newcomers early. But that right ear! Watch out, we were told, for it had compensated for whatever loss there was in the left. It was as if she could hear words before they were spoken. Sometimes Ruth could be soothing, like the time Naomi's bed was full and a recurring nightmare had driven me to seek comfort anywhere I could find it. The need to hear steady, rhythmic breathing, rather than marching feet, made me abandon all the pride a seven-year-old could muster and ask her if I could sleep in her bed.

She made a warm place for me and asked, "Did you have a bad dream?"

"Um," I mumbled.

"You can tell me."

I wasn't sure about that. I always told Naomi and she would assure me that dreams were not real or even prophetic.

"I just heard marching. I thought I heard the soldiers." Ever since returning to the home, soldiers came to my dreams, killing, threatening, harming—a piece of the history of life with my mother that would not come into focus.

Miss Ruth replied, "Sometimes I hear sounds at night and I don't know what they are. Sometimes they even sound like soldiers to me, too."

I exhaled long and deep. How could she know? Had she ever seen a soldier? And as though she read my thoughts she told me, "Some soldiers killed my brother—in the war. I loved him more than anyone in the world. Sometimes at night, I think of the soldiers, too."

Struggling to think of a way to close the gap between us, I fell into a deep sleep. It was barely light when I rolled over and watched as she dressed. She raised her nightgown, her back to the bed, and I watched as she slipped on a bra, then a girdle. She removed the gown as she stood in front of the closet to select a dress. Her body was smooth and firm, like Emma's, the oldest girl in the home. Her contradictions—such a young body on a woman whose hair was turning gray—constantly surprised me.

It was bright the second time I woke—and quiet, too quiet. In the distance I could hear the hum of voices, and I realized Miss Ruth had let me sleep in while everyone else was at breakfast. I panicked. I was angry with her and dread flooded me as I rushed down the stairs to take my place at the table. My fears were confirmed by Shirley's voice as I slid into my seat. Her jealous voice hissed at me, "Pet! We don't get to sleep in late. What makes you so special? You need a bottle?" She began to mock me by whimpering like a baby.

I wanted to smack the toast right out of her mouth. I wasn't going to let her get to me. "Yeah, I'm special. 'Cause I'm not a retard like you."

There's one thing I can't stand, and that's people who think they are better than everyone else. The high and mighty, Eliza used to say, put their pants on the same way as she do. Eliza used to say a lot when I lived with her. She didn't let no one accuse her of being a fool. She'd just stand face to face and tell them what she thought. Sometimes I wish she didn't do it so loud. Like that night she come lookin' for me, screaming out my name in the middle of the night till you could hear it clear to the next mountain range. I coulda' died. I can't hardly stand to look at her—no front teeth and stringy hair. Don't look like she never let a finger touch water. I could probably of took it if it hadn't been for one of them giggling in the dark and saying, "Shirley, ain't that your mom? She's come to git you. Ha. Ha."

I couldn't tell for sure who said it, but I'm just knowing it was probably that Jennifer. She thinks she's better than everyone else. Miss Ruth and Nam thinks so, too. They act like she is. If they only knew what I know about her. I saw her playing with herself in bed, and she saw that I saw her. I'm just saving it to tell at the right time, to let Nam know that Jennifer ain't no saint. Just 'cause she can memorize Bible verses faster than the rest of us, they take her on all those trips when they go raise money. Then she comes back talking like a fool, like she ain't from these hills. Too good for us, she thinks. Well, I make it my business to remind her she's the same as all of us. Maybe my mother is a drunk, but at least she does look me up now and then. Don't see why Jennifer is so proud. Ain't not one of her family come to see her. And Jennifer says her daddy is rich. Ha. Ha. Lot of good it does her. Like the Bible says, "Pride goeth before destruction and a haughty spirit before a fall." I figure Jennifer has a real fall comin' to her.

Wish Frankie would come git me out of here, before Miss Ruth kills me. Every time he comes to see me, he promises. He said when he finishes his work in Ohio, he and Eliza will have enough money for me to come home. I've been here ever since I was four. I keep telling him, "Frankie, one of these days I'm going to be too old to go home." He just laughs and says I never will. I wished he'd git a job nearby so I could go home.

He's the best daddy a girl could have. He calls me "Pet"; he says with my eyes so big and brown I look like a small doe. He treated me real good, better than Eliza. He'd bring a whole box of candy bars for me to eat, worried 'cause I was so skinny. Sometimes he'd tuck me tight inside his coat, all buttoned up, and I'd be pressed flat against him, with my legs around his hips. He smelled like licorice and I never felt so warm and good as when he'd carry me. He'd go ask Eliza if she'd seen me. Then he'd laugh and laugh when he pulled me out—like a surprise.

He was the only one that could tell Eliza to shut up when she got carried away—and she would. Nam did too that night she came late and yelled so the whole country could hear. Nam told her to leave and come back when she was sober. In my heart I was glad. Glad I didn't have to see her 'cause I probably would've gotten so mad she wouldn't never come back. I don't keer if they laugh at her. It don't bother me none. I'm not going to hold pride in my heart.

Nam says I have bitterness in my heart. She made me memorize Ephesians 4, verse 31 and 32. I can say it in my sleep: "Let all bitterness and wrath, and anger, and clamor, and evil speaking be put away from you, with all malice. And be ye kind one to another, tenderhearted, forgiving one another even as God for Christ's sake hath forgiven you." I don't know why she give me that verse. Maybe I do have bitterness. Well, at least I don't have pride. She says I shouldn't always be trying to git someone else in trouble and that I should look to myself. Well, I am. That's just what I'm doing—taking care of myself.

Nam's always talking about finding our calling. I think I've found mine. It's to make sure that someone don't think they're better than someone else.

From Shirley's perspective, it was easy to hate me, for Shirley was often the target of Miss Ruth's lightning-swift changes in moods. She would take a paddle, a belt, a coat hanger, a hairbrush, a book—she wasn't choosy—in order to drive the evil out of the child. Even though I, too, secretly thought Shirley was evil, I was sure Miss Ruth was on the wrong track trying to improve Shirley's nature, and Miss Ruth's tactics made defining evil all the harder for me.

We were all given chores as soon as we left the nursery. Mine were to waken the babies and get them dressed and ready for breakfast and after breakfast, before school, to clean and make the beds in Naomi's and Miss Ruth's rooms. Sometimes I would sit at Miss Ruth's vanity table. She had bottles with the scent of lilacs, a small drawer that contained white lace handkerchiefs she wore peeking from a pocket of a dress or a jacket, a jewelry box with the dog tags of her deceased brother, Lee, a few rings. The few items suggested something beyond the bleak, meager surroundings of my daily life—a hint of elegance in the midst of the harsh puritanical denial of body and materialism.

One ring's radiance and luster entranced me—a single white, brilliant stone set in a thin gold band. Holding the ring in just the right light would cause it to sparkle and cast its fiery splendor in tiny dots around the room. Ruth called it a promise ring. Someone had promised something to her but changed his mind, she said, but she got to keep the ring. It had a strange effect on me, this ring. Sometimes I found just the right spot to place it so that its star bursts scattered across the room and I would dance in its fire. Or with my arms straight out like a propeller I would slowly turn, eyes half-closed, as I watched the light freckle my body. Other times I was compelled to put it into my mouth, hoping to swallow its light, wanting its beauty to fill me, to reawaken the sleeping princess. With the ring's magic came music, a haunting melody never completed. The happiness gradually faded, replaced with a sadness that drove me to the bed where I would lie in a small, fetal curl until I could will away the darkness. Miss Ruth was like the ring to me—a promise, a hint of brightness that was snatched away by her blackened moods.

My desire to understand her mysteries was thwarted by my peers. They were afraid of her and called her names behind her back—"The Warden," "Ruthless" (a pun on her name, Ruth Lewis), "Queen Bee," and others. She got the name "Hammerhead" after she stopped Shirley and Millie from arguing by slamming their heads together. She wouldn't have quit, either, if Billy hadn't gone to get Naomi. Naomi came running, screaming at Miss Ruth to stop, trying to wrench her away from the children. Finally she managed to place herself between the girls so that their bodies were flung against Naomi's. Miss Ruth stopped when she saw she was battering Naomi. We were all on the front porch waiting for the last lunch bell to call us to assembly and all frozen with fear and disbelief. I watched the blood come from Millie's head and watched Shirley fall as if in slow motion. I heard Billy's voice say to Naomi, "She'll kill them. Stop her." I vomited over the side of the porch.

Billy was the only one I knew besides Naomi—and my best friend, Sunny—who was not afraid of Ruth. He proved it to everyone who was present one afternoon in the dining room. The confrontation had started with a new rule she made up (all her new rules were made when Naomi was away) that we had to eat everything on our plates or it would be served at the next meal. Being a finicky eater particularly disgusted by fat, I had carefully carved away any semblance of fat and left it in a small pile at the edge of my plate. Miss Ruth had decided to test our seriousness about the rule, probably believing I would be a compliant participant. But I took one look at that jiggling white matter and was determined that it would not slide down my esophagus. I sat for an hour after everyone was dismissed before she took my plate and sent me back to school. The plate appeared before me at the evening meal. I still resisted. It was there at breakfast. Billy sat at the next table watching and waiting for the outcome.

I saw him at school before lunch and he told me, "Sin, if you hold your nose when you eat it, you can't taste it because it's the smell that makes the taste." So when the plate appeared, since I was pretty hungry, I considered Billy's words. Close to the end of the meal I thought I'd give Billy's suggestion a try. I pinched my nose and took the first bite, but then let go of my nose as my gag reflex took over, and I vomited on my plate. Miss Ruth was mad. She was not going to be made a fool of. She was swiftly behind me, shoving my face into the plate, her angry voice telling me that I would not manipulate my way out of this. Suddenly a hush came over the room as a chair scraped the floor. Billy was standing near her, and in a low, steady voice he said, "You let go of her, Miss Ruth, or I will kill you." Her hand lightened as she turned toward him, and I looked over my shoulder and saw him with a raised chair poised to do exactly as he had promised.

In a surprised, disbelieving voice she said, "Put that back and go sit down. I will handle this."

Billy stood still. "No. Now I will handle this. Maude, go get the plate and dump it in the garbage."

My friend Maude had been assigned to wait tables that day. I tried to catch her eye and warn her to stay out of this. But she was looking at Miss Ruth, waiting for a signal from her as to what to do. Miss Ruth looked around the room and realized she was the only adult present. The others had left to prepare for their groups' return to their dormitories. She made a move toward Billy, but then several other chairs scraped across the floor, and I saw the new boy, Dillon, rise to stand beside Billy. Then Jake stood, then W. C. Even mentally retarded Millie rose. The quiet in the room made breathing seem loud, so I sucked in my breath, as though exhaling would create a catastrophe. I waited. Miss Ruth nodded to Maude and she ran forward, grabbed the plate, and knocked all the contents to the floor as she hit the swinging door going to the kitchen. A nervous twitter spread through the room. Miss Ruth pulled herself to her full five feet six inches, holding her head high and back straight, and announced that lunch was over.

The incident was never mentioned again. I had dinner that evening, and no one was punished for defiance. Why was a mystery. But I was bursting with pride over my brother's stand. He had mutinied against injustice.

———

One rarely escapes childhood without trauma. That's what friends are for, to carry one through when parents and adults go too far. Sunny was my best friend. She thought the way everyone stood up to Miss Ruth was a great drama, and there was no one who liked drama more than Sunny. She came to our new home at Lookout Ridge in the summer of 1950, a few months after we moved from the mission. I was five the day she came and so was she. Managing to escape adult supervision, I was sitting alone on the big front porch when a car slowly made its way into the long driveway. A man sat with his body turned toward the back seat and it looked as if he was having a conversation with himself. The car stayed parked for a long time until he finally got out and opened the back door. Out stepped a girl, an odd-looking child with tangled red curls wildly sticking out from under a small beret and horn-rimmed glasses that were too big for her face. She was tall, with arms and legs too long to go with her thin body. She was covered with a brown coat that fit too tightly, and she wore a knotted string of brightly colored scarfs that had been put together to make a long one and tossed carelessly across one shoulder. What obviously would have been a costume on another child seemed to fit with this girl's unusual overall appearance.

She let go of the man's hand as she approached the big white building and walked with an air of confidence and superiority. You would have thought she was auditioning for a part in a play the way she held her head up and nearly floated up the stairs. She was determined not to be defeated by what lay beyond those double doors at the top of the stairs.

When they got closer, I could see that she looked like the thin coughing man beside her. But she was less fearful than he. He hesitated and faltered before he asked me where he could find Miss Fraser. I had never heard Naomi's last name—we just called her Nam—and I stared back ignorantly. "Who is the director here?" he asked, so I took him to Naomi. But I had a strange feeling as I observed the coltlike child walk toward the building. I was sure we knew each other from before. I felt I had found a lost friend, and it was as though a fine invisible thread within my soul uncoiled and attached to her. As we walked together to find Naomi, I took her hand and said, "I will take care of you. You can sleep in my room."

"There, you see, Sunny, you have already found a friend," her father said. Sunny turned to me with a haughty glance that told me, "I can take care of myself, thank you," but for one instant when our eyes met, it seemed that she, too, had a look of recognition. Then the moment passed, and we stood before each other as strangers.

Sunny became my bunkmate, my mentor, my collaborator in story-telling, my reality check. She was indifferent to her surroundings, more prone to describe than to pass judgment, and she had a penetrating power of observation that could be unnerving. I remember the time I got into a disagreement with Franny, arguing fiercely that the real colors of Christmas should be brown and yellow, winter colors in a child's view. Sunny looked up from her book and said to me, "Drop it. You're just mad at her because she beat you in the drawing contest." When I went in search of Sunny, I often found her in a hiding place reading a book. I figured that's how she got to know as much as she did.

She came and went over the years. Her father would reappear unex-pectedly, taking her away for long periods and then just as unpredictably returning her. She never talked about her life, and as was common in the home, we never asked one another. Like all children, we evaluated one another on the present, not on the past or future. When Sunny returned, my bunkmate would be displaced and Sunny would resume her rela-tionship with me as though she had been gone but a day.

Miss Ruth did not like Sunny and tried to discourage our relation-ship by asking what I saw in Sunny. "I like her" was the only answer I could give. But I knew why Miss Ruth didn't like Sunny—because Sunny didn't like to pray. She was the first person that told me that there were different gods to whom people prayed, and she was waiting until she was older to decide which god she was going to pray to. Sunny never said much about Miss Ruth, she just stayed out of her way.

One time I told Sunny my true feelings toward Miss Ruth. "I hate her," I said simply, unable to explain my confusion.

Sunny challenged, "Why do you act like you like her?"

"I don't know."

"Yes, you do."

"No, I don't. Maybe it's because I like her sometimes."

"Maybe."

"Well, I just hate her when she's mean."

She stared hard at me and was silent.

"What?" I asked. "What do you think?"

"You're afraid of her."

"I am not," I said, lying. It felt like a bad thing to admit. Although I was used to Sunny's honesty, it still stung. And sometimes I thought Sunny was jealous of my relationship with Naomi and with Miss Ruth, even though she didn't seem to need anyone.

"You can lie to Miss Ruth, you can lie to me, but lying to yourself is the worst," Sunny said.

She didn't say it angrily, more like an afterthought. But I thought about that remark often, so I began a little game with myself at the end of each day, reviewing my lies and then stating my true feelings three times. For example, if I had agreed with someone that blue was my favorite color when it was really green, I would repeat three times my true feeling that I liked green best. I got to where I could do it on the spot. It was not my fault entirely that I couldn't spontaneously say what I really felt because the two most significant people in my life needed agreement, not honesty. To disappoint one caused too much sadness, which I could not bear, and the other too much rage, which I could not risk. It was a kind cruelty that put me in danger of losing my soul.

Sunny was right about the fear. I hated it and thought myself a coward. Why did I not intervene when Miss Ruth was mean to my friends? Instead, I looked away, then quietly went to them afterward offering comfort and hugs, but they angrily pushed me away. Millie got the worst. Pretty, green-eyed, mentally slow Millie. She was always in trouble, either locked in her room for long stretches at a time or beaten until she no longer had the strength to protest. Millie looked to me to defend her with our peers, and often I did.

Once when I sided wrongly with one of them against her, she threw me on the sidewalk and began slamming my head against the cement. "You didn't say she lied. You didn't say she lied," she screamed. I couldn't even be mad at her because I knew she was in the right and she didn't have the means to cleverly argue her point.

One day, however, I proved Sunny wrong. It was the week of the circus. Excitement was thick, and exuberant fantasies about walking on high wires and flying on trapezes dominated our conversation. It was important that no one got into trouble so we protected Millie, helping her with her chores. The day of the circus came, and Millie was slow to sweep the dining room floor. We had failed in our vigilance, for Miss Ruth walked in just as someone impatiently said, "Hurry up, Millie." Millie growled back.

Miss Ruth responded, too happily, "Well, I can see who is not going to the circus today. It was agreed that only those who were good and did their work well could go."

In her devastation, Millie threw down her broom, only making matters worse. Silence fell around us, and my quiet, buried rage began to rumble inside its volcano. To smother a spirit seemed worse than to harm a body. I could no longer look away. I turned to Miss Ruth and screamed at her, "How can you do this to her? You know she can't help herself. She can't help it. You are evil and I hope you burn in hell!" My words of blasphemy bounced off the thin walls. I was in risk of burning in hell myself for uttering such words. The effect on me was strange, miraculous. I did not feel evil, I felt cleansed, strong, unconcerned about my fate, even though I figured I had a good chance of being dead in the next twenty minutes. The look crossing the faces of my peers confirmed that possibility.

Instead, unpredictable Miss Ruth replied with a sarcastic smile, "Well, in that case, both you and Millie can sit on the front steps all day. Neither of you are going."

So I sat on the front steps with my rage and hate as company. But I was strangely less afraid.

Years later I argued with Billy over my cowardice toward Miss Ruth. He said I wasn't a coward, I was cautious. Cautiousness came from wisdom, he said, and cowardice from foolishness. The line is sometimes hard to distinguish.

I hope Jen don't hate me. She won't look at me. She didn't sit next to me, she sat three steps higher and way down on the other side away from me. She just sits staring across my head like I'm a ghost. She don't believe in ghosts, either. I know it 'cause of that time they put the sheet over me with lightning bugs stuck on it and made me go to the nursery saying, "Woo woo," trying to scare everyone and they cried and Jen got real mad and told them, "Ghosts don't ex . . ." I forget the word, but she said they weren't real and she made them hush crying. Jen is smart, real smart, not like me, but she is wrong about ghosts. I know for sure they are real. I got one and every now and then I see it—like in a dream.

I don't mean to get in trouble. If I go fast, it makes me slow. Nam has a sign on her desk that she told me says "The hurrier I go, the behinder I get." That's me. Fast, then slow. Fast, then bam! Wham! My head. I don't remember what happened, but I heard about it. Jen says I can't help it. She said it mean to Miss Ruth. That's why we're on the steps.

Jen's my friend. She makes me feel good. That's why I hit her when I did. Because she made me feel bad.

She was jumping rope, real fast. She can go as high as a hundred and not miss a skip. I was watching. She was laughing and playing with Shirley. Shirley told a lie about me, said I cursed, said the D word, but I never did. I never would. Jennifer never said nothing. She knowed it was a lie, too. I was just sittin' there minding my own business, watching Jen and the ghost jump rope. It was a little girl, jumping real good, easy—like—not getting mixed up, knowing all the numbers as she counted when she jumped. Her hair was falling around her eyes, and it was thick like chocolate frosting.

My hair is cut so short I don't hardly have to comb it. Miss Ruth says it's because I'm too slow to get dressed in the morning. She cut it off in a fit 'cause I was late for school. But I think it's 'cause she hates me and wants me to look ugly. It makes me look like a boy. I'm not a boy. I miss my pretty long chocolate hair—the way it felt around my face when I jumped and ran. The way I could twist it around my finger when I got scared. I got scared all the time after I left the hospital. I don't know nothin' about what happened 'cept what I was told. Before it happened I could jump and run and read and fly. I knowed I could fly. I dreamed it. Sometimes I remember a little bit before I came here. But I don't remember her.

They took her away right after it happened. The nice doctor said I would never have to see her again. But she wasn't so bad. I think it was probably an accident. She must have let the frying pan slip out of her hand. It just fell on me so hard it ended me up in the hospital for a long time. Then I came here. Grandma couldn't be no meaner than Miss Ruth.

I couldn't go fast anymore, not after I got out of the hospital. But I have a ghost to remind me. It has long hair that bounces soft when it jumps, like the day I hit Jennifer. I wanted to show her that I could jump rope, too, that I'm not bad. I wanted her to know I didn't do what Shirley said, but they talk too fast. I never git to start before they are over with what they are talkin' about. I tried to say it, to tell Jennifer I could jump like her a long time ago. It just jumbled up inside me and I got mad inside, real mad, because I couldn't jump no more and because Jennifer didn't say nothing to Shirley. I wanted to say it fast, but the words get stuck.

I hate slow. I always listen in church to see if being slow is a sin. It's not. Moses was called special by God and he didn't want it, to be called to free those Israelites, because he said, "I am slow of speech and of a slow tongue." And the Lord put words in his mouth. I wish he'd put some in mine. I sure wish Miss Ruth would remember that story. She acts like slow is a sin. I asked Nam to look up every verse with slow and she said slow was good, that God was slow to anger. Another place in the Bible it said that being slow to wrath—that's anger—is of great understanding. But being slow is why I'm on the steps.

I hope Jennifer ain't mad at me for being slow. She looks real mad staring over my head. I hope she is only mad at Miss Ruth. Before we sat down she told me she wasn't mad at me when I asked her, but her voice sounded mad, so I don't know. She looked mad when we watched all the kids climb inside the truck to go to the circus. Once I looked over at her and I thought she was goin' to cry. But she didn't. She just looked madder.

I don't hardly cry no more. Not even when I git hit. I scream real loud 'cause it hurts bad, but I don't cry. When you cry, it means the person matters. Miss Ruth don't matter to me. I cried after I hit Jennifer 'cause she matters.

She should believe in ghosts. Because when you have to stay in dark rooms all by yourself for a long time or you have to sit a long time on the steps, they keep you company.

CHAPTER 14

My home at Lookout Ridge was poised at the top of a five-thousand-foot mountain ridge. One traveled twelve miles from the valley floor, up a twisting, perilously narrow road, to arrive suddenly at the top of a plateau. A sign posted at the top announced a "Lookout," where a driver could pull off the road and gaze across undulating, multihued mountain ranges. As homes began to appear along the newly paved highway, the fledgling community took the uncreative name of Lookout Ridge.

We home kids found humor in the name. As a car rounded the final curve before the turnoff, we would call out in unison, "Look out!" In some ways it was a fitting name for this bedraggled group of lost, unwanted children. For some, "look out" might express a defiant, chip-on-the-shoulder attitude. For others, it might represent a vigilant, guarded position, keeping an eye out for the dangers they felt were ever present. But Lookout Ridge came to be home regardless of how we viewed the name.

By the time I started school across the street from the home, there were over one hundred of us. Outside the home we were like siblings—looking out for one another, defending a home kid against an outsider in a fight. Within the home, siblings sided with each other during conflicts. My brother Billy lived in the boys' dorm across the street. I saw him at mealtimes when we waved to each other across the room. We rarely sat together.

Sundays were visiting day, and because he and I never had visitors, we were sometimes allowed to spend an hour together. We played Monopoly or looked at books, but most of the time we caught one another watching the door. "She's not coming," he would say. Or, "What would you do, Sin, if she walked through that door right now?" That was the most we ever spoke of our past. I never asked about our mother. I didn't have to. But Billy did.

Every time he was alone with Naomi he asked in his most serious, grown-up voice, "Miss Nam, why doesn't my mother love me?" He asked without whining, without self-pity or fear. To him it was an established fact that she did not love him, and he wanted to understand it. What courage!

Naomi would sigh and say, "Well, honey, I think she does love you. I'm sure she does." Billy would shake his head and ask, "Then why doesn't she ever write me?" Naomi would fall silent. I knew Billy was still loyal to our mother because he called Naomi "Miss Nam," unlike me. I called her "Nam," the affectionate substitute for "Mom."

———

Our life at Lookout was centered around bells. The sound of a bell still causes me to turn my full attention toward it and stand speechless until it has finished ringing. Over the years at the home I made a game of trying to identify the ringer and his or her mood. There were bells that were urgent, bells that rang playfully, bells that were solemn, bells that were impatient, bells that simply conveyed the call to assemble. Bells could sound like music or like an angry outburst.

The bell tower was on the fourth floor of the big white building. A long rope ran down a shaft to the first floor, to a small landing above a stairway that led to the basement. The bell called us to meals, to church, to study hall, to special gatherings, and to prayer meetings. There were three separate bell ringings for each occasion. The first bell gave a thirty-minute warning of the forthcoming event; the second, a ten-minute warning; and the final bell called for immediate assembly.

Of course, there was also the other bell that was placed at the head table next to Miss Ruth, who rang the bell for silence at the beginning of each meal and called on someone to say the blessing. She rang the bell to quiet us when the volume of our voices became too high. We could tell by the way she rang the bell what mood she was in and whether we would have to sit through the rest of the meal in silence.

I attribute my awareness of the nuances of bells to Bobby. On a particular morning he asked at breakfast who had rung the first bell. When I asked him why he wanted to know, he shrugged and then said, "Because it choked."

Indeed it had. I had rung the bell and it sounded just as he said. It was my morning to rise early and help put on breakfast. Ten was the age when you could be assigned to breakfast duty. After finishing setting the tables, I asked Eleanor, the cook, if she needed some help.

Eleanor had come to the home as a teenager. She was slow, probably of below-average intelligence, but she had an even, pleasant disposition, and we all loved her. She had dropped out of high school and asked Naomi if she could stay on as a worker until she could figure out where to go. Eleanor was a hardworking, capable girl, but she could get easily confused and overwhelmed if a situation got too complicated or if unexpected interruptions required quick, flexible thinking. This particular morning, the milk had curdled during the night and she needed to go to the basement to get fresh canisters. The milk was often a problem. The state required that we pasteurize it and sometimes during the cooking it burned, forming thick globs of scorched cream.

The toast was already on large trays and the oatmeal was starting to give the first indication that it, too, was ready to burn. Eleanor looked overwhelmed, so I offered to stir the oatmeal to keep it from sticking on the bottom. Burned oatmeal alone could ruin an entire day.

I was standing on the stepstool to reach inside the three-foot-high pot. Absorbed in my task, I was suddenly pulled from the stool by an angry Miss Ruth, who demanded to know, "Just what do you think you are doing?" I started to explain just as Eleanor entered the room carrying the cold, metal milk canister. Miss Ruth turned on her before either of us could explain. Heatedly she informed Eleanor that it was not my job to cook. I thought her concern was for my safety, that she was worried I might get burned. But not so. She lashed out at Eleanor: "If you can't handle the job, just let us know, and you can find another place to live." Poor Eleanor. She would have if she could. We both realized she was close to being thrown out.

Just at that moment Naomi entered. "Good morning, everyone. Does anyone need help? I can smell the oatmeal." Her cheerful tone fell on the silence like a discordant chime. Eleanor stood frozen in place, confused, still clutching the heavy, large can of milk. Miss Ruth stiffened and in a much softer tone explained, "I found Jennifer stirring the oatmeal, which she is not allowed to do. I have just told Eleanor that if the job is too much for her, she should let us know. Perhaps we could find another place for her."

"Oh, Ruth, that won't be necessary. Everyone needs help now and again." She took the canister from Eleanor and set it on the table. "You get the toast, dear. I'll take care of the oatmeal."

Miss Ruth spun around, her back stiff, and with a choked, tight voice she said to Naomi, "You are always doing this. You are always trying to make me look bad. You spoil these kids and they will never amount to anything in life. You don't have the will to do the tough things. Somebody needs to be in charge here. Things need to change around here."

Naomi stood at the stove and I could see the tears brim in her eyes as the words stung her. She did not answer. The silence in the room was broken by the sound of the metal spatula lifting the toast from the tray to the plates. Miss Ruth asked me to go ring the first bell, then she exited. As I rang the bell, I choked back tears. The battles seemed to come more often now and Naomi never fought back. I was afraid for her and for our home. I could not imagine Miss Ruth in charge. How would she have handled little Wayne?

I was in the back office folding envelopes the day Uncle Adam, one of the workers, brought Wayne to Naomi to be reprimanded. I heard him say that she needed to "get him to shape up or else." I smiled to myself as I imagined Naomi raising her eyebrows with amusement and surprise because she did not think there were any bad children. But I knew Wayne to be the exception. He *was* bad!

"Thank you, Adam, for your interest in Wayne. Leave us and let us talk."

Wayne was eight, small and wiry, always with clenched fists ready for a fight. He walked like he was looking for a fight, too: his head cocked forward, his shoulders pulled up, and his mouth screwed into a little zero. When he got mad, language abandoned him. Instead, he'd start to whirl in circles like a little dust devil with his fist raised. Wayne didn't talk, he sneered and cursed and grunted. He was a hellion.

Naomi said, "Come, Wayne, let's go for a walk. It is such a beautiful day." When they returned an hour later, Wayne was in happy spirits. Naomi helped him write a letter to his grandmother. Then she sent Wayne off so that she could talk to Uncle Adam.

"Wayne reminded me that he has been here for over two years and has not had one word from his people. I tried to tell him about God's love, but when I mentioned a Heavenly Father, he told me he didn't care much about getting a father, it was a mother he wanted." They chuckled, and she went on, "I can't imagine what can be more devastating to a child than to feel that he is unwanted. These feelings have been building in him." She paused, reflecting, "I promised to send a note to his grandmother to remind her that he is here, but I'm sure she won't come." Her voice brightened. "I have an idea. I think it would be good to have him spend one afternoon a week with Mrs. Sheffield. If she agrees, you make sure he gets there."

So it was arranged. Wayne became Mrs. Sheffield's shadow. An eighty-year-old termagant with a kind heart and an eight-year-old troublemaker was a magical combination.

Mrs. Sheffield had retired to a small cottage on the home's grounds after Mr. Sheffield died. She and her husband had been large contributors to the home and instrumental in helping purchase Lookout. It was not with everyone's blessings that she remained, because she assumed the same role as the prophets did in relation to the Old Testament kings, admonishing and warning them when their hearts were not in the right place. She admonished Miss Ruth a lot. We kids learned to see through her cranky posturing and looked for an excuse to visit her. She always had cookies, but we had to tolerate her lectures, her evaluations of each of us, and her fussing over small matters. "Sunny, your hair is a mess. You should cut it. Mike, you ride your bike too fast. You will kill yourself. Shirley, you are too bossy," and so forth. Maybe she overdid the criticism most of the time with the majority of us, but she seemed just right for Wayne. Thanks to her he stopped cursing and one could have a conversation with him now and again.

I wondered what Miss Ruth would have done if Uncle Adam had brought Wayne to her. Wayne probably would have had his skin blistered. The differences between Nam and Miss Ruth were many, from their decisions about discipline to how they made you feel when you were standing next to them. Naomi's goodness pulled me toward her and held me in balance, like the balance found between negative and positive particles. When I moved too far away from her, I lost confidence in my goodness. With Naomi I felt good and lovable and even pretty. Around Miss Ruth I felt deficient, for she scrutinized my hygiene, posture, grammar, morals, attitude, and behavior, and I was always found lacking. Perhaps it was her way of keeping me grounded in reality.

I was an anxious scorekeeper of their arguments, and I had a foreboding sense that Naomi was losing ground. The incident that brought the problem sharply into focus happened in the summer of 1953. Two black children were brought to our home. One was a baby girl, who was placed in the nursery, and the other a seven-year-old boy, who was sent across the street to the boys' dorm. In our border state, laws existed, at least until 1954, mandating that public and private institutions were not allowed to racially mix children. I would not have thought much about their sudden departure—children came and went without explanation—had I not accidently overheard a conversation between Naomi and Miss Ruth. I was sitting on the swing on the big front porch, and I could hear their voices but could not see the two.

Naomi's voice was firm but agitated. "It's just not right. This is a Christian home, and I can't believe it is right to turn a child away."

Miss Ruth replied, "Well, of course, you are right, but we will be in violation of the law. There are *rules* we must follow. You know what this could mean. We could be shut down. They can't stay. You must call social services and have them picked up today, before there is a problem."

"I've already talked to them. There is no place for the children right now. I have decided they will stay here until the state can find a place."

That seemed like a logical solution to me. However, it was clear that Miss Ruth did not want to take the risk. She convinced Naomi that at least they should talk to the director of the board. (How quickly electing a board can turn a place from a home into an institution.) Miss Ruth made the telephone call. Her voice was warm, its tone imbued with admiration for the person to whom she was speaking. She wanted his guidance, she said sweetly, since she and Naomi disagreed on a matter. When she hung up, she turned triumphantly to Naomi and said that the director would arrange for the children to be picked up that afternoon.

The *rule* would rule! I was beginning to learn that there are written rules and unwritten ones, that legalism and ethics sometimes collide. It was confusing.

I don't know where the black children went. But Naomi's sigh of resignation lingered, alerting the listener to the sound of change, of acquiescence to another order, warning that the scales of power had been tipped.

CHAPTER 15

Although both Ruth and Naomi were like beacons in my life by which I navigated, my life was occupied by more than them. School, friends, work, and play occurred outside their guiding light but never without my vigilant eye glancing in its direction. Most of all, I was occupied with the task of trying to place my jagged, mismatched fragments of memory into an order that would bring back faces and places and a *me* that existed before this point in time.

On a Sunday afternoon in April, when I was eleven, a large piece of the puzzle fell into place.

The day had begun in a very ordinary way, without premonitions or any preparation for its ending. Every Sunday after lunch, between two and four, a hush settled over the buildings and grounds of the home as we settled into our beds to rest as the Lord had on the seventh day. Lying in bed, one could hear the music of nature that was usually drowned out by the swell of children's voices. These blessed two hours were free of conflict, a time to listen to one's thoughts. This time was also visiting hours, even though only a handful of children received any visitors. So I was surprised when my housemother gently shook me from my half-slumber to inform me that I had a visitor. My heart quickened. Could it be my mother? Could it be my father? Had they come looking for me?

No. It was only Mary Beth Baker, a friend from school, who was waiting for me downstairs. Would I like to sing with her in the evening church service? she asked. Her parents, who were town people, were famous in our part of the world for their musical talent. Her father played the guitar, her mother sang the lead and played the accordion, and Mary Beth and her brothers harmonized. The Bakers had a reputation as the best singing family in the county, probably in the whole state. Mrs. Baker's singing voice could make you cry the way it quavered and faltered, balancing on the edge of pain, reaching to the saddest parts of one's heart. I could never understand how such powerful emotional fullness could come from so shy, so slender, a woman.

I was given permission to walk with Mary Beth the five miles to church, where we would practice for the evening service. I was excited about the invitation, for I had sung with them before and, ah, what ecstasy. It was as though a closed door in me opened and a nightingale flew out. I soared to heights close to the sparkling, shimmering stars. It was as close to heaven as I figured one could get here on earth. As I hurried to get dressed, suddenly my heart sank. I had not seen Mary Beth since I spent the night at her house the last weekend. We were discouraged from spending the night with friends, but Mary Beth and I had become close and she had stayed over a few times in order to practice for a school play. The past weekend had been the first time I had ever been to her house.

The visit was awkward because I did not know how to fit into a family. I was an outsider in a mysterious and forbidden place, a place I often fantasized about. Who were these people that lived so close together, that loved and wanted one another? How fortunate they were to be one among few, how abundant must be the goods that were given to them. For I was one of many, and although I received much, everything was scarce, and I hungered for more. But I was good at finding the best in every situation and concluded that I was lucky. I had seen the way parents sometimes scrutinized their children too closely, and I welcomed the freedom that came with so few adults supervising so many children.

Unlike my home, Mary Beth's home lacked any routine or structure. Her family did not sit at the dinner table together but rather took plates of food to different parts of the house. The children did not have their own private beds, as we did at the home, so whoever went to bed last got the least desirable sleeping place. Because Mary Beth and I stayed up late, we shared a couch. The experience was oddly both liberating and disconcerting.

It was not the lack of order that unnerved me but rather the sadness that permeated the house. Mrs. Baker was quiet and withdrawn, anxiously looking toward the door. Mary Beth became nervous when her father came home and suggested we play outside. I ran back into the house later to find the bathroom, and just as I entered I saw Mrs. Baker at the sink, trying to cover her head from the blows that were coming from Mr. Baker's hand. I saw him stagger to a chair and heard his slurred speech. The boys' eyes, filled with fear and hatred, were fixed on their father. No one saw me, so I returned to join Mary Beth. She could see I was shaken, but neither of us spoke about the incident. We stayed out late and the house was quiet when we came inside. Long during the night I lay awake, fearing the man who was snoring in the next room.

For the first time in my life I was grateful to be an orphan. It wasn't that I had never seen abuse. I had. But somehow this abuse seemed worse because it was in a family, among people who were committed to stay together. I had divided the world into two camps—the wanted and the unwanted. I thought those lucky enough to stay together were the wanted, the loved. I believed that they knew how precious it was to have each other and therefore would treat one another with honor. The workers at the home were caretakers. We were their burden, their charges. I considered it a good day when I made it through without a worker losing patience with me. I was more forgiving of the workers than of Mary Beth's parents; I held them to a higher standard because they *wanted* their children. To me it was a greater misdeed to abuse someone you loved than someone whom you were in charge of.

I had not seen much of Mary Beth during the school week, and this outing would be our first time together since I stayed over at her house. I was sure she knew that I knew of her shame—of what I had observed the previous weekend. I decided that I would make her feel better by telling her about the one thing that I was most ashamed of, the one behavior that I could not control and that was sure to condemn me to hell.

Mary Beth surely must have thought I had lost my mind when I began a manic monologue about my great sin and my fear of hell.

"Do you worry about going to hell?" I asked anxiously as we walked to the church.

"No, I don't think about it," she said, sounding a bit puzzled.

"I mean, don't you ever do things that you think are so bad that you might not be let into heaven?"

"I guess. But I'm a kid and kids go to heaven, that's what my mother says."

I walked in silence, weighing her words. The conversation was not going as I wanted. How could I tell her about my terror that I would perish in a burning hell if she felt she was safe from it?

"Do you think your mom and dad will go to heaven?" I asked. Maybe if kids did not go to hell, she might understand my anguish about the possibility of someone she loved ending up there. By now I was quite certain that at least her father had a good chance of making it there.

She paused for some time, as if hesitating to reveal the next astonishing fact: "We don't believe in those things. We're not Christians."

People should be warned before such earth-shattering remarks are made so that they can brace themselves against losing their footing. I was speechless. How could someone come to church and sing songs with such conviction and help Reverend Charles win souls to God and not believe a word of it? Very slowly, imperceptibly at first, I felt relieved. For the first time I realized that not all behaviors were judged and sentenced by the same code. Maybe in someone else's eyes, I might not be so bad.

But I had a dual mission that afternoon. I wanted to help Mary Beth feel better about last weekend, and I was like a train out of control in my desperation to confess my shame to someone. I could not let it go, so I tried again.

"Mary Beth," I said solemnly, "sometimes I break the rules on purpose." So far, so good, I thought. I saw no reaction of alarm at my announcement.

"What do you do that is so bad that you think you will go to hell?" Mary Beth asked.

I agreed to tell her if she promised on her life and on her parents' lives, and on her brothers' lives that she would never tell. Then I told.

"We are only supposed to listen to religious music. But on Saturday nights when the staff have their prayer meetings—after ours—I sneak into Nam's room and change stations on the radio. I listen to this music—"

Mary Beth was laughing. She said they listened to all types of music in her family. She was sure it was not a sin. I hated her. She didn't understand the betrayal in which I was engaging, the hypocrisy, but most importantly she didn't understand the deep, disturbing emotions that came with the music. I did not have the words to tell her. I only knew that the music made my stomach ache and an unfamiliar taste spread across my tongue, and I would be imbued in the color purple, with sparkles, like jewels, bathing me. The sweet smell of gardenias (and another smell I could not identify—Mary Beth's father had that smell— maybe it was alcohol) made me warm inside. I did not understand from where these feelings came or the power they had over me, but I wanted more. I felt disloyal to Naomi.

Mary Beth started to sing a rock-and-roll tune. "Is this what you listen to?"

"No, it's different. It makes you want to sway." I stopped in the road to demonstrate with my body the rhythm, moving gently back and forth as I mimicked the sound of a saxophone and began to sing the words to "I Should Care." She joined me in the song—knew all the words.

"Yeah. I like that music too—blues. Torch singers, my dad calls them."

Torch singers. Singers on fire, like the fire of the diamond. Yes.

We walked the rest of the way to town singing every torch song we could recall. She sang some I had never heard. As we neared the town, we passed a side street near the church and she pointed out a pool hall where she had heard blues and swing and torch songs played. "Blues," "swing," "torch" were fitting words, exact words, that described the feelings that came with their sounds. Mary Beth told me that she went there with her dad and heard other music too, usually country songs.

We sat on the steps of the church in the warm afternoon waiting for her parents to arrive. A few dogwood trees in the yard had begun putting on blossoms. The two business streets in town were empty as the shops were closed. I could see the pool hall from where we sat. It was open, but no sounds, no songs, came from the open door. The only sounds I could hear were a few hungry bees searching for sustenance among a few early-blooming flowers.

I mulled over our conversation and felt somewhat better. Maybe I was not quite the sinner I thought I was. Mary Beth had said with convincing certainty that "All music is pure and one can't sin if one is doing something that is pure." But something still troubled me, something elusive I could not yet identify. Gradually it came into focus. The feeling I had about listening to the music was different from hers. Mary Beth did not have a *need* for it as I had; with me, this music was a compulsion. I could not resist temptation and allowed myself the indulgence of pure pleasure, of feelings I did not have about hymns. Maybe I loved this music even more than I loved Naomi. Guilt placed a frown on my face. I was betraying her for having separate feelings that I hid. Why, I was no better than the Apostle Peter, who betrayed his faith for his own needs. The feeling of dread returned.

The arrival of Mary Beth's parents rescued me from my rumination. A church not yet filled with people is indeed a sanctuary—a cool, quiet place untouched by the outside world. I knew in a few hours it would be filled with the hot passions of sin and regret, and Reverend Charles would make it so uncomfortable that sinners would plead for mercy. People came from long distances to hear Reverend Charles preach because he was the best around for saving people. In fact, he wouldn't quit until he saved at least one soul. One time I felt sorry for him because no one was coming forward, so I went up to the altar to get saved, just so he wouldn't feel bad. But that was a rare night because you couldn't help but get caught up in his passionate appeal. He began with a soft melodious voice, like a lullaby, and built to a frenzy, often ending by jumping over the railing in front of the altar, running down the aisle to a poor sinner, grabbing him by the collar, and exposing his sin to the congregation.

I was shocked the time he grabbed Mr. Jim, a neighbor who supervised the home boys in the fields, and told him in front of everyone that he should stop beating his poor sick wife. I never thought the same of Mr. Jim again. About a week after that I was riding the pony Natalie through the woods at the edge of his farm. I was thrown from Natalie when she saw a snake and halted. Mr. Jim saw me fall and came running across the field to help me up. Even though I had the wind knocked out of me, when I saw him leaning over me, I jumped up in panic and mounted Natalie and rode away before my breath returned.

We were practicing "Amazing Grace" when Reverend Charles wandered in and told us how beautiful we sounded. He was sure our singing would save a few souls that night. He asked me if I would sing one verse solo, backed by the Bakers humming the music, since he was so proud of his little cousin. He and I were distant cousins. He used to be drinking buddies with my father, he had told me. A number of times when I had sung at church, he would inform the congregation that I was his relative, a "precious gift from God." It embarrassed me to be singled out, to be known as a "home girl." I wasn't ashamed of the home or of Naomi, I was ashamed of not belonging to a family—and I was ashamed of being ashamed.

At six o'clock we gathered in the basement to eat a potluck supper. Families who wanted to socialize before the service came with bowls of food. Naomi and other workers brought food and the children. Throughout supper I weighed the risks of going to the pool hall to hear the music. I was afraid I might not get another opportunity for a long time. Maybe if I threw myself into temptation, I would get over my preoccupation with it—somewhat like getting really dirty before taking a nice, warm bath. The more I thought about it, the better rationalizations I developed for going.

At six-thirty I made my way toward the pool hall. I knew no one would miss me. The other home kids were running around outside the church, and the staff were socializing. I could make my way back before the service began at seven. I could even sneak in late—the door was left open for latecomers—and sit in the back with the home kids.

Dusk had come. I stood in the shadows outside the bar, away from the light that fell like a path outside the door. It was quiet inside except for the low murmur of voices drifting through the open window. The brick wall still held the heat of the day's sun. I leaned against the wall and let its warmth penetrate my back, which helped calm my nervous excitement. Only a few men were in the bar. I could hear the sound of glass mugs touching wood. Then I heard the clink of coins as they dropped into the jukebox. The first song was Kitty Wells wailing about how "It wasn't God who made honky tonk angels." Then another country song. Then I heard the music I had come for, the easy, tender sounds of the piano and the sad singer's lament: "It's a quarter to three . . . Set 'em up, Joe. I got a little story I think you should know . . ."

The old familiar feeling began. Maybe it was the heat or the purple glow of the sunset, but a powerful feeling took hold, so strong that it ripped away the veil covering my memory. As if a fog was lifting, images at first hazy and confused came into focus. It was as though I were swimming my way up out of a coma, and the feeling took my breath away. I gripped the building for support as the memory flooded me.

There she was, beautiful with long black hair, full and falling over her face as she rocked and sang and swayed in her lovely purple dress. A necklace grabbed the overhead light and threw out sparkles on the walls and faces of the attentive listeners—men in uniforms. The strong, sweet smell of cologne and whisky and shaving cream filled the room. "Mama," I whispered. She was looking at the boy who was looking up at her with bright, shining eyes. She was singing to him, her arms outstretched. The memory was clear and real and sharp. I could hear her as she sang, ". . . he's just my Bill." I rolled my tongue across my lips and could taste the liquid that came out of the bottle I was holding as I watched my beautiful mother sing to my brother. I knew this was not a one-time event; it was a place where we spent our nights with her.

Joy filled my eyes with tears. Oh, I had forgotten her—her face, her voice, her beauty, her laughter. The music led me to her. It had always been trying to lead me to her. Then I remembered something else. Mama was rocking me and singing softly, "You are my sunshine." Now it was no mystery why for a year after my return to the home, I sat in the swing nearly every day singing the same refrain over and over, "You are my sunshine."

Nothing more came. I felt weak, then exhilarated and powerful—the kind of power you feel when you have a secret that no one else knows. The memory had put one big piece of the puzzle into place and made me feel a little more whole. I wanted to stay against the hard, warm wall and hear more, remember more, but I could hear the music in the church begin. I ran back in time to hear Corbin, one of Reverend Charles's most fervent converts, open the service with a prayer. He was known to go on for nearly twenty minutes, so I felt safe. I could slip into my seat unnoticed since the people in church were supposed to have their eyes closed. I slid into the pew next to Billy in the back row. Only Dillon, another boy from the home, had his eyes open. He looked at me with his sea-blue eyes, eyes that you could drown in, and smiled.

The time came for the Bakers and me to sing. We first sang a song they had written. Its beat was a little too close to the sounds I had been listening to at the bar. Then we began "Amazing Grace," and the time came for my solo verse. Suddenly, I had no control. My mother was still too much with me. I threw back my head and raised my arms to her, singing with her as I had heard her sing at the request of a soldier before going overseas. My eyes were closed and I saw her smiling at me. She was singing with me. I stretched out the notes, making small vocal runs up and down the scale and adding a few more syllables to the words. With a fevered pitch of the blues, a new version of "Amazing Grace" was being heard in the small Church of God at the edge of town.

I did not hear the music stop. Mr. and Mrs. Baker and the boys had stopped singing and were staring at me in disbelief; Mary Beth jumped in, trying to harmonize and get me back in line, but then she stopped. When I opened my eyes, I realized something was amiss, for the Bakers and the audience had surprised—well, more honestly, shocked—

expressions on their faces. The home kids in the back row began giggling but were stopped with a stern look from a worker sitting nearby. Only Dillon started to clap.

Slowly, the full impact of what had just happened sank in. This was not the kind of music sung in a fundamentalist church. One could sing with passion, but not this kind—not with one's body swaying and moving to the rhythm. After what seemed like forever, the Bakers took up the last verse and got us back into the graces of the congregation.

After we left the stage, Reverend Charles stepped to the podium. He smiled at me, then said, "My, that girl has soul." I took my seat in the back row with the home kids. My face burned with shame, and I never heard a word of the sermon.

After church, outside in the cool night air, my brother came up to me. He slapped me and said in his most angry voice, "Just forget about her." Then he walked away. Oh, he remembered her, too, and it made the slap tolerable. The pain of having forgotten was worse than his slap. Maybe for him, remembering was worse.

Naomi put her arms around me and said, "My goodness, honey, where on earth have you heard music like that? You know, we Christians don't sing that way." I just hung my head and did not tell her that I had practiced those sounds in her bed.

————•————

I did not sing for months after that evening. I sang again after Candi came to the home. She had been picked up as a runaway from Chicago, a long way from the home, and had been placed with us until she could be transported back to Chicago. Someone must have forgotten about her because she stayed a long time. She was twelve, going on eighteen. She was in my dorm room and entertained us in the night with her experiences on the streets of Chicago. She shocked us with stories about sex with police officers and being accidently booked into an adult jail before they learned her true age. One night she started to sing a popular song of the day, one we had heard at school. She could barely carry a tune. Finally, a voice in the dark said, "Jen, you sing it. Sing it like you did in church that night. Please." Everyone in unison said, "Yeah." So I sang again. I closed my eyes and my shame faded as I allowed myself to sing again with my mother in the dark room of the dorm.

Stupid! Stupid! What on earth was she thinking, making a fool of herself up there. Honest to God, sometimes I think she hasn't a brain in her head. She thinks she can sing like Mama. Isn't a soul on the planet, well, maybe except Patsy Cline, that can sing as good as her. Don't she remember that it was her singing that caused all the trouble? She was probably too little to remember. How Mama used to take us to the club—us all ready for bed and in our pajamas. She'd leave us in that little room and make a bed out of blankets so we could sleep while she worked. But I never slept. I was her soldier and would look after her—and Sin. Sometimes she let us listen when it was early. I could never stop looking at her. She was the prettiest mother I ever saw, and ain't no one can sing like her. The men in that place wanted to capture her—just like in the story about the king who wanted the bird that sang so sweetly in the forest. Once he got it, it stopped singing. Same as Mama. After her work, we'd go riding in the car with them, them with their bottles, and next thing you know they'd be arguing. Or the parties at the house when she came home. She didn't sing then. It was like all she did was laugh. Then the laughing turned to arguing, and then it got so loud that Sin would start to cry. One of them soldiers would hit Sin, knock her against the wall, or lock her in the room while she was screaming like bloody murder. Mama tried to get to her, but some soldier would stop her. Then she'd get mad and then they would fight.

Mama called me her little soldier. I had a little soldier hat that Dad brought me when he came back from fighting in the war. He must have liked being a soldier because he acted like Mama was the enemy and they fought like it was a war. I wore the hat he brought me all the time and I tried to protect her, like a good soldier, not like those bad soldier men who hung around her. I threw myself between them, and she would grab me, holding on to me, screaming at the top of her lungs, "If you touch him, I'll kill you."

I begged and begged her not to let them come home with us after she sang 'cause they were so mean to her. She would laugh and say it was just a party. "Parties are fun." She said that sometimes parties could go bad. Me and Sin quit going to the parties. I took to hiding Sin in the room and put a chair by the door so no one could come in. I sat on the chair watching, making sure Mama wasn't hurt. You never knew when it could get bad. Most of the time she was dancing and laughing. I kept Sin quiet in the back 'cause when she cried, it got bad. Mama wanted to leave the party to check on Sin, but they didn't want her to. I told Mama I would look after Sin. She knew I would. Still do. That's why I got so mad when Sin stood up there like a fool trying to sing like Mama. Don't she remember how much problems that singing caused? She should give it up right now 'cause there is no way, anyway, that she will ever sound like Mama.

CHAPTER 16

"Fire! Fire!" Eleanor's voice, reverberating down dark halls and through the thin partitioned walls of the rooms where children slept divided by age, shattered the nocturnal quiet in the big white building and brought forth a cacophony of panicked voices and running feet. It was past midnight. The house was lit up like a soft pink, cotton-candy sunrise. In the hazy moments of new wakefulness, the beauty of the glow kept me motionless. Then the adrenaline hit. "I must find Naomi." I sprang from my bed. In times of danger, Naomi was the calm that extinguished fear and restored reason. I found her bed empty.

I ran down the long, narrow hall, down three dark sets of stairs to the first floor, and out into the cold night until I found her. She was beating back the flames that were creeping toward the propane tank, and at the same time she was battling to keep the fire off her nightgown. A burning truck lay on its side, the dazed and helpless driver standing nearby. I ran forward, but Naomi's wild, frantic screams stopped me dead in my tracks. She mistook me in the dim glow, for she yelled, "Zinnia, get back! Go back!" and she was waving like a madwoman. There was no calm here. I backed up and bumped straight into Miss Ruth, who had arrived fully dressed.

She spoke urgently. "Jennifer, tell all the kids to go across the street to the boys' dorm and stay there until we come for you. Hurry."

"But I'm not dressed."

"Just go. Now!"

I turned to face a scattered group of children who were running like thieves in all directions. I took my responsibility seriously and began frantically ordering everyone to the boys' dorm. Some of the smaller children were confused and crying. Maude, Sunny, and I went to the nursery, where we wrapped the babies in blankets and carried them outside. Mayhem was the night's visitor, mocking the children flying about in their long white nightgowns like miniature, mindless ghosts.

A few workers arrived on the scene. In an effort to establish order, they began to form a line to march us across the street. I heard someone say there could be an explosion. I slipped out of the queue when we crossed the street, sat on a patch of grass on the edge of the bank facing the fire, and kept watch. Naomi was still beating back the flames as they inched closer to the silver tank. Her long gray hair was loose, and she was whirling and stomping and beating the ground with her blanket. From a distance it looked as if she was performing an Indian dance. I was there to keep vigil over my Naomi, for if she were to die, so would I. I was as much her protector as she was mine. We were bound together by an unspoken, incomprehensible pact, which I was sure had to do with the miracle of her having saved my life.

Sunny once told me that when baby rabbits die, even if separated from the mother, the mother will display a grief reaction. She said it was true because she read it in a book. I reasoned it could be so, for I sometimes knew events were going to happen before they came to pass or before someone told me about them. I did not think prescience was unusual, I thought it occurred to everyone. Once in the third grade during the morning reading class, I was overcome with trembling apprehension and knew with certainty that Naomi was in distress. I was not allowed to leave the class, so I had to wait helplessly until the end of the school day. Then I ran to the office in search of her.

"She's lying down. Do not disturb her," Miss Ruth said and sent me off to do my chores.

When you *know* something, there is no quieting the knowing until you are sure. So I crept to Naomi's door and softly knocked. She invited me in. I stood in the center of the room until she reached out her hand to me and I ran to her.

"Are you okay?"

"Oh, I'm sorry you heard, dear. Yes. I'm okay."

"What happened?" My voice was trembling.

"I took a curve too fast this morning and the car rolled. But I'm okay. Miss Moses was with me. She is in the hospital." A soft, anguished cry escaped her.

Miss Moses was my octogenarian piano teacher, but it wasn't her that had dominated my thoughts all day. My antennae were pointed in Naomi's direction.

———

That is why I had to sit on the bank. I could not bear not knowing. I also believed that by watching, I could send Naomi protection. It worked. She was safe. The truck blew up, but everyone got out of the way, and Naomi saved the propane tank from exploding.

It was after this incident that a new rule was made. From then on, each older child was assigned a younger child to be responsible for whenever there was a crisis. The older children were to find their young charges and take them to an area of safety and stay with them until the emergency was over. Naomi was proud of me and Maude and Sunny for thinking of the younger children, and our actions had given her the idea. Several of the toddlers had wandered about lost and were found crying on the dark field of the boys' baseball diamond. If everyone had a child for whom to be responsible, then no one would be lost and afraid.

Older siblings picked their younger siblings to look after, older children picked younger ones, until all the little ones were taken. Since there was an odd number of children at the time, I had no little one for whom to be responsible. Naomi said not to worry, she was sure another one would come along.

———

A few months passed and summer came. One day I was awakened by the early morning sun. As usual, I lay in bed trying to recall the day of the week. The unpleasant thought that it was a school day faded when I remembered that school had just ended. Joy spread through my body and I stretched like a cat as I viewed my options—lingering in bed and enjoying the quiet or being the first to the bathroom. It was always an advantage not to have to fight with ten others for the two available toilets. I tiptoed down the hall.

As I approached the bathroom, I nearly stumbled on a child no more than two years of age. She looked exactly like the Kewpie dolls sold at

the county fair—large eyes, a turned-down mouth, and a small patch of
hair that curled like a miniature ocean wave on the top of her head. She
was pudgy in her long nightgown and stood rigid and doll-like, staring
at me without blinking.

It was not unusual to wake and find new children at the breakfast
table. Often children came during the night, brought by police or
drunken parents. We would not necessarily hear them arrive. Admission
took place on the first floor at the nurse's office, where children were
examined, bathed, and fed before being taken to the appropriate age
unit. The girls' wing, where I slept, was on the second floor of the big
white building at the opposite end of the hall from the nursery. We got
used to the sound of babies crying in the night and learned to sleep
through it. From age eight, my main work assignment had been the nursery, where I learned to diaper, toilet-train, nurture, and scold. I prided
myself on my skill with babies. Everyone called me patient, but it was my
daydreaming nature that caused me to ignore small misbehaviors.

At ease with babies, I approached the chubby, expressionless newcomer standing motionless by the bathroom door. "What is your name?"
I asked, squatting to her eye level.

There was no response.

"Do you want to go potty?"

Again, no response. The girl stared back with wide, unblinking
eyes. I opened the door to the bathroom so that she could follow me
in. She stood unmoving—no expression, no emotion, just a large,
empty stare. I picked her up and carried her into the bathroom. She
was heavy and smelled pungent and sour, scented with an unfamiliar
chemical aroma. Later I came to know it as the smell of ketosis that
comes with malnutrition.

I carried her back to my bed and tucked her in with me. Assuming she
was scared, I began to softly sing nursery songs as I had done many times
to quiet restless, fussy babies. No response. Then I tried nursery rhymes.
No response. I bounced her up and down on my belly, tickled her, played
"This little piggy" with her toes. Nothing. She stared back and not once

did she smile. Gradually the awareness dawned that something was wrong with this child. My years in the home had allowed me to see many children react to their abandonment. Some cried with heart-wrenching grief, some threw fits, some sat timidly in terror. This was different. This was—*nothing*. It was not natural.

I lost my enthusiasm for surprising my roommates with this new, doll-like child. I cuddled her close to me, rocking her quietly back and forth, softly repeating a singsong phrase, "Everything is going to be okay. It's going to be okay."

When the first bell finally rang for rising, I carried my broken child to Naomi. She was already dressed when I knocked timidly on her door.

"Look, Nam, I think something is wrong with her."

"Why do you think that, honey?"

"She doesn't smile. It's not natural. And she doesn't smell right, not like a baby is supposed to."

Naomi spent a few minutes interacting with the toy girl and confirmed my suspicions. She told me that the baby and her two brothers—one younger, one older—had been brought by the police during the night. The children had been abandoned by their mother about three days before, the neighbors guessed. The police had found a broken jar of applesauce on the floor, the children's only food. Because the nurse was away for a few days' leave, the children had not received the usual examination and attention before being placed in the nursery.

"You are very observant, Jennifer. And since you found her, she can be your little sister." That meant that when there was an emergency, I was to locate her, protect her, lead her to safety. But Naomi meant more than that. This child was my baby, my little sister. Her name was Maggie.

Naomi decided that drastic measures needed to be taken to help Maggie when after a few days at the home she still did not smile or talk. It was unnerving to walk into the nursery and find Maggie standing in her crib. Her eyes followed me, but they had no expression. She made no contact, gave no communication about whether she was wet or hungry, tired or happy.

Naomi gave instructions that Maggie was to be held by someone every minute that she was awake and was to be rocked until she fell asleep. All of us fought over holding Maggie. We made it our personal challenge to be the one who could put a smile on her face. We never gave up—not for one whole year. She became a familiar household fixture at every gathering. We joked about how we had a "growth" on our hip, referring to the expressionless bundle that we carried all day.

———•———

When Maggie's birthday came, we gave her a special party. Normally, all birthdays falling in a single month were celebrated on the same day. However, we sensed Maggie would get lost in a group celebration. When we brought in the cake lit with three candles, she raised her hand and pointed. I bent down and blew out the candles for her, then looked up into her face. Her eyes connected with mine as never before. Then it happened. She smiled! We all saw it. There was a second of silence as the fact sank in before we burst into celebration, dancing around each other, hugging one another, passing Maggie from one person's arms to another's as we took turns whirling her around the room. Such joy we all felt. And she smiled again.

Language soon followed. She was not a lost child. We had brought her back from whatever darkness had engulfed her. We all felt we had a part in resurrecting a lifeless child. By osmosis we had learned from Naomi how to work miracles.

———•———

Maggie's arrival had stirred in me a dark, mysterious region that awakened in dreams. Besides my soldier dream, I had another recurrent dream, which changed after Maggie came. The dream had a joyful beginning but always ended in sorrow. I would be engaged in normal activity when suddenly a few coins would appear at my feet. As I picked up several, more would appear, leading me down a path where they were scattered in clumps; I would gather them until my pockets and hands were filled. Then I would fill my skirt by making a sack out of my skirt.

The discovery of the abundant discarded treasure would end in my losing the coins or someone taking them from me, leaving me with a feeling that I was wrong to have gathered them and that they did not belong to me.

After Maggie came, the dream changed. In my new dream, I would be watching the babies in the playground when the coins appeared. As I ran about gathering them with great joy, the playground would suddenly change into an arid, desolate field. In the center of the field stood a scraggy, barren tree, and beneath it lay an infant. Overcome with joy, I would rush to the baby, repeating, "I found you, my baby, I found you." One night, the dream shifted to an ending that was deeply disturbing. The money, the barren tree, and the baby were present. But when I went closer to embrace the infant, a deformed, gargoyle-like Maggie stood guard over the baby. Thin, matchstick legs and arms extended from Maggie's distended belly. Her swollen, fat, disfigured face stared at me with great hollow, empty eyes. As usual, I ran forward to caress and hold the baby, but this time Maggie watched me and suddenly tears streamed from her eyes as she said, "That's my brother. You can't have my brother."

I woke from this dream sobbing, uncomprehending, and with more pain than I thought a small heart could endure. Needing someone to explain, to take the burden from me, I rushed to Naomi's bed. I could not control the sobbing that normally stopped as soon as my body found hers.

Between sobs I told her, "Oh, Nam, I had the saddest dream. I dreamed I found a baby brother. But he did not belong to me."

The dream reminded me that at times when I was baby-sitting, a feeling of déjà vu would swiftly appear, like a fleeting hallucination, and I would see the face of a toddler running on tiptoes toward me, reaching hands for me, calling to me. Then the feeling was gone. I searched for that face in every new child who came to the home and in every baby I saw in my travels. But I never saw such a face. Now I felt a great longing to know, so I risked sounding stupid and amidst my sobs I asked, "Nam, do I have a baby brother?"

She put her arms around me and squeezed me to her. "Honey, you have quite an imagination. You always have the most interesting dreams. Go to sleep, now. Everything will be better in the morning."

The coin dreams came less often after that. I never asked anyone again whether I had a brother. All the love and protection that I would have given to a baby brother I gave to Maggie. She came to replace the lost baby for which I yearned.

Maggie was the same age as Jamie, Maude's baby sister. As they grew up together, the little girls became friends, and like all friends, they had disputes. Maude was as fierce in her love and defense of Jamie as I was of Maggie. We would stand before them arguing over who started their fight, nearly coming to blows.

"She started it," I would insist. "You know how Jamie is—she always plays innocent."

"Watch what you say. I know Maggie. She don't share, and it always makes the kids mad at her. You should teach her to share."

"Well, you should teach Jamie not to be so sneaky."

As our fight began to escalate, the two children forgot their differences, staring with wide mouths at our behavior, and walked away to play. We couldn't have manipulated a better tactic to renew their friendship had we tried. Maggie came to count on my defense and affection. She asked for me when she was sick, when she was tired, when she was hurt, when she was upset. I would have done anything for her, and she knew it.

I don't know how to stop the dark. It comes quick and unlooked for. It's not like the dark at bedtime 'cause from my bed I can see the light from the hall under the door; and it's not like small dark places 'cause I like to crawl into them—and I'm not afraid there. This dark is big and black without one teensy bit of light and nothing close to me, nothing touching me to keep me from feeling I'll become jelly or maybe just go

"puff" into nothing. When the dark comes, my eyes stop seeing things around me and my mind just stops dead still like a TV with snow and no pictures. The only thing that keeps it from spreading is if I put my thumb in my mouth. But then I get in trouble. Miss Ruth says now that I'm seven, I'm too big to suck my thumb. She put pepper on it and tied it with a rag, and when I needed my thumb to keep my eyes awake I put it in my mouth—yuk! Seemed like it took me two days to start seeing and hearing again. Jennifer lets me suck my thumb when she rocks me. She sings so pretty. The best is when she sings me "You are my sunshine." When she holds me, she makes me feel like I'm not ever going to see that black place again.

Boy, Miss Ruth was mad when she found that nickel in my pocket. Nam heard her and came running before she hit me. I was goin' to give it to Jen to buy some jawbreakers that I could suck on besides my thumb. I told Nam I took it out of her desk, but I forgot to tell her about the jawbreakers.

Nam is teaching me to love Jesus. I told her about the dark, and she taught me a Bible verse from the book of Ephesians: "For ye were sometimes darkness, but now are ye light in the Lord: walk as children of light." I like that verse. I say it over and over: "walk as children of light." I'm hoping it keeps me seeing the light. No more darkness.

CHAPTER 17

Baseball! I fell head over heels, dumbly in love with the game for an entire summer at the age of eleven. I lived and breathed baseball, dreaming of someday being a great catcher in the World Series. When scoffed at, I publicly changed my goal to a sports announcer but privately kept my dream. The Cleveland Indians never had a more ardent fan. W. C. was a fan, too, and he taught me the rules of the game and how to calculate batting averages. We followed rookie Herb Score's season, and W. C. told me stories about the greatness of pitchers Bob Lemon and Early Wynn. I took up reading biographies of famous baseball players.

My love affair began when thirty of us were loaded onto the back of a flatbed truck, where we rode standing up until we arrived wind-whipped and sunburned from the long drive, at Lakefront Stadium to see the famous Indians.

Naomi was a Yankees fan and to my dismay had rooted for the Giants when the Indians played against them the year before in the World Series. I knew the Indians would come back. I counted on Herb to make it happen in '55, to restore the glow of '54 and '48. Not that I remembered that earlier year, but W. C. told me all about Satchel Paige and Bob Feller and Larry Doby.

W. C.—his real name was Winston Churchill Campbell—taught me how to hold a bat, how to keep my eye on the ball, and how to swing the bat to be a slugger. I owe all my home runs and my skill at sliding into base to him.

Almost every night after supper, we gathered on the baseball field to choose up teams and play. Maude and Sunny declined when they were chosen and sat on the bench watching the boys. Maude had eyes for W. C. and he knew it. He had come to the home with his cousin Jake a few years earlier. They were scrawny boys who worked in the coal mines but had been abandoned to the streets. Lately they had grown into hard, muscular, tall-bodied boys with square-jawed, hungry faces. Unlike his cousin Jake, who had a silver tongue that sometimes turned nasty and who looked too handsome for his own good, W. C. was painfully self-conscious. He spoke haltingly, mostly in monosyllables. Jake, on the other hand, could sell overcoats in the Sahara or ice in the Arctic. W. C. loved baseball, Jake loved trouble, and Maude loved W. C.

That summer I learned about how you can suffer for love. Normally Maude's hair was stringy and dishwater blond until it was washed, then it fell soft and straight and gleaming blond to her shoulders. Her oily hair needed more frequent washing than the once-a-week shampoo scheduled for Saturday nights. She sneaked extra shampoo and hid it so that she could wash her hair midweek. She took her beatings from Miss Ruth without protest so that she could smell pretty and her hair could swing when she turned to smile at W. C. The only effect the beatings had was that the hardness that was barely perceptible when she first came to the home was now growing in her blue eyes until it filled them up with a flinty, icy stare. She would look at Miss Ruth with a "Someday I'll kill you" look, and I was worried for Miss Ruth.

Although Maude never said so, I overheard that her mother had been a prostitute. Miss Ruth was determined to make sure Maude wasn't headed in the same direction. Truth was, Maude had a special way around guys that if it could have been bottled would have rescued a lot of spinsters from loneliness. Around men she became soft and pretty, and her hips moved and her head tilted in a way that made W. C. blush. She couldn't help herself for it was a rhythm as natural to her as her honey hair. In the summer evenings, she sat on the bench watching W. C. like a predator that knows it can take its prey in its own sweet time. Every time he got up to bat, he would swing the bat so that the muscles stood out on his arms, and he knew that she was watching.

Sweet Lordy Jesus. I can still taste him, a blend of tobacco and Juicy Fruit—his lips like silk, soft and wet, moving across my mouth, down my neck, onto my chest. His body hard, the part between his legs as firm as the hands that grip me, his shoulders and arms powerful and solid. Hard

and soft is how he is in my mind—hard on the outside, soft on the inside. Shy and puppy-dog soft in his ways. Last week in church, Billy was pass- ing around the Bible in the back row and Jake and Dillon were laughing and I could see W. C.'s face go red. Billy sent me a note to look up Song of Solomon, chapter 7. Well, you can imagine my shock to find all that sex stuff in the Holy Book. I mean stuff like "Thy two breasts are like two young roe that are twins" or "as clusters of the vine, and the smell of thy nose like apples." You could have knocked me over with a feather. As religious as Miss Naomi is, I wonder if she knows about this? She probably does, but I bet it's not her favorite part. I was sitting next to Jennifer, who knows the Bible backwards and forwards, and she pointed to some verses in the next chapter. I thought they were the most beauti- ful words ever written. So I sent a note back to W. C. to read them: "Set me as a seal upon thine heart, as a seal upon thine arm: for love is strong as death . . . the coals thereof are coals of fire." The chapter went on, talking about how almost nothing can quench love. When I glanced back at W. C., I could tell he liked it. He don't have to talk much 'cause his eyes do all the talking. I can tell when he is mad or sad or happy. Those freckles in his eyes are what give him away; they move like a dance when he is glad and seem closer together when he is mad.

It's funny how just the smallest thing about a person is the most telling. I guess I learned that from Ma. She had a way of knowing peo- ple before they became known to her. She said you could tell about them by watching the way they used their energy—and that you could use your own to fit with theirs. I watched her do it: calm the excited and excite the calmed. Said you could tell what kind of lover they were, too, by studying their energy. I figure W. C. will be steady and lasting. Ma knew a lot about men. She knew whether to let a man in the house or send him on his way, knew it from just a few seconds of talking to him in the dim yellow light of the front porch. She stood behind the screen door and talked to the stranger a few minutes before inviting him in or sending him on.

I knew what she did before she told me. I would wake up to soft tap- ping on the door late at night and stand in the shadows of my room watching as she invited the man into her bedroom and then shut the door. I mean, I didn't know all at once; it came slowly over time. At first I thought it was a dream because the men were always gone by morning. I knew, but didn't know, not until that nasty little Adina said it in front of all those other kids at school—just because I wouldn't go to her stupid birthday party. Turned her nose up when she walked by and said loud enough for everyone nearby to hear how she didn't want no hooker's daughter at her party anyhow. I ran all the way home, plumb out of breath, and lay on my bed fixing to never get up again.

Ma came home and found me there. I swear I wasn't never going to speak to her again. How could she do that to me—shame me in that way? She sat on the bed and I guess she figured I knew by the way I was acting. She lit up a cigarette; I can still see the smoke swirling above her head like a halo as I stared into the mirror, acting like I wasn't looking at her. I didn't want to, but when I stealed a glance she sat there picking at her lip and looking real worried. It was the first time I knew she was scared of me. Her voice shook a little, and she was trying to find the words to say to me—something about her not being perfect and how everything she did was for me, for me to have the best of everything, not like her, who had to work her fingers to the bone.

I stopped listening to her because I thought those were the lamest excuses I'd ever heard. She could take two jobs to pay for those things if she really cared about me. She didn't have to shame me the way she did. Everyone was laughing at me in the whole school, so I just quit going. It was after that when the social worker came out to find out why I wasn't in school. I was so mad at Ma that I said outright that she was a hooker. Man, I'd have kept my mouth shut if I knew how much trouble it would cause. Ma was sent off to jail and I was sent here.

At first I didn't care. She was a whore and they should just shoot them for all I care. But when I saw her for a visit after court, just before me and Jamie were brought here, she looked like she was going to puke, she was so upset. I felt sorry for her. I put my arms around her and said I loved her and I was sorry for getting us in this mess. She told me there

was worse things in the world than what she did. She never killed any-
one. She made a lot of guys feel good that couldn't feel good any other
place. She didn't see a reason to lock someone up for something that
made others feel good. She said that the worst thing in the world was to
lose your kids—for us to have to live someplace else because she was a
bad mother. I told her she was the best, and Ma said, "I tried to be."

As far as I'm concerned, they should lock up people like Miss Ruth,
who for the life of her can't make one person feel good, or that social
worker who testified that my mother was morally corrupting me. Her
tight little puckered face could do more moral corruption than my ma
ever dreamed of. That's right. They should lock up people who make
other people feel bad; just get them out of the way, and let all the hook-
ers and Naomis who run around trying to make people feel good, let
them have full run of the planet.

I wish I could tell Ma that I understand about how virtuous it is to
make someone feel good. I know how I feel about W. C. "I am my
beloved's and my beloved is mine." I ain't never going to let someone
separate me again from the one I love. Never!

One evening during a baseball game, I hit a grounder to shortstop.
Running fast to first, I got there just before Dillon stepped on the bag.
Everyone started yelling, "You let her be safe." Dillon turned to the
group and laughed, making an exaggerated "Who me?" gesture.
Furiously, I protested that I made it to first fairly. The onlookers kept
taunting him, and out of embarrassment I reacted angrily, out of pro-
portion to the incident.

Dillon turned to the group and said, "I don't know what makes a person run fast or slow. I just got here after she did."

Dillon was a slight, athletic boy with clean-cut features and a small
gap between his front teeth. He would have looked average were it not
for his large eyes, which were the color of a clear, bright sky. He had a
habit of tilting his head slightly back and to the side, as though he were
looking down on others, even if he was shorter. And that disarming

grin—it would be his undoing one day. His mouth questioned, Are you for real?—not so much as a challenge as a sincere question. I noticed how he held himself sideways to people, turning full face only when he felt someone was sincere with him, which seemed to be rare. It could give others the impression of indifference.

Uncle Adam, a worker acting as the umpire, tried to settle the dispute by suggesting that we run the bases and determine whether I was safe or out by whoever got to home first. I was determined to beat Dillon, and he seemed to stay effortlessly close behind me as we ran. The boys were cheering for him, and just before touching home he pulled ahead and I was called out. He was welcomed back into the males' good graces, but I was left somewhat befuddled by an emotion I could not name.

———•———

Dillon was my brother's friend. I remember the first day he came to the home. A rumor spread fast that he had never been to school one day of his life, and he was ten at the time. People said he was stupid, but when I looked into his alert, bright blue eyes, I knew they were wrong. After one year of schooling, he was placed in fifth grade.

Credit has to go to Mrs. Greeley. She taught us for the first three grades. Then we were released from the warmth and protection of her brilliant tutelage to go across the street to the public school. Mrs. Greeley was a fine woman with a fine mind, a very fine mind. However, she was completely overtaken by gravity. She piled her fine, curly gray hair on the top of her head, but before breakfast was over, her curls were falling in strands around her face. She was tall and heavy. Her breasts hung, her buttocks hung, and her stockings hung. If one caught a glimpse of her in the morning before seven, she was tidy and neat, but by half past seven she had come undone. I can still see her, unendingly pushing up strands of fallen hair or pushing up glasses that were always sliding down her nose in a valiant effort to defy gravity's hold over her. While everything else about her seemed to fall, her mind was always rising to an observant, creative realm. Building character was as important to her as writing a proper sentence. Despite Naomi's mild protest, she illustrated moral character from stories of the Greek heroes and gods. (To appease Naomi, she also told stories from the Bible.) She read from Kipling's *The Jungle Book* and Tolkien's *The Lord of the Rings,* and she told us about some great men in history. But the best time was at the end of each day when we would wind our way through each other's imaginations. She would begin a story with a few sentences and then each child took turns adding a sentence, expanding and altering the story.

Dillon was lucky to get Mrs. Greeley as his first teacher, for certainly few have her gift of inspiring a love of learning. Always patient, Mrs. Greeley treated the most and the least gifted the same. Because the majority of the parents in our community had no more than a sixth-grade education, she tutored after school at the big brick building across the street. I learned that she had been a teacher of teachers before she came to our home. She came after her husband died, but I can never imagine her doing anything other than standing in front of the little classroom located behind the living room in the big white building.

Mrs. Greeley had one flaw as far as I was concerned. She hated baseball. She also hated television and made no bones about its being the downfall of civilization—especially advertisements. She railed against them, warning us that they were produced with the sole intent to exploit and manipulate. She took it upon herself to shield us from such influences.

We gathered in the living room on Saturday mornings after chores from eleven until noon to watch a western. We were allowed one hour of television on school weeknights and two hours on weekends. We sat on the floor in front of the set. Mrs. Greeley stood at the back to supervise and "correct" errors on the part of the screenwriters. To our dismay, she would tell us whether an outcome was possible or not. Every time a cowboy was knocked out, she disgustedly exclaimed, "Concussion—it will take several hours, maybe days, even years to recover; he can't just jump up like that. What do you think just happened in his brain?" We would groan and plead for her to stop. But she was a relentless self-appointed critic and censor.

The most irritating part of her supervision came during any adver-
tisement for alcohol or cigarettes. Scattering children with her large body,
she forced herself forward to the screen to turn down the sound and
stand in front of the set to block us from seeing the ad. I can still hear the
jingle "Winston tastes good, like a um um cigarette should" since she
usually got to the set just as it was about to end. We complained and
pleaded for her to move before the program resumed. She would turn the
television up and wade through the bodies of children to the back of the
room just in time for the next forbidden commercial, most likely for alcohol. Into action she would spring, back to the set to start the whole
process over again. Often we missed the opening lines following the
break and were left to fill in the missing parts ourselves. No matter how
we protested, argued, or pleaded, she never relented.

I agreed with Mrs. Greeley about the dangers of television. I saw it
come between us and our baseball. Not everyone shared W. C.'s and my
passion for baseball. So sometimes we were out on the field with too few
for a team; he would hit and I would catch or he would throw and I
would catch or he would pitch and I would catch. Maude would sit on
the bleachers watching.

The summer that I was in love with baseball was the summer
Daniel came for a two-week visit, and he liked baseball, too. Daniel
was Miss Ruth's sister's boy. His mother was too ill to travel, so he
came with Miss Ruth's mother. Even though he was about a year and a
half younger than I, he was strong and could hit and throw almost as
well as I could, but not as well as thirteen-year-old W. C. No one was as
good as W. C.

It is strange that I think of Daniel when I think of baseball, for really
it should be when I think of music. I first met Daniel at his home in New
York. Miss Ruth had formed a choir, and for about two weeks a year we
traveled up and down the eastern states, singing and raising money for
the home. I played a little piece on the piano and quoted from memory
the Twenty-seventh Psalm. Sunny drew a picture in charcoal of three

crosses on three mountains as we sang "The Old Rugged Cross," and the choir sang a number of other pieces. Our performance usually made a lot of people cry and part with more money than they had intended to.

It was during one of these trips that I stayed in Daniel's home. The minute we laid eyes on each other, we knew we were meant for one another. I felt sorry for him being alone in that big, sad house, with a mother who seemed on the verge of death and a father who never spoke. He was different when we were alone and away from them. He laughed a lot more. He taught me little fast runs on the piano and how to jazz up a hymn. Miss Ruth didn't take kindly to that, but because we were in her sister's house, she did not make a fuss. Daniel and I had a special bond. I know he felt it, too, because while we were sitting under a tree, he said, "You know I feel like me and you were born for each other. Let's get married when we grow up." I pledged my word.

Then something strange and inexplicable happened that I thought might end his admiration. The day of our departure, I could not say good-bye to him. A spirit must have invaded my body because I threw a fit that thoroughly embarrassed Miss Ruth. Clinging to the banister, I screamed at the top of my lungs, "I'm not going without Daniel. You can't make me go." It was Daniel that convinced me it was okay to leave. I didn't know you could fall in love at the age of nine—another one of nature's hints I suppose.

When Daniel came for the visit, I was a bit shy around him at first. I worried that he might think I was crazy after that performance at his house, but if he did, he didn't let on. He seemed happy to see me. Miss Ruth must have wanted him to feel welcome, for she allowed me to spend extra time with him.

Daniel and I re-established our close feeling almost at once, and he told me, "I feel like you are the only one who understands me." Billy liked him, too, but didn't pay him much mind. He slept in the bunk next to Billy, and Daniel told me Billy taught him to identify some bird songs. Daniel was from the city, and Billy felt sorry for anyone who didn't know something about nature.

Daniel was helping the day we had to strip and wax the dining room floor. We had moved all the furniture to the front porch—the dining room tables and chairs, even the upright piano. Daniel and I stood on the porch picking out tunes on the piano when he started playing a simple version of Scott Joplin's "The Entertainer." I watched his fingers as he arranged C, G, and F chords into a melody. He motioned for me to try. Hesitantly at first, then with gathering confidence, I began to play out the tune. Each time I missed a note, my hand flew to my mouth to push back the "oops" that followed like a burp. Some of the kids gathered around to listen. Dillon was leaning against the piano, his eyes following my fingers, anticipating the next note. When I looked up, he became embarrassed and turned away.

"You try," I called to him.

"It's not my thing," he said, and he walked away. I could tell he was jealous of my attention to Daniel.

Miss Ruth came to tell us to get back to work and did not even get mad at our loitering. It was puzzling. At first I thought the change in her was because her mother was visiting, but it was also something about Daniel. The way she fussed over him was downright maternal. I started to wonder if there was something more, especially because Daniel didn't seem to fit in his family. He didn't look like either of his parents. If anything, with his handsome looks he took more after Miss Ruth. I thought about the ring on her dresser; I began to imagine that maybe she had gotten married, and her husband had promised to take care of Daniel but broke his promise, so she gave Daniel to her sister. It seemed more plausible than anything else I could come up with to explain her altered state. In my world, parents casually gave away their kids all the time. Why would a single woman keep her child? This ill-formed belief was given some credence after I overhead Miss Ruth argue with her mother.

Having just finished making Miss Ruth's bed, I heard the tapping of a cane as it approached Miss Ruth's room. I knew it was Miss Ruth's mother. She used that cane like Moses used his when he intimidated the Egyptians. Its purpose was to strike fear into the hearts of those she sought to change. Whenever she encountered a word or behavior she disapproved of, she would bring her cane down hard and thump the floor, often accompanying the crack of the cane with a loud "Harrumph." If she could have turned that cane into a snake, I'm sure she would have.

Suddenly I knew why Miss Ruth couldn't hear out of her left ear. The woman frightened me, and it made me sad to think Daniel had to spend time with such a mean person. He had no Naomi in his life. I didn't know then that you couldn't miss what you didn't have, so I thought he must be the saddest boy in the world because I couldn't for the life of me see where he might be getting any love.

I slunk against the wall, trying to make myself invisible, when the old, cranky woman entered. She spotted me but ignored me as she turned her attention to the vanity table. It was as if she had x-ray vision. What she was looking for wasn't there, so she turned and walked to the bureau, where she opened several drawers until she seemed to find what she was seeking—a small bundle of envelopes tied with a ribbon.

The need to know overcame my apprehension and I blurted out, "You hit her with it, didn't you?" My eyes were looking at the cane in her hand.

"What?" She turned toward me, startled by the voice.

"Miss Ruth. You hit her in the head so now she can't hear on the left side." I said it as though I were Sherlock Holmes using deductive reasoning. I was so smug with my conclusion that I forgot myself for an instant.

"It's none of your business, and if you're not careful I'll give you some of it for your impertinence."

Just then Miss Ruth entered. "What do you think you are doing? You have no business going through my things. This is my private room!" She was shaking mad. I wondered if she would hit her mother, and I began to worry about that cane.

"You don't think I know what is in these?" her mother said, shaking the envelopes at Miss Ruth.

Suddenly Miss Ruth did not look so big and scary. She stood trembling before her mother. "Can't you forget anything? It is the past. This is all I have of the past." And she was choking back tears.

Her mother tapped her cane on the floor. "You thought Daniel would be an answer for your sins? You are a fool."

"He does make a difference." Miss Ruth reddened when she suddenly caught sight of me. "I will not discuss this here. Not in front of her." She nodded toward me.

"Well, you should." And her mother turned and walked out of the room, carrying the bundle with her.

I could not make sense of the conversation, but Daniel had something to do with a payment. It must have been as I thought. She gave him to her sister because of her sin.

I stood looking out the window, wondering about the mysteries that surrounded Miss Ruth. I saw her below walking side by side with her mother. Even from my high perch, I could see they were somber and in deep conversation. Miss Ruth was gesturing with her hands, as she often did when she was serious about something. She turned to face her mother, and as she did she stood partially in her mother's shadow. As the sun moved, Miss Ruth's shadow shrank until it was engulfed in her mother's shade. Only the shadow from her moving arms could be seen as belonging to Miss Ruth. It looked as if she were dancing in her mother's shadow.

I don't remember seeing Daniel again in my childhood, but one thing I felt certain of: there are some places lonelier than orphanages. For even when I was on the outs with one friend, there was always someone else I could count on to be in my corner, to understand. The loneliest place in the world is a place where there is no understanding.

I was glad for my home and for baseball.

CHAPTER 18

Early that fall, at the end of baseball season, the doctor said I had rheumatic fever, but I knew it to be a sickness of the soul. I had been feverish for three weeks, ever since my encounter with the stranger in the church. Guilt over an impulsive act gnashed its teeth, threatening to devour me. Four times in three weeks I had gone to the altar to be saved. Sitting next to Naomi at the Saturday night revival meeting, I moved to go forward again. She whispered, "Honey, you don't have to go more than once. Once you're saved, you're always saved."

That wasn't what Reverend Charles preached. He was constantly calling backsliders to come forward and "get right" with God. I whispered back, "I don't feel saved," and made my way to the front again.

I was seriously bargaining with God. If he let me get by this one time, I would never again do anything wrong, and I'd be what Naomi wanted me to be—a missionary to Africa, even though I seriously doubted my talent in that department. One day after being hit by a wave of guilt about the stranger, I approached the meanest boy in school to "witness" to him; I'd put my talent to the test. Boldly, I approached fat Jeter and said, "Jeter, have you thought about turning your life over to God? If you did, more people would like you and you wouldn't feel like being so mean." He stared back at me for a second as he gathered his thoughts, and with all the contempt he could muster he replied, "Little, ugly, freckle-faced snot, have you thought about having a fart in your face?" So ended my missionary efforts.

At first, time and daylight helped ease my guilt. My fears appeared as a raging storm only during the night hours. Gradually, like a malignancy, the guilt spread until it consumed my daytime thoughts, causing me to ignore small daily pleasures. Just when I was on the verge of confessing to Naomi, an event happened that changed my mind.

Sunday afternoon, after rest time, I was sitting alone on the large stump in the front yard when a man came staggering down the highway, pronouncing the imminent destruction of the world. The way he seemed so excited about it, I was certain he meant the end was due either that night or by the end of the week. "God appeared to me. Told me to warn y'all, to tell you to git right. The end of the world is nigh, and those of you living in sin will be separated from your family and God's face for eternity." He didn't have much credibility with most of the kids listening since they had already been separated from their families. They just stood by the road with little curiosity about the unsteady man who was hollering.

But for me, it was that word "separated" that caused me to spring into action. I rushed to Naomi, out of breath. "Will the world end tonight? Will I never see you again?"

"Where did you hear such a thing?" She was rubbing my forehead to soothe my fearful, agitated state.

"A man on the road, he says it's so."

She walked outside with me. The man had stopped in front and had a small gathering of children around him. He was no longer shouting but continued a rambling outpouring about his vision while trying to keep his balance.

Naomi called the children to her and yelled to him to move on. She laughed and said, "Oh, that's ol' Chester. Drunk again and hasn't a bit of sense. He doesn't know what he is talking about."

I was puzzled. He sounded just like Reverend Charles, who said nearly the same things every Sunday morning and Sunday evening and especially during the Saturday night revival services. I guessed it must be true only if you are sober, but I'll be darned if I could tell the difference between Chester and Reverend Charles.

Naomi put her hand on my forehead; my face was flushed and wet with perspiration. She took me to see the nurse, who put me to bed. The next day I saw Dr. Hudson, who became our doctor after we moved to Lookout Ridge. He diagnosed rheumatic fever and recommended complete bed rest for one month. The isolation gave me ample time to reflect on my deed and a false sense of security because Sheriff Mac wouldn't arrest a sick child. God had arranged this sickness both as punishment and as protection, I reasoned.

––––––––––

The act that had brought on my sickness had occurred at church three weeks earlier. I had left the sermon, as I often did when I became bored, making an excuse to use the bathroom, which was downstairs. I knew of a special bench hidden in an alcove on which I would lie looking out the small window high above, which let in the starlit sky. I loved the cool, large, empty, dark space of the basement where I could lie unnoticed and observe occasional intruders. Once I saw Maude kiss W. C. Another time Butch, a community boy, gave Doug, a home boy, two cigarettes. Seeing others' secrets reassured me that I might not be so bad as I imagined.

Ever since remembering my mother, I had felt a battle raging in me. I longed for the sounds of her music and the fast, wild side of her personality, but I could not reconcile the two sides of me—the little pious "Miss Missionary" and the passionate torch singer filled with sinful desires.

I was thinking about my mother when a man appeared in the shadows of my alcove. I saw him before I heard him. He was breathing heavily and looking frantically around for a place to hide, holding his hand to his side to keep the blood from dripping on the floor. I could tell he was in trouble. He swore softly. My eyes were accustomed to the dark, so I saw him before he saw me. He was a handsome man, wearing dark slacks and a soft shirt with jeweled cuff links. Unlike the local men, who wore boots, the stranger wore shoes that barely made a sound when he walked. The faint odor of cologne and cigarettes, so unlike the smell of the men upstairs, awakened in me an urge to help him. I handed him my hanky. Our eyes met. His fear softened when he saw the eager, scrawny child before him. Before I had ever heard the expression about eyes being the windows to the soul, I had searched the eyes of others, seeking to find what they tried to conceal. I could see fear when a voice spoke confidently; anger when the person's words spoke sweetness; sadness behind laughter. This man had kind eyes, eyes that said he would never hurt a soul.

He spoke. "Help me. I need to get away. Fast. A place to hide."

I rose from the bench and pointed to the high window above. He leaped on the bench and reached for the latch to open the window. Just before he lifted himself, I spoke, as if anticipating his thoughts. "Follow the row of eucalyptus trees behind the church. There is a path and it takes you to the railroad tracks. A train comes by at 8:30 every Sunday night. It's the coal train and it's slow."

He looked at his watch. "Ten minutes," he said. Then he hoisted himself up and slipped his body through the narrow window. Once outside he turned and looked down. "Thanks. Please don't tell anybody about this."

He waited to hear me say, "I won't."

I moved forward. My hanky fell to the bench and I ran forward to pick it up. It was covered with his blood and his smell. I heard myself choke out the word. "Wait." But he was gone. Then softly I added, "Take me with you." He did not hear.

My words startled me. I ran into the bathroom, locked myself in a stall, and tried to still my shaking body. What was wrong with me? Why had I asked a perfect stranger to take me with him? A longing had erupted, like a volcano spewing forth fire, its lava threatening to bury, to destroy, the child in me and from its ashes bring forth a woman. But I was overwhelmed and ashamed of my need. Why, oh, why couldn't I be like Naomi and just need God? How could I betray Naomi to go off with a stranger to find my mother?

The fire inside me only singed and I remained a shaken, abandoned, waiflike child, wondering what to do with the hanky.

I stood at the sink washing it with my back to the door when Sheriff MacFarland entered. Mr. Mac, as everyone called him, was a big man with a stomach that hid his belt. He poked his head into the room and yelled, "Did you see anyone come down here?"

My head felt light as the blood drained to my feet. I squeezed the hanky into a ball so that it fit into my palm and kept it out of sight. Opposing voices jumped around in my head: "Tell the sheriff, he's the law." "You gave the man your word." I continued letting the water run over my hands, putting more soap in my palm. After a pause that seemed like a whole school day, I finally shook my head.

"Did you hear anything? Like someone running by?"

The first lie is the hardest. I answered more easily, "Nope."

Hurriedly, he turned to his men and shouted, "See anything?"

"No."

"Let's go. Jones, see if he's upstairs, I'll look outside."

He had no more use for the little person at the sink, so I rested against the porcelain, wondering what I had done. I slipped upstairs in time to sing the closing song, "Rock of Ages," and belted out the phrase "Let me hide myself in Thee."

After the service, the word spread quickly about the manhunt. People said the man had robbed somebody; a fight had broken out and he was stabbed. Some of the men volunteered their hunting dogs to help the sheriff find him. They swore that before the night was over he would be in jail. We children were quickly rounded up and secured in the station wagon to return home. If they found him, would he keep my secret, as I had kept his? I worried.

Now with my fever, I lay in bed going over and over the scene. The men never found him. I was guilty of helping a fugitive from the law escape. I was more guilty than he. I envisioned myself in jail, lying on a slab of concrete, looking up at the small, high window and seeing his face as he bent down and said, "Don't tell." I wasn't protecting him now, for he was free; I was simply protecting myself. I knew the right thing would be to take my punishment. In a confusing way, not betraying him was being loyal to my mother. I was trying to defend her and the her in me. But by not telling I was betraying all I had been taught and was denying Naomi. I wanted to tell Naomi, but she could look so disappointed, so sad. It seemed she was sad a lot now, and I didn't want to make her more so. It seemed a great sin to have secrets. It created that dreadful monster Separation.

Day and night I lay in the hospital bed in the small white infirmary, which overlooked the front yard. During the day, I could see the boys come and go from across the street and I watched for Billy. Often he stopped in front of the infirmary window after meals and waved. "You okay?" he would call out before he was hustled off by a staff member. It was so hard to be an outcast. I was sure he would disapprove of my act as much as Naomi would if he knew.

Daily I heard the school bell ring for classes to begin, for recesses, and for announcing that school was over for another day. I heard the sound of laughter and arguments among my friends as they returned home. Naomi often would spend a half-hour in the afternoon reading to me. Most of the time I lay with my eyes closed so that I did not have to look into her clean soul. One night, during a furious lightning storm, I crept out of bed and sat waiting next to the window, wanting the lightning to strike me, to end my anguish. Something had to happen to end my internal torment.

One night there was a meteorite shower, and I figured the prophecy of Revelation was about to be fulfilled, for it was written how in the end times the stars would fall and the earth would be consumed by fire. I was doomed. The big separation was coming. My fever spiked. Nurse Ann came to check on me before going to bed and rushed to get Naomi. Thrashing about in a feverish state, I knew it was time to confess. "I hid him. He got away," I blurted out.

Nurse Ann whispered to Naomi, "She's delirious. I'll get something to bring down the fever."

"No, no," I murmured, "it's true. Send me to jail."

They didn't listen, believing I was delusional. "Shush," Naomi was saying soothingly. "You'll feel better by morning."

She was right. I felt deeply relieved for having told. If no one chose to believe me, then that was their problem. Absolved, I was free of my fever and my guilt—at least for a few hours before the doubts returned.

Naomi came to see me. "You look better today. Would you like to see your brother? He's been asking to see you."

Yes, I longed to see him. His easy laughter and irreverent way of speaking made me think he wasn't afraid of anything, but it also made me worry about his soul. He was even so brave as to speak up in Sunday school class and ask the teacher how she knew for sure there was a God. She got really mad at him and told him there were some things that he would have to accept as fact. He laughed and said, "Is that the best answer you can give?" The teacher immediately went to Naomi, who made every effort to restore him to the faith. Billy never told me whether he was restored or not.

He sat at my bedside and gossiped, asking me about Laura, a girl in my class, which made me feel a little jealous. But it was good to talk about trivia; our talk released me from self-preoccupation, refreshing me like a bath after two days of sleeping in sheets wet from fever.

We were playing Monopoly, our favorite game. Our favorite part was trying to cheat on the other without getting caught, creatively diverting the other's attention to gain an advantage. Our true game was to catch each other, not win the game. He caught me and he said, laughing and wiggling his finger at me, "You cheat as bad as ol' Sheriff Mac. Well, maybe not as bad as him. Nobody could be as bad as he is."

"What do you mean?" I asked, catching my breath.

"Everyone knows he cheats. He has these gambling games every Sunday night at the pool hall down the street from the church. You know the one?"

I nodded. "I didn't know he cheated." My heart was beating fast. I didn't like talking about the sheriff.

"You probably haven't heard—I think you were sick when it happened—but about a month ago this man came to town. He came with two of his buddies. I think they were from Florida. Anyway, he was smarter than the sheriff. He beat the pants off the sheriff, won all his money. The sheriff got mad and tried to arrest him for cheating. They got in a fight. Someone said he got hurt, but he got away." Billy was laughing like it was the best joke he had heard in a long time. "Can you beat it, Sin, that he would accuse someone of what he did every Sunday? The whole town is laughing about it. Glad he got away. Serves the sheriff right. You owe me; you landed on Boardwalk."

I lay back against my pillow. Oh, what joy, what lightness comes with redemption. I felt as light as the breeze that came though the window and gently swayed the curtains. Suddenly, the air felt fresh, I could feel the warmth of the sun as it bounced off the sidewalk below, and I could feel myself rising on its thermal breeze, carried above the trees, away, away from all that had imprisoned me.

"I've missed you. I'm glad you are my brother." For I doubted anyone else would see the humor in the escape as Billy had. Oh, I wanted to tell him, to thank him for transporting me out of my inner prison, but I had promised not to tell anyone. Wanting to share my other side with him, instead I said, "Billy, I think of her a lot."

"Who?"

"Our mother."

His mood darkened. "Well, don't. It's no use."

Dr. Hudson was pleased with my progress and soon afterward pronounced me cured. I escaped without developing a heart murmur, even though I wouldn't have minded having one because then I would be like Naomi. I'd also be excused from having to go to Africa. The only trace left of the disease was the confusion that came with the collapse of my black-and-white world. All the cues, measurements, markers, symbols, and indicators that guided me through the mist of childhood were scattered in the wind. I was left to reassemble the pieces into a new order. It felt a little like walking a tightrope with my safety net removed. Goodbye, childhood; welcome, adolescence.

PART IV

SET ME AS A SEAL UPON THINE HEART, 1956–1964

CHAPTER 19

I was at that awkward stage between childhood and womanhood the summer before I turned thirteen. My passion for baseball was waning and had not yet been replaced with another. Sunny, Maude, and Franny were chosen to spend half the summer with couples who wanted to feel good about doing something for a "needy child," and I was left friendless. I had twice tried going to strangers' homes and had failed at it.

The first time was clearly my fault. I was nine, an unfortunate age of moral rigidity, and turned my nose up at the couple's plans for me. They had picked me up on a Saturday afternoon and we drove until evening to another state, leaving neither of us much time to adjust to the other. The next morning I put on my church dress, expecting they had plans to attend services, but instead they informed me that we were heading to the stock car races. Well, that seemed sacrilegious to me, and with a sullen, down-turned mouth I went along, praying in my heart that God wouldn't be mad and I wouldn't get into trouble if Naomi found out.

The first time I saw a pileup on the track, I headed to the bathroom and sat on the floor, trembling with terror and covering my ears to block out the noise. For the life of me, I couldn't understand how people could make entertainment out of catastrophe. Maybe they had never had any and didn't know how catastrophes felt. The couple took me back to the home and said I "didn't fit in." Naomi said, "Why, Jen is our best child," and she gave me a puzzled look. They should have chosen another child; there were any number of them who had not been in the home as long as I and would have welcomed getting out of mandatory church attendance.

The next time I was asked, I was eleven and, under the impression that I would be swimming to my heart's content in the couple's pool, I accepted. Instead, I had to baby-sit their four-year-old hyperactive daughter and their seven-year-old brain-damaged boy, who came by his dementia from having fallen in that pool. It was my job to keep both of them away from it. The couple were gone all day and by the time they got home in the evening, I was so worn out I would have drowned if allowed in the pool. I declined summer holiday invitations after that, preferring the known to the unknown.

But Sunny got a much better deal, one that lasted for at least three summer vacations. While Naomi and I were traveling to Iowa to sing and raise money for the home, we stopped off to see Sunny. She was the only child in a big house in the country that smelled like homemade bread and spices. As my envy grew, she told me that she rode horses in an open field, learned to cook, and could read all she wanted without someone making fun of her or scolding her for not doing chores. Naomi shook her head, not believing that Sunny had been successful at staying in a stranger's home and I hadn't. She never understood Sunny and asked me after we left, "What do you see in her?" I knew Naomi was worried about Sunny because Sunny never would go to the altar to get saved or baptized. I guess that's what I liked about Sunny, that she wasn't as eager to please as I was.

The summer was passing slowly. Each year we were sent to camp for two weeks if we could recite five hundred Bible verses, and I had only sixty more verses to learn before camp. We all learned the short ones first: "Jesus wept," "For all have sinned and come short of the glory of God," and so on. The hard part was not getting mixed up about where the verse was located. Camp wasn't for another six weeks and I was bored.

Then something wonderful happened. Teresa Thomas invited me to her house. This was a miracle—Teresa was the envy of the school. Her mother, Mrs. Thomas, taught fourth grade and was as pretty as her daughter; her father was the town lawyer. The Thomases lived in a big brick house at the edge of the home's property. By the standards of our community, they were rich. Every orphan dreams of being someone like Teresa, of having golden ringlets and good-looking, rich parents. The first time I saw Teresa, I was sure she was a little princess right out of the fairy tale books. Wearing a pink angora sweater that gave her the appearance of being wrapped in cotton candy and little white patent leather shoes, she looked edible. Standing next to her, I looked like I had been dropped in the dirt a few times, and I appeared far from edible in my worn cotton dress and scuffed shoes. Teresa never paid attention to the home kids, except for Billy. Her best friend was Nell, a dark-eyed, feisty daughter of the Methodist minister.

Teresa must have found herself bored that summer as well. Or maybe her mother persuaded her to ask me. I got the impression when I was her student that Mrs. Thomas wanted Teresa and me to be friends, but Teresa had a way of making me feel that she regarded me about the same way she did grasshoppers. I once saw her bat at one, flinching with disgust and shrieking, "Get away, get away," when it landed on her pretty, soft sweater. So I kept my distance. Besides, standing next to her brushed curls and creamy skin only accentuated my straight brown hair and freckled face. She was as clean and fresh as Dove soap, and I still had the stains of baseball dirt on my elbows and knees.

But Teresa asked for me, and I felt the possibility of metamorphosis. Maybe Teresa could make me different. I sat on her white, chiffon-curtained canopy bed and believed myself to be a demi-princess. I tried not to show my utter amazement at the decor in her room. She had so many toys that some were displayed in a glass-cased cabinet, obviously untouched. I looked at them only when she left the room. We listened to "Love Me Tender" and "Jailhouse Rock" over and over. I was ready to betray my torch singers for her music. "Yes, it's so wonderful," I heard myself lie. I had no preferences, no choices, no ideas of my own. I was whatever she wanted me to be—because I believed she could make me her. That's a problem for orphans: they run the risk of selling their souls for acceptance.

I wanted to be Teresa, so I ignored how she belittled my friends and I betrayed my friends to her. I told her about Maude loving W. C. and that I had seen them kiss. I told her that Sunny believed that she had led many past lives, one as an Egyptian king. I told about the time that Shirley begged at the national park, how she pulled her swimsuit down around her crotch, so that you could see everything she had. She wanted people to think she was pathetic. She told them she was from the orphanage and begged for money to buy ice cream.

I told Teresa how Holly liked to beckon girls into the large, dark closet where we hung our clothes and how she would lie on top of them and rub her hands gently all over their bodies. No, she never did it to me, I lied. Teresa and I howled with laughter. It wasn't until I left that I felt uncomfortable about my betrayals and shuddered uneasily when I thought about the shriek of Teresa's laugh. But I was on my way to becoming a princess and this was the way to get there.

————

A few visits later, Mrs. Thomas opened the door to greet me, her eyes red and her face swollen from crying. Teresa came from behind her, speaking to her mother in a contemptuous manner. I was even more shocked to hear Mrs. Thomas respond with a pleading, supplicating tone: "Teresa, that isn't nice. Teresa, don't talk like that." I would have been sent to my room for a year had I dared speak in half the tone Teresa was speaking. As Teresa directed me toward her room, she turned to her mother and said accusingly, with icy hatred, "It's all your fault. You are so stupid."

I hesitated. "Maybe it's not a good time for me to be here."

"Oh, don't be silly. It's nothing. She'll get over it." And she rushed to put on an Elvis record. Her demeanor rapidly shifted to a relaxed, gossipy spirit. "I'm bored. I need an adventure."

We let our minds drift, turning over ideas for excitement, when she came up with the notion that we look for a mystery to solve. We were to be detectives. Spies. It was my job to find a mystery worth solving. It certainly could not be found among my friends since most of them were away, and those left were too uninteresting. But I was vigilant. A few days later an opportunity presented itself during kitchen duty.

Agnes, our new cook, was in unusually good spirits, hinting about what a wonderful day off she had had the day before. Shirley scoffed, for she could not imagine six-foot, plain-looking, sour-mouthed Agnes having a life. Agnes seemed to resent us all, mocking us when we complained, "Oh, you have it so bad. Poor you. Poor, poor little you." She never gave us a break for having ended up at a children's home. "You think life here is tough, you just wait. Wait until you get out into the *real* world." And we hated working with her, hated hearing anything close to the truth. But Agnes was annoyed at Shirley's scoff, for she knew what it meant. She knew how we perceived her.

"What was so great about your day off, Miss Agnes?" Shirley asked.

"Wouldn't you like to know, Miss Nosey?"

Shirley rolled her eyes at me, and I smiled. Our insolence threw Agnes into revealing what she most wanted to guard.

"You can't imagine anyone looking at me. Well, you aren't half as smart as you think you are."

Our mystery was right in front of me. Who could this man be? How could I find out? I certainly couldn't follow Agnes into town on the bus. I told Teresa. She was halfheartedly interested, as if she had forgotten our plan to solve a mystery. I was worried that she was losing interest and I would lose my invitation to the clean, quiet all-white interior of the house where one might become a princess.

I requested kitchen duty the day after Agnes's next day off and approached the topic of my concern with her. "Gosh, Miss Agnes, you must have had a bad day off. You don't look so happy."

"It is none of your business, Miss Smarty-Pants."

"Oh, I'm *sooo* disappointed," Shirley said sarcastically. "I thought you would tell us all about him."

To my astonishment, Agnes replied, "I only tell my diary. It's beyond your years to understand, anyway."

That was it. We could solve the mystery by reading the diary. I was eager to tell Teresa. She thought it was a great idea. I should steal the diary, bring it to Teresa's house, where we would read it, then write a note letting Agnes know it had been read. On her next day off, I was to make entry into her room, bring the diary to Teresa's house, and place it back in the room before Agnes returned.

The next week, the day of the break-in, I was nervous. I had decided that right after lunch, when those without chores were to remain in their rooms until the staff prayer meeting was over, I would sneak to the fourth floor where Agnes roomed, enter quickly, take the diary, and then go to Teresa's later as planned.

I hated to miss after-lunch cleanup because we assigned someone to listen at the door of the room where the staff prayed and gather the latest news. During those meetings we learned about who was having problems with whom, we listened to Naomi mediate, and we learned about the weaknesses of our leaders.

It was during one prayer meeting that Mrs. Beal accused Miss Ruth of having an affair with her husband. She had proof, she said. I knew I had been found out. Miss Ruth had sent me across to the boys' dorm a day earlier with a note for Mr. Beal. I knew from Billy that the boys hated and feared Mr. Beal because he beat them with a strap and he ran the boys' dorm like a military school. He even looked mean, with his dark moustache, his square, muscular build, and his cold eyes that ran over you from head to toe, as if he was looking for sin. Miss Ruth had told me not to give the note to anyone but Mr. Beal, but when I got there, only gloomy-looking Mrs. Beal greeted me. I asked for Mr. Beal, saying I had a note for him, but Mrs. Beal talked me into giving it to her. She outranked me and Miss Ruth wasn't around to back me up. Besides, what could be in a note that a wife couldn't see? So I gave it to her. That same little note was being waved around in the prayer meeting room amid tears and yelling. Mrs. Beal stormed out of the meeting, and later that day the Beals packed up their car and their two ugly children and left. I was never questioned, and Miss Ruth never spoke to me about the incident. We all acted as if we didn't know why the Beals were leaving. And I was never thanked by the boys for indirectly having sent the Beals away.

But now I had a greater mission than hanging around for the news from the staff prayer meeting. I made my way to the fourth floor to Agnes's room and tried the doorknob. It was locked. I had not counted on this. When I thought I heard someone coming, I slipped out the window at the end of the hall and I stood anxiously waiting on the fire escape landing. What was I to do now? Looking around, I suddenly realized that a small ledge ran along the front of the building, passing Agnes's room. I could get access to her room by crawling along the ledge and opening the window.

Cautiously, inching my way slowly, I crawled along the ledge. My skirt kept getting caught under my knees so I lifted it, gripping the hem by my teeth to be free of it. I heard a car pass on the highway below and for the first time looked down. I was high above the tall pine tree in the front yard. I froze. It was a long way to earth with nothing to break my fall until I hit the ground. Perspiring, with my heart pounding, I looked back. I was midway between the fire escape landing and Agnes's room. It seemed more frightening to go blindly backward, so I continued forward, my hands clammy and my head dizzy. What I wouldn't risk to be a princess! When I got to Agnes's room, the window did not give at first. I pushed again with panic rising in my throat. It opened a crack. I slipped my fingers onto the sill and braced myself, for the first time feeling secure. I slowly raised the window, grabbed on to the frame, and pulled myself in.

Standing in the room, shaking and out of breath, I felt the exhilaration that one feels when one has faced down death. Triumphant, I looked around the room. It was sparsely furnished with a single bed and a small table with a drawer next to the bed and a high dresser against the wall. What would warrant her locking the door? The secrets in her diary?

On top of the dresser were photographs. One picture showed a young Agnes standing between a man and a woman. At their side was a tall, handsome man with eyes like Agnes's. Her brother, I thought. Genetics had played a cruel trick on Agnes, awarding her the worst features from each of her normal-looking parents. A small shudder of confusion began as I looked at the picture. Agnes belonged to someone. Strange, odd-looking Agnes. She was someone's little girl. The man in the picture was looking at her with affection, and the older woman had her arms around Agnes and was smiling proudly. I felt as if I was back on the ledge, about to lose my balance.

I pushed the feeling aside and began my search. Spies cannot afford to be sentimental. I found the diary in the small drawer next to the bed. As I began to read, I felt ashamed of my voyeurism, for I was reading the words of a woman longing to be chosen, to be wanted, to be recognized. I was not yet of that world. I was between childhood and adulthood, that awkward place where girls first look upon womanhood with awe and fear, knowing themselves to be outsiders, somewhat fearful of belonging, yet envious of the mysteries that surround their older rivals.

Slowly, as I read, I discovered that Agnes had an unrequited affection for a stranger, a clerk in a department store, a man whose name she did not know. I skimmed over phrases: "Please look my way," "Let it be me," "See past my homely self to the beauty that lies within." She wrote of adolescent schemes to catch his eye the next time she went into town. Her hopes, her dreams, her expectations for another life were wrapped around this fantasy man. For a moment I recalled the stranger I had helped in the church basement. Was I so different from Agnes?

I thought of Teresa's shrill laugh and her eagerness to jeer and shame. I remembered how she stood in the hall at school with her friend Nell, pointing and sneering at those of us who tried to mimic her. What would Teresa say to me if she could look into my soul? What would she say if she knew about the secret affection I felt for the criminal-stranger? Suddenly my sympathies were with Agnes. I would not let Teresa mock her, degrade her affection, shame her. Agnes's feelings suddenly seemed fragile, delicate, and easily blown to smithereens by the slightest carelessness.

I put the diary back into the drawer as I had found it. I straightened the bed, took a long, last look at the woman who had parents, and left through the front door, locking it first from the inside.

I told Teresa that I had been unable to get into the room. She didn't seem to care. I was already being dismissed by her; I was used up. I could feel it in her disinterested and disdainful attitude toward me. Our brief friendship faded like one season giving way to the next.

Teresa did not return to school in the fall. It was the talk of the school about how her parents had separated after Mrs. Thomas found out her husband had been having an affair with his secretary that summer. The house was sold and they moved away. I never saw Teresa again.

It was all so complicated—the complexities around love, the longings and betrayals. But I discovered that summer a thread that binds us all—that brittle, breakable, banal thread called love. It was something we all wanted—me, Teresa, Mr. and Mrs. Thomas, Agnes, and even Miss Ruth.

CHAPTER 20

At graduation from eighth grade I was honored with the valedictorian title. I always wondered whether Naomi had a hand in that decision. The honor should have gone to Roger, who lived in town. Even though he missed more school days than I, he never missed an assignment. Being the oldest son in a family whose father had black lung disease, the responsibility fell to him to do the heavy chores or take small jobs to earn extra money to feed his seven siblings. He spelled better and scored higher on the math test than I. When I gave the departing speech about the great opportunities our future held for us, I could not look at Roger. I was on my way to a private girls' boarding school, on a full scholarship courtesy of the same railroad that had helped us buy our home at Lookout Ridge, and Roger most likely would not finish high school. Opportunities were given to us orphans that were unavailable to the community kids.

By this time a tiring, lingering gloom had settled over the home like a gray, overcast day—the worst kind that brings neither rain nor sun— because Naomi and Miss Ruth could not repair their disaffected relationship. My longing to step outside my holy temple and face worldly challenges grew stronger as I neared the time to leave. I was leaving behind the many who had taught me about human nature—all except Sunny, who was going with me. Excited and scared at the same time, I was ready for the new adventure before me.

The others my age chose to attend the local high school five miles away. Billy and Dillon had left the year before for a working school established for poor Appalachian students. Recognized for its high standards, the school offered tuition in exchange for work. In addition, students made salable arts and crafts to finance the school. My heart was set on joining Billy, but Naomi had other plans. She believed that Billy had lost his soul at that school, or at the very least was drifting away from God, and she was bound to preserve my soul by sending me to a religious girls' school.

Naomi was right about Billy. I had hard evidence about what she only suspected. His small green army trunk, with his name printed in white tape boldly across the top, was placed in the main office when he arrived home, waiting to be taken to the boys' dorm in the evening. Curiosity had inspired me once to lift its lid in search of clues about my brother. Among his belongings were writings—poems and essays mostly—about whether a God really existed. In one essay he declared himself to be agnostic. (I had to locate a dictionary to know what the word meant. It was not a word ever spoken in the home.) Reading his words had jarred my mind, but because of them I was prepared to be less shaken by the information I was to receive at my new school.

I loved my new school completely—its large brick buildings in the shadow of old oak trees; its long, wide, manicured lawns; the marble floors and the mahogany shelves that held leather books; the outdoor amphitheater where Greek tragedies and plays about the Civil War were performed; and its students and teachers. Teresa had not accomplished the metamorphosis in me for which I had longed, but it was certainly bound to happen here.

It is a mystery why Naomi believed the school to be religious. It was more secular than Billy's school. The school was loosely affiliated with a Presbyterian church, but other than mandatory chapel attendance on Sunday, there was no mention of God, not even grace before meals. A "finishing school" where grade levels ranged from high school through junior college, it provided young ladies a liberal arts foundation in preparation for attending a university.

Even though I was not at school with Billy, he was close by, and he and Dillon often came to visit. Why shouldn't they? They had their pick of girls. Dillon called me "Freckles," and he didn't pay much attention to the other girls the way Billy did. He sat quietly with me while Billy joked with my friends. I asked Dillon once what he was learning in school, and he said, "To weave." He made blankets, but when he was rotated out of that job, he learned other skills as well—to make brooms, to milk, to do hydroponic gardening. He never said what he studied. He asked me what I liked best and I said playing the trumpet.

Sunny and I were housed on different floors. Because of her physical maturity, she was placed with older girls on the third floor. I roomed with Amy, who had been reared by her grandmother. Amy welcomed me immediately as her closest friend, and I liked her, too, perhaps because I felt we were not so dissimilar; she, too, had known early loss. She had not yet lost her baby fat and looked a little like an overfed lap dog with rumpled hair that covered her eyes and a tiny, flat nose. Her home was on an estate where Thoroughbred horses were raised. Amy's grandmother would occasionally arrive with a chauffeur and take a group of us out for hamburgers. On one of these outings I saw my first movie, *South Pacific*. I had never seen anything like it, and it was the most thrilling moment of my life up to that point. There in the dark, as the music flowed over me, I had an indescribable experience. Both myself and not myself, I was mesmerized, seduced, and exalted.

Whereas Amy introduced me to a monied world, my teachers presented a wealth of ideas. Mrs. Mueller, a buxom, large, Germanic woman, arrived in class every day with her tiny, stroke-shrunken husband, the former eminent historian Dr. Mueller, whom she dressed tidily in a suit and bow tie. He sat staring out the window as she lectured to us from the writings of historians Gibbon and Livy. On Saturdays when I chose to stay on campus rather than return home, I had tea in her small apartment on the school grounds, where she allowed me to handle the treasures she had brought from their travels and showed me slides.

I was lucky to have Amy, for she was totally accepting of the way I tried on new identities the way most girls changed clothes. When I read Brontë, I became Jane Eyre, then we read Dickens and I was Little Dorrit for a while—infinite possibility presented itself as new stories were introduced. I could be anyone I wanted to be. When I told Amy's grandmother that my father was an executive in a large international corporation, she became concerned about my fantasies. It was the truth, even though no one believed me. But buried in the story was an implication that I lived with him, and that caused Sunny to make a rare appearance in my room.

"You shouldn't make up stories," Sunny scolded.

I didn't see the harm in it; everyone around me seemed to be pretending. Naomi was pretending to be happy, Miss Ruth was pretending to be a virgin, and Sunny pretended, too. I challenged her: "You do it, too. You tell stories about your past lives."

"Those are true. Besides, one can't prove it one way or the other. Everyone knows you are from the home. They see the car."

How could anyone *not* know? The station wagon that pulled up to the school to take us home was like a neon sign, with the name of the home written in iridescent script lettering across the driver and passenger doors and Bible verses written in small print all over the other doors. On the back door, in bold black letters, was the scripture verse "Train up a child in the way he should go, and when he is old, he will not depart from it." The car embarrassed us, and some of the older kids would slide low in their seats when they went into town so as not to be seen. Frankly, we all would have rather arrived and departed unnoticed, for we did not appreciate the value of advertising. Naomi did, because when merchants saw us pull up in front, they often gave us free supplies.

Sunny's words stung. It was as though I was wearing a scarlet *H* on my forehead, branding me as a "home kid," a stamp that meant "product inferior." I wanted to embrace my new bright world and leave behind the crumbling, dark sadness that permeated the walls of Lookout Ridge. I didn't want to be known by my history but by the present, my newness. But in reality, my world alternated between home and school. Sunny made me see that it was so.

When we went home on break, a new girl my age had arrived. She was unlike any girl I had ever seen. She was so lovely—dreamy and ethereal like an angel. She had been petted and carefully groomed, attentively cared for like a prize rose to be shown for competition. I knew this because she had bright red-painted toenails. Her name was Chloe and she walked as if strolling in a daydream, with wide open, unseeing eyes and a faraway look. Perhaps she was looking back at where she had come from. Even her voice was low and soft, as though she was fearful that she might wake up. She was not going to surrender to the present and held herself aloof, apart from us.

Naomi was worried about Chloe, who had come to the home after her parents were killed in an automobile accident. Her only relatives lived across the country, in California, and they were taking their sweet time about deciding on Chloe's future. Naomi was fearful that Chloe was not adjusting well. She never caused problems and always did her chores on time, but she kept to herself, never relating to anyone. The only change I observed was that one day she no longer had red toenails.

At the semester break, Naomi decided to send Chloe to school with me and Sunny. "Look after her, honey. She needs a friend. This is a very hard time for her."

I nodded, but in truth, I forgot about her as soon as I got back to my school activities. She drifted in and out of my daily routine, maintaining her dreamlike state. It was usually not until we were ready to go home for a weekend visit that I would suddenly remember my promise to Naomi and rush to seek out Chloe, inviting her to join our activities. She rarely came but smiled a vacant "thank you." All seemed well. We rode home together, Chloe sitting quietly, looking out the window in her spacy way. Naomi would ask, "How is she doing? Is she making friends?" And I would say, "She's fine. Just fine."

"One, two, buckle my shoe; three, four, shut the door; five, six, pick up sticks; seven, eight . . . One, two, buckle my shoe; three, four, shut the door; five, six, pick up sticks; seven, eight . . . seven, eight . . ." Can't remember what comes next. Eight. Eight months here. It's a strange place. Not at all like I thought it would be. I thought that kids who ended up in orphanages were treated mean. Everyone is pretty nice. Most of the kids don't like Miss Ruth, but she's been no problem to me. She drinks too much coffee, that's for sure. I never see her without a cup, early in the morning until late at night.

I know what too much coffee did to Mother. It made her so tight, like an out-of-tune, overstretched guitar string ready to snap. Daddy would tell her to lay off awhile until she could get control. That's probably why she started drinking. She said her coffee was to "pick me up" and the wine was to "bring me down." Up and down she would go all day. Miss Ruth doesn't have anything to come down with, so she just keeps going until she snaps. The only problem I have here is they overdo it on this church business. They are always talking about what's in your heart, getting your heart right with the Lord and always saying that whatsoever a man thinketh in his heart, so is he—or something like that.

Miss Naomi says California is a long way off—where my Uncle Sam is. She said his attorney wrote and they are "looking into it," about my getting adopted by him. I don't think I want to be adopted. That's for babies. I'm too old. It would be hard to take on a new name. Chloe Goodwin. Sounds strange. I'm a Taylor and always will be, no matter what. Miss Naomi says that a name's not important, it's whether I like my uncle. She thinks I should tell him to give us a "trial period" to see if we like living together. I guess if it doesn't work, I could come back here. I like Miss Naomi. She's nice, but I don't look at her because her eyes see inside me and I think she knows. I don't look at anyone, just look far away and stay to myself. I want to go far away, far away from where I lived. I like that verse that says, "Oh that I had wings like a dove! For then would I fly away, and be at rest."

Mother told me that she and Uncle Sam used to be really close. They didn't talk because of Daddy. She never said exactly why, but I can guess. Daddy didn't like anyone being close to Mother but him—not even me. As soon as he got home from work, he would send me out of the room. Then he'd start on her.

He didn't used to be like that. It started after she got that job. Sometimes she would come home tired and late. I would start watching the clock at five, praying "Don't be late, don't be late." The questions would start soon as her feet hit the doorway. Mother could never answer his questions right—where had she been, who had she seen, what had she done? Over and over he would ask her, accusing her.

Don't drink, Mother, don't drink, I would say to myself, like she could feel my hope and it would stop her. I hope Uncle Sam doesn't drink. It makes one change. Mother changed. She'd drink "to come down," then she'd be too tired in the morning to fix my hair for school. She could barely get herself to work.

I learned how to comb my own hair and get ready without her; I fixed it so good no one even guessed at school that she didn't help me with it. I even got breakfast ready for us—cornflakes and milk. Soon as she figured I knew how to fix breakfast, I got to do supper, too—whenever there was food in the house. Most of the time, Daddy brought takeout food home. It was better than when we went out for dinner. I stopped going. They argued so bad in the restaurant until I was so embarrassed I nearly died. I couldn't even eat.

I made up my mind I was never getting in the car with them again. "One, two, buckle my shoe; three, four, shut the door . . ." They didn't even stop their arguing in the car; three times they almost had a wreck. No, four. That time Mother just got out of the car when it was moving and said she would walk home. "Shut the damn door!" he screamed at her; it was almost an accident. She said she wasn't going to ride with a paranoid maniac, and the way she said it, really exaggerated and drawn out, it sounded like he was the scum of the earth. Par-a-noid ma-ni-ac.

After that fight, Mother quit her job and Daddy moved out. Mother would cry at night when talking to him on the phone. She'd tell him over and over how much she loved him. She told me he just got mad when she was late. I hated them both, the way they acted like children. I wished they were both dead. I think Miss Naomi knows I felt like that— when she looks at me I can see her wanting to forgive me. I keep worrying about that verse about what a man thinketh. Am I a murderer?

Sometimes I can't tell whether they were killed because of what I thought or whether I thought it because I knew it was going to happen sooner or later. "Create in me a clean heart, O God; and renew a right spirit within me." I don't think it's a clean heart I need but a new one. Mine feels like stone.

It was me and Mother for a while after Daddy left. The house was quiet and waiting. Mother would drink and then start telling me all about Daddy, how good-looking he was and how all the girls wanted him because he was the quarterback. How everyone counted on him to be the future pride of the school. He wanted it, too, to be a success. He did the right thing, though, by marrying Mother before they were out of high school—after she was getting on with me. We sat in the kitchen talking, my feet up on the chair and Mother leaning over them, painting my toenails. Her long hair barely touching my legs, tickling them like feathers, her head moving as she painted and talked. She told me about how much I was wanted, even if Daddy couldn't go on to school. He loved me, too, she said, no matter what he sometimes said.

"One, two, buckle my shoe; three, four, shut the door; five, six, pick up sticks; seven, eight . . . seven, eight . . . don't be late!"

I was wrong about Chloe being okay. The awareness came on a weekend when most of the students had gone home and I was left without distractions. Deciding to spend time with Chloe to make good on my neglected promise, I went to her room on the second floor, where I saw her sitting like a model posed for a painting—expressionless, her eyes cast to the floor, her hands softly folded. She was still wearing her bathrobe. Obviously she had not made it to breakfast—or lunch.

"Chloe, would you like to come hang out with us?" I asked.

She did not acknowledge me. I tried again, but there was no indication from her that I was even in the room. "Chloe," I called out, "are you okay?"

Something was wrong. Should I go for help? Had she fallen into a trance and should I awaken her? I crept forward, tentatively touching her shoulder. She did not move. I looked at the lovely mannequin before me and instantly realized that her wide-eyed, frozen stare was a mask of fear behind the veil of dreaminess. She was in shock. I was afraid for her and for myself—for my limited abilities. Could I reach her? It had taken a whole year with Maggie. How long would it take for Chloe? But I wanted to help because now I understood. My mind raced for solutions. Then I recalled something that might reach beyond the catatonia.

Where could I get it? It was school contraband, not allowed on campus. But I remembered Leslie had snuck some in and was away for the weekend. She would not mind if I borrowed it, and so what if she did? Some rules were made to be broken for a greater good. This was a matter of life and death—Chloe's! I ran down the hall to Leslie's room and found what I was looking for.

I came back to Chloe and sat on the floor in front of her and began painting her toenails bright red. I talked to her, or rather to each toe as I painted, and then softly sang "My Love Is Like a Red, Red Rose." I realized that she had heard when a tear fell to her feet. Her tears started as a trickle, then became a downpour, then a dam bursting. Her body convulsed as she slid to the floor sobbing and choking out the word "Why? Why?" And with each "why" I kept saying, "I don't know." I didn't know because I thought bad occurred only to those who had flaws, like myself, not to the good and the perfect. And we cried together, rocking back and forth, until we used up all our tears.

Chloe did not stay at the boarding school, nor did she stay much longer at the home. Someone came for her soon afterward. After she cried she lost much of her dreaminess, but she never lost the aura of being a prize rose among daisies.

———

Chloe's unbridled grief stayed in my memory, tugging at me, puzzling me about the sorrow that had erupted in me. Being around Chloe had started me thinking again about mothers—but in an entirely new way. I constructed an imaginary perfect mother based on what I believed Chloe lost. This perfect mother was gentle but strong; protective but not overly so; soothing yet encouraging; someone who instilled confidence and dignity yet was careful to teach proper etiquette so her child would not make a fool of herself. She would dress her child in the most stylish clothes and paint her toenails. I had come to believe Chloe had such a mother, and this explained her boundless grief. What about my grief? How could I grieve a loss I barely remembered? Was my mother more than what I had been told? Idealizations are created in vacuums and I had little to go on. It was a time before I discovered that the greater the idealization, the more bitter the disillusionment.

My real problem with mothers was I had too many—each competing for my loyalty. Naomi, who said, "You belong to me; your father gave you to me in writing." Miss Ruth, who said, "You are like my own; I could not love you more had I given birth to you." And the shadow mother who sang to me when I was lonely and lost. Each had given me a part of herself: Nam made me know the power of love; Miss Ruth, the power of achievement; my mother, the power of music. Often I felt like a toy clown made of wooden blocks strung together. When you pull the string, the clown bends, wobbles, twists. Each of these women was pulling my string to bend me in her direction. Back and forth I teetered trying to embrace the lives their dreams held for me.

One day, while reading a magazine in the school library, I discovered my destiny. I took the magazine home to discuss it with Naomi. "Look, Nam, here is an article about a woman who works with kids, who understands them, like you. That's what I want to be when I grow up." And I struggled to pronounce the word "psychologist."

"Well, write her. There's her address at Columbia University. She will tell you how to reach your goal."

It wasn't until later that I realized Naomi had not said a word about my being a missionary in Africa. Had she forgotten? Had she given up on me? Maybe she knew I would never really make it. Had I too much of my mother's soul and not enough of Naomi's? I kept the letter the psychologist wrote to me, telling me each step I had to take to accomplish my goal. It would serve as a map to carry along a road marked with detours.

School provided a safe and fun sanctuary. My comings and goings from home gave sharp focus to the changes taking place there. Miss Ruth was openly critical of Naomi's "leniency," as she labeled it, proclaiming it a weakness. With Ruth assuming greater control over functions and decisions, a gradual erosion of Naomi's authority was occurring. More important was the erosion in Naomi's self-confidence that came with the increasingly vituperative criticism from Miss Ruth. I often found Naomi lying down with a migraine. I sat quietly with her in the darkened room, wondering about her surrender.

Orphans are normally very forgiving. They overlook imperfections in others because they believe that imperfections within themselves brought about their abandonment. They forgive because in forgiving others, they are trying to forgive themselves. I forgave Miss Ruth for her lack of gentleness, for her possessive kindness, for her sexuality that she could not control, for her cruelty, but I could not forgive her when she brought Naomi to a place of despair.

In the midst of a happy school day, Naomi made an unscheduled visit to see me. Gone was the spring in her step, gone the lightness in her voice, gone the sparkle in her eyes. Melancholy and hopelessness were all that now propped her up. She said, "I have nowhere to go, so I came here." What did she mean? She had her home—Naomi's place! She sat broken and silent, and I watched with alarm the transformed figure before me. I was scared, angry, ashamed—and embarrassed that my roommate had to be dislodged for the night so that Naomi could sleep in my room.

Slowly the story came out. There was to be a board meeting in a few days. Either Naomi or Miss Ruth would have to leave; the differences were too great between them, she explained. Nam's fear was palpable. Sentences hung unfinished as she stared blankly at the floor, as if she was staring into a dark ocean of betrayal. She needed me and I wanted to be all things to her in this moment of crisis, but I was a child, self-indulgent and powerless. I was angry at my uselessness and disgusted by her weakness. "Nam, you must fight back. Fight for what is yours. It is your home; it belongs to you. You must not let them send you away. Where would you go? What would you do?"

"What will I do? Where will I go?" she parroted softly.

"You can teach. Yes, you are a wonderful teacher."

"My dear, I haven't taught in over twenty years. The world is much different now."

"Nam, I will speak for you. I will go to the board. I will tell them about Miss Ruth, how she beats the kids, how she slams their heads together, how she leaves bruises on their bodies, about her affairs. How she has probably slept with every man on the board in order to gain control."

Naomi's eyes widened as if she realized for the first time that we saw what she thought she had kept hidden from us. I was puzzled and disappointed by her response, for she was not heartened by my loyalty and determination to defeat injustice.

"At one time she needed me. She turned to me for spiritual guidance, for comfort, for protection. Now I am no longer any use to her. But I cannot hurt her. *You* must not hurt her. She has been hurt so much already." There was a long pause, separating the prelude from the main theme, then she added, "I love her."

Furious, I lashed back, "Well, love is—" Not sure what love was, I shifted course. "I don't think love is lying down and letting someone kick you. Besides, you have greater loves—your calling, God's work, and us," I added hesitantly. "Can't you fight for that, for us—with love?"

I could see in her eyes that she saw me for what I was—a child. She could not make me understand. Suddenly I remembered a night when I was sick with fever and my bed had been moved into Miss Ruth's room. Naomi arrived back from a long trip, late into the night, and came to Miss Ruth's bed. They lay together and talked in hushed whispers. Naomi told Miss Ruth about news of some missionaries who had been tortured and killed. She was questioning whether she could endure such suffering for love, for her faith. Miss Ruth leaned over and kissed her and said, "If anyone could endure, you could. I do love you." With that memory came a crystal-clear understanding of martyrdom for the first time. I still drew my lines—Naomi was the victim and Miss Ruth was the victimizer. The black-and-white colors of childhood still remained.

I never knew what compromise was reached at the board meeting, but the eruption that threatened the stability of my home eased again and routine was re-established, with Naomi spending greater amounts of time on the road. By summer, she had moved to a small trailer up the hill behind the main building, near Mrs. Sheffield's cottage.

The following summer, Sunny, Maude, and I visited her one afternoon, pleading with her to come back to the main building, to send Miss Ruth away. She said the arrangement was fine, that it would give her more time to do what she wanted most, to give individual attention to the children who needed her. We abandoned ones felt again abandoned, for we knew Naomi had been shuffled into a powerless, useless role, and the children would not have free access to her. How could she not see that? Maybe because, as like the poet said, love is blind.

An earthquake was rolling across my life, shaking the foundation on which I planted my feet. My world was changing. And at the same time, Naomi effected her last act of authority. She removed me from the boarding school I so loved and sent me instead to a fundamentalist religious school where for the next three years my soul was to be scrutinized, terrorized, and pulverized. But the greater discomfort was the separation from Sunny, who remained behind at my beloved school, and from Billy, who would be a day's bus ride away. It was an incomparable loss.

CHAPTER 21

The note in my mailbox startled me. I rarely received any mail, but I routinely checked anyway so that I could appear normal. I squeezed in and out the door along with others who went each day to the mailroom and left carrying stacks of letters and checks from home. The little note bore an ominous threat because notes usually meant demerits for having slighted some rule or a request to visit the dean of women. It certainly was not going to be a love letter, I believed. I was partly wrong.

The small, handwritten note requested me to meet with Nadine Love, the dorm monitor, for a get-acquainted personal chat. My heart sank. What had I done to draw her attention? God knows I had tried to keep as low profile as possible. My heart raced and a lump swelled in my throat. Had she found out about Sunday? If she had, it was over. I would be expelled.

I ran into Eva outside. "Did you get a note?"

"From?"

"Love, the dorm monitor."

"No, did you?"

"Yeah. What should I say?"

"Deny everything."

"Yeah, but if I lie and Jane tells, I'll be in worse trouble."

"Jane?" Eva laughed scornfully. "She'd never tell anything. You're the one we're worried about."

All this had happened because I wanted to make a friend. Since I had come to the fundamentalist school, I avoided all social events—because of money. I had been promised that money would be sent, five dollars a month, but it came unpredictably, and it was used immediately for notepaper, pencils, and the required nylons. Nothing was left for after-school lingering with schoolmates in the cafeteria, where they bought French fries with gravy and Cokes. There were eager invitations for me to join them in the beginning, but my evasive excuses eventually caused them to stop asking.

Last Sunday, Eva and Jane had asked me to skip church services, hide
in the room until the room monitor had checked to see that everything
was clear, then afterward meet in Jane's room and listen to the Platters'
new records. It was a mystery how Jane had snuck in the records, bypass-
ing the monitor who checked all packages and luggage when we arrived
on campus. I went along with the plan, having a miserable time because
Jane and Eva had nasty mouths. The minute they were outside authority's earshot, they competed with each other, showing off who knew the
most sailor language.

Now here I was sitting before Miss Love, scared and acting sullen to
hide the fear. In spite of her name, Miss Love's pinched and narrow face
looked as if all the love had been squeezed out of it—and she was only a
few years older than I was and a student the same as me. I had observed
that the homeliest students were the most righteous. Maybe they had
fewer temptations to resist, I mused. I sat across from her desk on the
chair she provided for me. With a sanctimonious tone authorized by her
position, she began, "It is my job to make sure that you are right with
God. I have observed in the small group prayer meetings that you rarely
share a scripture that has touched you personally." She paused, her narrow birdlike eyes sharply focused, looking for the slightest hint of
rebellion. I waited—was this a trick? When was she going to bring up
Sunday? She continued. "And frankly, Jennifer, when you do pray," a
self-righteous sniff escaped her nose, "your prayers don't seem *sincere*."

Sincere? I screamed silently. I could run circles around these people
with sincere-sounding prayers if that was what she wanted. I had been
trained by the best—Reverend Charles, Corbin, and of course, Naomi.
Why only last summer, we had had another crisis—the state was threatening to shut us down because we did not have a fire-alarm system, and
we certainly did not have the five hundred dollars to install it. But Naomi
stood before us again and worked another miracle with her simple, sincere "It will be so" prayer. The next day a man had a flat tire in front of
the home. The boys helped him fix it and answered his questions about
the home; he asked to meet the director. "How do you run this place?"
he asked. And Naomi said, "God supplies." I was standing next to her

and heard the whole thing. I heard him say, "Well, I've never done anything like this in my life—I don't even believe in God—but I believe in
what you are doing." And he wrote her a check for five hundred dollars.
Naomi said, "God believes in you even if you don't believe in him." And
she told him how he had answered her prayer. Miss Love didn't know
anything about prayer!

Ironically, I believed that I couldn't tell Miss Love or anyone at the
school the stories of Naomi's miracles. I could have told Amy, who
wasn't religious, and she would have understood and believed without
question. Miss Love would have probably accused me of heresy, not
that I cared one bit for what she thought, if only she would stay out
of my life. If she wanted to hear sincerity, I'd give it full blast in the
next prayer meeting. I was powerfully relieved that she was concerned
only about my prayers.

With my cold-hearted, defiant spirit kept hidden, I assured Miss Love
that I would examine my heart. I would have agreed to anything she proposed because I was feeling so lucky to have escaped the inquisitor. But
I also knew Miss Love was right. My prayers were not sincere, and in
truth, I had stopped praying. In the beginning, I had prayed with all my
soul, as Naomi would, that I would get some extra money so that I could
pay the fees to go to the annual picnic with my classmates. I tried to get
a job, but I was on a full scholarship, with my books and tuition paid for,
and the jobs were given to other students who needed assistance paying
for their tuition and board. The hardest thing for an orphan is to be
excluded, and that was the situation in which I found myself. Unable to
participate in many of the activities that required extra fees, I had withdrawn into myself. And that's how it had come about that I agreed to
skip church—to get back into the "club." After my reprieve, I shied away
from Eva and Jane.

———

Adolescence is a trial by fire—a time when cruelty forges one into
a new shape. And I had never before met quite the number of cruel
students as those that gravitated to this holy institution.

Despite my shy, withdrawn state, I exchanged tentative glances with a good-looking dark-haired boy named Matt, who sat near me in class. It led to his asking me for a date. Now a date meant sitting side by side on couches in a large lobby, with monitors walking around inspecting, making sure there was no handholding or touching or lingering gazes. Matt and I sat uncomfortably side by side, searching for topics of common interest. Since I was not going to tell anyone I was from a children's home, we did not have much to say.

Our mutual attraction was quickly interrupted when Eva and Jane decided to fix Matt up with Angie. Although boys were given passes more readily than girls, Angie managed to get an off-campus pass when her older sister came to visit. Through Eva and Jane's manipulations, Matt arranged a date with Angie during her weekend pass. The girls were getting back at me for refusing to join them in skipping church services.

When I found out, I only withdrew more, ignoring the conspirators' whispers and sideways glances toward me. But sweet revenge came without even my wishing for it. Two months later, Angie and Matt were both expelled because she was pregnant.

Maybe that's the lesson Naomi was trying to teach me: "Vengeance is mine; I will repay, saith the Lord." I feared for myself, for my withdrawal in the face of battle felt uncomfortably familiar. I was acting like Naomi. When pushed, I rose to any challenge and fought back with the fierceness of Miss Ruth—and that worried me even more.

My English and drama teacher, Miss Elizabeth, rescued me from my isolation when she discovered a prodigy in me after I read "The Hound of Heaven" in English class. Since age five I had traveled with Naomi up and down the states quoting chapters of memorized Bible verses, telling missionary stories, and singing, so I was at home on the stage—it created no terror for me as it did for so many of my classmates. I became a protégée of Miss Elizabeth's, and she encouraged me to compete in dramatic reading competitions. Once again I found myself on center stage. The school valued drama and even had its own film studio. Hope was renewed, for I had found my niche.

But I was homesick and on the periphery of social life. I counted the days until I could go home and see Sunny and Billy and be back in an environment where I had already earned acceptance. Christmas break neared and I could hardly wait. I was determined to talk to Naomi about my expenses when I got home. I would have three whole weeks at home, away from the hazing and pettiness of my peers. Christmas evoked images of security, stability, and happiness and overshadowed any feelings of apprehension. Home! Where child-made decorations filled the halls and doorways of the dorm rooms, where the Christmas tree cut down by the boys in our own woods was hauled into the main dining room and decorated by us teenagers. Christmas meant rising in the crystal-frosted mornings when night stars still refused to surrender to light and walking to the gym to practice the Christmas play to be given on Christmas Eve. What part would they give me this year? And after the play on Christmas Eve, we opened presents in our small groups—presents that we bought with the dollar allotted for Christmas spending or those that we had made.

After midnight, Naomi made her rounds, distributing a stocking at the end of each bed. Every year she would linger a moment to whisper "I love you" before moving on. On Christmas Day, we gathered in the dining room, nearly one hundred of us, to unwrap the beautiful presents under the tree—presents that Naomi, Miss Ruth, and other staff had worked diligently to provide, keeping a careful count of the number so that one child did not get more than another. Then came Christmas dinner in the glow of candlelight, which fell on our well-used china carefully displayed on linen tablecloths. It was for this I waited, knowing that even after all the effort, work, and sacrifice made for us, an emptiness would remain in hidden chambers of the children's souls, a longing for the one thing the home could not give. In the dormitories, this longing came in a

muffled sigh, an occasional cry from the lips of a sleeping child—the
desire to *be* the special adored child whom we dwelt on all season.

It was still my home and I eagerly looked forward to the day when I
would be returning, daily awaiting the arrival of my bus ticket, checking
the mailbox several times a day. School ended with the excitement of students hugging and sharing rides to airports and train stations with the
few who had cars. The evening came and I sat alone in the dark room,
wondering what to do. There was no ticket and the school was shut
down for the holidays. That meant no mail delivery. I heard footsteps
coming down the hall. It was Miss Conners, the supervisor of my dorm.
She heard my sobs as she walked by.

"What are you doing here?"

"I don't know."

"Well, you can't stay. What about your family? You must contact
them." Then she paused as she looked more closely at me. "Oh, you're
from the orphanage." Her voice was unsympathetic.

I nodded. "They didn't send me a ticket." I could not bring myself to
say, "They forgot about me," so I added, "It's a busy time for them."

"Well, get on the phone and call them." It was long distance and I did
not have the dime to make the call.

I sat motionless on the bed. "Well, go on. Use the phone."

"I don't have any money."

"Reverse the charges." That had never occurred to me. I asked her
how it was to be done. She stood at the phone as I called and heard the
hardest words I ever expected to hear, "Oh, we thought you would go
home with some friends you had made." That was Miss Ruth. When I
asked to talk to Naomi, she said Naomi didn't have a telephone up at the
trailer. Then Miss Conners got on the phone and said in an authoritar-
ian voice that could get even Miss Ruth's attention that they had to
arrange that night for me to leave. No one could stay past the day that
the school closed.

I took a midnight bus that got me to the home at noon the next day. Naomi greeted me, looking tired and rushed. Even she seemed burdened with my arrival. For the first time in my life, I truly felt like an orphan.

This painful experience more than anything else prompted my next action. Over the holiday vacation, I was left alone in the office one lunch period to answer the phones. I found myself staring at the file cabinet before me—a cabinet I had often seen opened and shut by Naomi and Miss Ruth as they pulled files, then replaced them, then carefully locked it. I reached over and pulled on the handle and the drawer slid open without resistance. I saw that it contained folders for all the children in the home. I quickly closed it, as though I had opened Pandora's box. I sat down again, but my eyes kept wandering back to the cabinet. Curiosity finally hypnotized me and there I stood holding the file with my name on it. To my astonishment, in it were cards addressed to me. I opened the one on top. It was a birthday card with a mushy love poem and a note. The note was written in neat, small script and said, "Dear Sin-Sin, I hope you get this, darling. I think of you every day. I don't know if you are still at this address or have gone to live with your father, but each year I keep hoping that you will get this message from me and that you know I love you. Never doubt my love." And it was signed, "Mother."

I slammed the file back into the drawer. I was too weak to stand, my heart was pounding, and my head felt ready to explode. The dark-haired singing woman had written, had been writing me every year. She was as close to me as a three-cent stamp. The thought brought me back to my feet. What was that address? What was her name? I had never heard my mother's name. Hurriedly, I memorized the name and address on the envelope. I wanted to look inside my brother's file. Had she written him? Just when I gathered enough nerve to look again, Miss Ruth entered and relieved me of my office duty.

While feeling I was losing one home, I wondered, might I find another? I would write her, pour out my heart, tell her I remembered her—her beautiful singing voice. She would rescue me from the dreadful school and the mean, intolerant students with whom I lived. I would be liberated!

Once back on campus I carefully wrote my letter. After countless revisions, it was constricted to a brief, formal, and polite letter of introduction—something along the lines of this:

> Dear Mother,
>
> I have recently learned of your letters to me and would be interested in meeting, if you are. I still live at the home but am here at boarding school. It would be best if you wrote me here. Billy is fine and he used to ask about you a lot. I hope you are fine. Please write.

I signed it "Jennifer," wanting to distance myself as much as possible from "Sin."

I waited so long for a response that I almost forgot I had sent the letter. Then one afternoon a lone letter sat waiting for me. I could see it through the small glass door of my mailbox and my hands trembled as I opened the lock. It was from a woman whose name I did not recognize but from Florida, where I had written. I waited until I was alone, fearful of what reaction I might have in public. The response was not what I expected.

> Dear Jennifer,
>
> Your letter came to my address. I have lived at this address for many years and did not recognize the name to whom it was addressed. I beg your forgiveness for opening and reading it. I was very touched by your letter and I have hired a private investigator to find your mother. I hope we are successful and that you and she are eventually united. I wish you the best, dear, and would appreciate it if you would let me know the outcome.

Hope lay shattered. I must have mixed up the address. Surely they would never find her. Maybe she had moved far away. Discouraged, resigned, I went back to my routine of living without her. But in the spring, the week before my lead performance in *Our Town,* I heard my name being echoed down the hall, "Jennifer, telephone!" I thought it might be Billy, who infrequently called. Instead, I was greeted by a breathless staccato voice.

"Baby, my baby," said a voice choking on tears. "Is it really you, Sin-Sin?" Once our identities were solidly established, my mother explained that she was en route to see me and would be arriving the next day, Friday. Before she hung up she asked about my brothers. I told her about Billy. "What about Daniel? How is your brother Daniel?" I said I didn't know.

But I knew shortly after she arrived. She showed me his baby picture. It was the face of the baby that ran on tiptoes reaching for me in my dream, the baby I found under the tree that Maggie claimed. And slowly, as though I had been asleep and now gradually coming fully awake, I realized that Daniel, Miss Ruth's nephew, was *my* Daniel, my baby brother. Oh, what sweetness comes with validation. I wasn't crazy. There was a brother. I didn't just have "such an imagination," as Naomi had said.

My mother entered my life with the force of a whirlwind, seducing me, making me shed layers of myself before her, leaving me languid, defenseless, and tongue-tied. Her effusive hugs and words of adulation confused me. She pulled me toward her without giving me a chance to brace or steady myself. However, in moments when I observed her without her awareness, a familiar, haunting memory gave rise to a vague feeling. She reminded me of a worn Christmas ornament: lovely yet tarnished, fragile, seasonal.

My mother chain-smoked nervously and kept filling her glass from the liquor bottle on the dresser in the motel room where we tried to get to know one another. Gone was the lovely teenage mother in my memory. She now had a face that had seen a hard life, a figure that revealed a trend toward indulgence. She gave me intimate details of her life, telling me things I wasn't sure a daughter should know about her mother—the fights she had had with my father, their betrayals of each other. She even told me about the barroom fights and how I used to cry and cry when the noise got too loud and the men got too physical. But I stubbornly held fast to the mother I wanted her to be. Even though I was troubled about what I saw, I pushed it aside.

She pieced together some of the frustrating, fragmented memories that had defeated me. We had a cat named Bloomers. She remembered the red-plaid dress I was wearing the day I ran into a barbed wire fence, cutting my face. I still had a small scar on my cheek. She tenderly touched the scar and told how Billy held my hand, "fearless, like a soldier in his little soldier hat," when I got a tetanus shot. She couldn't stop crying about Daniel, expressing heartbreak and fury over his being separated from us. I told her I thought he had been adopted, but I didn't want to make trouble, so I kept what I knew to myself. I was worried about how tipsy she was getting.

During the weekend, I heard a phrase repeated so often it started to sound like a melody. When she began, "If it hadn't been for . . . I would have . . ." I began to absently hum a tune to match the rhythm of the phrase. I came to think of it as her theme song. Any hardship, any failure, any loss was explained with "If it hadn't been for . . ." I tried believing her totally, for there were moments when she was the perfect mother—a Chloe mother—that weekend. I was consumed by her energy, and in spite of catching disturbing glimpses into her, I surrendered to her.

She took me to a beauty salon before my big night's performance—a place I had never been inside before. She bought me new dresses and new underwear, things I had never had before. At the home, we dressed in used clothing sent by churches or hand-me-downs from older girls. The experience of shopping for new items introduced a powerful joy, bringing me about as close as I ever thought I would get to being a princess.

She witnessed my stage performance. I was her star, her extended self, for she was more of an actress than I. In a vague blur, I sensed her acting would not end when the part was over. She gave me money and promises and compliments and hugs and more promises. Then she was gone. I was left to assemble the pieces strewn in the wake of risk and betrayal.

As the weekend had progressed, so had my pangs of conflicted loyalty. Had I betrayed Naomi? There must be something dreadful about
my mother that would cause Naomi not to give us her letters. I needed
Naomi's blessings on this visit. Having found myself flying high on a tra-
peze without a net, in desperation I reversed the charges to call to Naomi
but instead got Miss Ruth. "What's wrong, honey?" The maternal, caring voice made me feel worse.

"Is Nam there? Can I speak to her?"

"She's at the trailer. Is there anything I can do for you?" Her voice,
secure and familiar, made me feel like I had fallen back to earth, so I told
her that everything was fine, just that my mother had dropped by for a
visit and I wanted to talk to Naomi about it.

An icy silence followed. We spoke a moment longer and then hung up.

The visit left me confused and afraid. No one had blessed the visit and
I was afraid to lose what security I had. Questions burned during the
night, robbing me of sleep. What was a mother? The one who gave birth
or the one who taught you to count at her bosom? Whom would I
choose if I was forced? Did I want to turn out like my mother, worldly
and sinful, or like Naomi, kind and saintly? The two mothers became
polarized. My fear caused me to focus on my mother's liabilities rather
than her strengths. If forced, I was willing to give her up.

———

The following Monday, a note appeared in my mailbox from the dean
of women. Terrified, I made my appearance at the scheduled time. All the
students were afraid of her because she could expel you in a flash, even
for as obscure a reason as your soul's not being right with God. A visit
to her office generally meant your soul was in hot water. I feared her
because of her wrinkle-free, sixty-year-old face. I was of the firm belief
that compassion was accompanied by pain, and its evidence was etched
in small lines on the face. Naomi had them. Miss Ruth did not. Neither
did the dean.

I sat expressionless before her, ready to be condemned for my "outra-
geous behavior." I later tried to remember all the adjectives she used to

describe me—words like "ungrateful," "deceitful," "unchristian," and one I didn't know, "insolence"—as she admonished me for the audacity I had to contact my mother and to invite her on campus, giving misleading information that she was an authorized visitor. I was informed that she was not an authorized visitor, that she did not have custody of me. Unbeknownst to me, I had violated some holy dictum of the school, and there was hell to pay. The dean was not interested in my whys and wherefores—not that I was even going to try to explain matters to her—for I was judged and condemned without a hearing. My penalty was that henceforth I was not to be trusted and that any mail coming from *that woman* who had no legal right to me would be returned.

I knew without asking who had betrayed me—Miss Ruth. Well, I suppose she had something to fear. Hadn't she given away *that woman*'s child to her sister? Could one do that? I wondered? And I had not betrayed Miss Ruth to *that woman*.

I concealed my true feelings from the dean. I did not feel contrition, as she demanded. Unknowingly, she had let me off the hook. I would not have been able to decide. The beautiful, dark-haired singing lady would remain a dream, a melody, a past. It was this image that I would keep, consolidating it with the best of the new image. A small inner voice warned me that eventually I would be abandoned again by my mother, for I could see that she had two loves, alcohol and herself. Not once in the visit had she asked about my interests, my life at the home, or my aspirations. But perhaps I should not have been so hard on her, for she was probably as frightened of me as I was of her.

I let someone else bring to an end what I didn't have the courage to face. I was afraid of what I would be drawn into—another mother, who seemed lost herself, who might confuse my course. And I did not have the strength to ally myself with her and risk losing my security. But I was grateful to her—grateful that she had confirmed my dream that I did indeed have a baby brother. And from the short moments spent with her, I discovered our likeness as well as the value of spontaneity and the ability of surrendering oneself totally to the moment. Together we were enthusiastic about the moment and we let the past take care of the past. I had been getting used to oppression and necessity, and she showed me a freedom from oppression in her spirit and her extravagances.

And so she was gone. I surrendered my longing for a mother. It was both terrifying and liberating at the same time. I was left to find my own future.

CHAPTER 22

I passed through my eleventh school year in a fog, with a sense that there was no ground beneath my feet. An unscreened telephone call escaped the operator's vigilance and I had one last communication with my mother. Her slurred speech confirmed my fears about her relationship to alcohol. Although I had not placed any hope in her stability, another safety net had been removed.

Having worked over the summer, I had fewer financial concerns. If frugal, I could make it comfortably through the year. I was ready to move beyond basic survival and attend to my social needs. Pushing aside all doubts, I embraced the fundamentalist culture surrounding me. I declared myself a future missionary candidate to Africa and joined the Women's Prayer Circle. I was determined not to let adversity weaken my faith, and I struggled to deny myself all pleasures of the flesh. My prayers were once again sincere. I had almost convinced myself—until my encounter with Duke.

Duke was a college man who had returned to school after a stint of working in the world. He assisted in the arts department and knew of me through my dramatic readings. He had Dick Clark's looks but without his Howdy Doody smile. He asked me one morning at breakfast, "What are you going to do with your life?"

Piously, I informed him of my plans to be a missionary to Africa. At that point a roaring laugh escaped him. "You're kidding! You?"

"Yes. Why not?"

"Because you are no more missionary material than a baboon. It wouldn't take long before you'd be dancing around the bonfire in a grass skirt with the natives instead of telling them what to believe."

How could he have seen what I had so carefully, cautiously, hidden? His insight fueled my anger and determination. I worked even harder at my prayers and donned an even more self-righteous bearing. A few weeks later I passed him on my way to class. He stopped abruptly, giving me an intense stare and, breaking a rule about males and females speaking, blurted out, "Don't do it. Don't try to be something you are not. Be yourself." And he walked away.

I guess I needed permission from someone I admired to drop the charade. My resolve began to melt, and I turned once again to my earlier dream of becoming a psychologist.

———

Throughout the year I floated from one class to another, viewing others as annoying intrusions into the dreamlike world where I lived. Only Miss Elizabeth was welcomed as she met with me weekly, coaching me in elocution and drama. We pored over readings, selecting ever more challenging ones for the bi-annual competitions. I portrayed the meeting of Elizabeth I and Mary, Queen of Scots; I enacted both Sampson *and* Delilah; I performed a dramatic reading of the love correspondence between Elizabeth and Robert Browning. Miss Elizabeth had a whole cabinetful of readings from religious, historical, or classical periods that were edited to be acceptable to a pious audience. Shakespeare and the classics were permitted at my school but not Tennessee Williams or any other modern writer that stirred the murky depths of human nature.

An unspoken understanding about these competitions, however, decreed that I would always finish second when competing against the school president's daughter. In truth, she was better than I, and I studied her carefully, gleaning what I could. I won the competition once, when she was away touring in Israel. I gave my best performance in a piece about the relationship between Aeneas and Queen Dido. Inspired by how Aeneas gave up all, even love, to fulfill the gods' call to found Rome, I was untroubled by his indifference to the bodies that lay scattered in his wake. Queen Dido's unrequited love fit comfortably into my adolescent angst about boys.

Being more comfortable onstage than off, my encounters with boys were awkward and superficial. I placed myself in a dilemma for which I could find no solution. When a boy eventually got around to talking about my history, my family, I cleverly avoided the questions by turning the focus back to him. The topic filled me with dread. It wasn't that I didn't *want* to talk about my home; I didn't know *how* to. And I wasn't sure "home" was even mine any longer. The situation was too complicated and too personal to be shared casually. But another little demon stopped me—I was terrified to test new ground, to find out whether I was good enough to belong. I was still wrestling with the same monster: who wants castaways, damaged goods?

Once, when I did allude to some truthful (my parents' divorce) but misleading particulars of my family, I landed into difficulty. Larry was infatuated with me and pressed me for a phone number where he could reach me over the summer. "Will you be staying with your father? or at your mother's?"

Evasive and deceptive, I told him I would let him know. I said it would be best if I called him. I was afraid that when he heard the greeting "Lookout Ridge Children's Home," he'd probably faint with shame! He was spared the shame, and so ended our budding relationship.

———

That summer, Sunny and I got jobs waiting tables at the lodge in the national park fifteen miles away. We commuted daily—one of the workers would drive us—making sure we were there by 6 A.M. to set up the dining room and begin serving meals. The unpredictable monthly allowance had stopped completely after I got my first job at the end of my sophomore year. Naomi had worked hard during our young years to rid us of that sense of entitlement all orphans have. In her wisdom she knew it would defeat us if it got the upper hand. Every Thanksgiving we participated in taking baskets of food to the poor in the community. In December we made gifts or donated something we cherished for a child who had less than we. One Christmas I gave away my doll, Esther—a treasured gift I had received from my father. Naomi rescued the doll and returned it to me as a Christmas present, with a note that it is the willingness to give, more than the gift, that matters.

I was happy to be home again and to be with Sunny. The life split between school and home ended during the summers. Whole once more,

Saturday, April 29 2017
10am - 1pm

at
529 W. Santa Clara

I didn't have to hide my history. But again I observed changes—at home and with Sunny. The population of the home was shrinking. No new children were coming to offset the ones who left. Naomi said something about "politics"—that the government felt children were better off with their families. None of the ones I knew at the home would be. Then she told me about "foster homes," which I mistook for "frosted homes," and I had the image of children streaming into cold homes where they shivered in icy beds.

Sunny, too, had changed. She was distant, aloof, withdrawn when I arrived. Though our worlds created vastly different experiences, I never thought anything would separate us. But I could feel something slowly nibbling away at the friendship that bound us. With each reunion, fewer names she mentioned from my beloved former school sounded familiar. Mrs. Mueller left after Dr. Mueller died, and Sunny did not know much about Amy since Amy ran in a different circle of friends. My stories about school seemed dull compared to Sunny's, and when I tried to make up for it with funny anecdotes, she saw through the pretense.

Sunny's attire had changed along with her looks and attitude. She wore loose, flowing clothes with exotic scarfs and small hats. What would have seemed like a stage costume on me was stunning on her. I fought my jealousy. Not only had she gotten to stay at the school I longed for, she was getting the looks I wanted as well.

But what separated us the most were the faces in the small, silver, heart-shaped frame that sat on the table next to her bed. When she was not present, I held the picture, studying it closely, noticing the way she rested her head against the tall, handsome boy's shoulder. There was a look between them that made me blush. Sunny had crossed a barrier I had not dared to. How did she tell him about herself? Did she tell him everything? Even about the winter she was twelve and what Miss Ruth had revealed in front of us all?

———————

That crisis had centered on a hat. Sunny loved hats. When we were allowed to rummage through the used clothing sent by charities, she searched for hats to go with various outfits. She had an eye that could imagine the redesign of almost any piece of clothing. But the crisis between Miss Ruth and Sunny was less about hats than about Miss Ruth's sudden awareness of the changes occurring in Sunny's figure. She was the first in our age group to transition from childhood to womanhood. We all showered together, and there were jokes and shrieks about the changes. As we crossed one stage of development and waited for the next, we listened anxiously to the older girls tell us what was to come. Since they were trying to impress us, most of what we heard about sex and having babies was exaggerated.

Sunny had selected a perky little hat to wear to school that morning. Miss Ruth told her that it was not appropriate attire and demanded that she remove it. Sunny argued that it was cold and the hat kept her warm, but Miss Ruth insisted that if she was cold she could wear a scarf, and she produced an ugly woolen one. We all stood by watching the scene unfold. And we all knew what Miss Ruth did not—that she was annoyed with Sunny's attractiveness. It wasn't the first time Ruth had been upset with one of the older girls for looking sexy. We concluded that Miss Ruth did not want any rivals.

Sunny rejected the scarf. Miss Ruth should have let the matter go, but it became a battle of wills. Miss Ruth said Sunny was not going to school unless she put on the scarf. And Sunny retorted that she would not be caught with that scarf on her head. Sunny was not one to seek out confrontation, but she would not back away from one either. She looked squarely into Miss Ruth's eyes and said, "Because you can't accept who you are is no reason why I shouldn't accept who I am."

Miss Ruth stood frozen in momentary shock. It was rare for her to be stood up to, but rarer to have truth placed so bluntly before her.

"You don't know what you are. You are illegitimate, young lady, and don't think that you will ever be anything more than that!"

Sunny turned pale. Then she turned and walked into her room. We heard a chair being placed beneath the doorknob to secure the door. Sunny refused to come out.

Miss Ruth sent us off to school, saying she would deal with Sunny later. I worried about Sunny all day. What did "illegitimate" mean? Why had Sunny become so pale, as if she had gone into shock? What could be so terrible about being illegitimate? Was she a criminal? At lunch I got the nerve to approach my teacher and, with the most casual and indifferent interest, I told her I had read the word "illegitimate" in a book and wondered what it meant. She said, "Not legitimate; not real." Well, I reasoned, that was possible. Sunny had once said she was born on another planet. Then the teacher added, "Its common meaning is that a person was born out of wedlock, that their parents had not been lawfully married."

What could be so terrible about that, I wondered? Many of us hardly knew our parents or our origins. It must be connected somehow to Sunny not feeling wanted. I would tell her not to pay attention to Miss Ruth, that she only wanted to hurt Sunny. And besides, it didn't matter to any of us about her parents. Some of the kids had parents in prison or who worked as prostitutes. They loved their parents and we liked the kids.

When I returned home from school, Sunny was still locked inside her room, where she remained for three more days without food or water. She wouldn't even let me in and I had to bunk with one of the other girls. We no longer lived in a big open dorm room. When the state began to establish and enforce regulations for institutions, partitions had to be installed in the large dorm room, ostensibly to give us privacy and to prevent disease. The partitions didn't protect the young against the childhood diseases that came seasonally. And as far as privacy, no one ever knocked politely to enter.

But I knocked on Sunny's "private" door, begging her to let me in. She didn't answer. The next day, after several attempts, she opened the door a crack. I could see red, swollen eyes peering at me.

"I brought you some food. Please eat. We all decided to sneak you some after each meal and Miss Ruth won't know."

"You don't have to. I'm not hungry." She started to close the door, then opened it a crack and added, "Don't get in the middle of this like you always do. I'll be okay." And she closed the door, putting the chair back into place beneath the doorknob.

I realized this was more than a "get back at Miss Ruth" game. What Miss Ruth said caused a devastating injury to Sunny, one that I could not understand. When Naomi returned at the end of the third day of this crisis, she made Miss Ruth apologize to Sunny. An uneasy truce existed thereafter between Sunny and Miss Ruth. Ruth never took on Sunny again.

That incident was the only time before now that Sunny had closed me out. We shared everything, all our secrets. She had told me all about Kent, the boy in the picture, on previous visits and even how they "did it" one weekend. She didn't go into all the details because she was private, but she never shut me out, not like now. Now there was silence, and Kent's picture was often placed in a drawer where it would remain for weeks. Then it would pop out again and be sitting where she could look at it when she lay down.

"Did you and Kent break up?"

"Not really. He's going off to college."

What kind of answer was that? I wanted to know how she had jumped the hurdle of telling him about the home.

"Does he know? You know, about your being from the home?"

"Of course. He's met Naomi." She eyed me with a funny expression on her face. Of course, it would be easier for her, living nearby. The revelation would happen naturally. There would be less to explain.

I felt bewildered and lost with Sunny's apparent abandonment of me. We had been the closest of friends throughout childhood. Now she preferred the friendship of Aunt Rose, a pretty, single worker in her twenties who had come several years before. They spent hours in hushed conversation. Sometimes they seemed to argue, and it made me glad. I was angry with both of them and resented the exclusion. In the few weeks after my return home, their friendship grew until Sunny was spending her days off from work with Aunt Rose, going to town with her instead of me. Trips to town had been our special times in the past. We would take the bus, eat lunch in a fancy restaurant, and walk through stores as if they belonged to us.

———•———

About a month later, Sunny came home late in the evening from spending her day off with Aunt Rose. She crawled into bed, and Aunt Rose came in with a washcloth and rubbed her head, asking how she felt. She brought Sunny some little pills to take to make her feel better. I made small noises with my throat to show my disgust at their intimacy. After Aunt Rose left, I thought I heard soft weeping come from Sunny. Why didn't she share with me? Oh, I resented that she shared her pain about Kent with Aunt Rose. Didn't she think I was mature enough to understand?

The next day I approached my room and stopped outside when I heard Aunt Rose and Sunny in quiet conversation. Sunny was telling Aunt Rose about being illegitimate. Then she said, "I could never bring a baby into this world and have it be illegitimate. Kent would not marry me. His family would not want him to marry an illegitimate girl."

Aunt Rose was saying, "But you didn't tell him. You didn't ask."

Sunny was silent. Then I heard her say words that ripped the floor and ceiling from my space and left me spinning. "You know, I always thought that it was because I was illegitimate that my mother went crazy—after I was born—and had to be locked up. She never got better."

"Oh, Sunny, I wish you had told me before the abortion. Because your parents weren't married when you were born had nothing to do with your mother suffering a mental illness. Nothing. It happens to a lot of women when they have a baby, married or not."

They sat in silence until Aunt Rose asked, "Would you have made a different decision about the baby had you known that?"

I could barely hear her reply, "No."

I heard someone coming, so I backed away from the door, I was reeling and I needed a place to find my balance. I ran outside into the rain, then sat on a stump sheltered by a large walnut tree and wept. It seemed the world was weeping for Sunny, too. I cried for her courage, her loneliness, her grief. And for my selfishness. She was my best friend in the whole world and I never knew anything about her life outside the home, what the trips home with her father had meant—Sunny's sudden disappearance and what she was going back to face and then her reappearance and what she was returning from. All those events coincided with either her mother's release or rehospitalization.

Now I understood what I could not know at age twelve. When she called Sunny illegitimate, Miss Ruth had thrown her dagger at the heart of the matter, crushing Sunny's fragile effort to resist the blame for her mother's illness. To Sunny, it was an accusation that she had caused her mother's craziness. No wonder she had collapsed, for what child can bear the knowledge that she has caused her parent's destruction? Sunny knew the price paid for intimacy—the price her mother paid and now the price she paid in losing Kent.

My anger was replaced with a deeper love and compassion for Sunny. I did not judge her. I discovered that others also carried heavy secrets, ones that could twist them on the inside yet leave them appearing normal on the outside. I had thought that I alone was burdened with demons that needed to be kept under tight security. The awareness gave me comfort. It reassured me that the secret, crazy fears about myself that surfaced periodically might be as irrational as Sunny's belief that she had caused her mother's insanity.

I made a fool of myself today in class. I offered the word "mad" as a heteronym. I understand why it isn't a homophone—'cause it has to be spelled different: like pain, pane. When she called on us to think of examples for a homophone, I wrote down twenty in less than two minutes: birth, berth; bawl, ball; pray, prey; liar, lyre; see, sea. It was easy for me because it was the kind of word game I played with Mother. But

when we got to heteronyms, I answered too quick when she said think of words spelled the same but differing in meaning. I didn't stop to listen to her add that the pronunciation had to be different. I raised my hand, and before she even called on me I blurted out, "Mad, first definition, crazy or insane; mad, second definition, to be carried away by anger." Then she explained it had to be a word pronounced different. And I said, "Tear, a liquid cry, and tear, to rip apart." I guess I redeemed myself. I hope no one made anything of it. The teacher was nice and said we might find a way to use "mad" when we come to studying figures of speech. She explained that mad is a word like many that is pronounced the same, spelled the same, but has different meanings.

Mother would have liked my English teacher. She loved words. She'd misuse them on purpose so me and Dad would have to guess the proper word. Like when Daddy asked if anyone was hungry and she would say, "I feel famous." We'd have to say, "You mean famished." And we'd laugh and laugh. That's how we tried to pass the time in the car. Those were the good times. Before they turned bad. Before the benign words became bitter ones.

Daddy kept believing she was cured. He would come get me, telling me how he thought Mother would stay out of the hospital this time. "Sunny-girl, she's so much better. This is the last time I'll have to leave you at Lookout. Wait till you see her." After a few of those promises, I quit hoping. Self-deception seems like a horrible waste of time and energy. My way of thinking is that it is easier to accept things, including oneself, for the way they are.

We would pick Mother up and head across the country, helping Daddy search for antiques. Mother always started out good, but we could see her fading, disappearing slowly into some foggy place. Was it Byron—no, I think Shelley—who wrote "She faded like a cloud which had outwept the rain"? You could see it, the fog settling in slow at first and then covering everything until there was nothing more than ghost outlines. Daddy would disappear, too. I was the only one that seemed to stay alive because I had stopped believing in wishful thinking. I tried all

*the word games I could think of to keep Mother and Daddy from evap-
orating. They were too involved in disappearing to hear. It was worst
when the silence would start, when she stopped talking, 'cause I knew
what came next. The fear. I tried to stop her from feeling it by staying
close. I couldn't even go to the store—by the time I got home she would
have worked herself into such a state, thinking I'd been killed.*

*Oh, Mother, why did you go and do it—call the police saying that we
had all been killed and our dead bodies were hacked into pieces, strewn
about the living room floor? Well, when I answered the door, the look of
surprise on that policeman's face was something to behold. There were
at least four police cars out front. I figured things out pretty fast when he
asked me if everyone was safe and then asked if he could talk to my
mother. He was nice. Daddy told him he would take her to the doctor
that day. That was the last time she came home. The fear just wore her
out. She said to me when she kissed me good-bye, "Sunny-girl, I'm too
exhausted to be a mother. You took the life out of me." Daddy said she
didn't mean it, but I know it to be the truth.*

*They did not sanctify their relationship with marriage until I was four
years old. I was the offspring of their sin. Mother paid. We both did. Me
and Mother, both institutionalized, imprisoned. Both feeling like we
don't fit in the world where we have been sent. I look around and know
I am not a normal girl. I devour everything, have a need to understand
everything—I guess so there aren't surprises.*

*Sometimes I'm afraid that life will run out before I'm finished with it.
Maybe that's why I rushed with Kent. I opened the Bible to find comfort,
to find guidance about what to do, and what verse did my eyes come
upon? Psalm 89, verse 45: "The days of his youth hast thou shortened:
thou hast covered him with shame." Shame has followed me all the days
of my life. It sets me apart from the others. I'm different. For the life of
me, I wish I could be ordinary, but I'm not. It's a waste to try it.*

*Mother gave me some of her differentness. It could be my karma. I
couldn't tell Aunt Rose, but I was afraid I'd pass it on. It was for the best
anyway that Kent left. I nearly left him exhausted, too. He said he was*

going crazy over loving me. Me, too. It's best not to let love make you mad. It will never make me mad again.

CHAPTER 23

I began to look at others differently after I learned of Sunny's secret. I saw them as couples, envisioning them entwined in passionate embraces, enfolded in one another, their bodies wet and hot with violent kisses and burning caresses. I could not imagine everyone that way—not Naomi or Mrs. Greeley, even though I knew that Mrs. Greeley had entwined at least once because she had a daughter. Visualizing some unlikely people—Agnes or Shirley—made me laugh. When I imagined Sunny or Maude, I felt afraid—as if I were standing before a fury that could threaten annihilation. The wedding made me think about these matters even more.

Mr. Wetherbee, a deacon in a church that had long supported the home, came on a sunny summer afternoon. He had an amazing effect on Miss Ruth. She blushed in his presence and self-consciously straightened her skirt as if she were caressing her thighs and stomach. Less sure of herself, more awkward and fumbling in her speech, she was kinder, almost motherly, toward the younger children.

Mr. Wetherbee showed his admiration in other ways. He watched her every move approvingly but stoically, like a deacon looking down on his congregation from a lofty position. He wore only black, which was striking with his silver hair and fitted my image of how a deacon was supposed to look. That was what we all called him, "the Deacon." He came for a visit, but stayed on.

He and Miss Ruth looked like brother and sister. He was a few inches taller and was slender and rigidly straight like her. Both had a pious brow, a thin, tight mouth, and an unwavering attitude about what was right and wrong. They fit together like a reflection in a mirror. Most people I knew seemed to choose an opposite, someone that complemented and completed them. The two making one, each somewhat less without the other. But the romance between the Deacon and Miss Ruth was a twinning.

I couldn't quite picture Miss Ruth as a bride. Was it because she was in her forties and I thought of brides as being around eighteen years old? Or was it because the married women who came to the home always seemed to be subservient to their husbands and I couldn't imagine Miss Ruth being that way? Maybe it was the way she shamed and punished the older girls for evidence of sexual interest. Oh, I knew she had a passionate nature. Twice, couples had left when she became involved with the husband. Her duplicity around sexual matters made it more difficult to get a fix on just what this marriage was all about.

The problem was complicated by the Deacon. He just seemed too tight, too self-controlled, to fit my idea of what mating required. Then I heard Miss Ruth respond to Nurse Ann's tease about the honeymoon with, "If you knew what we knew, you wouldn't needle." What could it mean? I concluded they were going to avoid sex and instead have a spiritual experience.

The Deacon asked Miss Ruth to marry him the same afternoon they met. She didn't give an answer until she went for a ride with him that evening. Aunt Rose told Sunny and me the news on the drive back from our jobs late that same night. I asked Aunt Rose what she thought about it and she said it would probably be good for Miss Ruth. I had an uneasy feeling.

The wedding took place on a hot Saturday afternoon in September, shortly after the courtship began. We all returned home for the occasion. The boys' gymnasium was revitalized and turned into a chapel, with gleaming new varnished floors and a flower-covered trellis placed in front of the elevated stage at one end of the gym, where the couple would take their vows. The piano was moved off the stage and onto the floor near the trellis. The chairs were placed in straight, even rows, with ribbons tied carefully on the first few rows, which were reserved for board members and special guests. Large bouquets were placed like pillars along the aisle and in the front near the piano, and the perfume from the flowers masked the usual stinky smell of the gym.

There was a bit of scandal in the community when Reverend Charles was slighted in preference for the minister from Mr. Wetherbee's church. The mountain people saw him as having "airs" and some boycotted the wedding.

The Bakers sang "I Love You Truly" as Miss Ruth marched down the aisle. When the choral director from the Deacon's church sang "How Great Thou Art," I saw Miss Ruth look at Mr. Wetherbee, and I could tell from the way she was looking that it wasn't God's greatness that was in her mind.

It was hot and stuffy in the gym. No breeze came through the high windows to cool us. The only moving air was from the fan Sunny had made from the program and was waving across her face. I sat between Sunny and Maude. Maude kept turning in her seat to steal glances at W. C. The only one who had expressed any feelings about the wedding was Maude, who said, "Lord, have mercy on his soul. Only a fool would marry that battleaxe."

It wasn't until I saw Naomi walk down the aisle to give Miss Ruth away that I understood why I was uneasy. Naomi was looking at the floor as she walked toward Mr. Wetherbee, ready to hand over her closest friend and confidant. Lost, hopeless, defeated would have been good descriptions for the look on her face. When her part was finished, she was supposed to sit on a designated chair in the front, but she absently walked to the back and sat alone in the last row. I turned to look at her. She held a handkerchief over her mouth to hold back the sound of her sorrow, but her eyes were not hidden and I could see the tears streaming down her face. They were not the tears of happiness one lets flow at weddings but more like the tears shed by a jilted lover.

When the ceremony ended, there was a reception on the front lawn. Long tables were set up for food and drink. Standing in the shade of an oak tree cooling myself, I watched the activities with a surreal feeling of detachment. A small ache, like heartburn, filled my chest and I tried to understand its meaning.

Jake wandered over. Handsome, irreverent Jake held the distinguished
role of speaking what none of us dared say aloud. "A shame, isn't it?' he
asked, looking at Miss Ruth lustfully.

"What? What's a shame?" The minute I asked, I wished that I hadn't.

"That he couldn't have tasted her fruits when she was a younger
woman."

"Oh, I don't know," I said in defense of her. "Love is sacred no matter when you find it." I did not have the slightest idea of what I was
speaking.

"Wonder what he will think after tonight when he finds out he
wasn't the first one?" His loud laugh caused some people in the reception line to turn in our direction. I blushed at his remark, feeling as if he
had crept inside my thoughts.

"Is that all you've got on your mind?" I retorted.

"Honey, it's what we've all got on our mind. Can't think of nothing
better to think about. Bet that's all she has on her mind, too," he said,
nodding toward Miss Ruth. "Why else would she have said yes to his
proposal the first afternoon that they met?"

Jake moved off to join W. C. and Maude, who were sitting at a distance. That was the question that had been sitting like heartburn in my
chest: Why the rush? Desperation? I looked back at the reception line.
The board members and their wives had come. You could tell who they
were by the friendly but formal way they gathered around the couple.
The others, the staff and some of the community members, were more
casual. The home kids were indifferent. To them the wedding was just
another event in the long days of waiting to become adults so they could
be free. A few of us had wondered how the Deacon's presence might
affect the running of the home. So far it seemed positive—certainly positive for Miss Ruth.

The scene before me began to slow, like a film when motion and
sound become elongated. Words of congratulation, comments on the
bride's appearance, sounded thick and distant. Miss Ruth did look elegant in her simple satin dress with a matching shirtwaist jacket with

embroidered buttons. A small bundle of posies, forget-me-nots, and baby roses was pinned at the top of the jacket, securing it against exposure of skin or bosom. Her face was flushed, not with happiness but with a sense of impatience, as if she wanted this to end quickly.

My eyes rested on Naomi, who stood at the table serving punch. She seemed to be a servant to the newly married couple, having no status, no rank, no position of authority. The board members did not gather around her as they had at other social affairs.

Suddenly prescience woke me from my self-absorbed repose. I knew what it meant—the hasty engagement, the quick wedding. I thought about Naomi's unhappy visit to my first boarding school a few years earlier when she told me about her struggle for power with Ruth. Now I understood the meaning of Naomi's tears at the ceremony. Had Miss Ruth found a new way to win?

The couple left for their honeymoon in Niagara Falls.

Look at her. Isn't she a beauty? That's who I'm fixing to marry in a few years—when she comes of age. I won't call her Vicky but by her full name, Victoria, like the queen, 'cause she has the makings of one—that is, with a little help. She'll clean up good with the right clothes and a good haircut. I look past the dirty elbows and tangled hair and I can see a Shirley Temple. She's got spirit, too. It makes her so mad when I tell her, "I'm gonna marry you when you come of age." Miss Naomi says, "Jake, stop teasing her." But what Miss Naomi don't know is that I'm not teasing. No, sirree, I want me an unspoiled, untouched, pure virgin, one I can shape to be proper, to be what a man wants—pure on the outside but a wildcat in bed. Someone I can take back home and show them what a prize I've got. That'll change their minds about who is white trash. But that means waiting six more years, then she'll be eighteen. They're be seven years difference in our ages.

Wouldn't Miss Naomi have a fit if she knew the truth? She thinks I'm still seventeen. I pulled one over that ol' sheriff when he arrested me. I heard him tell the deputy he couldn't send me to reform school 'cause he thought I was about twelve. He said, too, that he didn't have it in his heart to send a kid up for stealing food, even if he knew I was a born thief—like the whole family. To be safe, I told him I was eleven 'cause I sure didn't want him to know I was thirteen. I guess living in that cardboard box for six months must have stunted my growth. Hell, I wasn't going to go back to my uncle's after he threw me out. No way was I going back to work in no coal mines no more, especially after that accident. Lucky for me that when the sheriff talked to him, my uncle said he didn't care what they did and he couldn't remember for sure how old I was. That's how I ended up here and not at the juvenile reform school. So now they think I'm seventeen and I'm really nineteen. I didn't mind being put back in school. Never saw much of it before, so I had some catchin' up to do.

I just wish I hadn't grown so fast after I started getting fed. I was afraid all the time someone would figure it out. I thought maybe Miss Ruth had. She'd always send for me to help her in the clothing room. Said she needed someone with strong arms to lift the boxes and I was the biggest kid. Seems like she'd find ways to brush against me, then act like it was my fault. I'm no fool when it comes to women.

One afternoon I was standing beside the table and she had to pass. It was tight there, not much space, so I backed up against the table, but I swear she didn't. She turned sideways to get around me. Then she stopped, or maybe I . . . it happened so fast. I started to move my hands up so I could step aside and the next thing was her falling into them and we were laughing. Her eyes looked bright, and the way she threw back her head so her neck was right next to my mouth, well, I did what any man would do. I grabbed her. Then we heard Dillon come and jumped apart. Wonder how far she would have let me go if Dillon hadn't come in? So what if I bragged to everyone I had her. I wouldn't be the first. I bet she's a firecracker. Sometimes the hottest are the ones you least expect. Like Sunny. She's always behind her books, but I figure she'll be the first one to go down, even before Maude.

I didn't figure on Miss Ruth telling Mr. Beal. He stripped me down and beat me with a belt until he drew blood. Said he would teach me not to defile a woman. Wonder what the hell he thought he was doing with Miss Ruth? Did they think we didn't know? I think the Ten Commandments say something about adultery and lust. I think he broke two of them with Miss Ruth.

Mr. Wetherbee is in for a surprise. I bet he thinks he's got a virgin. Wouldn't I like to be a fly on the wall to hear how she explains her carnal sins to him. In my mind, there are girls you play around with and there are girls you marry. And I'm going to make sure the one I marry is no whore. That's why I'll write Victoria every week when I leave here after high school. I'll make something of myself and she'll want me. Maybe I'll join the air force. I always wanted to fly, to be up there above everyone else—looking down on them, having them look up to me with jealousy. I'll tell her just how to keep herself pure for me, how to be a lady, and say that I'll teach her everything she needs to know. I'll win her over. She's just young now.

CHAPTER 24

The evening after the afternoon wedding, a group of us went to the annual county fair, which was held on the grounds of the local high school. The school sat on a large plateau above the town of Hampton. One could reach the top of the leveled mountain either by climbing some steep stairs or by taking a winding road to the top. From the town below, one could see the lights of the fair and hear the music coming from the rides. Traditionally, the home kids participated in the fair. The boys entered a pig or a cow or made a science project. The girls produced a sewing project or did a cooking demonstration. Art and writing contests were held, with the winners' exhibits posted on the large bulletin board in the main hall of the high school—a ribbon for first, second, or third attached to each work. Each year, on a Saturday evening, there was a community performance, somewhat like a talent contest, where anyone could compete in either recitations or music.

Maude, Sunny, Jake, W. C., Dillon, and I had wandered into the cool auditorium to get out of the heat. We were sitting in the back observing Mrs. Thomas, who was up front making out the program for the order of the performers. The program always began with first graders, moving to the upper grades, with adult performances scattered among the grade school performers in order to relieve the boredom. Feeling nostalgic, I was remembering my first grade performance of "The Raggedy Man." The poem was performed every year by one of the grade school students. I was surprised to see Mrs. Thomas. From a distance, she looked younger than when I had seen her last. Maude said she was dating the principal.

Jake, Maude, and W. C. attended the community high school and wanted to go to the performance because Jake wanted to see the girls. The event was usually fun and spirited. It wasn't to begin until eight o'clock. We were just killing time, cooling off from the climb up the hill before heading for the rides. Then we'd return for the show. Earl and Luke, cousins, were onstage practicing their fiddle pieces, "John Henry"

and "Foggy Mountain Breakdown." They always won in the music category. They were considered the local dance musicians.

As we sat in the back laughing and talking, Dillon was leaning forward, watching the cousins intently and nodding to the music. When
they finished "Foggy Mountain Breakdown," he leaned back and said—
to himself, really—"I'd play it different."

Jake, who was next to him, said, "Well, get up there, boy, and show
them how to do it."

Dillon said, "I don't have a fiddle."

We all looked at him in disbelief. Maude laughed, "Do you really play
the fiddle?"

"A little. I used to at home. I've taken a few lessons at school."

"Hey, you've been holding out on us. Come on, man, don't let those
guys have the whole show." Jake was nudging Dillon in the arm.

I asked, "If I get you a fiddle, will you play?"

He glanced sideways and half-smiled. "I will, if you will."

"If I will what?"

"Will you do something? Play the piano or recite a poem or something?"

"I haven't prepared anything."

"Neither have I."

We sat playing chicken with our eyes. Finally, I got up and started
down the aisle toward Mrs. Thomas, who was still scheduling the
program rotation. Maude whispered loudly to call me back, "Don't
ask about Teresa. She eloped this summer. She—" Maude looked at
Mrs. Thomas—"took it hard."

I had not seen Mrs. Thomas since the afternoon of the red, swollen
eyes. As I got closer, I was startled by how pretty she looked. A divorce
had done wonders for her. Maybe getting rid of her nasty kid helped, too.
She smiled as I approached.

"Jennifer, I haven't seen you in a couple of years. How's school?"

"Great!" I lied.

"My, you are sure turning into a lovely young woman. I wish Teresa
were here to see you. You know she got married."

"Yeah. I just heard."

She looked hard at her list. Then she brightened. "Are you performing tonight?"

"Well, if I can get a fiddle."

"Do you play fiddle now?" She said it like it wouldn't have surprised her. She had heard I tried the trumpet.

"No, it's not for me. For Dillon. He wants to play if there is a fiddle available. I'll do a reading if he plays the fiddle."

She placed a hand across her brow, searching the auditorium. "Dillon, come up here. I'll get you a fiddle from the band room. Come on down, I want to know what you are going to play."

So it was settled. Dillon would play two songs. I would give the last reading I'd done at school, the one about Aeneas and Queen Dido.

Dillon stayed behind to practice while we made our way toward the rides on the high school grounds. We were excited about the change of events. None of us even suspected that Dillon could play. Suppose he couldn't—or didn't play well? Suppose he got stage fright? Maybe he was pulling a joke on us. He had a great sense of humor, but he usually preferred an offhand pun or satirical remark. If you weren't paying attention, his remarks would go right over your head. I thought he was the funniest and cleverest person I had ever met. No, he wouldn't pull a joke and play the fool in public—Jake maybe, but not Dillon.

It seemed the moment of the performance would never come. First one student from each elementary grade performed. Interspersed for variety, adults performed. Then came the high school students. We were seniors and had to wait a long time. Recitations followed the music competition.

Then came the announcement that Earl and Luke would perform first, then Dillon would follow. They would each play "Foggy Mountain Breakdown" and, for their second piece, something each had composed. Earl and Luke got thundering applause following their performance.

Then it was Dillon's turn. He entered with a self-conscious stroll, looking small as he stood alone in the center of the empty stage. He stayed perfectly still until an anxious hush came over the audience. The silence was shattered when the bow crossed the strings, sending out a strong, sure, pure reverberating note. Then he paused as the violin came away from his face and his hand fell to his side. He turned his profile to the audience. We giggled. It *was* a joke; he was going to play one note and walk off. But his chin came up and he lifted the fiddle back in place. Down came the bow again and the earth began to shake. The hills had never before heard such a nervy rendition of "Foggy Mountain Breakdown." He turned it inside out, upside down; he embellished, inverted, extended, and augmented the notes. He came under and around the melody until it seemed to hide behind a veil of rapid sonorous slides. One arm moved with confident speed, and one foot tapped to the rhythm, but his body stood straight and still. The boy was hidden behind the powerful music. Before he finished we were on our feet, shouting, stomping, whistling. When he finished he stood still—like an awkward boy not knowing how to behave—until the thunder subsided. In a quiet voice he announced, "I have a piece I made up. It doesn't have a name."

The composition began with a slow, haunting, longing melody and progressed to an elevated, ethereal euphony. A shimmering eddy of notes swirled around the velvet curtains and musty concaves of the walls, soaring, diving, lifting again to an escalation of crescendos, then falling into a cascade of *glissandos*. A sad, tremulous cry rose to the highest, thinnest pitch to fall back happily, hopefully, to middle range. Grace notes and trills, syncopation and rests held the listeners captive. The sublime beauty of the music opened me to my highest self and for the first time made me desire perfection. Hypnotized, my soul bowed before it and worshiped its beauty. Like the sirens, it left me powerless, surrendered, devoted. And like the sirens, it took my breath, leaving me filled instead with its splendor.

Then the music ended. Weighed down by the fullness of it, the audience paused before it broke into deafening applause. I dared not move for fear it would disturb the loveliness, the magnitude, the power of the moment. The music warmed me with a new heat I had never known. If I remained still, the moment might last.

Dillon left the stage and walked back to his seat. Maude was punching me, saying, "Hey, how about that? He's great. I bet that knocked ol' Earl off his high horse." Her words were far away for I was nowhere near. I swear my soul had left my body and had floated a few rows over to be next to Dillon. I felt like we were two notes floating in the room— incorporeal, weightless, embraced in perfect harmony. I was in love.

I heard Mrs. Thomas announce the upcoming events. I was to be third. A slow panic began, for I could not remember a line of my reading. What was I going to perform? Oh, yes, Aeneas and Queen Dido's parting. I heard my name called. I rose, still in a dream, and walked toward the stage. I stood for a moment trying to regain control. The words sounded distant as I began. As Queen Dido spoke to Aeneas, I suddenly understood her desperation at his leaving. The man she worshiped was abandoning her to follow his calling. With anguish and frenzy she saw his ship in full sail in the harbor and she lost her will to live. Now I knew why she plunged the sword into her body on her funeral pyre, why life would hold no meaning with his absence. I saw Dillon's face as I, Queen Dido, spoke:

> If only, if before thy flight, my arms
> Had clasped a child of thine, if in my hall
> Some tiny-limbed Aeneas played, to bring
> Thee back at least in feature, I had then
> Not been so wholly captive and forlorn.

I was trembling when I finished. Sunny was right. Once I heard her say that love was a music box that goes off inside you when you meet the right person and it plays "I want to have your baby."

It was music that had once reconnected me to my mother, and now it was music that had awakened me to womanhood.

Dillon and I took first place in our categories. I was relieved that I was sitting in a different part of the auditorium. It gave me time to get control before I went to congratulate him. He must not know how he had changed me. We were friends; we must remain friends. Suddenly, I remembered all the times I had played the piano so carelessly, heartlessly, passionlessly. I can't imagine what must he have thought with such a matchless talent as his.

I was surprised when I approached him to see that he looked the same. He had not changed—the same slender frame, slightly tilted head, sandy hair spilling over his forehead, curled from the heat of the energy he had expended, and cerulean eyes. But he was now greater than the sum of all his parts.

"Congratulations," I said, feigning a casual indifference.

He smiled. "Same."

He looked down at me; I looked back, trying to find a way to stay detached but still connected. "I liked your music . . . a lot." The compliment sounded empty, silly, small compared to the grandness of his sound.

"I liked your piece, too."

I groped for words. "So you have no name for it?"

"I thought about 'Freckles,'" he said, laughing.

I blushed. "That's so plain for something so, so . . ." I could not find the word without giving myself away, but I blurted out, "so everlasting."

He laughed and said, "I'll name it 'Everlasting.'"

Was there hope somewhere in his words that he felt something for me? I was restless, dissatisfied, out of sorts, and out of touch. Everything that had been comfortable and easy between us was gone.

After the performance, we all left the auditorium for the fairgrounds to enjoy the rides before they shut down for the evening. Everyone was in high spirits. I pretended to be.

CHAPTER 25

I had not seen Dillon since the wedding and school fair in September. My drama teacher, Miss Elizabeth, had invited me to her home for the Christmas holiday and I accepted after hearing from Billy that he and Dillon had found work and would not be coming home. I wrote to Billy before spring break, telling him when I was coming home. I added that I hoped both he and Dillon would be there. It seemed my feelings for Dillon grew stronger during our separation. He dominated my every thought and inspired me toward perfection. I poured myself into my studies and music with new zeal, inspired by Dillon and my newfound love.

On the bus ride home I rehearsed every possible scenario of how to face Dillon should he be there. Should I be indifferent? Hint that my affection belongs to someone else? Taunt him by flirting with Jake to see if it makes him jealous? Tell him boldly how I feel? Each ploy left me dissatisfied. The butterflies inside my stomach beat their wings more rapidly as the bus neared home. My preoccupation with Dillon overshadowed my concern about Maggie's letter.

Maggie had started writing me when she got into trouble or needed advice. She wrote about the day Mr. Wetherbee accused her of talking at the dinner table after the dining room bell for silence had been rung. Maggie was truthful—to a fault, we all knew that—and she informed the Deacon that he was wrong about her talking. He placed her on room restriction for a month because of her defiance. "He didn't want the truth, he just wanted to be right," she wrote. Maggie told how she went straight to Naomi's trailer "because I wasn't going to take no punishment for something I didn't do." Naomi talked to the worker who was at the table and the worker sided with Maggie. Naomi got the restriction reduced to just a day. Maggie went on to write that she overhead Mrs. Sheffield tell Aunt Rose that Miss Ruth came storming up to the trailer and threatened that if Naomi interfered again she would be gone. I wondered how many changes I would face when I arrived home.

The one ritual we all counted on had not yet given way to the new authority. The kitchen belonged to the teenagers on Saturday nights. Nam had encouraged the teens who attended the local high school to invite their romantic interests home. We made popcorn, played board games, but mostly spent time flirting, teasing each other, or arguing. A staff member was assigned to make an occasional visit to the kitchen to be sure our adolescent passions did not get out of hand. Mrs. Greeley was our monitor for the night. W. C., Jake, Dillon, Shirley and her boyfriend, Jim, Sunny, Maude, and I were hanging out. Our group was smaller than usual because Billy had to serve as dorm monitor for the weekend and he had stayed at school. It was also stormy and some of the kids from the community stayed home.

Everyone was in a good mood. A talent scout with the farm team for the Cleveland Indians had interviewed W. C. There was a good chance he would be signed. Jake was full of himself, threatened by W. C.'s upstaging him. He was bragging about having gone to see Ruby the night before. The boys had more freedoms than the girls, and it was easier for them to get passes to be absent from the home in the evenings, especially on weekends. These evenings out were unsupervised; that's how Jake had been able to visit Ruby, who had been my classmate in elementary school. It was rumored, and verified by Jake, that she was exchanging sex for money.

It didn't surprise me. Years earlier I had gone to Ruby's house, only once, with Naomi. Ruby's mother had rheumatic fever, so Naomi had taken over a basket of food. The house was filthy with unwashed clothes and smelly dishes scattered around like confetti. I moved some clothes aside and sat on a chair. Ruby's brother, Jeter, came into the room, paying me no attention. He staggered over to a cot in the corner and started to yell at the clothes. The clothes moved and Ruby's thin body rose to yell back at him for interrupting her sleep.

"Get up and make me something to eat."

Then he called her a word that I'd never heard before. I must have made a sound because he turned toward me and began laughing, his

piglike face bloated and red. Jeter was a few grades ahead of me and a
known bully. I glanced at Naomi and saw her biting her lip. She shook
her head slightly.

Jeter turned back to Ruby.

She scowled and hissed, "Don't you touch me, pig."

At first I thought it was funny when she called him a pig. But then I
began to suspect that something was wrong here. Ruby looked angry and
something else. Frightened?

"I just bet you wish I would," he said, leaning toward her.

She pulled back and got off the cot to walk toward the small stove
across the room. He turned to me and said, "You know the ol' saying,
little girl—if it ain't good enough for family, it ain't good."

Naomi blushed and hurried me toward the door. I wasn't sure what
he had meant and why Naomi had reacted the way she did. I wanted to
ask her as we headed back, but when I started to, she shushed me. "It is
hard to be well in a home where the air is polluted with hopelessness and
defeat," was all she would say.

Hearing Naomi's voice inside my head, I told Jake that his visiting
Ruby did not make life any better for her. I was trying to be virtuous
because Dillon was sitting silently in the corner, watching the exchange.

Jake laughed loudly. "Honey, she has more fun and makes more
money than you ever will. She likes what she does. She's not uptight, like
you little goodie-goodies that go off to school and think the most fun you
can have is with your brain."

The sexual overtones of the evening had begun. Maude answered his
dare by suggesting that we play spin the bottle. Before, I would have
kissed Jake or W. C. or anyone else on a dare. Now, such games seemed
irreverent, unholy, unthinkable. Jake was egging us on. Maude said,
"Let's take a vote. Who wants to play?" She just wanted to kiss W. C.
She didn't need an excuse; we'd have covered for her if she wanted to
step out on the back porch.

Shirley declared, "You act like kids. What's the big deal about kissing?
I kiss Jim anytime I want. But I'm not kissing in front of all of you."

Maude kept pressing. "Five minutes on the back porch. Those inside
have to keep an eye out for Mrs. Greeley." Mrs. Greeley was reading in
the living room, which was separated from the kitchen by the dining
room. It was easy to hear her heavy, slow walk across the room.

Sunny protested, "It's raining outside. It's cold."

Jake laughed, "Honey, you won't notice it when I'm finished."

She retorted, "Don't flatter yourself, Jake. A man can't warm a
woman unless she's willing."

I sat anxiously awaiting the outcome, filled with excitement and
dread. I glanced over toward Dillon. Our eyes met. It was as if a circle
enclosed us, dulling the noise, transporting us to the center of the universe, where we stood exposed and vulnerable in our knowing. I tried to
break the contact, to hide from him. I could not stop my hands from
moving to my hair, my mouth—such small gestures could betray my
heart. *Stop. Stop. He'll know.*

I heard Maude ask, "Who wants to play?" and Dillon—still looking
at me—said, "I do." My fever rose. The tension was high; something
about this game seemed taboo. We laughed too much, said ridiculous
things to each other. Jake and Sunny went outside on a dare. No one was
really playing, but Dillon casually picked up the bottle, spun it slowly,
and put his finger in front of it so that the open end pointed to me.

Everyone laughed. Sunny and Jake came inside arguing. Maude said,
"Go, Jen, go for it. Go get your first kiss."

My face was hot and red and my legs, like rubber, were propped up
solely with desire and anticipation. Dillon stood up and held the door
open. I walked outside. The rain was falling hard and the roaring sound
in the wind-torn trees made the world seem wild and dangerous. I
wanted to climb inside Dillon's jacket and be warmed and sheltered. But
we stood in the dark, neither moving toward the other, waiting for our
eyes to adjust. I leaned against the wall, clutching my sweater, wrapping
it tightly around me. He placed both of his hands against the wall above
my head, enclosing me, and leaned his body toward mine. His nervous-
ness seemed to disappear when he noticed me shivering.

"You cold?"

I shook my head, then nodded. It was the inner heat, not the external cold, that produced the trembling. I closed my eyes for fear of falling into his and let the warmth of his breath and body bathe me. I waited, but he did not move. Opening my eyes, I found his face was close to mine, studying me as though I was a rare treasure. Again I felt myself falling into the deep fathoms of his honest blue eyes. Might falling into them make me everything I admired, aspired to, and worshiped? How could it be wrong to want him? For he was honesty. "And the truth shall set you free."

"Jen, I won't kiss you unless you want me to."

"Don't kiss me unless you want to." It felt as if my pounding heart was muffling my words.

"I want to."

"Yes, yes, I want you to."

An unpracticed, timid kiss was planted next to my hot, quivering lips. With his cool mouth next to mine, I wanted him to extinguish the fire in my body, but I held back.

He pulled away and perhaps from my response found the courage to leap to the next level. Tenderly, with my face in his hands, confided, "Jen, I love you. I have from the first day I saw you." He looked toward the door, knowing our time was short. "Tomorrow, during rest time, can you slip away? Meet me behind the gym. There's a place I want to show you." Unsatisfied with partial truth, he added, "I want to spend time with you before we have to go."

Before we walked back inside, he kissed the top of my nose and said, "I'll be seeing you."

We walked back into the kitchen, but the game was over. Maude and W. C. were arguing. Soon afterward, Mrs. Greeley came into the kitchen and told us to wrap things up for the evening.

———·———

The storm passed during the night, bringing forth a clean, freshly washed, cool day. I flashed Dillon a smile as a way of letting him know

I would be at our meeting. I slipped out of the building during rest time and crossed the street down the road from the main building so as not to be seen. I made my way to the edge of the woods behind the boys' dorm where Dillon was waiting. He motioned me to follow. We walked along a small footpath that sloped gently, taking us deeper into the woods. The path narrowed just as we turned along the edge of a cliff, and Dillon instinctively placed his arm around my waist to protect me from the precipice. My heart raced at his touch. The path widened as we rounded the bend, and below us appeared a small, natural pool. Across the chasm a waterfall cascaded. I gasped at its beauty. This was my first time in the boys' woods. The girls had their own hideaway, but it did not include a natural swimming pool; instead, we had a large rock that held at least five of us, where we stripped to our panties and sunbathed. It was on that rock that Maude let me have a puff of a contraband cigarette.

Dillon and I sat on a ledge just above the water. The sun filtered through the trees, spreading dancing light. The smell of the woods was pungent—decay and life were all around.

"You like it here?"

"Oh, yes."

We sat quietly, staring at the scene below us, waiting for our estrangement to fade. Grasping for a topic, I asked, "Where did you learn to play the fiddle?"

"My uncle. He gave me one, three-quarter size, when I was eight. He showed me a little, how to find a few chords, then I picked the rest up myself."

"You were born with talent."

"I guess." There was a long pause, and then he said, "It was the only thing that made sense to me. My parents were always moving around, fighting, separating. The fiddle became my friend. I discovered that music was language; I could make the fiddle speak."

"You never get visitors. What happened to your parents?" The only thing I knew about his history was that no one had bothered to send him to school.

He flinched as though I had touched a wound. "My dad shot my mom. I guess he's still in prison. It was the worst punishment for him; he loved his freedom." He fell silent like he was imagining it. "Yeah, it would be the worst—to be in prison."

I understood the power of music to befriend, to erase loneliness, to distract from adults' anger. It could become a surrogate parent—reliable, constant, stable.

"What happened to your fiddle?" I asked, as if I was asking about his mother.

"I don't know. My uncle brought me here. I haven't heard from him since—let's see, about seven years now. Maybe he's keeping it for me." He lapsed into silence once again. He seemed relieved to get the ugly part out of the way, and I sensed he didn't want to linger there. He brightened. "It's okay. I'll get another one someday. I use the one at school now. I have a great teacher." He started mimicking his teacher's exaggerated reactions to his errors.

"Will you have your teacher write down the music to 'Everlasting'? I want to play it on the piano."

He looked startled, as if he'd never given it any thought. "Sure. I'll do it for your birthday."

We laughed a lot. It was a way of telling each other how clever and special we each thought the other was. I admitted that I knew I was in love with him the night he played the violin. He said he never knew a time when he had not been in love with me. Then, as if trying to hold on to the future, he asked, "What are you going to do after graduation?" Even though he was a year older, he was a senior like me.

I didn't know. I wanted to talk to him, but we were entering a dark, threatening territory. Could I risk sharing the confusion, the disgust I felt about the event that had happened at school? It had dramatically changed how I felt, and I swore a silent oath that I would never return after graduation to attend the college there. I stumbled forward. "Dillon, what do you think about President Kennedy's assassination?"

He shrugged. "It's a damn tragedy."

I sighed with deep relief. "You know, at my school, when the teacher announced it to the class, all but a handful of kids stood up and cheered. I was shocked! They said the 'anti-Christ' had been killed. The school lowered the flag for only three days, not thirty like the rest of the country."

"My God!"

His reaction gave clarity to how I felt. Then in a low but determined and firm voice, I announced, "I'm not going back after I graduate. I'll lose the scholarship to the college. But if I were to return, I'm afraid I'd lose something more precious than that. I don't know what I'll do—yet."

He nodded. "I don't blame you for not wanting to go back. It is not a place to encourage free thinking. You'll soon be on your own. You could transfer to our school, go to college with us—me and Bill."

A perfect solution. "Yes, I could!" A free, deep inhalation told me a burden had just been lifted. I took my stand against three years of brainwashing and turned away from it unharmed. I felt like I might find who I was before I completely lost myself.

"What do you want to study?" It was amazing that either of us considered college. We owed that to Naomi.

"I'm thinking about agriculture. I'd like to join the Peace Corps— maybe go to Africa."

I nearly choked. Maybe I would get to Africa after all. "What's the Peace Corps?" We didn't get outside news at my school. No television was allowed, and the school had its own radio station, so we got a slanted view of the world.

"It's the program President Kennedy started, where college graduates serve their country by helping other countries build themselves up, help them get out of poverty."

"Some of them should come here."

He laughed. "Jen, there are places in the world a whole lot worse than here."

He seemed so wise, so sure of his future. And for the first time since the moments I spent as a little child counting bushels full of love at

Naomi's bosom I was so blissfully happy. I had finally found a place to plant my feet. I had a future and a pure and simple love. Dillon and I stopped talking. I leaned against him and he placed his strong arms around my shoulders and pressed my back and shoulders close to his chest. We both stared into the mist of the waterfall, dreaming of a beginning.

The evening dinner bell sounded, shattering our reverie. We wanted to linger, to discover more about each other, but perhaps too much had been learned already in so short a space. Dillon turned me slowly to him, and that crooked smile that could be his undoing lit up his eyes. He exclaimed, "Those freckles!" and with a great big playful bite, he pretended to eat them. Then he kissed me again on the tip of my nose and said just before we parted, "I'll be seeing you."

Now I knew the secret of how angels fly, what gives wings to lift one's feet above the ground and makes one's soul soar. It is a love that inspires, that elevates people above themselves to new heights. I floated, I flew, I danced on the top of sunlit pines all the way to the girls' dorm. There would be more meetings and many more hours of unraveling the mysteries of one another. I could let him go because he promised, "I'll be seeing you."

It was easy to sneak back to the girls' building because the Sunday evening meal was held in each group, rather than in the main dining hall. I took the Greyhound bus back to school late that night, too full of happiness to sleep. So this was what it was like—what others already knew—to be wanted! I had looked into the eyes of goodness and it washed away my confusion and left me clean and whole. I was ready to take on whatever challenges were ahead; nothing could stop me from being the best. Dillon and I would build a life together—I knew it!

I waited eagerly for his promised letters. They did not come. Each day brought me closer to discouragement and disbelief. One could be careless in love and fail to notice small signs pointing to deception and fraud. Had I not seen something hidden? What had happened? Was it again my clever "imagination" that assured me I was wanted—yes, even loved?

Doubt nearly drowned me. I doubted Dillon's honesty, then my own, and finally my intuition, my instinct, my reality.

I did not get a letter, but a few weeks after my return to school, I did get a visitor.

CHAPTER 26

Billy was waiting for me in the lobby. I saw him from a distance and he looked awful, as if he'd slept in his clothes for days and hadn't eaten in months. He was pacing aimlessly but stopped when I entered. He greeted me with a hug. He smelled like cigarettes and coffee.

"Hey, Sin, how are you?"

"Good," I said frowning, wondering what on earth had brought him so far from home. "How are you? You don't look so good."

"I'm getting by." He looked around the large room. "Man, I need a cigarette. Where can I smoke?"

"Probably not within a mile of the campus."

He slumped into the couch nearby, resigned to tough it out, surrendering to the reason that brought him to my part of the world. "You doing okay, huh?" He asked again.

He's stalling, I thought. "What's up? Why are you here?"

His faced turned serious and my heart kicked into a higher tempo. He leaned back against the couch, studying me. "Come, sit next to me." I was still standing, becoming stiffer by the minute. I didn't want to sit. I wanted to know why he looked so disheveled—so lost.

"I've quit school, Sin. I'm joining the navy. I came by to say good-bye and warn you—to take care of yourself."

"What do you mean you've quit? Warn me? About what? Why? What's happened?" And for one brief moment, the news made me forget to ask about Dillon, who had been on my mind constantly but especially the minute I saw Billy.

"Listen, I don't know how to tell you this, but something's happened. Everything's changed. Jake, W. C., and Dillon, they all got arrested and sent off to reform school."

"Prison? Dillon?" The tempo stopped and with it my breath. I felt as if my blood dropped into my feet. "No, please, no." I sank to my knees.

"Hey, I didn't know you'd take it so hard." He looked at me as if seeing me for the first time. "You and Dillon? A thing?"

I nodded, then shook my head. "The last time I was home, we . . . talked." I did not want to diminish the memory by speaking about it. For the moment, I wanted information. "Tell me everything. Why?" I sat on the floor looking up at him.

"It's crazy, really. Jake stole some meat from the home's cooler that he sold to buy some liquor. He and W. C. were seen in town, pretty messed up from the booze. They were celebrating W. C. having that interview with a baseball farm team."

"The Indians. He was going to get signed—with the *Indians.*" The loss I felt could have been my own.

Baseball had never been Billy's passion. He went on, "Miss Ruth and Mr. Wetherbee came to school to interview Dillon about the break-in of the meat cooler. Dillon knew about it, but he wouldn't say anything. He was hanging out with them the night they got drunk; Miss Ruth and Mr. Wetherbee figured he knew about the break-in. Even if he didn't do it, he was considered an 'accessory to the crime,' they said. They took him out of school and sent him to the jail where Jake and W. C. were being held."

"They can't do that. He was innocent." I was coming out of my paralysis.

"Well, information that Jake and W. C. gave to the sheriff indicated that Dillon knew."

I was searching my mind as to when it could have happened. We were together Saturday night—I blushed—was it after I left on Sunday? Probably Friday, the night Jake went to see Ruby.

"There was a hearing at the courthouse in Hampton. Miss Ruth told the court that the boys' behavior had been getting worse. This was not the first time that Jake and W. C. had gotten drunk. She said none of them could be managed at the home any longer. She said they should be sent to reform school. Even Dillon."

"But Dillon doesn't live there. He's only home a few times a year."

"I know."

I stared at Billy, trying hard to understand how such an injustice could happen. He was silent for a long time. He rubbed his hands through his hair as though it would make him remember or clear his head and make sense of this. "I don't know, Sin. I wonder if Miss Ruth had it in for him. You know, it was Dillon who walked in on her and Jake that time in the clothing room at the boys' dorm. He always thought she was a hypocrite. I think she knew how he felt about her."

"I thought that was just a rumor—her and Jake."

"Dillon told me what he saw. Jake was standing close to her with his hands on her blouse. Dillon doesn't lie, but he doesn't gossip either. It was W. C. who told Maude, who told everyone else."

"You don't think she would get rid of them—I mean, now that she's married—because they might say something?"

He shrugged. "Who knows what her motives are? I think she'd like to get rid of all the teenagers. She only wants them small, when they can't challenge her."

"What did Naomi do?"

"I went to her, argued that Dillon wasn't in on this, that she had to intervene." He was bending over, his elbows resting on his knees, and holding his face in his hands. "She's finished, Sin, the world has moved past her. She doesn't have any power anymore. She said she talked privately to the judge, but he took Miss Ruth's side. He said the boys were setting a bad example for the younger ones, that they were *incorrigible*,"—he emphasized the word and mimicked Sheriff Mac—"and he told her that he didn't like Dillon's smirk as he sat through the trial."

I knew that look would get him into trouble, that it would be misunderstood. I could see him as he watched the sham unfold, with that "Are you for real?" look on his face. I wanted to scream to him, "Dillon, the world does not want truth. It wants order, and truth brings chaos."

"What did he tell them in court? Did he defend himself?"

"He wouldn't tell them anything. They wanted him to rat on W. C. and Jake, especially Jake, who they knew was the ringleader. But you know Dillon. He probably thought the whole thing was a joke, that they couldn't be serious."

Oh, Dillon, all this time I thought you had forgotten me and instead you were in the fight of your life, smiling through it. Oh, God, what will I do? How will he survive prison? "The worst" he had said when he talked about his father's fate. I wanted to vomit.

"I'm sick about this, Sin. I just want to get away."

He *was* away, but I knew what he meant. He wanted another world, far away from the one collapsing around us. It wasn't like the ground had been pulled out from beneath us, it was more like we'd been standing on an ice sheet that had been slowly melting and we had finally plunged into the icy waters to swim without direction, without a lifeboat, without a raft in sight. I wanted to cling to him, to save him. But clinging could make us both drown. We barely had the resources to save ourselves. I could see Billy was a mess. His hands shook like an old man's. All these years I had never thought about how he felt about the home, what effect it had upon him. I always thought of him as above it— bigger, stronger, untouched. I had forgotten that even boys cry.

I stood before my wrecked hero too much in shock to cry, but a gallon of tears lay just behind my eyes. Gone was the promise of college with Billy and Dillon—a dream crushed with senseless and cruel disregard.

Then I asked, "Did you see him before he was sent away? Did he say anything . . . about . . . me?"

"Yeah. I went to see him. He said to tell you—I can't remember— something about everlasting. It wouldn't be—or maybe it would be— everlasting, something like that. It didn't make sense."

"Can I write him?"

"I think you have to get permission from his probation officer. I don't know. He's out at that place near the school where you used to go—by Brownsville—where Sunny is. I don't have the address."

He was looking out the window as if he wanted to leave so he could smoke. I didn't want him to leave. He was all that was keeping the veneer over my emotions from shattering. I blurted out, "Billy, you want our mother's address?"

He looked shocked. "You have it?"

"I think so. She came to see me here—my sophomore year." I wanted to make him feel better. "You know, she wrote us every year at the home. She cares. She does. Maybe she can help you."

To my surprise, he rejected my attempt to throw him a lifeline. "Thanks, Sin, but it's too late. I don't need a mother now. I need a job."

For the first time since we last saw her together, we had a long conversation about our mother. He listened as I shared my impressions of her. It seemed to make him restless and impatient. When I told him about Daniel, he said, "Yeah. There was always the three of us." I was shocked. It had never dawned on me to ask him if he remembered. He turned from our past back to the present with as much ease as dismissing an unimportant intrusion.

"Sin, be careful when you go back. Everyone is upset, and there are repercussions when they talk about it. I'm worried for Maude. I know you are friends, but be careful what you put in writing. Your letters might be read."

"I will. Please write me. Let me know where you are sent and how you are."

One last tight grip, one last bear hug, and I was separated from him. "We're all we've got and we have to stay in touch," he insisted. "I wish I could take care of you. Let me know if you need anything. Take care."

I watched him walk toward the highway to hitchhike a ride. Then I collapsed. The world was upside down. A snarling, red-eyed wolf tore at the door, threatening to devour everything I had learned. Now good was bad; evil was sanctified. What craziness! I had to fight a battle with new, confusing rules. I had nothing to hold on to.

For a time, rage consumed me. It ate up all desire to study, eat, and sleep. Frantic but hopeless, I could do nothing to save Dillon. When rage wore me out, apathy took over and I quit everything—no homework, no activities. To class, then to bed. I put forth the smallest effort, enough to keep from getting expelled, because I didn't want to be sent back home. It was not my home, not a place I would claim any longer. Gradually it dawned on me that I had no place to go. What was I to do after graduation now that Billy and Dillon were gone? The despair had overshadowed everything else. All I could see was Dillon sitting in a small cell, sinking, sinking, sinking. I could see no future. An adolescent without hope, without a future, is in a dangerous place.

I wrote to Sunny, whom I trusted—the only soul in the world I trusted.

> Dear Sunny,
>
> What are you doing after graduation? I don't want to go back home or come back to this place. There must be another way. I'm not doing so well. Please write as soon as possible. School will be out in a few weeks.
>
> Love,
> Jen

She wrote back immediately.

> Dear Jen,
>
> Aunt Rose got me a job at the lodge where I can live for the summer. Then I'll be going to Orlando to stay with friends of her family and go to school there. Come back. Work with me over the summer. We'll figure something out for you. Listen, I've started to study Zen. They believe all things are predetermined and have already been decided. No amount of energy can change the course of things. Don't destroy yourself over what you have no control of. Believe me, I know. Don't think I don't feel the pain and tragedy of this. What it cost W. C., Dillon—even Jake. The more I live life, the more I wonder if it isn't bad that wins out. I'm just learning to stay out of harm's way and hope I have good karma. Keep your head, girl.
>
> Love,
> Sunny

And high school ended with me in a daze—uncaring, not participating in the hoopla following graduation. It did not feel as if I had passed a milestone. Instead it felt as if I had been handed an enormous burden: I had to figure out on my own how to face a grown-up world in which the hero does not always win, where playing straight does not always bring victory, where I could no longer trust the masks on the faces of my mentors. More importantly, I was now being asked to transition out of complete dependency into total independence—without assistance, without a road map, without a guide.

It was a challenge for which I felt ill prepared.

CHAPTER 27

The bus stopped at the post office a quarter of a mile from the home's main building. Since no one was there to greet me, the driver took me to the front entrance and dropped me off, depositing me by the side of the road with my small metal trunk and garbage bags filled with clothes. The drivers of this route were uncanny in their ability to spot the "home people." I had changed buses at Madison Creek, and after I boarded, the driver glanced at me and asked, "Headed for the home at Lookout?"

"Have I got a sign on me or something?" I replied sarcastically.

"Yeah," he grinned, "you got the look," whatever that meant.

I sank into the seat and stared out the window, dreading the arrival, wondering if I could keep my rage under control for these last few hours until I would be gone. I had only to drop off my trunk and take a few necessary articles for work at the lodge, and I'd be free of what now seemed my prison rather than my home. I felt feverish and weak, fearful that reason and control would be abandoned as soon as my feet touched home soil. How does one face evil? Does kindness conquer, as Naomi had taught? Her way didn't seem to have worked. Does hate or denouncement work? It seemed the better choice. Hate could be cold; maybe cold hate was even worse than raging hate. I would be cold!

As I stood there, I heard the door of the bus shut and the roar of its engine as it gathered speed. The front door of the main building swung open and Maggie raced down the steps to greet me. She was out of breath as she hugged me tightly. She picked up an end of the trunk and a sack of clothes and we carried my belongings toward the building.

"Maude, she done run off. Ain't no one seen her. Not for a week. Miss Ruth ain't lookin' for her. Says it's no use, that she's a big girl now, can live on her own."

It didn't surprise me that Maude was gone. I had wondered how long she would stay after W. C. was sent away. The only reason to stay would be for her sister, Jamie. I wanted to tell Maggie not to worry, that Maude would be back, but I knew she wouldn't. I smiled and said, "She *is* a big girl. I'm sure she's fine. Probably went home."

"Jamie cries every day. I can't make her stop. Will you talk to her, Jen?"

"Sure, I will." How could Maude have left Jamie? She fretted over her, babied her, protected her. She had lost one sister before she came to the home. Maude said that she died of food poisoning. She said it was the saddest thing that ever happened to her. Before losing W. C., I thought.

We carried the trunk and sacks to the third floor where the few remaining teenagers resided. As I walked down the hall, it looked small, narrow, and dingy. I never remembered it as being so dark. Everything looked smaller and dirtier and lonelier. The emptiness in me swelled and I felt as if I had fallen into a hole. Where was the light? Where was the end?

I dropped my luggage in Maude's room since I no longer had one. For the last few years when I came home for holidays, makeshift arrangements were made to accommodate me. It gave me the feeling that I kept trying to fit into an old, familiar, comforting coat that I had outgrown.

I sat on the bed sorting through the things I would need to take with me. I heard Millie tell Shirley that I was back. Shirley lowered her voice and spoke in an urgent, harsh whisper. I could only hear parts of it: "If you tell her, I'll . . . You know how she feels . . . can't trust her." Millie protested, but Shirley was persistent, threatening, then persuading.

Normally I would have interrupted: "Tell me what? What can't you tell me?" But I was tired, wrung out by my own torment, and frankly, I didn't give a hoot about their squabbles. I was leaving; I was out of here in two hours!

Then I heard Sunny's voice. I wandered down the hall, as I had so many times over the years when my emptiness was too much and I needed companionship. Tired of my own thoughts, I was eager for Sunny's. She was sitting with Eleanor, who still had not found another place to go. Their conversation stopped when I made my appearance. I thought I heard them mention Maude.

"I just heard from Maggie about Maude. What about her?"

"Don't know, just left," Eleanor replied a little too casually. I saw the look pass between her and Sunny, and I knew she was lying.

"What happened?" I pressed.

Sunny changed the subject. "Have a good trip?"

I was studying Sunny. She was wearing sandals and a long flowing dress with strings of beads. Her wild hair was fastened down with a bandanna. What kind of style was this? I wondered.

Just then Miss Ruth appeared. "Oh, there you are. Are you girls staying for dinner?"

She approached me, placing her hand lightly on my shoulder. A shudder went through my body as though a reptile had slithered by. She dropped her hand when I stiffened and said coolly, "You need to let the kitchen know—for supper count."

Sunny spoke, "We have to be checked in by six for our assignment. Aunt Rose said she would drive us over around five-thirty. We'll eat there."

An awkward silence followed while Miss Ruth hesitated as if she wanted to join our conversation, but she turned and abruptly left. We breathed a sigh of relief and laughed. I had remained cool in round one. The three of us were united in our feelings toward Miss Ruth, and I felt encouraged to ask again.

"Come on, you guys, tell me what's going on, for God's sake. With Maude."

"Later," said Sunny. "When we leave. It's better." Eleanor shot her a hard look, and Sunny looked away.

But it was not Sunny or Eleanor or Shirley who told me. It was Millie—slow, slightly retarded, loyal Millie. She told me in a hushed whisper on the steps between the third and second floors.

"Don't tell no one I told you. They said don't tell you because you like Miss Ruth. But you don't. Maude tried to kill her. She did. She tried to kill Miss Ruth. It didn't work, and she ran away."

"What?" I was trying to grasp the meaning of the words tumbling out in Millie's mildly slurred speech. Then, "Why?" knowing full well why.

Millie answered with a grave, sincere look on her face. "Because of what she did to W. C. She loved W. C."

"How?" I stammered.

"With soup," Millie said confidently. Then she looked frightened. She had told all, the guarded secret of the clan. I was leaving and could not protect her if the others found out that she had told me.

"Soup? How did she try it, Millie?"

"I don't know. They won't tell me."

I looked deep into her eyes, mustered as much firmness and seriousness as I could, and said, "Millie, I won't tell anyone you told me. And you must promise that you will not tell them you told me. Promise me. Now!"

"I promise."

"Now, promise me something else. Promise me that you will never tell any other person; you will never say it out loud again; you won't even whisper it; you won't even think about it." Her eyes were widening, but she was nodding. "You will never say again that Maude tried to kill Miss Ruth. Promise me. Cross your heart and give me your hands so I know you are not crossing your fingers."

She gave me her hands and I put them on my heart. "Millie, if you tell, it will break my heart. It might kill me."

"Oh, I won't tell. I won't ever tell."

I went to find Jamie to comfort her before I left.

On the ride to the resort, I pretended fatigue and rested my head against the window. I was trying to sort through what Millie had told me. My first reaction was "Yes!" Maude had tried what we all felt. Bravo for her. After all, Miss Ruth had killed in her own way—she had killed love, a chance for happiness; she had destroyed a life, taken W. C.'s chance to be a great ball player. But more than that, she had killed hope and crushed innumerable spirits. Is that a crime no less than murder? But my conscience admonished me. I knew there was a difference, but I kept weighing one against the other, never completely sure.

After we checked in at the lodge, Sunny and I sat on the porch in the warm night air, talking about the court hearing, where the boys were, whether we could get in to see them. Eventually, she told me about Maude's foiled attempt to kill Miss Ruth.

"Ever since W. C. had been sent away, Maude had watched as the lid on a can of soup in the storeroom had been slowly expanding. You remember that Maude's little sister died of botulism, food poisoning, from a can of contaminated soup. Maude was sure this deformed can held the answer to her rage."

We both fell silent. We could visualize her going daily to the pantry to inspect the can, moving it behind others, to be saved for her use only. We could see the satisfaction settling in her cold blue eyes as she watched the can. Then one day she would decide "Today is the day." It would occur on a day she had resolved to leave Jamie, a day when she could no longer hold the rage—and a day that soup was on the menu.

Eleanor told Sunny that the day Maude ran away she was scheduled to make vegetable beef soup. Maude was waiting tables at lunch. Eleanor said she later remembered hearing the "whish" from the can when it was opened, but she didn't pay attention at the time. After it was all over, she remembered washing the small pot that contained the special soup for Miss Ruth.

"How did Maude get it to Miss Ruth? All the soup is served in large bowls and placed on each table."

"Right. She didn't put enough in the bowl for Miss Ruth's table. Miss Ruth serves the kids first. Maude had to go back to the kitchen for more. She refilled the big bowl and then brought out the small bowl with the contaminated soup and put it in front of Miss Ruth's place. Miss Ruth had gotten up to go to one of the other tables to speak to one of the kids about something. She wasn't watching Maude. I got all this from Eleanor, who pieced it together by asking the kids some questions."

"So it didn't work. Did Miss Ruth get sick? Discover what Maude had done?"

"No, she never ate it. Just as Maude was turning to go back to the kitchen, Jamie—who was sitting at the place next to Miss Ruth's—

reached over with her spoon for a bigger piece of meat. Maude saw it. She dived toward the table to knock the spoon from Jamie, but she hit Miss Ruth's bowl, knocking it to the floor, spilling it all over the place.' "

I thought Sunny was finished, for she was quiet, and I sat listening to the crickets and frogs, listening to nature's cry for love and survival. Then Sunny spoke again, "She came back into the kitchen crying— Eleanor said, 'crying like a heartbreak'—and as she was at the sink wringing out a rag to clean it up, she was saying, 'She deserved it. She deserved to die.' That's what made Eleanor ask questions, figure out what had happened.

"Maude went back into the dining room and cleaned up the spilled soup. She was gone right after lunch. Didn't even take W. C.'s high school jersey, just the clothes on her back. Miss Ruth did not know that Maude had left until nightfall." Maggie was right about Miss Ruth; she didn't bother calling the police. Sunny and I agreed that Miss Ruth was glad that Maude was gone. We wondered if she would come back for Jamie.

———

Sunny and I settled into summer, a final act in our passage to adulthood. Our living quarters at the lodge were in the old section of the resort, where we lived for the first time in our lives without surveillance or examination from adults. Lifeguards, concession stand attendants, waitresses, and ground employees who lived too far away to commute bunked here, a mixture of high school graduates and college students. After work hours the staff gathered in the lounge area. Some played the guitars they had brought, some drank, some just hung out.

If only I were not so out of sorts, how I would have loved the liberty. Instead, I pushed my body to its limit with work. Rising at 5 A.M., working through until 11 P.M., filling in for others, taking extra shifts. Work. Work. Keep moving. Don't stop. That was my mantra. I didn't join the frivolity in the lounge. I fell into bed exhausted. Pain of the heart is worse than any physical pain. With the physical pain, one knows one is alive; the cells scream it. But this pain was numbing, a welcomed numbing. Putting one foot in front of the other, working like a robot,

I ignored my body. But my body reacted to the fatigue by vomiting at the end of the day.

Sometimes at night, the sleeplessness made me restless and I wandered into the lobby or sat on the porch staring into the blackness. Often I came across Sunny and her friend Mark sitting in the dark, a candle lit between them. They'd be listening to Bob Dylan's music, staring deeply into one another's eyes, and smoking cigarettes that didn't smell like tobacco. Mark was studying botany at Antioch College and working as a trail guide. He called me *Cypripedium calceolus*, the Latin name for lady's-slippers, after my yellow bedroom slippers. One night while I leaned against Mark's chest as he rubbed my temples, he told me that lady's-slipper was named for Aphrodite's association with Cyprus, a city whose people worshiped her. He said Aphrodite was the goddess of sexual love and beauty, and did I know that she was the mother of Aeneas? I shuddered.

———————

We were at the lodge about a month before given a day off. Sunny suggested that we take the bus to the reform school and maneuver our way in to see Dillon, Jake, and W. C. She wanted to let W. C. know that Maude was gone. For the first time in weeks, joy filled me. Might I see Dillon again? I had chosen to give up happiness. Since he was being deprived of freedom, I imprisoned myself. I did not smile because he did not smile. To suffer with him was to stay bound to him. I had nothing of his to hold but a refrain of "Everlasting" that reverberated through my brain like a phrase that one can't shake. It held me steady and kept me looking toward tomorrow.

Sunny and I took the bus as close to the institution as it went and then walked the last mile along a paved, tree-lined road past large brick mansions set far back from the road. Horses grazed behind rock fences. I thought of privileged Amy and a time that seemed like another life. Maybe that's how Sunny came up with the idea of having lived other lives. God knows that she had—with her comings and goings from the home.

Sunny was talking again about Zen Buddhism, about how Buddha received Enlightenment. She was saying, "He denied his body, suffered extreme privations, until he looked like a skeleton."

Now why is she telling me this? I wondered. I knew Sunny well enough to know that she was not informing me about the religions of the world. Was she trying to urge me to find understanding in my suffering, that it would bring Enlightenment? Or telling me to give up suffering and get a life?

When she added, "He found the answer to life," my ears pricked up. What could it be?

"Man should not live with either self-indulgence or deprivation. Leading the middle path will bring knowledge, calmness, and peace."

"That's it? How stupid. I don't believe in the middle path. I think it is the extremes that give meaning to life."

Sunny was thoughtful and answered as if she had already long ago passed that reasoning, "Well, it will be a difficult life if you make that choice."

"So you're going to play it safe?" I asked. I thought of her and Mark. I didn't think she was playing it safe; it seemed dangerous—reckless—as if she was paying back Kent.

I wondered if I would ever feel sane again—calm and dispassionate like Sunny—if the numbness would ever end. Jealous that she seemed untouched, I boldly declared, "I don't believe in God anymore," as though announcing I had outgrown Santa Claus.

She stopped without warning, jolted. "You what?" Her arms flew out with a questioning exclamation. "Why?"

"I believe life is random. It begins and ends with chance. No purpose."

"Well, of course it can seem that way if you don't understand the bigger purpose. A universal force, like—"

I cut her off. "Nothing is behind anything. You get one round—one go of it. And you never know when it will be over."

"Come on, Jen. I know this thing that happened to the guys—you took it hard, but you can't give up believing. You don't have to believe like Miss Ruth or Naomi because only a third of the world believes like them, but almost the whole world believes in a god."

Astonished by her last remark, I wondered if she was right. My impression was that most of the world was Christian, except for the pagans, who were in the minority. But I wasn't going to challenge Sunny, who seemed to know more about these things than I, for I was becoming aware of how narrow my education was in these matters. At that moment, I was in the rank of the nonbelieving minority.

"It's not about Dillon—not completely." Then I told her about the day I stopped believing. "Just after I heard about Dillon being sent away, I was sitting on the grass near the highway behind my dorm. There is a huge supermarket on the other side of the road. A woman pulled her car into traffic. She had just finished grocery shopping and she had bags of groceries stacked up in the back and her three little kids with her. They were hit by a speeding car. I could see it coming. I saw that she was looking in the other direction and didn't see the car. I couldn't warn her. I couldn't do anything but watch. They hit and she—" I was still shaken by the memory. "They were all killed. They fell onto the highway along with the tomatoes and eggs—smashed, broken."

Sunny was quiet for a minute. "Wow. That's heavy."

"Now, if God wanted to take the whole family, why would he make them waste all that money on groceries that would never be used? There should have been some mercy shown for her family. They had the expense of burying four people."

"Yeah. But it doesn't matter. That's a small thing in the scheme of life. Maybe they were finished here." She paused. "You know, when you stopped believing in Santa Claus you didn't stop believing in the spirit of Christmas. Santa Claus is the child's way of first learning about giving and love. One day, you drop the myth but understand the purpose behind it. That's the way I feel about God. *It's* probably not one gender, or anything like we know, but it does exist, if for no other reason than we need it to."

I was weighing these new ideas, but anger made me stubborn. I wanted the world to be just and fair and reasonable. Sunny was sure shaking up my way of looking at life.

"I'm leaning toward the Zen way myself. It would explain that accident in several ways—karma or that we don't always see the bigger picture. Take, for example, Dillon coming home the weekend that Jake broke into the meat locker. Why that weekend? Maybe the real reason he was sent away was that it's not the time for you to be together." Then she added, "Or because Miss Ruth didn't think he was good enough for you."

I stopped dead in my tracks. "What are you talking about? She didn't know. We only just—it was that weekend."

Sunny laughed. "Jen, we all knew. The way Dillon looked at you—chose to sit next to you when he could. You seeking him out when we were all together. We were all wondering when you would wake up and figure it out."

I couldn't buy Sunny's explanation. Miss Ruth was too involved in her own new relationship to have been paying attention. She wasn't even paying enough attention last summer to figure out what was going on with Sunny and her abortion and Aunt Rose. But I wondered, what was the real reason Dillon was sent away? He was no trouble—working, making his own way, seldom coming home.

The small kernel of hardness that had begun to grow inside me grew larger. I dismissed my belief that pain brought about compassion. Pain left one both tender and hard—and cold and lonely.

"I loved him, Sunny. He loved me, too." And the tears fell. She put her arm around my shoulder and we walked the rest of the way in silence.

———

When we arrived at the reform school, I was startled by its appearance. It looked nothing like what I had expected. A beautiful stone building was surrounded by manicured, rolling lawns. It was similar to one of the gracious estates we had passed on our walk. However, on closer inspection, I could see a high, wire fence behind the main building, which I found out was the administration building. Behind the fence were multiple buildings where the inmates resided. Dillon was in one of them. We sat on a bench under an old oak tree and plotted our strategy. We would announce ourselves as the sisters of W. C. and Dillon. As we plotted, we could hear the excited voices of boys rising from the area behind the fence. From the sounds reaching us, we knew they were playing baseball. It was not as I'd imaged. I had envisioned Dillon locked in a small cell without sun and exercise. It struck me that the feeling I had about reform school might be the same that some children had about orphanages.

While we were deciding what to say, a man in a uniform approached the building. He stopped in front of us and asked if he could be of help.

"We're here to see our brothers," Sunny lied confidently.

"Well, visiting days are Saturday and Sunday, and you have to have a pass from their probation officers. Only parents are allowed to visit. Friends and sisters," he emphasized the word "sisters," letting us know he doubted our story, "have to have a special authorization."

"Oh. Well, can you tell us how they are?" I blurted out.

"Who are they?" He studied us, especially Sunny, who wore the look of a free-spirited gypsy. Sunny responded confidently, giving their full names, and then added that she wanted to know about Jake, too, since he was her cousin.

He answered that Jake and W. C. were fine. Then he said something that made me glad I was sitting down. "Dillon isn't here. He was released about two weeks ago."

Stunned, I could not hear the rest of the conversation Sunny had with him. She told me later that the man agreed to deliver the message to W. C. that Maude had gone home.

How could it be that Dillon was not there? Released? He was free? Where had he gone? Why had he not come looking for me? He knew that I worked last summer at the lodge. It would be the logical place for him to look. My head was spinning. The numbness began to diminish and in its place came a raw, powerful pain that made me feel reckless.

As the man turned to enter the building, I asked, "Who was he released to?"

"I don't know. Maybe to his probation officer."

Now I had no place to picture him. The last branch I grasped on to gave way. I was falling and there was nowhere to fall but into the yawning cavern that threatened to never let me see sunlight again.

CHAPTER 28

Sunny helped lessen my loneliness. Tired of my self-absorbing grief, tired of my nocturnal wanderings and restless pacing, she looked up from her book one evening and said, "Catch," as she tossed me a book off the stack by her bed.

Thank you, Sunny, for throwing Faulkner at me. I opened *Light in August* and spent the next few days feeling a cool breeze fall across my heated brain. The smooth, achingly beautiful phrases soothed and encouraged me: "Thinking goes quietly, tranquilly, flowing on, falling into shapes quiet . . . Memory believes before knowing remembers . . . In the quiet and empty corridor, during the quiet hour of early afternoon, he was like a shadow, small even for five years, sober and quiet as a shadow." Faulkner knew about psychic pain, about the amorphous orphan-child fears of being defective, unwanted, desperate. And Sunny knew there were better ways to cope with days of desperation than aimless roaming.

The rest of the summer I worked and read. I waited for Enlightenment, for guidance on what I should do, where I would go. I decided not to return to the college affiliated with my high school, and I had not applied to any other college.

Serendipity had a hand in the choice I made. I was serving lunch to a family in the dining room when the child asked her mother, "Is she Tinkerbell?" Her parents apologized for her, saying they had just returned from Disneyland in California, and the child made a game of imagining people as Disney characters.

"Well, I'm glad I wasn't Minnie Mouse."

As was common at the resort, the family freely gave personal information about themselves. They were on vacation and seemed willing to reveal themselves before a total stranger.

"We're moving there," said the older boy.

The mother added, "Yes, California is a great place for college. They are practically free."

Enlightenment arrived like a thunderbolt with one word: "California"—where dreams of college come true. I was giddy with relief, feeling free of indecision. The highways were already traveled by kids on the move—uprooting, relocating. Being a girl of my time, not extraordinary or exceptional, I thought it seemed natural to travel to a faraway place—to leave behind a ground that was forever shifting, to search for a more solid one.

Sunny did not try to dissuade me; instead, she astonished me with another piece of information that I hadn't known about her. She had been born in a city within sight of Los Angeles. Sunny came into this world while her parents were traveling in search of antiques for her father's store. Several times he had come to the home for her so she could accompany him on his buying trips. She never talked about her travels. Based on a childhood memory, she thought I would like San Francisco the best. So it was decided that was where I should go to fulfill my destiny.

———————

I had one last reason to return to my childhood home—to say good-bye to Naomi. Aunt Rose came for us early Sunday afternoon when the season ended. Sunny and I would be departing for our separate destinations in the early evening.

As we approached the home, we fell silent. It was the kind of uneasy silence that occurs when one is asked to pause out of respect for the memory of strangers who have experienced some great tragedy. One struggles to find the appropriate emotion but instead is too burdened with one's own preoccupations. As I stood before the home, I felt as though I were trying to mourn a stranger.

I leaned against the car as I looked up at the big white house for the last time. I cannot say that any profound truths came to me. I was standing before the home with anger and sadness, not yet able to feel gratitude. A place that had sheltered me, nurtured me, disciplined me, and shaped me received only my resentment. For I was still an adolescent—idealistic and demanding perfection of its adults. It takes maturity to be able to balance good and bad, both within oneself and in others. That was a journey I was just beginning.

———

Sunny and I went together to Naomi's trailer to say farewell. She greeted us in her usual enthusiastic manner, laying aside her pen and paper. But sadness hung in the room, heavy like humid air, making it difficult to breathe and to find words. I had come with anger, but her sadness engulfed me and I could not look into her eyes for fear I would fall into the abyss of her despair.

We talked with a jerkiness as people do when avoiding a topic as unbearable as permanent separation. Sunny casually made reference to a movie we had seen over the summer. I was furious with her. Why did she have to bring controversy into the parting? She knew Naomi believed movies were evil. I could never reconcile how Naomi could love television and be opposed to movies. However, she explained that the dark theaters tempted young couples, causing them to "give in to sins of the flesh." I suppose she was right about that.

Sunny never lied about her beliefs, unlike me. I would keep quiet rather than stir up a conflict. But did she have to bring up this topic? Was she trying deliberately to hurt Naomi? Or was Sunny dealing with separation on her own terms?

Sunny left to pack and I was alone with Naomi. The scene had left me exhausted and I sat immobilized in the chair. Oh, God, I was bad at separations. Sorrow erased my cavalier pretense of courage and I broke down. The tears were of fear—fear for Naomi's survival, of guilt over my inability to save her, of bereavement over an era ending for her and me. I was frightened to let go and fall back solely upon myself.

Naomi held me tenderly. "Why are you crying so?"

"Good-bye," I gasped between sobs. "I don't know when I'll see you again. I love you and I can't stand the changes. Everything is changed."

She smoothed my hair as she had always done and lovingly said, "My dear, life is constantly changing. Make it change you for the better. Never forget how much I love you. You can always come home if things don't work out."

I shook my head. She did not understand—there was no home when it was no longer Naomi's place. Home had become an institution where rules were more important than relationships, where discipline had become loftier than learning.

There was something I had always wanted to ask, and the picture of the small mission that sat like a small trophy on her desk reminded me. I reached over and held it, trying to see beyond the flat surface to a place where happiness once reigned.

"Nam, who was Zinnia?"

Her eyes became soft and misty, and her whole being transformed into a familiar figure that I thought had vanished. The sparkle suffused her like an aura as she answered, "Oh, she was a precious spirit. She was my first little girl. She used to come to my room at night and say, 'Can I sleep in you's bed?'"

"Me, too. That's what I used to say."

"Yes, you reminded me so much of her. Sometimes, I . . ." Her voice faded and she took the picture from me, rubbing her hands across it, as though she were tenderly caressing Zinnia.

"What happened to her?"

"She died in the fire." She was silent for a long time, and I felt a little jealous of this child who could captivate Naomi so entirely. Then she sat beside me and took my hand. "Perhaps it wasn't fair of me to love you so deeply. You reminded me of her; you had so much of her magic dust— her spirit and her capacity to love. I suppose at times I held on to you so tightly because I wanted to keep the past. My heart was always at the mission. But, honey, things do change. And it is not good to cling to the past. It is now your time to find your dream. Go with my blessing. You will always be in my heart."

"Will you be okay?"

"I have made my choices. It's your turn now. Make them with care and prayer."

I nodded. "I will write you. I love you."

I leaned into her, allowing myself to be comforted once again, locking the feeling inside my heart so that I could find it when I needed it. And, oh, how there would be days when I would need it. How graciously she permitted separation. I had seen partings all my life but never with love or with the acknowledgment by both parties of the necessity. That afternoon Naomi gave me her last lesson: there is a time to let go. No matter how much pain it causes, if one's survival depends upon it, let go.

I did not fling the words of blame at her that I had come to deliver—blame for failing to protect Dillon, Jake, W. C. In the confusion and desperation of parting, I knew that she had also failed to protect me and Sunny and Maude and Bill. Her surrender felt like a betrayal.

But what did I know about the anguish of a middle-aged woman who found the only world she had known was collapsing around her? Society no longer wanted orphanages—she was soon to be a displaced missionary. Maybe she knew; maybe she felt the reins should be turned over to someone younger, someone she thought more capable to lead the home into the next, more institutional, era. Maybe she never felt she belonged anywhere other than with the people and the hills for which she had first come.

She was a woman who had a great capacity for love. But I saw that her love for Miss Ruth was like that of a wife who loves a husband who has stopped loving her. The wife clings, fearful of the loneliness that might come, unaware that it already has arrived; she believes that just staying will make love return, not understanding that it is in the fighting that bonds can be reforged and the fracture healed.

But I was seventeen and stubbornly believed that anything you fought for you could win. And that if Naomi had fought, she would have won.

I left her. No, I fled from her that day with a determination to close the door behind me and never look back. I left with my sorrow, my anger, my disillusionment, and my despair, not realizing that I was taking more than these with me. I was also taking everything that Naomi had hoped for me. Our relationship would not end at the trailer; it would go on through the years, seeking resolution in every new relationship I had.

I walked back to the main house to gather the few items I would be taking with me to my new life. I was ironing, standing with my back to the door, when I heard a sniffle behind me. It was Maggie.

"Someone said you are leaving tonight. Is it true?"

"Yeah, it's time for me to go. I'm going to California to go to school."

"Where is California?"

"It's a place far away from here."

There was a long silence, and in a whisper she said, "Who will love me when you are gone?"

I turned to her and took her in my arms. Oh, I knew that demon—how every separation is an abandonment.

"Maggie, people don't stop loving you when they leave. Sometimes they have to go away for other reasons. I will always love you. When you have one of those days when you feel like no one in the world loves you, just stop and say to yourself, 'Jen loves me no matter where she is. In her heart, she still loves me.'"

We stood crying, slowly rocking back and forth, me smoothing her hair like Naomi taught me. I told her that I would send her my address and made her promise that should Dillon ever return asking for me, she would give him my address. Maggie knew that I would not be returning.

———

Sunny and I were standing in front of the building, our trunks loaded into the car, waiting for Aunt Rose to take us to the bus station. Miss Ruth came down the wide concrete stairs toward us to say good-bye. What would I say to her? To a woman who demanded of those she loved that they stand in her shadow, have no will, no voice, no separateness apart from her? Her price was too high. I knew these truths then but was too young to give voice to them. My rage had frozen into an iceberg, and I stood as stone before her. Sunny gave me a long, steady "be wise" look.

"I came to say good-bye and to wish you luck."

"I bet you do!" I said sarcastically, coldly.

Her smile faded, and Sunny said brightly, "Good luck to you, Miss Ruth. Watch your back. Someone may try to do you in."

I suddenly felt strong enough to stand before Miss Ruth without fear, to step outside her shadow and face her as an equal, not a cowering child. "Miss Ruth, I have nothing to say to you." I turned my back, hoping that she felt the worst pain that one could inflict on another—the hardest to bear—that of abandonment.

We left in that hour before day closes and twilight begins—always the hardest time of day for me—a time when night approaches with its uncertainty. Will it bring peace or demons? Sunny and I waited together at the bus station and exchanged gifts. We laughed when we discovered that we had bought each other charm bracelets with a half heart. On her bracelet to me she had inscribed "Enlightenment." On hers, I had put "Find truth. Jen."

Before I boarded my bus, she hugged me and said, "Hey, put memories on that bracelet. The next time I see you I want to see it filled with memories. Write me!"

I left with all my worldly possessions: a few clothes, a bus ticket, and four hundred dollars in my pocket. As the bus pulled away from the terminal, I leaned out the window and waved to Sunny until she disappeared. And the silver thread that had linked me to her so many years before kept unwinding.

EPILOGUE

Naomi eventually lost her home, and though she sustained a loving and forgiving outlook about her defeat in the power struggle with Ruth, she never found herself so wholly fulfilled as when she was at the center of our small world. She tried to start another children's home, to do what she knew intuitively that she did best, but she came to realize with full heart-rending reality that an era had ended. Costs had become increasingly prohibitive and innumerable new regulations were threatening to destroy the remaining homes. Naomi lived out the remainder of her life in a missionary retirement home.

Many children's homes across the nation later became residential treatment homes for troubled children or were converted into juvenile detention facilities. Miss Ruth finally got her way when Lookout Ridge became a correctional center for youths. This kind of institution probably better suited her. She remained there until her death.

As for the rest of us, Jake wasn't accepted into the Air Force pilot's program but served honorably as an airman. His uniform dazzled Victoria, the pretty, feisty girl of his dreams; they married, then divorced. He worked in construction and eventually established his own small but successful business building family homes. W. C. joined the military and stayed in Vietnam after his discharge. I hope he found a place he could call home.

Surprisingly, I ran into Maude on a midnight flight from San Francisco to Los Angeles. We both eyed one another skeptically, and I might not have approached her had I not heard a soft "Sweet Lordy Jesus" escape her lips as she lifted her luggage to the overhead compartment. We spent the fifty-five minute flight catching up with each other. Self-consciously, and with only superficial shame, she revealed that she had served time in prison for killing her abusive husband. The hardened edge that was scarcely visible in childhood now adorned her like a shield. As lost as W. C. had been, she had never forgotten him. It

seemed her bitterness over their separation was all she had left to hold
on to.

Shirley worked her way up to the position of office manager of a
small fabric firm where she was respected in spite of suffering from
chronic bouts of depression. She never married. Maggie and Eleanor
married their teenage sweethearts. They swore that the most precious
treasures in their lives were their children. In defiance of the well-known
1960s monkey studies in which abandoned infants failed miserably at
parenting, most of the home kids turned out to be attentive and caring
parents. If they erred, it was in being overly involved with their children.

Sunny had the worst luck. Her life was changed forever by a car accident at age twenty-one in which she sustained severe brain damage. Her
childhood terror of losing her mental faculties and becoming institutionalized like her mother became her fate. Mercifully, she had right frontal
lobe damage so she was protected from being able to fully understand
the impact of her disability. I still think of her as she was back in childhood: wise, philosophical, and nonjudgmental. These qualities remain
and she continues to see with clarity when my vision becomes clouded.

Dillon. Now there's a story that would probably fill another book. He
survived, but not without lasting wounds that made him choose the life
of a wandering minstrel. After his release from reform school, he was
given an extended probation period in which he was forbidden to make
contact with the home or any of its inhabitants. I heard he made an effort
to find me even before his probation ended, but that was long after I'd
left the home. While in graduate school, I attended a professional con-
ference in Vancouver, British Columbia, and during a nocturnal
wandering in search of music, I heard the sweet sound of a violin coming from a club and thought for a fleeting moment it was a short measure
from "Everlasting," a melody that refused to fade over time. Bearded and
long-haired, Dillon was unrecognizable, but his name was on a flyer
introducing his combo. I thought my heart would burst from its pounding when my eyes found his. I stayed at the club all night, talking with
Dillon between sets. I learned he had migrated to Canada to avoid the

Vietnam War. I learned much more, but that remains to be told at another time and place.

Daniel learned of his adoption when he turned twenty-one. He played in a rock-and-roll band through college, writing some of his own music. Professionally, he teaches mathematics and computer science to high school students and coaches a girls' track team.

Bill is still my close friend, a steady guide when I need one. He became a lawyer.

I am a family therapist. In that role I have had a front-row seat as I watch the failures and deficiencies of the foster care system. I often turn back in time to my home, thinking of how it offered stability, continuity, a work ethic, discipline, and opportunity. I shudder when I see children go through the legal revolving door from one foster home to another, back to their homes, and then back into the system. How can they escape catastrophic damage from these multiple broken attachments when even one broken bond, one separation, takes so long to heal? I say a little prayer of thanks for every good foster home, but the system is overburdened and needs a helping hand. Should society so carelessly, so myopically, write off children's homes? Contrary to prejudicial, Dickensian images of orphanages, many of us home kids emerged with few scars; we healed because of the continuity and love that existed in the homes. The peer parenting we received and gave was often more honest than what many children receive in their own families.

But children's homes will become institutions if they simply house children and they have no one like Naomi. All the rules, guidelines, fire alarms, square-footage requirements, legalities, and structure cannot fill the hole and heal the wound of a castaway child as can a forgiving smile and the words "I believe in you." Essential is someone who will stand beside children through all their infractions and failures. Infractions will be many with abandoned children because all the rules were broken with them. Love alone cannot solve all the problems, but it can help children soar above the very hurdles created by their histories. Love becomes the tensile cord to grasp, the thread to lead one home when one's way is lost, the fiber to keep one from falling asunder. Naomi's love saved me, carried me through my anger, and healed me.

———————

Just as the invisible silver thread bound me to Sunny, it also kept me attached to the home, despite my efforts to sever it. Looking back at my home is like peering into a kaleidoscope: images shift into endless patterns as I view the picture with an ever-changing emotional eye. No, my home was not perfect. It was caught in a crosscurrent of philosophical differences. All philosophies start with the philosopher's view of people as either intrinsically good or inherently evil. Polarized in their philosophy of child-rearing, Naomi and Miss Ruth never found grounds for compromise. They were also polarized in their beliefs about love. Naomi had learned well the lesson of her generation, that love was masochistic submission. Miss Ruth rejected this definition but, through her rebellion, demanded that others submit to her. Each had learned her mother's lessons well. Fighting my way toward adulthood required me to understand and accept without malice the imperfections of those who influenced me.

Each era, and indeed every life, carries its own congeries of deceptions. I had to weave my way through mine. I gradually came to understand that lies are inextricably linked to humanness. As a child, I was surrounded by lies. My mother told lies out of desperation to be reunited with her children; Naomi would not face the truth because of her love for Miss Ruth; Miss Ruth told lies of self-deception; I told lies of distortion. Over time, the lies of my childhood have faded to paler shades.

Coming to a place of repose, I have accepted that the adults who cared for me did the best they could but did not always do right. I have accepted that what was given to me was enough to help me face the challenges and demands of adulthood—to love work and to work at love. I have found that it is easier to resolve anger and let go of blame when there is happiness and fulfillment in one's own life. These gifts were mercifully given to me.